THE OCCUPIED

Center Point
Large Print

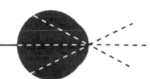

**This Large Print Book carries the
Seal of Approval of N.A.V.H.**

THE
OCCUPIED

CRAIG
PARSHALL

CENTER POINT LARGE PRINT
THORNDIKE, MAINE

This Center Point Large Print edition
is published in the year 2016 by arrangement with
Tyndale House Publishers, Inc.

Scripture quotations are taken from the New American
Standard Bible,® copyright © 1960, 1962, 1963, 1968,
1971, 1972, 1973, 1975, 1977, 1995 by The Lockman
Foundation. Used by permission.

The Occupied is a work of fiction. Where real people,
events, establishments, organizations, or locales appear,
they are used fictitiously. All other elements of the
novel are drawn from the author's imagination.

The text of this Large Print edition is unabridged.
In other aspects, this book may vary
from the original edition.
Printed in the United States of America
on permanent paper.
Set in 16-point Times New Roman type.

ISBN: 978-1-68324-134-8

Library of Congress Cataloging-in-Publication Data

Names: Parshall, Craig, 1950– author.
Title: The occupied / Craig Parshall.
Description: Center Point Large Print edition. | Thorndike, Maine :
Center Point Large Print, 2016.
Identifiers: LCCN 2016028058 | ISBN 9781683241348
    (hardcover : alk. paper)
Subjects: LCSH: Paranormal fiction. | Large type books. | GSAFD:
Suspense fiction.
Classification: LCC PS3616.A77 O28 2016b | DDC 813/.6—dc23
LC record available at https://lccn.loc.gov/2016028058

PROLOGUE

I keep monsters in my peripheral vision. When you've been attacked by the horribles, you never forget.

I lean against the railing of the car ferry as it plows the waves of the Pamlico Sound, the body of water protected from the full force of the Atlantic by a chain of white-sand barrier islands. I can only afford to close my eyes for a second or two, feeling the sun on my face and the wind moist with sea spray. My Mets cap is yanked down tight against the hard gusts blowing across the steel deck as I head back to Ocracoke Island, a place laced with fishermen, odd-jobbers, and occasional hurricanes. Things are peaceful for the moment. Yet that could change in a heartbeat. The horribles don't give much warning.

Life has become a razor's edge. I pray for a trip safe from mayhem. I am ready in case it isn't.

The ferry is motoring me along the North Carolina coast, taking me back to the island that is now my home. I lean over the railing, look down to where the water is the color of gray-green slate, and watch the sea curling as the ship cuts it into whitecaps.

But I can't linger. I have the growing sense that one of them may be on board this ferry with me.

So I shift position, eyeing the deck stacked with vehicles so I can study the strangers milling along the guardrail.

I catch sight of a passenger who is standing toward the rear of the ferry. He is a tall man, wide of girth, unshaven, wearing a dirty denim work shirt over a mechanic's jumpsuit, and he is standing alone at the very end of the ferry, looking out to the waters of the sound, where the wake is churned into froth. He pulls back his head and spits loudly as he launches a gob of phlegm from his mouth down to the sea.

One of my senses tells me that this man might be one of them. One of the horribles. Though I can't be sure.

Then I notice on my right, along the railing, about twenty feet away from me, a mother and father with their boy. They are smiling and talking. The man says something to the woman, and she laughs generously and links arms with him.

The couple reminds me of the women I have known. Courtney, of course. The princess of excess and regret.

And the others. How can I not think about them after everything that has happened? Marilyn Parlow, the young love of my much younger life. The flirtatious, insulting, mysterious Marilyn.

And Ashley Linderman, the smart, gutsy detective I met recently during my harrowing return to my hometown, after being away so many years.

And of course, there is Heather. Whose life remains all but a mystery to me.

I glance over to the tall, wide man standing by himself at the end of the ferry. I could be wrong. It's possible that the special sense I have about him might be due to the ferry's diesel engines, nothing more.

To my left, I also notice a young man along the railing who looks to be in his early twenties, and judging from his skull-and-crossbones T-shirt, he is likely a tourist. Everything about him is in black—his pants, his shoulder-length hair, and, as I look closer, his eyeliner is black too. He is reading a paperback book that appears to be a paranormal novel, which grabs my attention.

I call out, loud enough to be heard over the wind and the water, "You into horror?"

"It's just vampires and demons and stuff."

"You say 'just' like it's a trivial thing," I reply. "Supernatural suspense, they call it. But I'd say *horror* describes it best."

"Describes what?" He is looking at me with his head tilted back, keeping his distance, treating me like I've morphed into a Komodo dragon.

I look straight at him. "You think dark forces are just a fantasy. The ones breaking through from the other side. Bringing death. Destruction. But that's exactly what they want us to think."

The kid snorts again and says, under his breath, "Dude, that sounds a little paranoid."

"Dude," I shoot back, "not if it's true."

I get a laugh from him. Then a question. "Dark forces, like what?"

I don't usually converse with strangers about invisible monsters, but he seems interested. So I feel compelled to lay it out. "Like the three mortal enemies."

"Wow." He takes a second. Then, "Okay. Three enemies . . ."

"I'm telling you something important," I warn him. Even as I say it, I know I must sound like a crackpot. But then again, who knows when the truth might break through to somebody? "First, there's the world, and all that's in it and all that we see, but also what we can't. Second, the flesh—all those desires, arrogances, strivings—when we let it rule us. Last, but definitely not least, there's the devil. That's in reverse threat level."

He looks out to the sea and then begins to open up the paperback to the page where he has his finger as a bookmark. "Good luck with that."

I decide not to verbalize what I am thinking. Which is, *Young man, luck has nothing to do with it.*

He drops his hand to his side, still clutching the paperback while he walks away, perhaps looking for his car parked on the deck of the ferry. Perhaps just wanting to get away from some kooky guy with a demon complex.

I scan the other passengers on the deck again, knowing any one of them may be harboring a monster.

It wasn't always like this. There was a time when I would carry professional business cards in a sterling-silver case tucked into the left pocket of one of my handmade Italian suits, just over my heart. The cards were heavy stock with black and gold embossing that read, "Trevor Black, Attorney-at-Law, Criminal Defense & Major Crimes," followed by the address of my law office on the Upper East Side.

But no more. If I handed out those cards to people now, I could be arrested. The Dunning Kamera murder case changed everything for me.

I notice off to my right, a half mile from the ferry, fishermen on the far shore casting into the surf. I think about launching my forty-footer at the marina and out to the Gulf Stream. The yellowfin tuna might be running, but even if not, out there on the blue expanse of the ocean, with no land in sight, there is a chance I could get a vacation from *them*.

Or so I've guessed, thinking there might be safety on the open water. On the other hand, I keep an eye on the big guy who spits again over the railing. We will see whether my theory holds true.

Soon I will catch sight of the little harbor at the island, so I decide to wander back to where my Land Rover is sandwiched among the line of other cars, bumper to bumper, on the deck. Like other passengers now, I climb into my vehicle and shut the door and will wait until the ferry eventually docks. I can't see the harbor yet, but eventually the ferry is going to slide to a halt against the big wooden pylons that are roped together and slick with greenish ocean slime.

Then I realize that the driver's-side window of my car is down, instantly followed by a feeling like a slap in the face. That I was right all along. One of the monsters is aboard this ferry and is very close to me. And getting closer.

I turn my head slightly to the left, toward my open car window. Then out of the corner of my eye, I see him. The large man with the dirty denim shirt over his mechanic's jumpsuit who is slowly approaching my car.

A crackling sound comes over the loudspeaker, followed by a voice giving the familiar instruction about starting our vehicles and keeping them in park and how one of the ferrymen in the tan naval uniforms will motion for us to drive forward when it is time.

The big man in the mechanic's suit has stopped next to my wide-open driver's-side window. His beefy fist is now gripping my door, so close to me that I can see the bristles of hair on the back of his hand, and he grunts in a tone that is deep and feral.

But I see another man through my windshield. He is dressed as a ferry officer, in a tan uniform, marching, arrow-straight, toward my car, and he looks unstoppable. Then, in an instant, the big man at my window vanishes. I look in my rearview mirror to find where the man has gone, but I can't see him. I look for the ferry officer. He has disappeared too. It's part of my everyday life now—this clash of kingdoms, darkness and light. The invisible war. Except, by an extraordinary series of events, I am able to see it. And I have chosen sides.

I lock my door and roll up my window. I will wait in my car for the rest of the ride until we eventually reach the island, when the steel gate of the ferry will be lowered down with a metallic groan and then a clank, creating a runway for the cars, and shortly after that I will be connected to the land. I steady myself. Soon I'll be home, though I now realize my island is no longer a safe haven. But then, I should have known that anyway. Mere geography never is.

11

THE
FLESH

1

I was thirteen years old when my father died. His funeral was held in a large stone chapel on the grounds of the cemetery. It was my first face-to-face with death. But it would not be my last. I couldn't put it into words, nor understand it, but somehow the fact that the ceremony was being conducted in a graveyard hit me with an almost tangible image of death. Like a sad fairy tale full of ink drawings about a powerful, pitiless giant standing guard over the land of the dead, while I, hopelessly and haplessly small, shivered in his looming shadow.

My mother's muffled sobs during the service that morning were heartbreaking. Even more than her unceasing wails on the day she'd answered the doorbell and spoken to two men from the foundry. One of the men had taken me into our television room, presumably waiting for my mother to collect herself. When she finally appeared, she sat down next to me and, in a quavering voice that was barely capable of transmitting facts, reminded me that my father had loved me. And then the worst. She told me that he had been killed in an industrial accident. I tried in my own dizzying numbness to console her, but nothing I did seemed to ease the pain. Despite that, she gathered me in

15

her arms and told me, laboring on each word, "We are going to make it." But I didn't see how.

When the funeral service ended, there was a flood of faces that came up to me saying they were sorry about our loss, some familiar to me, many not. A few chose to remind me that at least death had come instantly. "He didn't suffer," I was told. I am sure it was meant to be consolation, tinged with wisdom. But it imparted neither. When you're thirteen, and you know your dead father is lying over there in that burnished wood casket, the proffered wisdom of a grown-up sounds hollow and distant, and the faces of all those strange adults don't register. Except for two faces—the ones that even now connect that day to this one, haunting my memories. I can still see those two faces.

Hoskins Opperdill was one. My father had been a quality control engineer at the Opperdill Foundry, which operated along the banks of the Little Bear River. From the few occasions my father had taken me to the foundry, I remembered it as a place of infernal noise and gargantuan machines. The plant was owned by Hoskins Opperdill, who I had always heard was the richest man in Manitou. I never heard my dad say a negative word against him. After the funeral, Opperdill strode over to me in his suit and tie and starched white shirt. I had heard that he had a son of his own, about my age, but I'd never even seen him. He might as well have lived in a different world.

Opperdill had the stern, stiff look of a man who had kept to matters of business his whole life, et when he held out his hand to shake mine and patted my head, I sensed a different side.

"Your father was a fine man."

I nodded.

"I am very sad that he's gone. Would give anything to change that. Do you believe me, son?"

Here was a grown man—a wealthy, powerful man—asking a thirteen-year-old boy for his opinion. I kept my head down at first, hot tears blinding my eyes, and I almost felt ashamed. But while the man's face was stern, his eyes were gentle, so I worked up the boldness to answer. "I'm not sure if I can believe that. I just know that my dad is gone, and it was your foundry where he died."

He gave a sound, like he was clearing his throat. "A straight shooter, huh? Well, that's okay." Then he reached in his pocket and pulled out a roll of hundred-dollar bills and shoved them into my hand. "Your mother's too proud to take it. Make sure she gets this. If the money-grubbing lawyers have their way, it'll be quite a while before the workers' compensation payments are straightened out."

Everyone stepped outside and strode silently down the gravel path for a short graveside service.

The pallbearers strained cautiously against the weight of their load under a brilliantly blue sky, which seemed grotesquely out of place. A smaller group gathered around the vacant space that had been dug in the ground. I was given two red roses. One was to put on the coffin while it was still poised at ground level, which I did. The other rose remained clutched in my hand. The minister droned in vague generalizations about a man he'd never met. I focused on the rose, trying to follow the spiraling of its petals from the outside into the center, then out again. Keeping my mind occupied, steering it away from the raw fact of why I was there. After the service was over, as I stood beside the box containing all that was left of my father, I felt a hand on my shoulder, too heavy to be my mother's. Almost too heavy to be a hand.

I turned my head and started at the sight of Mason Krim, a neighbor of ours who lived in a huge brick house at the end of our block. The word among my neighborhood pals was that Krim had poisoned cats and dogs that had ventured onto his property, supposedly leaving tainted food in bowls on his back stoop for that purpose. But then again, that could have just been urban legend, spread abroad by imaginative teens.

Krim stood hunched over and pointed to my father's casket, which had yet to be lowered into the ground, and spoke. "I know what you're thinking."

Even overloaded and shell-shocked, I still found this statement exceedingly odd.

"You're thinking," he went on, "that's all there is. Dead is dead. Gone." Then he bent toward me, closer to my face, his breath filling my nostrils with the scent of something rotten and barely camouflaged with peppermint. "Just make sure you keep your mind wide open to anything. There's things out there you don't know yet. Things that can happen. Even when you can't see them."

Krim looked down at the blooming rose in my hand and reached out, as if asking to take it. For some reason I felt compelled to lay it in his palm. He closed his hand slowly around the soft, ruby-red petals of the rose and held it there for a few seconds. Then, with a crooked smile on his lips, he opened his hand and offered the rose back to me.

I held it by the stem, and at first just stared at this very strange man with the bent-over posture. Then my eyes drifted down to the rose. The petals that had been red and velvety were black and brittle. It was as if that flower, full of color, had been instantly transformed by Krim into something lifeless. As dead as some forgotten plant on an untended grave.

The sight of that was so startling that I dropped the rose and took a step backward. "Are you a magician?"

"The magic you're thinking of, that's for tricksters. I'm no trickster. I told you, there are things that can happen."

My mother must have spotted the interchange, because she had started to approach. As she did, Krim turned, gave her a curt nod, and then lipped out.

I had little comprehension what Krim was talking about and no idea how he did that with the rose. But in the midst of my grief and the swirling confusion of my young life, I knew that it had actually happened right in front of me. And it had to do with death, and things that I didn't know yet, things that were mysterious and inviting, and it was whispering a story to me, like a fairy tale about how, with the right secrets, the departed might be within reach, and the land of the dead could be tamed.

2

Manitou, my hometown, was located in central Wisconsin. Back then it had a population of thirty thousand and was surrounded by farmland. By late March or early April, you could tell that spring was coming because the snow and ice would start thawing and the melt would rush down the streets and the curbs, and the scent of manure from the fields would come drifting in.

It had the look of a relatively safe town, nestled in the heartland with a turn-of-the-century main street, quiet homes, and leafy avenues. On the surface, just one small cog in the slowly turning wheel of the natural order of things. But the visible things tell only part of the story.

My mother was a nurse, and for a while after my dad died and until she finally collected on his workers' compensation settlement, she had to pull double shifts to keep food on the table. She carried a wearied look on her face most of the time, but did the best she could for me. I had this distinct feeling that I could have pitched in more to help, but I didn't and worked hard not to think about that, trying to shuck the guilt.

With Dad gone and Mom working all hours, there was nothing for me at home but empty rooms and watching rock bands on MTV. So gradually, I gravitated to a gang of new friends, most of them following in the mold of brothers or uncles serving jail sentences. Over a span of almost two years, they showed me the finer points of shoplifting from record stores, garage thieving, vandalism, and smoking Camel cigarettes. Street fighting was their thing, not mine. But I did end up joining the boxing club for a while so I could take out my inner turmoil on the other kid in the ring. Living with abandon had a certain appeal.

In the end, my misdemeanors caught up with me. When my mom received a second call from the officer in the juvenile squad, she read me the riot act, cut off my questionable associations, and grounded me for three months.

During my home internment, I was surprised to find how little I missed the gang I'd been hanging out with. And only slightly less surprised that they never came asking after me. So during long stretches of solo evenings and weekends, I had plenty of time to wonder what else life had to offer. I would lay on the floor, staring at the ceiling and listening to music on our Crosley portable turntable that had to have been almost twenty years old. That is when I discovered the soul-rending sound of the blues harp—the deep-throated, soulful, scale-running harmonica that typified the sound of blues greats like Paul Butterfield, a man who became my music hero during high school.

My mother was talking all the time about how the Berlin Wall had just come down. But I couldn't be bothered with that. I had managed to get my hands on a copy of an old Butterfield album called *The Resurrection of Pigboy Crabshaw*. I hadn't the faintest what that weird title meant, but I knew what his music meant: his music ripped into subjects on heartbreak, trouble, running out of time, and bells tolling for things I couldn't describe yet, but could somehow feel deep inside when I listened.

When I stopped showing up, my old friends all

too easily cut me loose, but as soon as my long "house arrest" finally ended, I probably would have looked them up if it hadn't been for Dan Hoover. He was a classmate of mine, someone I had known since junior high. He was crazy serious about music—took guitar lessons twice a week and was in two different rock bands until our junior year. Just so happened, the first week I was allowed out of the house, he needed a player in his second group, called Nagasaki. I could play basic rhythm guitar chords, nothing fancy, but the real reason Dan wanted me in was because I had taught myself how to play the blues harp, which he thought was cool. Plus, I could actually sing on key. But after I'd been playing with them a few weeks and Dan asked me to break out the blues harp, the other guys in the band called it lame and said rhythm and blues music sucked, which Dan and I took to be heresy.

I told them what they really wanted was for Mickey Mouse to sprinkle magic on them and turn them into Duran Duran or A-ha—groups that Dan and I couldn't stand. A blowup followed, and Dan and I stood by each other. Nagasaki had a less-than-amicable breakup, and Dan and I decided to take the road less traveled and become blues men.

We put together another band called The Soul Assault, which later morphed into simply The Assault, and played Marvin Gaye, the Butterfield

Blues Band, James Brown, Muddy Waters, and even some classic acoustic stuff from Mississippi John Hurt that we jazzed up.

Bobby Budleigh was our drummer. Smaller than me, but with an athletic frame, he had a square, handsome face and a blond shock of hair. He was a heartthrob with girls, engendering envy among the rest of us.

Augie Bedders, our bass guitarist, was a first-string lineman on the football team. We put up with it during the football season, though Dan and I continually threatened to replace Augie on bass with someone else. But Bobby stuck up for Augie and argued us down.

To my surprise and delight, The Assault started making some money on the weekends, playing private parties and frat house beer bashes, first around our county and later in different parts of the state. Things really took off during our senior year, when we entered a statewide "Rising Stars" pop music festival that was held in the Milwaukee arena, and I got a taste of how fantastic success and fame could feel. The Assault ended up winning first place by nosing out a black soul band called The Royals—a dance-stepping, sax-playing, tightly melded seven-man ensemble from an inner-city church with a female lead singer who could belt a tune like Aretha Franklin. By all accounts we should have come in a very distant second at best, but in the middle of their second number, The Royals suffered from a blown amp and obnoxious feedback on the mic. It was as if their electronics had been bedeviled.

Back at the home front, though, things had become strange. Our neighborhood, though not affluent, was well maintained. No peeling paint. The yards were mowed.

Mason Krim's home was different. It was a dilapidated mansion that got worse as the years went by. A Spanish motif castle with crumbling turrets and spires and terra-cotta tiles missing from the roof. The yard remained uncut and sprouted tall, stalky weeds and bushes that had grown into vegetative monstrosities.

By the time I was a senior in high school, Krim, who was then in his eighties, had suffered a stroke. He was back home from the hospital and was apparently semi-mobile, but needed to be checked periodically. As a nurse, my mother had the inside scoop on all of that and told me, because Krim didn't have any relatives in the area, checking on him would be my job.

I tried to weasel out of it, but my mother insisted it was our duty to be "charitable," even to someone as peculiar as Mason Krim. "He was nice enough to come to your father's funeral," she said. "His wife and daughter both died a while ago. He lives alone. Let's try and return the favor."

Right. I certainly remembered him from the funeral. His strange reputation had only continued to grow over the years. I wasn't looking forward to my encounter with him.

On Friday afternoon, I stepped up to Mason Krim's front door and clanked the big iron knocker that was shaped like the head of an ugly animal, like a jackal. After hearing someone yelling for me to come in, I entered his mammoth house for the first time. The place was full of dark-purple curtains pulled shut, frayed velour furniture, and mahogany paneling. Every wall sported weird art, some of it abstract.

On one wall there was a large painting that showed the pale corpse of Christ, lying dead, face up, and bearing a visible chest wound, having been lifted off the cross so his body could be readied for burial. There were sad angels on both sides of him.

Floor-to-ceiling shelves were crammed with books, and on the coffee tables and in curio cabinets were a few strange objects that looked like archaeological relics. The place had the musty smell of an untended museum or a library that had been closed for a decade. And the air felt thicker somehow, like how it must feel inside a pyramid where the mummies are buried. There was the aura in Krim's house of my being watched by things that were not living and not visible, yet they were there in some nonphysical way, just beyond reach.

I found Mason Krim bending over his walker in the middle of the large foyer, with his head jutting out like the figurehead of a ship, and staring at me. His pale, saggy face had a droop on one side, and his head sported a few wispy hairs on top. He addressed me in a loud voice that quavered a little bit. "You checking on me?"

"Yeah. Mom told me to come over."

"You're Black's kid, aren't you? What's your name?"

I reminded him.

He nodded with recognition. Then he gave me some wacky instructions. "Always knock six times. Then six times again. That way I know it's you."

I nodded.

He asked, "You're not a Lutheran, are you?"

I didn't know exactly what I was, but I certainly was not that, so I shook my head no.

He added, "And don't stick your nose in my business."

I said okay to that too. Actually, I wanted no part of his business, whatever it was.

He kept going. "And don't ever intrude where you're not invited. Ever. You've been warned." But just as quickly he gave me a creepy smile. "Now if you mind your own business, I might have something for you."

As I started toward the door to leave, Krim

began to follow me with his walker thudding on the ground, then halted with a jerk and looked up at the painting of the dead Christ. He said, under his breath but loud enough for me to hear, "It's on the wrong side."

I asked him if he wanted me to take the picture down and to put it up on another wall, somewhere else in the house. Mason Krim didn't respond, but just stared at me with eyes that, for the moment, looked black and lifeless.

I took that as my cue to exit and hustled out the front door.

3

Through the rest of our senior year in high school, as a result of our burgeoning fame as blues musicians, our band started attracting female groupies who followed us around. Bobby Budleigh was a chick magnet. But he was too polite to return the favor. Besides, he was dating a girl from a private Lutheran school, and Bobby was the true-blue kind of guy. Unlike the rest of us, who weren't picky or loyal or anything else except ruled by the powerful subterranean streams of testosterone and hormones that coursed through our veins.

I had my share of flings, all of them self-conscious tangles of sweaty, awkward bodies. I recall each time silently arguing the case to myself that it had been great, and there were no regrets, but I never could fully convince myself. Besides, there was only one girl that I had squarely in my sights. Her name was Marilyn Parlow, a curvaceous blonde who was the captain of the girls' swim team. Whenever the swim meets were held in the high school's Olympic-size pool, Marilyn, in her form-fitting red swimsuit, helped fill the bleachers with ogling boys.

One Friday I stopped her in the hall on the way to the next class. "Hey, nice job at the swim meet."

"Thanks."

"You're Marilyn, right?"

She clucked her tongue, tilted her head, and said, "Uh, yeah."

Then I added, "Exactly. Marilyn. As in Marilyn Monroe."

She shot back, "And you must be Alec? As in the school smart alec?"

I tried not to reel after the kidney punch to my ego. I played it cool. "So you really don't know who I am?"

"Yes, I know. You're Trevor Black. Lead singer and blues harp player in The Assault."

The bruise was immediately healed, as if by some miracle.

She tossed me a Mona Lisa smile and said, "I like your music." Then the smile disappeared. "Just don't use that macho, chauvinistic line with me. Ever. About Marilyn Monroe. She was a beautiful spirit who died because men used her and abused her. And threw her away."

I paused. Then I said, "Okay. Sure. But do me a favor. Next time tell me what you really think."

Marilyn laughed.

I advanced, this time from the flank. "How about coming to our next gig? As my guest?"

The bell rang for class. She hurriedly said, "Tell you what. I'll come to your next music thing. Even stand right in the front. But not like a groupie or anything. Only you have to do something for me."

"What's that?"

"Have to dedicate a song to me."

"You've got a deal."

We both ran in opposite directions to our classes. As I turned around to catch one more glimpse of her, I noticed that she had turned around too. That made my day, and it helped me forget, at least for a while, that after school it was my day to check on Mason Krim again.

It was late afternoon when I did the magic knock on Krim's front door: six knocks, then a pause, then six more. I heard the clump of his walker on the other side of the door. He let me in and then walker-shuffled himself to the middle of the room, with his back to me. "Come here," he called.

I walked around him until I could see his face.

"Things have been happening."

I waited for more.

"A couple of vases. Falling off my shelves." Then he pointed to the far corner of his living room, to the right of the bookshelves, across from his easy chair, where there was a display case with an assortment of ancient-looking pots and figurines that looked like crudely fashioned women with multiple breasts. But the glass door was open, and there were two vases that were shattered into pieces on the wooden floor in front of the case.

"Get a broom, in the kitchen closet. Dustpan. Sweep up." He motioned to the shards of glass and pottery on the floor. "Throw the pieces away in the wastebasket in the kitchen. But do not let them touch your hands under any circumstances." Then, like a cover-up posing as an afterthought, he added, "Wouldn't want you to get cut." He flashed the creepy smile.

After I got the dustpan and bent down near the pieces on the floor, I felt strangely drawn to pick up one of the fragments and take a closer look, but I remembered Mr. Krim's warning and thought better of it. As I stared at the pile of broken pieces, I thought I heard whispering. I looked up at Mr. Krim. "Did you say something?"

He inhaled sharply. "I haven't said anything. Just get it out of here."

When I was done, he asked, "Have you talked to anyone about me?"

"No."

"That's good. You have any girlfriends?"

I smiled. "Yeah."

"That's good too. You like school?"

"It's okay."

"You like to read?"

"When I have to."

"You need to change that. Books are good for you. The human mind is meant to be filled up. What is your mind filled with?"

As a lusty teenager I knew exactly what my mind was filled with, but I wasn't about to share it with Captain Creepy. So I lied by half. "Music. I play in a band."

He scooted across the floor, leaning on his walker, until he reached the bookcase. He bobbed his head around, looking for something, then pulled a book out of the bookcase. It was a thin book with no dustcover. The title was faded but still legible. He handed it to me. "Read this."

I nodded.

Then he stared at me, and I noticed he was shaking a little. I thought maybe he was having another stroke. But he kept looking around, like something was about to happen. He stared hard at the painting of the dead Christ. Then he said, "One thing, and it's important. Regular people can't see them. They're invisible, unless they want to be seen. You only see what they're capable of, and only after they've done it. Then it's too late." Krim gave out a husky chortle, then dropped the creepy smile. "Just remember. You have to be the one in control. You. Not them."

I didn't answer, wondering, *How do you reply to something like that?*

His expression changed into something disturbing. "And one more thing. You ever tell anyone about what goes on in here, you'll be sorry."

Again, I was at a loss for words.

"Now you can go," he said.

I turned to leave, but had a thought, trying to be neighborly. "Next time, Mr. Krim, if you want something out of that glass case over there, I'd be glad to get it for you. You know, so you won't drop them and they won't get broken."

He pursed his lips tight together for a second. "Haven't you been listening? I wasn't the one who opened that glass case."

When I got home I tossed the book he gave me into a corner of my bedroom and, for a while, forgot about it.

The end of the school year was looming, and a bunch of our classmates had raised a pile of cash to throw a party the last weekend before the beginning of summer vacation. Some of it was to buy a modicum of soda and a huge amount of beer, and the rest was the talent fee for The Assault. We happily took the cash and carted our equipment to the edge of a private beach park at Silver Lake. Somebody knew whoever it was who ran the park, and we were assured that he wasn't the kind who would call the police and report underage drinking. He must have been paid off.

That evening, ready to light the night on fire with rhythm and blues music, I looked out into the crowd, and there, in the very front, was Marilyn Parlow. She was wearing a pair of short shorts, a tight-fitting tank top, and a flirtatious smile.

I was ready for her. I whispered the name of the first number to Dan and Augie, then strode back and told Bobby, who was engulfed by his drum set. It was a number that I had picked out especially for Marilyn.

Augie started thumping a bass line, slowly. Then Dan's guitar let out a slow, shivering scream that originated at the high frets way up there near the body of his Fender Stratocaster. Bobby was riding the foot pedal with a chest-pounding beat.

Then I put on my Ray-Ban sunglasses and gave the intro. "Ladies and gentlemen," I shouted into the mic, with the vamp building in the background. "The Assault is happy to be with you tonight."

The crowd went crazy.

"We have a very special number for you."

More cheers and screams erupted.

"This one goes out to someone very special. Marilyn Parlow."

I could barely hear my own voice over the noise.

"This one is dedicated to you, darlin'. Hope you like it."

Music pounded, swelling slowly up the scale. *Dundt dundt dundt dundt, dahhhh* . . . Then I wailed out in a falsetto, the first line of the James Brown hit—

" 'This is a man's world . . .' "

Even through my shades, I could see Marilyn's expression. First, mock anger at my insult to her professed feminism. Then, as if she couldn't help it, the surrender to a grimace that was hiding a smile, and then finally her full-blown belly laugh as she shook her head.

I figured that was it. That I had her. But with Marilyn, it was never so simple.

After we finished our set, Bobby climbed out from behind his drums and started talking and joking around with me, when Marilyn wiggled up to us. She put one hand on my shoulder and one on Bobby's and pulled us to her. She kissed both of us on the cheek, first Bobby, then me. "I love your music."

She looked at Bobby. "When you're hitting those drums, I can't tell whether you want to hurt them or make love to them."

Bobby's face turned scarlet.

Before she walked away, she said to me, "And thanks for the dedication. I guess?"

Marilyn had successfully messed up my head in a very serious way. Did she know what she was doing? Of course she did. She had to.

Bobby started packing up his drum kit. "I think I'm gonna take off, guys."

Dan put an arm around Bobby's shoulders. "C'mon, stay awhile. This is your chance to party."

"Aw, let him go," Augie cut in, sauntering over. "He doesn't know how to have fun anyhow."

Bobby gave a half smile. "Yeah, not really my scene. Besides, something just feels . . . off about this place. Like something bad happened here and it left its mark, you know?"

I looked at Dan, who shrugged. Augie shook his head and just laughed and made a spooky noise, then wandered away to tap a keg.

"You guys don't feel it?" Bobby asked.

"Maybe," I said. There was something uncomfortable hanging in the air. "But it's nothing a joint and a few beers won't remedy."

Bobby said he'd see us at practice, then hauled his gear out to his dad's Pontiac. Dan, Augie, and I hung out at the party into the wee hours. In the past few months, Augie had practically become a one-man drug cartel, so we spent our time smoking weed and draining down beer.

I finally dragged myself home near dawn, feeling spent and empty, and trying to concoct in my head a headline for the evening, something like "Best Night Ever," even though on the inside I wasn't buying it. By that time the starry night had already started to change and darkness was turning into a hazy gray. The morning light was starting to break over Manitou, revealing what the world really looked like.

4

On the last day of school, an hour before the bell was to ring, I was called down to the principal's office. I wondered if someone had ratted on the drinking and other nefarious goings-on at the party at Silver Lake. But it wasn't about that. It was a message my mother had delivered to the school secretary, who in turn handed it to me.

> I know it is your day to stop by Mr. Krim's. But please come straight home after school, and do NOT stop at Mason Krim's house.

That message was intriguing enough to drive me crazy, so I hustled home. When I arrived at my house, I noticed that down the street there was a big black station wagon with no windows in the sides or the back.

My mother met me inside the door, and she had

that look in her eye, something serious. "On the way home from work, I saw some envelopes sticking out of Mason Krim's mail slot, and the newspaper was still on his doorstep, so I decided I'd check on him myself." Then the kicker: "Mr. Krim has passed away."

My body went cold. "How did he die?"

"Well, he was old. Already had a stroke. You know that. It was just his time." My mother was a nurse, and I knew she had experience with death, but she seemed more uneasy than she'd ever been, even after a shift at the hospital.

Plus, I had my own reason for probing. "Yeah, but . . . where did you find him?"

"In the living room."

"By the bookcases? Across from the glass display case?"

"No, Trevor. Not there . . ."

"I really want to know. On his walker?"

"Yes. I guess he must have been standing with his walker when he collapsed."

"But where?"

"By a wall. Under a painting."

"The dead Christ? That one?"

She eyed me closely and took her time answering. "Yes, under that picture. But you needn't worry about any of that . . ."

I couldn't let it end there. "Were his eyes open?"

She sighed. "Yes, they were. Now, Trevor, you don't need to know anything else."

"I do. I do need to know. Was he looking at something?"

"What difference does it make? He's gone. I'm sure he appreciated what you did for him—"

"Was he looking at something? It's important to me."

Long pause. "Does this have something to do with your father passing? I know it was so hard for you when it happened, you were so young."

"No. Nothing to do with Dad dying." I raised my voice. "Mom, I need an answer. What was he looking at?"

"Maybe looking at the picture, I really can't say—"

"Did Krim look surprised? Shocked?"

Longer pause. Finally she said, "Yes, he looked surprised. Probably a physiological response. It happens at death sometimes." Then she raised one eyebrow and added, "Trevor, how did you know all this?"

I just shrugged, and then I sprinted up the stairs to my bedroom and shut the door.

After rummaging around my room, I found the book that Krim had given me. It was titled *Piercing the Supernatural Veil*, but no author's name was listed. The publishing date was 1929 by the Theosophy League.

I started reading, and I kept reading until I finished the book at around two in the morning. It was the eve of summer vacation, and in a few

39

days my summer job with a construction company would be starting. I also knew that Dan Hoover wanted several band practices lined up as soon as possible.

But suddenly, none of that seemed to matter. By the time I hit the last page of the book, my view of the physical world had been rocked with the idea that there might truly be another dimension out there, one that could wilt roses and shatter ceramics . . . and scare a man to death. And as the title of that little book implied, there might be a way to connect with it. As Mason Krim had told me as a boy that time, in his weird monologue at the cemetery, *"There's things out there you don't know yet. Things that can happen."* Whatever those things were, I wanted to find out.

The question that was haunting me, as I drifted off to sleep, was whether Mason Krim, gripping his walker moments before his death, had some kind of experience as he looked up at that painting, the one with the pale Christ off the cross as he lay on the ground in death with his chest gashed. I thought back to my first visit with Krim at his house. And what he had said to me when I was with him and he was staring at that picture on that wall.

"Wrong side."

Wild dreams with crumbling houses and sad angels and strange whispers and doorknobs that turned into jackals' heads. I slept late the next day—almost until noon. My mom must have taken pity on me; it was my first day of vacation, and she hadn't wakened me before heading off to her shift at the hospital.

After prying my eyes open, I slumped around the kitchen in my gym shorts, filling up a mixing bowl with Cheerios and dousing it with milk, when the doorbell rang. I put down the bowl, shuffled to the front door, and opened it. Marilyn was standing on the front porch.

She laughed. "Wow. Bad hair day!"

I discovered a cowlick in my tangled hair and smoothed it down. "Hey, what's up?" I was trying to play it casual.

Then I looked out to the curb and saw Bobby behind the wheel of his parents' Pontiac. He waved. There was this bitter taste of disappointment. But I thought to myself, *Okay, so I guess the three of us is better than the none of us.*

Marilyn had her hands on her hips. "We're going on a picnic. Shake your booty."

I dashed into the kitchen, tipped the contents of the cereal bowl into the sink, and sprinted upstairs to get dressed. Fifteen minutes later we were cruising west toward the end of town where the country club was located.

I asked where we were going.

"Up by the golf course," Marilyn said. "There's a service road up there. Lots of grass. Great view."

"Yeah," I said, noting that she didn't call the place by its local name, Makeout Point. "I know about that area. How'd you know?"

She burst out with, "Everybody knows, stupid!"

After parking the car, we found a grassy hill with a view of the marsh and Pebble Creek directly below. If you looked farther you could see some farmers' fields, and even farther above the trees, the high cement tower of the incinerator at the Manitou landfill, which was illuminated at night with rows of vertical lights so you could see the eerie outline of the tower, like a surrealistic Christmas decoration. On "animal burning days" it would send up a disgusting odor of smoke and death.

Marilyn spread out a bedsheet and opened up a picnic basket. She had stuffed it with fried chicken, peanut butter and jelly sandwiches, and chips. My kind of food.

The three of us lay down on our backs with our bellies full, staring at the blue sky, not far from a hedge of lilac bushes that were exploding with fragrance.

After a while I said, "What's out there?"

Bobby asked, "Out where?"

"After life. After death."

"Don't know," Marilyn said.

"Heaven," Bobby said.

I narrowed it down. "I'm talking about something else."

"What?" Bobby asked.

"Supernatural things. Angels and demons. Another dimension."

"I don't like scary movies," Marilyn said. "I like love stories."

I needed to make my point. "Maybe some things seem scary because we don't understand them. Like an invisible supernatural veil. And we're on one side. But what if we were able to walk through it?"

Marilyn started laughing. "Oh, you are in such a weird mood. Where do you get that stuff?"

Just then, Bobby jumped up, looking at his watch.

"What?" I asked.

"I just remembered I need to get to the dry cleaner's at the Crestview Plaza. I promised my dad I'd swing by and pick up his shirts before they closed."

Marilyn started packing up her picnic accoutrements, but Bobby cut her off. "Don't bother. I'll be back in half an hour or so. You guys just chill."

We watched Bobby drive his dad's Pontiac down the road until it disappeared. Marilyn rolled over on her side closer to me, and we made small talk for a while. About her plans for school and how she had been accepted at a girls' college in Virginia. And about her summer job at the YWCA swimming pool as a lifeguard, and how she was bummed because it was an inside pool and she couldn't get a suntan that way. She joked about my construction job, and why I couldn't hurry up and finish the city's new outside swimming pool where my summer job had me pouring cement. The air was filled with the scent of lilacs, and I was trying not to stare at Marilyn, but it was hard not to.

I decided that she was flirting, so I made the move. I kissed her, and she seemed like she enjoyed it. She kissed me back, and I felt myself being swallowed up in her perfume, which had the fragrance of exotic flowers.

But when I tried to go further, she slapped my hand and pulled back. "I'm not easy like that. Why would you think that?"

I tried to be nonchalant. "I don't think that."

By then she was lying on her back with a serious look on her face. Then, after a minute or so, she burst into laughter. "What was that thing you were saying? About a supernatural whatever?"

"Supernatural veil."

"Yeah. What were you talking about?"

"Just something I read."

"Do you believe everything you read?"

"Of course not."

"Good. Because there's a lot of ridiculous stuff out there. What's important is what you can see and touch with your own body. And what you can feel with your own heart. Not some invisible make-believe."

I was trying to figure her out. But before I could, she sat up quickly and said, curtly, "Just don't be stupid, Trevor. You're smarter than that."

"Stupid about what?"

"You know, about me. Us. Everything."

As soon as she uttered that last word, she stood up and went back to packing the leftovers and the trash and putting it in the picnic basket. By then we could see Bobby's Pontiac, winding toward us up the road's serpentine twists and turns.

I grabbed the picnic basket, and Marilyn and I started walking toward Bobby's car. I was leaving behind the grassy hill and the lilacs and the drifting scent of her perfume.

Like Adam, I had been tossed out of the Garden. But unlike him, I didn't realize it yet.

5

That was the only romantic interlude I had with Marilyn before the start of summer, or even up to the fall for that matter. And it had been a failure.

In early summer The Assault had a few performances. But then things tapered off. Dan Hoover had always handled the bookings, but he had been accepted into the Juilliard jazz program and more and more was disappearing for music camp or private lessons. I knew he was talented, but it didn't hit me at the time what an incredible honor it was for Dan to be accepted into the program. All I cared about was the fact that our blues band was slowly disintegrating and I didn't like it.

With Dan not around, and Bobby going AWOL working six weeks straight at a church camp, Augie and I started hanging around together more. He had tried for a football scholarship at UW Stout, but didn't get in. He decided to start out at the local community college and then planned on transferring to Stout after two years, in order to save money on tuition.

One weekend my mother had to attend an overnight nursing conference out of town. She made a point of ceremonially handing me a set of keys with a serious mother look. "I'm giving you the keys to Mason Krim's house. We're expecting some relatives of his to arrive any day now to claim the estate and check out the house. In case they come while I'm gone, you'll have the keys, and you can let them in."

Then, an even more intense mother stare into my eyes. "And no parties in that house. Understood?"

I nodded approvingly. I couldn't imagine a worse place to have a rocking party than in Mason Krim's house.

After my mother left early that evening, Augie and I were at my house sucking down cans of Miller beer, killing time, when Augie gave a mock shiver. "Man, I get the creeps sometimes just driving down your block."

"From what?"

"That place on the corner. It looks like a haunted house."

"Yeah, that's where Mason Krim used to live. Don't worry. He's got some relatives coming to claim the place. I'm sure they're just going to knock it down and sell the lot. They're supposed to stop by here anytime to pick up the keys." I took a swig, then glanced at Augie. He had a strange look of concentration on his face. "I ever tell you I used to check in on Krim?"

"Like, face-to-face in his house?"

"Every Tuesday. He was a lonely, creepy old man. Always trying to scare me with talk about death and stuff. Even has this huge painting of a dead Jesus right in the entryway."

"Sick." Augie went quiet for a moment. "So what did he talk about?"

"He never came out and said it. Wanted to keep it hidden, I guess. Just implied a lot. Like there were these, I don't know, artifacts or something that fell off a shelf and broke, but he insisted he never opened the case. Like it was spirits or something. He even gave me a book about all this weird stuff he was into."

Augie was getting cranked. "What did it say?"

"The book?"

"Yeah."

"Hey, school's out. I'm not giving you a book report."

"But it talked about, like, ghosts and stuff, right?"

"Not exactly. Just about the world of spirits. And how to connect with them."

Augie was starting to laugh. But not funny laughing. More like laughing at the thought of something that was indescribable. "And that dude died in that house down the street, where some weird invisible force had knocked down his glass jars or pitchers or whatever and busted them." He took a second to think about what he had just said. Then, "Hey, you've got the keys to his house."

"That's right. So?"

"This is awesome. I say we hustle on down there and look around."

I hesitated.

He started taunting me. "What's the matter? Scared?"

"Are you kidding?"

"Well?"

"Okay," I said, taking the dare. Then I upped the ante. "How about we go over there, but even better, let's see if we can pierce the supernatural veil . . ."

Candles were lit and the little thin book was in my hand. Augie and I sat on the floor of Mason Krim's musty living room, our only light coming from the flickering circle of candles.

Augie was on a roll. "Let's go, big daddy."

I flipped through the book until I found the page I was looking for. But just then I felt a caution, like a personal smoke alarm going off inside. So, hedging my bets, I said, "No need to go through all of this."

"No backing out now," Augie countered. "Got to do it all." He grabbed the book out of my hand and looked at the page where I had it opened. Then he spoke up, mangling the pronunciation of the heading of that section of the book—*Incantation*. And he looked at me again, and I gave him the go sign.

Augie started to recite the Latin phrases. I had taken Latin as my language class for two years, but I don't think he knew that, and I didn't tell him. I just let him bungle through the words out loud. I wondered silently in my head whether that still counted as a real incantation or not. Or whether it was something else, something internal and having to do with the intentions of the heart that mattered, and if so, if that was the real hinge that would swing the door open to whatever was waiting on the other side.

He finished and handed the book to me. "It says here that everyone has to join in. Otherwise it won't work."

I knew what was next. What I was supposed to do? I looked around because I was hearing sounds, but I knew what it was. The wind was picking up, and the maple trees outside of Krim's house had not been trimmed, so the branches were scraping against the windows.

"Get on with this," Augie whispered.

"Okay."

In the flickering candlelight I said what I was supposed to say. It was simple. At the end, I spoke out in a loud voice. "Is anyone there? Is anyone listening?"

Then I said it again. "Is anyone there? Is anyone listening?"

Augie was stone still, his eyes half-closed, like he was listening real close. Waiting. I don't know how much time went by. Maybe several minutes. Neither of us said a word. In my mind I knew that one of us had to blink, had to call the game to an end. But neither of us did.

Then a deafening noise. We jumped. It was the jangling of a telephone.

I was startled. Augie went bug-eyed. It kept ringing, and ringing, and ringing. I thought, *Why doesn't it stop? Why is it still ringing?*

Augie tried to get to his feet, but in the process he kicked over one of the candles. The telephone kept ringing with that obnoxious, tinny, jangling sound, and it wouldn't stop. I pointed to the candle that was burning sideways on the floor and yelled to Augie, "Put out the fire!" Then I leaped over the candles toward the sound.

I found the telephone at the other end of the

room on a small table. I let it ring once more, hoping it would end. But it didn't. Another ring. I put my hand to the receiver and picked it up.

I never said hello. On the other end there was a voice. A masculine voice. What the voice said was very simple and sent a chill over me like someone had dropped ice down my shirt: "Is anyone there? Is anyone listening?"

I couldn't move. Augie looked at me and recoiled at first, as if my face was melting. Then he jumped over to me, almost tripping, and grabbed the phone out of my hand. He put it to his ear and stood there for the longest time, listening and not saying anything, his mouth half open. I could faintly hear a voice on the other end, but none of the words.

Finally he placed the receiver very slowly back onto the base.

I needed to know. "Who was that? What did he say to you?"

At first Augie wouldn't say. I asked him again. Then this smile came over his face, almost like the smile of Mason Krim that would creep me out.

Finally, after staring out in space, he answered. "It was Casper the Friendly Ghost. He says hi." Then Augie burst into a belly laugh. He always did have a weird sense of humor.

Augie never asked me what I had heard on the telephone. And despite my asking him several times that summer what he had heard on the other end of that call, Augie would never tell me.

6

When Bobby Budleigh arrived back in town after working at his church camp, he looked me up. Augie was out of town for a family reunion and Dan was at a guitar clinic, so it was just Bobby and me. I was driving my Ford Fairlane with the top down and the radio blaring. Bobby loved my convertible. He was sitting in the passenger seat, bobbing his head to Poison's "Fallen Angel," tapping his hand on the side of the car.

"You like that stuff?" I asked.

Bobby went along with my penchant for rhythm and blues, but his pop music tastes ranged wider than mine. Instead of answering, he just stared at me with a comical smile on his face, then burst out singing the Poison lyrics at the top of his lungs: "'Just a step away from the edge of a fall. Caught between heaven and hell.'"

It got me thinking about something. So I turned down the radio. "Bobby, you ever think that heaven and hell stuff is really real?"

"You know what I think? It's more real than you and me and the wind blowing through our hair. Just because we can't see it doesn't mean it's not there."

I nodded and swallowed. "Augie and I . . . One weekend while you were at camp, we snuck into Mason Krim's place and . . . I don't know. Had a séance or something."

Bobby waited a bit, but when I stayed silent, he flipped the radio dial all the way off. "And?"

So I told him. About the book and the candles and the incantation . . . and the phone call.

Bobby lit up. "Oh, man, you've got to talk to Rev. Cannon. He'd be the perfect person."

"Perfect for what?"

"He does exorcisms."

"Shut up," I catcalled.

"Not kidding."

"Really?"

"True. I think it got him into trouble with the synod."

"The what?"

"Our church, Good Shepherd, is part of this Lutheran organizational thing—a synod. Rev. Cannon is our pastor. I think the higher-ups didn't dig his being an exorcism stud. And his preaching about the devil and all that. Some people left the church. It was a big deal."

Part of me was interested. Another part wanted nothing to do with Bobby's church. I let it go.

But Bobby didn't. "I'm telling you, you ought to talk to him. He's been to South America. Cast out demons down there in the jungle. Really amazing stuff."

"Okay. Let's go over there. Sometime, maybe."

"He works on his sermons in his study at the church on Saturdays."

I threw him a nasty look.

Bobby laughed. "I'm just saying . . . but if you're freaked out about it, fine. No problem."

I wasn't one to pass up a challenge. "Fine. Okay. Where is the church again?"

Twenty minutes later I was sitting across from Rev. Cannon, a man in his late fifties with a square face and wire-rimmed glasses, who was seated against a backdrop of floor-to-ceiling books. He was in his shirtsleeves, wearing a clerical collar.

Bobby did the opening, describing everything that I had told him. I was surprised how he got it all right, down to the smallest detail.

After Bobby finished, Cannon ratcheted up the solemnity by scrunching his forehead and folding his hands on his desk. "The devil is real, you know."

I shifted in my seat and looked out the window. "I'm kinda new to this stuff . . ."

"No mistake. The devil, the prince of the air, is real."

"If you say so."

"No. God says so."

It was just the opening volley in the conversation, but already the reverend was bringing out the big guns. I was stymied for a comeback.

Cannon said, "Satan is a dark lord who commands legions of demons under him. When he tempted Jesus in the desert, it wasn't a metaphor. Nor an abstraction. The devil is an existing personality of intense evil. And young minds like yours are easy prey."

I had a single thought. *Get me out of here.*

But he kept it up. "The Word of God is clear. Read it for yourself."

I saw an opening to throw a curveball and I took it. "I heard your church is sort of upset about all the devil stuff you talk about, though."

He paused. I could see in his face something like, *Well played, lad.* He countered with, "We're Lutherans."

"Yeah, I guess I knew that."

He pressed the point. "Martin Luther himself felt so oppressed by the devil that he threw an inkwell at him."

"Did he hit him?" I never missed an opportunity to smart off. And I knew I had scored because Bobby was red faced, trying to hold back a snicker.

But Rev. Cannon wasn't fazed. Instead he asked, "You consider your activities that Bobby described here, your dabbling in the supernatural, a small thing?"

"I guess so."

"Then you'd better take care with those kinds of 'small' things."

I waited for the big finish. The rim shot from Rev. Cannon. A version of what Bobby had perfected on the snare drum. I figured it was coming and I was right.

Cannon ended with, "Small fires consume big forests."

Bang. There it was.

Walking back to my car, Bobby asked, "What'd you think?"

"Strange." I was still trying to untangle Rev. Cannon's metaphor about the forest fire.

"Thing about Rev. Cannon is, you always know where he stands."

"Right. I got it. He hates the devil."

Bobby stopped walking, just short of my Fairlane. He turned and gave me a look that was almost paternalistic. "Yeah, but assuming the devil's real, and I pretty much think he is, then I wouldn't want you tangling with him. You could get messed up, majorly."

"Look," I said. "I know there might be some kind of supernatural something out there. I'd like to know what it is. But do you actually think the devil's sneaking around, plotting bad stuff? I mean, come on, really?"

Bobby gave me a big grin. "Forget what I think. I stick with what God says. Just be careful with what you're doing. I don't want my buddy Trevor getting turned into a zombie."

7

By summer's end The Assault was no more. Everyone had scattered. I was getting ready for New York University and Dan Hoover was already situated at Juilliard. Because our schools were both in New York City, I naively figured we could easily hang out together. I guess I pictured that mega-metropolis as simply a bigger version of Milwaukee, the closest "big city" in our part of the country. Nor did I realize how all-absorbing college studies would become. And I was determined to shake off any small-town stigma and show all the city kids what I could do.

Bobby was on his way out west, after getting a science scholarship to the University of Idaho. He was a smart kid, so that didn't surprise me.

Augie was the only one hanging back in the hometown, going to the community college. His girlfriend, Susan Cambridge, was attending Stout. Augie planned on going up there to visit her on the weekends.

During the first months of college, the rigors of school were overwhelming, and I had little time for anything else except for binge drinking whenever I could pay a senior to buy booze for me and my fellow freshmen. Strangely, pot was easier to come by, but by then alcohol had become countercultural and therefore preferable from my standpoint. I liked being contrarian.

Then in November, just before Thanksgiving, I was in my dorm room when I received a call. I was shocked to hear Marilyn Parlow's voice on the other end. She had enrolled at Sweet Briar, a small women's college in Virginia. She said offhandedly that she had just returned from a short trip and would love to catch up with me in New York some weekend.

"Really?"

She clucked her tongue. "You sound surprised."

I needed to exude nonchalance. "Well, I'm pleasantly surprised. Great to hear from you. Yeah. I'd love to see you."

We worked out a date in three weeks. She would take the train up. I told my dorm roommate, Gary, that I would need the room that whole weekend. I knew I was putting him out, but Gary's family lived in New Jersey, so it wasn't that big a deal for him to go home and visit the parents while I entertained Marilyn.

There was another benefit that Gary provided. He had an uncle who used to work at the legendary Bitter End, which wasn't too far from campus. So when Marilyn showed up on the Saturday of her visit, I had already arranged for a table for Marilyn and myself. I had to pay Gary forty bucks for the privilege, but it was worth it.

I didn't tell Marilyn where we were going. When we strolled along Washington Park and into Greenwich Village and finally onto Bleecker Street, and when she recognized the famous blue awning over the entrance of the folk-rock club that had hosted every celeb music group ever worth listening to, she was visibly impressed. We stayed until after two in the morning listening to a blues group called Hard Road, and then we cabbed back to my dorm. I had a bottle of wine stashed in my sock drawer, which we quickly dispatched.

But during the visit Marilyn seemed different. She was a naturally beautiful girl, but she was wearing too much makeup and harboring an edgy attitude. And there was a sadness there too that I couldn't put my finger on.

During the conversation in my dorm room, we sat next to each other on my bed, downing the bottle of wine, drinking it out of coffee mugs. We made only small talk. Discussion about classes. Schools. Plans. No deep discussions about life, or death, or the "supernatural dimension" that I had raised with her on the hill at Makeout Point the summer after graduation.

I asked her where she had been on the trip that she had vaguely mentioned in her phone call.

"Out west," she said.

"Yeah, but where out west?"

"Idaho."

That was a kick in the shins. "You mean you met up with Bobby?"

She gave a labored smile. "Yeah. It was so nice to connect."

Now it was a punch in the kidneys. "I always thought you had a thing for Bobby."

"Don't be that way."

"What way? I'm just calling it the way I see it."

She stood up, a little unsteady, and started unbuttoning her blouse. "Let's make love."

I would later question the "love" part. But my hormones doubled up with my fascination with her, and it drove me forward. After we finished with our encounter, unemotional and mechanical, I lent her my bathrobe, escorted her down to the bathroom, and guarded the door until she was done, then whisked her back to my room.

She pulled on her underwear and climbed into Gary's bed. "Good night."

I was at a loss for words. What was going on? I tried to make conversation, and she gave me only one-word responses. Finally I laid it all out. "Why did you come up here? Why did we just have sex? I don't understand any of this."

"Really?"

"Yeah. Really."

She had turned on her side, away from me, and stayed there for a long time until she answered at last. "I have a question for you."

"Fine. What is it?"

"Is it wrong for a woman to love two men?"

I answered in a flash. "Only if you don't choose."

She left New York early the next morning. She changed her train ticket to get out earlier. That was the last time I would ever see Marilyn Parlow.

I finished the semester with top grades, though most of my straight-A mentality was just habit. I probably thought more about Marilyn and Bobby than about all of my coursework put together. I stayed in New York through the Christmas break. I know it broke my mom's heart, but I couldn't countenance seeing Manitou again. I made plans to meet up with Dan on Christmas Day, but he had to cancel when he got picked up for a major concert at a midtown cathedral, so I spent the holiday with a bottle of blackberry brandy. When classes started up again, at least I had some distraction.

Then in February, right around Valentine's Day, I got one last call on the phone from Marilyn. A bolt of lightning. The sinking of the *Titanic*.

"Trevor, I'm pregnant."

I cursed the news.

"Don't worry, I'll get rid of it. I'll take care of everything. Just wanted you to know."

The coward in me accepted that. Didn't challenge it. Didn't offer to be there with her. Never suggested that we think this over. Never considered that she was carrying a human life and that it was ours. Nothing.

I tucked it away. Life would go on. School. Lectures. Research. Papers. Grades. Binge drinking. Friends. More drinking. Eventually getting serious about future plans, and beginning to think about pursuing law school after graduation. But Marilyn never fully disappeared from my mind. Nor did my friends, nor Mason Krim, nor the strange way the supernatural veil, previously opaque, had become frighteningly transparent in Krim's house . . .

I'd given in to the flesh. The sensual. The experiential. The supernatural. I didn't consider any of the revelry to have been extraordinary, blind to the fact that I had already opened a door to a realm that I didn't understand.

It seemed harmless enough at the time. In retrospect, it looks different now. Back then I didn't know if there was such a thing as hell, and I hadn't the faintest idea that there could be hell to pay for things done, or undone.

THE
WORLD
25 YEARS LATER

8

The law offices of Tobit, Black, Dandridge & Swartz were tucked inside the Woolworth Building on Broadway. The one-hundred-year-old skyscraper was an icon of Gothic design, a commercial tower with the kind of ornate, brooding architecture, complete with spires and gargoyles, that would have made it a perfect setting for *Ghostbusters*. I spent twelve to thirteen hours a day in that office suite or at the courthouse, immersed in my criminal defense law practice. The courtroom was my altar, and I suppose it was the closest thing to a religion that I had.

My three fellow partners all did commercial transactions and estate planning—the civilized, white-glove stuff—and it was left to me to represent the scoundrels. Occasionally, though, I would get a few clients who, for all the world, looked like they might actually be innocent. I don't mean merely *not guilty* in the legal sense. But truly innocent. Those were the scary ones. You'd lose sleep when you handled those cases.

At the very earliest stage, that was where my head was at in the Dunning Kamera case before I started to dig into it.

I had already heard things on the grapevine

about the Kamera case even before my senior partner, Hal Tobit, gave me the nod. As it turned out, Hal was an old friend of Dunning's father, Slovan Kamera, who'd had a respectable career on the New York City Supreme Court until health problems pushed him into early retirement. The distraught judge called up Hal and said that his son had been indicted for the grisly murder of a prostitute, and Hal recommended me, of course. After I was retained, and when the papers got ahold of the story, the news splattered through the city like sand in a wind tunnel.

I conducted a short jail conference with Dunning. Following that, he shuffled under armed guard into the courtroom wearing cuffs and leg irons and sat next to me at the counsel table. When the case was called by the clerk, I made my pitch to the judge for release from custody.

During the bail hearing, the assistant DA, Betty Verring, practically went apoplectic as she argued why my client ought to be held without bail pending trial. I was aware that there had been a string of call-girl murders and the district attorney's office was catching heat for not bringing the culprit to justice. At the same time, they had to know that the son of a local judge would make a lousy suspect.

More to the point, as far as the bail hearing was concerned, Betty was a good prosecutor who had to know that the odds were against her. Dunning

Kamera made a great candidate for bail, even aside from his father's stellar standing in the legal community: Dunning was a local man, with numerous ties to the community, gainfully employed, no prior record, and no flight risk. He didn't even own a passport. Predictably, I prevailed. The judge set reasonable bail for him, despite the sensational nature of the crime.

As I was strutting out of the courtroom, feeling the momentary rush of invincibility, Betty handed me a manila envelope. "Here's a little present for you, Trevor."

I smirked. "Thanks, Betty. And I didn't even have to file a discovery motion to get this. You're tops." A few minutes later I was in the parking garage, having eased myself into the soft leather comfort of my Aston Martin DB9 coupe. I clicked on the reading light and opened the envelope. As I studied the contents, things got serious very quickly. I could see why the ADA had been in a hurry to make sure I had copies of the forensic photographs of the victim, a nineteen-year-old runaway named Heather who was turning tricks to support her coke habit.

I never had a weak stomach, but this case got to me. Heather's throat showed extreme bruising. The autopsy protocol would later explain that her larynx had been crushed; incredible pressure had been exerted. But after viewing the rest of the photos I knew that wasn't the worst part. Not even close. I had to talk to Dunning about these pictures.

On the other hand, the evidence laid out in the indictment showed only a gossamer-thin connection between my client and the crime. In fact, only one piece of evidence created the circumstantial link. My job would be to smash that link like I was wielding a ball-peen hammer, banging it until it broke. And I was good at my job. My acquittal rate at trial was 65 percent, which was impressive considering how deeply the deck is stacked against the defense. The prosecution always has the upper hand, especially at the start, when they can put their case together quickly and efficiently, marshaling police investigators, forensic experts, you name it. Most criminal defendants are actually guilty of something, whether or not they've been charged for it. Aren't we all? And most clients on the other side of a metal mesh or a thick pane of glass aren't eager to divulge the facts that have put them there. It usually took some cajoling and a heavy dose of threatening before I could get them to come clean. Even when they did dump the real facts on me, my cases often sagged under the weight of incriminating evidence like a garbage bag loaded with bricks.

The Kamera case looked like it would be another for the win column. But first I needed to size up my client.

A few days later, we were seated in my office while Dunning Kamera, a thin, thirty-four-year-old man with pale skin, extolled the aesthetics of my decor—the rich walnut paneling, my original art, and on and on. I interrupted him, sliding the pictures across my desk toward him, and asked him to study them.

He glanced through the photos like someone paging through an issue of *National Geographic*, with mild curiosity and interest, but no discernible disgust, although he did take the time to shake his head slowly at each photo of Heather's murdered corpse. When he was done, he spoke.

"Yes?" he announced, more like a statement than a question.

I asked him, "Did you know this girl?"

"No."

"Never met her, even casually?"

"No, I'm sorry."

"Sorry? Why are you sorry?" It was time to shake things up a little. So I added, "Did you do something to feel sorry about?"

He smiled. "Just a figure of speech." Dunning Kamera looked unperturbed.

I decided to press him on his alibi. "You say you were at the movies that night. Right? The Cineplex was only about four blocks from where they found her body in the dumpster."

According to the indictment, the medical examiner had concluded that Heather had been dead for only an hour or two before an apartment building super found her body in the trash.

"Yes, at the movies," he answered, pulling something out of his top pocket. It was the stub of a ticket for the movie he saw that night. He said that he went to the theater alone. The film ran two hours and ten minutes, and it ended about twenty minutes after Heather's body had been discovered. He handed me the ticket stub. His alibi defense was that at the moment of death he was several blocks away, in a movie theater, but with no witnesses that he knew of. Far from a perfect defense. Still, I've had cases that were a lot tougher.

"These pictures of the victim, did you notice anything unusual?"

"She looks dead."

"Other than that?"

He shook his head.

"Nothing else?" I asked.

He shook his head no, a second time, with a questioning look on his face. Then he added, "Why do you keep asking about the photographs?"

"Just wondering," I said. "Because they show that the killer cut her heart out of her chest."

9

I can't say exactly why I decided to cut my workday short, but I did. I left immediately after my office conference with Dunning Kamera and headed home to my condo on the Upper East Side and to my wife, Courtney, a beautiful, curvaceous redhead who had a taste for parties and the good life.

Courtney had been my secretary earlier in my law career, which is how we originally met. She knew that when it came to the law, I was highly disciplined, certainly; but more than that, in terms of wanting to win my cases, I was like a man possessed.

But then again, I was also a full-blooded male. After working with her at the law firm for only a few weeks, I fell for her quickly. She responded just as quickly and said she would be more than happy to adjust to the demands of my law career. We waltzed into a wedding six months later. Courtney was never timid about flaunting her obvious assets, and I became the envy of my legal colleagues.

Courtney knew full well about my slavish work habits and my long hours, and the schedule that I kept. I worked at the office until eight and got home around 8:45. The only exceptions to my regular 8:45 arrival time were Friday nights, when I would occasionally take her out to a play or a concert, or maybe a movie, unless I happened to be locked in a jury trial, in which case I might be staying at a hotel close to the courthouse. We always ate late. Occasionally I would call ahead so we could rendezvous at a restaurant. Otherwise, Courtney would order out for food and have it delivered to the condo so it would arrive just about the time that I walked in the door. To her credit, she had it down to an art. My schedule was as predictable as the constellations in the sky. And maybe that was part of the problem.

On that evening, I pulled into our parking space in the passkey underground garage very early, around six o'clock. I turned off the ignition but didn't exit my Aston Martin at first. Instead, I just sat there, thinking about Dunning Kamera and those photos. And about Heather, the victim. Criminal defense lawyers do think about the victims. The thing is, when we talk to the juries about them, while we express honest remorse about the senseless killings, we usually find ourselves arguing something like, *"You need to acquit my client so the police can find the real killer, because he is still out there. Convict my client, and the real culprit will never be found."*

As I had many times before, I silently rehearsed all the rationale for adversarial law. The system only works when both sides punch it out, and spill blood, and put everything into it, like the whole world depends on it. Then, and only then, can an attorney sleep at night because, regardless of the verdict, your client got everything you could give and you played your part in making sure that a rough-hewn kind of human justice had been achieved. *Besides,* I told myself, *who really knows, in the final analysis, who is guilty and who isn't? God only knows.*

And all ideology aside, losing sucks. I don't know a criminal defense lawyer who doesn't feel the same way. Judging ourselves by our wins in the courtroom, not our personal integrity. Hence the long, salt-mine hours, and the obsession. And the drive for the perfect defense. Often at the expense of things that matter. Sometimes the things that matter most.

But as I sat in my parked car that night, a vehicle that cost more than a lot of the houses in the Bronx, I was not thinking like a defense attorney. Something else was going on. Something metaphysical. I wondered, regardless of whether it was my client Dunning Kamera or someone else who committed the crime, how the murderer could have acted so savagely toward a forsaken street waif like Heather. Where does that kind of evil come from? Of course I knew the psychological explanations. I had used so many psychiatric experts in my cases, I was practically a lay expert in the field. I knew most of the diagnostic labels in the *DSM* backward and forward, as well as the presenting psychological symptoms that characterized each of them. But the textbook answers didn't address the ultimate, underlying question.

I trudged through the parking garage, then took the cement steps to the lobby, where the elevator carried me up to our condo. When I walked in, the place looked disheveled. I found Courtney in the shower. It was 6:15 p.m., and we had no plans that evening, but I quickly conjured up an explanation in my mind, hoping for the best. Until I detected the scent of a man's cologne around the place. I fished around in the kitchen, looking for more clues, and I found them in the wastepaper basket. Two Marlboro butts. It was like a dagger in the guts.

When she came out dressed only in her robe, she looked flustered, gave me a peck on the lips, and then, like a waitress in a cafe after the meal who asks the perfunctory question about dessert, asked me whether I wanted to make love.

On any other day that would have been an easy question to answer. But not tonight. "No," I said. "I'd rather have dinner. And then a talk."

"Oh?"

"Yes. About your day."

"Nothing out of the ordinary in my day."

"Even so," I said, "let's talk."

"Okay. But I am feeling a bit tired."

"Why is that?"

She tilted her head. "Trevor, I don't know. Just am."

"Oh," I shot back, "I think you do."

"What's that supposed to mean?" When I didn't respond she added, "Why am I feeling like a witness in one of your trials?"

"I didn't intend that."

"That doesn't matter. You make me feel like I am being cross-examined. Always. Every time we talk. I don't like being attacked."

"You're kidding," I shot back. "All I did was ask a legitimate question—"

"A nasty little question. Insinuating something . . ."

"Like what?"

"I don't know," she retorted. "Maybe that I don't have any reason to feel tired. That I don't work like you do. Whatever. I really can't go through this again."

Nice head-fake by Courtney. Once again, the banter was falling into the same conversation we had been having for quite a while. Way before that evening. Like two electrical fields that couldn't get close without a shower of sparks.

I gave a shot across the bow. "I know you have something you need to tell me. So let's get it out in the open. Or don't you have the guts to name names?"

But Courtney didn't reply. Instead, she turned and strode into our master bedroom. Then there was the dull click as she locked the door behind her.

I downed a couple stiff drinks and eventually skulked into the guest room and mindlessly popped on the TV, but paid little attention to it as I skipped through the channels on the remote, feeding my silent outrage. Underneath, there was another emotion. The restless despair that had become the hallmark of our marriage.

I toyed with the idea of banging on the master bedroom door and bringing it to a head right then. Asking Courtney straight up who the guy was in her life, and how she could do that to me, and whether she was ready to beg me for forgiveness; because if she didn't, then I was ready to kick her out of the condo that night, along with her thirty-four pairs of designer stilettos, from the Jimmy Choos to the Christian Louboutins.

My phone buzzed on the end table to alert me of a voice mail. Must have just missed the call when I stepped out to mix myself another old-fashioned. I nearly ignored it, but as a defense lawyer, I had a complex about full discovery. As if there was something on my cell about my wife, Courtney. A smoking gun. Something I needed to know.

Instead of that, what I heard was the voice of Elijah White, a former client of mine.

"Trevor Black. Hey, man. Been thinking about you abundantly. But this isn't about me. Or my parole either."

Elijah was a black man in his early fifties who

had been in and out of prison on drug charges. Then, while serving his last sentence, something happened. The rumor was that he had found religion, and he became a model prisoner, got his GED, and was released early on parole. A minister from Harlem had hired me to represent him at the parole hearing that ended up springing him from prison. Thereafter Elijah began volunteering at his church, a place that sounded like it was full of the Holy Ghost and rock 'n' roll. His day job had him working as an intake person at a drug rehab center.

In his voice mail he sounded even more excited than usual, with "usual" being along the lines of someone who'd won a medium-size lottery or just witnessed a bank robbery.

"Okay, listen. I had this dream," he started out. "Twice. Same dream. Actually, more like a nightmare. Not about me. About you. *You,* man. So you have to talk to me, 'cuz this is heavy stuff."

Against my better judgment I decided to return Elijah's call. I almost hoped I'd get his voice mail, but instead he picked up.

After our initial greeting, there was a little pause before he said, "I read in the papers how you signed onto this Dunning Kamera case. Listen up, I'm here to warn you. This is what the Spirit is telling me. I was told it in a dream. As clear as a bell ringing. Now, I've got only one question for you: is there something in your retainer agreement with Kamera, anywhere in that lawyer-client contract, about your soul?"

Then he laid it on me. "I'm of the opinion that the dark prince of the air, he's going to sift you and winnow you. Shuck you like an ear of corn, and that is no joke. So you better stay safe."

I groped for words. I regretted calling him and tried to get him off the phone with an edge to my voice, telling him, "Look, Elijah, I know you meant well by calling. Just don't do it at night like this. If you need to tell me something, do it during office hours."

"Just remember. You know where you can find sanctuary. I know you do." After that, Elijah hung up.

I never made it into the master bedroom that night. I told myself it was because I needed to cool down and think things over. Give her the benefit of the doubt. Maybe even give some thought to my failings as a husband. While there was truth in all of that, I stayed put for a different reason. It was because of my telephone chat with Elijah.

Elijah's words, and the prophetic ring to them, dangled over my head like a smashed-up car on a magnetic crane in an automobile graveyard.

At the time, though, I had no idea what was coming for me. All I knew then, as I clicked off my iPhone and tossed it on the bed stand, was that Elijah's message had rattled me to a surprising extent, and I needed to find a way to fall asleep.

10

I tossed and turned in my bed that night, finally slipping into fitful dreaming around three in the morning. My alarm was set for six, but by that time I found the coffeemaker in the kitchen on, a half-eaten box of donuts left opened on the counter, and a dirty dish and a coffee cup in the sink. Courtney had already left the condo. That was strange. She liked her beauty sleep, and I was always the first one up. Things were already percolating in my brain.

I pushed back mentally against a vague sense of doom, assuming instead that it was life as normal. After downing a cup of coffee, I checked the time, laid out my suit and tie, and jumped into the shower and soaped up. But I kept thinking back to our argument the night before. And the little things there were about Courtney that I hadn't focused on previously, even though I knew all the symptoms.

There were the sugar rushes and the repeated bouts of what my wife called the flu. Symptoms easily dismissed. Like the nausea and vomiting. Then it would disappear. Then reappear. I knew she couldn't be pregnant. We had both been checked out years before, and it turned out she couldn't have babies.

As I wiped the fog off the bathroom mirror and started shaving, I visualized her occasionally bloodshot eyes and, when I could get close enough to check, her dilated pupils. When you live with someone, it can be hard to track their slow disintegration. But at some point you have to admit it.

All the signs kept popping up in my head as I checked myself in the full-length mirror, knotting my tie. Maybe it had something to do with Bradley Yelsin.

It so happened that I was to have a client conference that day with Bradley, who was a floor trader on Wall Street and an arm's-length friend of mine. We ran in some of the same circles. Bradley had a penchant for throwing exotic, edgy parties, sometimes with multiple sexual encounters in his bedrooms and lines of high-grade coke on the mirrored coffee tables. I took Courtney to a few of his bashes, against my better judgment. After a while I began to notice the look in Courtney's eyes, and I knew immediately that something deep inside of her had been captivated by the whole scene.

I warned her that cocaine was a fierce monkey with a powerful grip and sharp teeth, and she needed to avoid it. She smiled and nodded, but in retrospect, it's painfully clear that she wasn't convinced.

Bradley tried to lasso me into seeing him at 7:30

that morning about his case so he could still make it over to the New York Stock Exchange in time to check the wire services and the news on the Bloomberg terminal before the opening bell for trading. But I said no, 8:30 instead. He didn't like that, but he didn't have a choice. He showed up at the scheduled time wearing his blaze-orange trading jacket and a really ticked-off expression.

It was time to get him ready for a settlement of the SEC fraud charges against him. The deal that I had worked out with the federal authorities was a sweet one. Bradley would agree to a federal monitoring of his trades for a year in exchange for a deferred prosecution. If he kept his nose clean for twelve months the whole thing would be forgiven and forgotten. *Poof.* Disappeared. No criminal record. Nothing.

After walking him through the drill and explaining what to expect in the next week's meeting with the assistant US attorney, I decided to take a chance. So I got personal.

"So, how have you been, Bradley?"

"Fine." There was a forced grin on his face. Then he shot a glance at his Rolex. I got the point. The opening bell for floor trading would sound in about forty-five minutes.

"What I'd like to know," I continued, "is whether you've seen Courtney recently. You know, over at your parties."

He laughed. "You want me to tell you what

your wife's been up to? Geez, Trevor. Really?"

"Yeah, really. I've told you before. I don't want her doing substances. Period."

"She's a big girl."

"Do you know where she is today?"

He tilted his head to the side, sizing me up. Bradley was still a client, and I knew I was wading neck deep into an alligator swamp by mixing the personal with the professional. He shrugged and replied, "Who knows?"

"Look, Bradley, I'm more than your lawyer. I thought we were friends. Maybe I don't dig the stuff you're into. But I thought we could tell each other the truth. Until now. Frankly, I'm hurt."

He huffed cynically. "Oh, wow. So does this mean you and I aren't going steady anymore?"

That lit me up. "Okay. That's it." I leaned toward him, across my desk. "You tell me right now where Courtney is. I've never busted a client's nose before. But there's always a first."

Actually, I hadn't landed a blow like that since I was sixteen years old, competing in the Wisconsin Golden Gloves competition at the Racine community center. The other guy was a tough Chinese kid with fast hands who was pummeling me something fierce, but he let his guard down for a second, and that's when I nailed him. A lucky punch.

When I delivered my warning to Bradley, his eyes opened wide. Silence for half a minute.

"Hang on," he finally said. "I remember now. Ginny and her and some of their girlfriends were going to have a girls' day out. You know, with Courtney. All day."

Ginny was Bradley's live-in girlfriend. I had no use for Ginny or most of her friends. As I considered the worst-case possibilities, I felt a sense of weightlessness and nausea in my gut.

Then Bradley remembered something else. "Oh yeah. And here's for your last bill. Paid in full." Then he reached into the top pocket of his colored trading jacket and yanked out a check. But in the process he also inadvertently pulled up the cigarette pack that was in that pocket. Marlboros.

At that point I wasn't interested in breaking his nose. I wanted to toss my client out the window of the Woolworth Building.

Before I could respond, Bradley jumped up and flipped the check onto my desk. As he turned and started to hike out of my office I yelled after him, "I'll be talking to you about Courtney. Outside of this office."

I muddled through the rest of the morning on several other cases. Then I worked through lunch on the Dunning Kamera file and into the afternoon, not stopping to eat, finding it difficult to focus but still trying to push through. I called Courtney several times but she didn't pick up.

I dug into the pile of police reports on my desk.

Assistant District Attorney Betty Verring had sent them to me in response to my discovery demand. Even in my fuzzy state of mind, I could see with crystal clarity that Detective Dutch Alreider, the investigating officer, had seized my client's bloody handkerchief without a warrant, and without probable cause. He had gained access to Kamera's apartment under the pretense that there might be a building code violation. That was the excuse he had given to the building manager in order to gain entry. Something about the electrical wiring in the apartment not being up to snuff. But it was an empty ruse, laughable actually.

The cop ended up finding the handkerchief in the pocket of one of Kamera's sport coats in his closet. Dunning Kamera considered himself a kind of fashion dandy, always wearing a smartly starched handkerchief in the top pocket of his sport coat. The blood on the handkerchief matched Heather's blood type.

My next step was obvious. I needed to file a motion to suppress from evidence the improperly seized handkerchief, a motion I expected that the judge would grant. After that, the prosecution would have no alternative but to grudgingly dismiss the case against Dunning Kamera.

But before I could start drafting my motion to suppress, Catherine, my executive assistant, buzzed me. She sounded breathless. I knew something was wrong.

"There's a call for you, Trevor," she said. "It's urgent."

"What's it about?"

Catherine made a little sound, like she was trying to swallow but had something caught in her throat. After a second she finished her message to me. "It's about Courtney."

I told her to put the call through. The numbness was already setting in, even before hearing the police officer ask me if I was Trevor Black, and whether Courtney Black was my wife, and if I knew anything about her whereabouts that day.

"No," I said in a stumbling voice. "I don't know exactly where she was going. Not exactly . . ."

"One of our officers will be speaking to you personally," the cop said. "Thank you for your cooperation."

Five minutes later, as I sat at my desk staring out into space and steadying myself, there was a knock on my office door. A uniformed officer entered with a look on his face that was different than I might have expected. I am sure he knew who I was and what I did for a living—mostly making cops look like the bad guys and the bad guys look like they were innocent.

But even so, at that moment the expression on his face said something else: regret for what he was about to tell me, as if he knew how hard it was going to shake me when he said the words.

"I'm sorry, Mr. Black. But there's been an incident with your wife, Courtney."

More numbness upon numbness. Then shock.

"I'm sorry to inform you that your wife has passed away. You'll need to come with me to the coroner's office."

11

Some images you don't forget. That day I found myself standing inside the morgue, staring at the cement floor that was painted in a thick, shiny gray, like the kind of paint you might expect on a battleship. My focus was on the floor, because five feet away there was a metal gurney with a body lying on it, covered by a sheet. I was clinging stupidly to the hope that there had been a grotesque mistake, and my legs were momentarily struggling to bear my weight, feeling like the marrow had been sucked out, or like my entire skeleton had vanished and I was just some ocean invertebrate, like a jellyfish.

A staffer had gone to fetch the coroner and had left me alone with what I had been told was the body of my wife. The sheet was still veiling the body, but the coroner's assistant assured me that it was Courtney. A patrol officer had found her dead behind the wheel of her Mercedes about a block away from Bradley Yelsin's penthouse.

A few minutes later the coroner strode in, said he was sorry about my loss, and pulled the sheet back from over her face. Courtney had always been so proud of her reddish-auburn hair, and she paid exorbitantly to have it styled. *Movie-star hair,* I used to tell her. But now her hair was a straggly, tangled mess, and it framed her face, which had a whitish-gray pallor.

It struck me how Courtney was absolutely unmoving, as if her very atoms and molecules had stopped, frozen in time. And there was nothing I could do to restart it all again. Or to go back. Or to change any of it. Ever.

"Yes," I told the coroner, "this is my wife." I wished somebody had offered me a chair, but I was too shaken to ask for one. I just stood there, my knees trembling, looking at the woman I'd promised to love and cherish till death parted us. I looked away from the body, bracing myself for an answer I already anticipated. "How did she die?"

"There will be an autopsy," the coroner replied, "but my preliminary impression is that it could have been a drug overdose. Her posture in the car suggested congestive heart failure, indicative of a possible cocaine overdose. Traces of the drug were found in the car and on her person." The coroner looked up at my stricken face, maybe realizing he was talking like a pathology report rather than a person. He licked his lips and looked away. "Unless . . . Did your wife have a history of heart problems?"

My mind was blank. I just shrugged. Courtney's heart was a mystery in several ways.

In the blur of the days that followed, I drifted between grief, rage, and regret, not able to really separate them. But one thing was clear. If I saw Bradley Yelsin, I would beat him to within an inch of his life.

I avoided the office altogether. Catherine and my paralegals kept things going for me. On the day of the funeral I was a mess. My friends came, along with the entire law firm staff. Neither Bradley Yelsin, nor his live-in paramour, nor any of his sordid party hangers-on attended.

At the graveside when the service was done, and as I turned to walk away from that open hole in the ground and from the casket that contained the mortal remains of my wife, I noticed that Elijah White was in the crowd. People were beginning to disperse. A few hugs and hand-shakes and many murmurs of *So very sorry* from friends and from my law partners and from my secretary, Catherine.

But I had to chase down Elijah. I followed him and called after him as he was passing quickly between two leafy trees in the cemetery. He heard me and turned. A stocky guy with a shiny bald head, Elijah had taken to wearing reading glasses, which hung around his neck on a chain, like he was a librarian or a schoolmarm. He had a smile on his face. No one would peg him as a former felon whose time in prison was spent fighting off Aryan Nation inmates and even members of a black power gang that he had refused to join. On one occasion he had pulled up his shirt in my office to show me the jagged scars from knife wounds that marked his torso.

Elijah trotted up to me and wrapped his arms around me and squeezed until my ribs could feel it. When he let go he said, "Man, I am cut to the bone over this. So sorry, Trevor. My heart is just breaking for you."

I thanked him. The two of us were alone then, on the spongy, perfectly manicured grass, standing near headstones and grave markers.

But I knew I had to bring it up. "I need to know something."

"Anything," he said.

"About Courtney. How did you know?"

"Know what?"

"When you said that about how the prince of darkness was coming after me. How did you know that something bad would happen to Courtney?"

Elijah gave me a look like I had been speaking Mandarin. "Hey, bro, not sure what you mean . . ."

"You must have had a premonition about Courtney dying. That must have been what you meant about my facing some kind of demonic attack."

He paused. Then, "Oh hey, Trevor, my man. This is a bad day for you. Not sure we ought to be talking about any of that right now."

I insisted. "You've got to tell me. You have to. How could you have known that I would lose Courtney like this?"

"But I didn't know," Elijah said.

"But all that stuff you said about the demons coming after me, or the devil, or whatever . . ."

"Trevor," he said. "My dreams. What the Spirit of God was speaking to me. The things I said about the evil one. There's something I got to tell you about that." Then he clapped me on the shoulder and looked at me real close. Uncomfortably close. Right in the eye. "Those warnings—they weren't about Courtney. They were about you."

12

Law work would keep me from going crazy. That was what I thought. When I finally dragged myself back to the office a few days later, there was a letter from the district attorney's office, from the DA himself, and an e-mail from ADA Betty Verring. There was also a pink slip with a phone message from Dunning Kamera.

The letter from the district attorney for New York City expressed condolences about the loss of my wife and that the entire staff was saddened at the news.

The e-mail from Betty shared her personal regrets about Courtney as well, but added something else. "I am sorry to hit you with this. However, Mr. Kamera was caught in northern Maine trying to leave the United States at the Canadian border, in violation of his bail terms. A passport was found in his possession. A detention hearing is scheduled for tomorrow because he violated his bail. Considering everything you have been through, I would be glad to agree to an adjournment for a week or so, but of course, you will need to clear that with your client."

I shot her a quick reply e-mail saying that I would forge ahead with the hearing as scheduled. My client deserved a quick decision about his being held in custody.

Not surprisingly, the message from Kamera was his single call from jail, telling me that he had been picked up, but that it was all a misunderstanding and he needed me to spring him from lockup.

I made arrangements to attend the court hearing the next day, and looked over the file. But by then, emotionally speaking, I had started to tank dramatically and I was ready to call it a day. I didn't even go through the rest of my mail, but grabbed my car keys, fled the office, and went home.

I walked in the door, and it hit me again. I almost expected to see her sitting at the table with clams and oysters from that upscale market or carryout chicken tikka from the Indian restaurant. Or maybe stepping out of the bedroom in one of her designer kimonos. There were traces of her everywhere. A bottle of kefir in the fridge. Cosmetics littering the master bath. Her specialty soap from Harrods still perfumed the shower stall.

After eating only a few bites of yesterday's carryout Chinese, I dropped into bed but couldn't sleep. Maybe I dozed off here and there, but my eyes had already been open for a long time when I saw the sun coming up around the curtains of the guest room. For some reason, I couldn't bring myself to sleep where Courtney had slept. I just left the bed in the master bedroom unmade. Exactly the way it was—when she left that morning ahead of me.

Later, in the courthouse, when I was on my way up to my detention hearing for Dunning Kamera, two women trotted into the elevator with me. One had a briefcase. The other had the nervous look of a client. They both got out at the next floor. I stayed in. While I was ducking my head down to leaf through my briefcase and make sure I had the Kamera file, someone else walked in. Then the elevator door closed. I looked up.

It was Bradley Yelsin. We didn't talk, but as the elevator stopped at another floor, he tried to scoot out when the door slid open, but I got there first and blocked his exit. The door kept closing on me and then banging back open as I stood there, staring at Bradley.

He spoke first. "I've got nothing to say to you, Trevor. About your dead wife. Or anything else. So let me pass. By the way, I've dismissed you as my lawyer. I'm meeting with my new legal counsel right now."

"Then you're not my client anymore," I said. "Which makes it easy for me to do this." I dropped my briefcase, took a step toward him, and punched him in the face.

Bradley crumpled against the side of the elevator and slid down to the floor, not moving. He was out for only a few seconds, and then he slowly came to, whimpering and grabbing his nose, which was gushing bright-red blood. He screamed something after me, but I didn't much care what it was.

I plodded through the sea of people in the courthouse hallway, wading through this world as I had known it: fretting lawyers, harried clients with puzzled looks, impatient witnesses, bored jurors heading to courtrooms where they would be impaneled for jury trials, vagrants off the street, clerks with stacks of files, and court-curious retired folks reading the paper and looking for some juicy litigation to view.

None of it made much sense to me at that

moment. I was suddenly aware of the grime on the floor, the ugly institutional aesthetics of the government building, and the miserable cynicism, selfishness, and punishing aggression that populated this place. Why was I there? I was on my way to plead the cause of a man who may well have cut the heart out of a nineteen-year-old runaway.

Something was happening to me.

13

I made a heroic effort during the hearing, arguing for Dunning Kamera's release. But the judge had no use for it. Bail was revoked and my client was ordered to be detained in jail until trial.

My pitch to the court had been straightforward: that we didn't lie in our argument in the original bail hearing about Kamera not having a passport. In point of fact, he actually didn't have one.

What I didn't know, because my client hadn't bothered to tell me, was that before the murder he had applied for a passport and was waiting for it to arrive in the mail. But in the end, none of that made any difference. Kamera had been ordered not to leave the country as a condition of bail, the judge pointed out. He was then caught trying to slip across the Canadian border. It was a clear violation.

But there was more bad news for my client's case. I knew that the prosecution might try to inject the whole sordid event into the trial as evidence of an accused's attempt to escape from the country—flight as an implied admission of guilt. I had to now prepare a motion in limine to keep that out. More damage control.

As Dunning Kamera was led away in his jailhouse jumpsuit, he turned around and threw me this strange look while lifting up his manacled wrists and spreading out his hands, as if he had a question. At the same time, the grin on his face seemed to tell me that he already had the answer, even if I didn't.

I wasn't sure why, but that last view of Dunning Kamera triggered something in my head. About the photos.

After passing through the doors under the Gothic spires and gargoyles of the Woolworth Building, I made my way up to my office. The first thing to do was to pull out those crime scene photos of Heather, the victim. Especially the one that most clearly showed the horrible, ragged cut beneath her breast and slightly to the side, where her heart had been removed. That was when something jumped out that my subconscious must have caught, though I had missed it before.

On the extreme left of the photo, there were the faint edges of red strokes on her belly. I had to stare at them for a long time before I decided what they might be. All that was visible was part of an arc and a dot beneath it. It looked like someone had painted a red question mark on her flesh, perhaps with her own blood, but the photograph had caught only the extreme border of it. Perhaps intending to exclude it altogether. There had to be more photos showing her entire torso and what had been written on her. If that was a question mark, then what was the question? The prosecution had been holding back.

I needed to demand the rest of the photographs. Another motion had to be prepared. I would have my law clerk do the legal research and my paralegal put together a rough draft of the motion papers. But I still needed to supervise the effort. Edit it. Do some of my own research. Redraft it. I would have to force myself.

I knew that on the exterior I would be going on cruise control. Like a droid. While on my inside there was a black hole growing, like some catastrophic cosmic event, swallowing up everything in its gravitational pull and sending it all to that place from which no light could escape.

When Catherine buzzed me on the intercom, it broke me momentarily out of the darkness that I was in. An overnight FedEx letter had just arrived. She said it was marked *confidential,* so I told her to bring it into my office.

Inside the envelope was the letterhead of a local attorney I didn't know. A guy named Carson

Tunney. The letter said he had just been retained by Bradley Yelsin to represent him and confirmed that I had been discharged as his attorney. Then the kicker. I was being reported to the New York State Bar Association for unprofessional conduct in having committed serious battery upon the person of Bradley Yelsin, a former legal client. I clenched my teeth and did the man-up thing by making light of it and telling myself with chagrin that at least there was a little good news: the beating had been ranked as "serious." Considering the fact that he probably supplied my wife with the cocaine that took her life, that was some consolation.

But in the logical part of my cortex I was aware that things were starting to fall apart for me. Swirling into oblivion.

I fought against it. There was the inclination that I could simply keep my head down and push through. The option of grinding on. Even if the gears had no oil. Thinking, *All of this will pass.*

Another part of my brain, emanating from who knows where, but just as cogent, and equally plausible, told me that I needed to take a chance. Find some meaning in all of this. Make a change. Perhaps I had been sailing through life on a skiff made of balsa wood and tinsel. But now that the rogue waves were coming, it was time to look for an island. One that had a harbor.

I went for the second option. Compelled to do

so. I found myself balling up my fists as my eyes filled with tears of regret, rage, guilt, and despair. I mirrored the Jimmy Stewart scene out of *It's a Wonderful Life* where he sits hunched over the bar at Martini's, praying. I pleaded with God, wherever he was, to give me some help down here. I thought back to Elijah White. As I did, a flood of the homilies that he had shared with me over the years came pouring back and took shape—the fall of man, and Jesus, and a blood-soaked cross, all of it—and the truth suddenly lit up my brain, so I prayed all of that too, and as I prayed, I meant it, every word.

I'd never poured out my soul, not even to my wife, so as I sat at my desk—the oval, vintage, mahogany number with the inlaid leather surface I had ordered from London—I had no pre-conceived notion what might happen next. Certainly no anticipation that some pleasantly bumbling angel out of a Hollywood script would show up, trying to earn his wings. And none came.

Yet I realized that, without even knowing how I got there, I had just been at a crossroads. Taken one route, and not another. And there was something numinous yet real going on. The kind of thing that could raise the hair on the back of your neck.

And despite the way my rational brain tried to scream that only the empirical mattered, that only the sensate was reliable, I couldn't deny what was going on. Invisible, yet overwhelming.

I sat in my leather executive chair for a long time, collecting myself. I was basking in a moment of relief. Able to actually feel my body, down to my fingertips. But suddenly aware that I was more than that. And that something began dwelling with me that had not been there the day before.

I gazed over at the framed photo of Courtney that was on my credenza. Then I reached over on my desk and picked up the silver blues harp that I had hung on to from my days in The Assault and had been using as a paperweight. The traces of things past.

At the same time there was the feeling that something else had happened. Something altogether new.

But just as quickly, another thought came filtering in. I dismissed it at first, but it kept returning. Like a spoiler at a wedding, where the couple is in love and meant for each other and everything seems right with the world, but the spoiler whispers that one of them is unfaithful and it's not going to last.

The spoiler was whispering to me about Elijah White, who had been busted on cocaine charges years ago. How did I know that he was really clean? He had called me the night before Courtney's death, delivering his doomsday message. Then the next day my wife was found dead in her car from a cocaine overdose. I didn't want to think about Elijah that way, but I couldn't help it. Humans do horrendous things and sometimes they claim that God told them to do it. I had handled a few cases like that myself. I needed to figure out how Elijah and his phone call fit into all of this.

I looked back at the grisly photos on my desk. The forensic pictures of the dead nineteen-year-old girl, Heather. And the one photo with the faintest edge of a bloody question mark. The evidence of dark deeds done by a heart of unimaginable cruelty.

But I had to stop looking at the photos, because of something in the air.

That exact moment was the very first time that it happened for me, though it would not be the last. There was an actual scent. One that I recognized immediately, even though I hadn't experienced it in decades. The Manitou landfill incinerator that was out on the edge of town, and how on Fridays they would burn garbage and waste, and dead animals. For miles around, you could smell it. The faint scent of smoke, incineration, and death. That exact same odor was in my office. And the tingling feeling on my skin, an eerie sensation that someone was there in my office with me, even though I was alone.

I jumped up from my desk and searched for a

fire. Maybe something electrical. A short circuit in one of the lamps. But there was nothing.

And then the alarm sounded. A fire alarm in the ceiling above my head, screaming with an obnoxious wail. Catherine bolted into my office. "Where's the fire?"

"Can't you smell it?" I yelled. "The smoke from a fire?"

She shook her head. "No, not really. The alarm battery must be on its last legs." She disappeared, ran down the hall to the storage cabinet, and came back with a new battery. I dragged a chair over to the spot and climbed on it, reaching the alarm, which was still sounding. I popped off the cover and yanked out the old battery. The wailing continued.

I snapped in the new battery. More screaming from the alarm.

I was stumbling into a rage. So I yanked the wires clean out from the side of the alarm. Catherine was watching the whole thing, wide-eyed. But the alarm was still wailing, even after that. There was no earthly explanation for it.

"Can't you smell the fire?" I yelled again over the screaming siren.

Catherine just shook her head no.

I jumped off the chair, grabbed a heavy brass bookend from my bookshelf, got back on the chair, and smashed the ceiling alarm, busting it into shards that fell to the floor. The alarm finally went quiet. But I could still smell the powerful odor of the Manitou landfill fires.

Turning to the doorway, I noticed my partner Hal Tobit standing there in his shirtsleeves. His client conference had been interrupted by the alarm. He looked up at the ceiling and down at the remnants of the alarm on the floor, and then focused on the big bookend clutched in my hand. "Trevor, what in blazes are you doing?"

"Fire . . ." I started to say. "Hal, tell me you can smell it."

He screwed up his face and said, "I don't smell anything. You need to get ahold of yourself."

After Hal left, I heard him remark to someone out in the hallway, "Obviously he's not ready to come back."

I thought to myself, *Wait till he finds out what I did to Bradley Yelsin.*

Catherine was still standing in my office with a sympathetic but helpless look on her face. I was about to ask her yet again about the foul, burning odor that still lingered in my office, but I caught myself.

She said, "I'll get a dustpan and clean this up." I cut her off and told her it wasn't necessary. I made the mess, and I would pick it up. I asked her to close the door to my office behind her. Then I dropped into one of my tufted leather client chairs.

A tangle of thoughts and a cast of characters

were racing through my head like the second lap at a NASCAR event. Courtney, of course. Bradley Yelsin. Dunning Kamera. Elijah White.

But others too. The reminder of Manitou had stirred them. The landfill fires had kindled something from way back. Suddenly I was thinking about faces from high school. Marilyn Parlow. How long had it been? And there were still others. My friends from those days so long ago—Dan Hoover, the guitar virtuoso. And Bobby Budleigh, and Augie Bedders.

But enough. I had to force myself out of those memories and back into the present moment. To that file on my desk, and to the murder case that was my task. Assuming mistakenly that my past had nothing to do with any of that or with what was about to happen.

But this I knew: I had the urgent need to find my way. To separate the light from the darkness. And to choose the one and not the other. Choices like that were becoming clear.

14

I went to bed early that night, again in the guest room. But this time I slept hard and long.

As I pried my eyes open the next morning, the same first thought came crashing in. It had recently become routine: *Courtney's dead.*

Then the avalanche of emotions. The feeling that I had failed her. My trial practice had sucked much of the life out of me. So when I would finally be off the clock on the weekends, when I should have spent more time with Courtney, instead I pursued my own indulgences: the Saturdays with my collector's edition Browning Belgium twelve-gauge shotgun at the skeet-shooting club in Hyde Park. Or trying to improve my miserable golf game at the Pound Ridge Golf Club. Or all those sport-fishing jaunts and drinking binges with friends, and with the wealthy clients of my partners.

But that morning, following my spiritual ablution of the day before, there was something else: a feeling like a window had been opened, and a fresh breeze was ventilating my insides. Even in the middle of my shock, loss, and professional maelstrom, I had a strange calm. Having lacked peace for longer than I could recall, maybe always, I hardly recognized it at first. There was clarity of mind, too, even in the swirl of internal pain.

Yes, I had failed Courtney. I could see that. And somehow I would have to sort all of that out. The true regret would be if I were unwilling to learn from what had happened. That would be the double tragedy.

Only two things were on my schedule for today: a conference with Dunning Kamera in the holding cell in the courthouse, immediately followed by a short status conference with the judge on his case. Perfunctory. Routine.

Before I left for the jail, I turned on my cell and went through a few messages. The only important one was from Detective Dick Valentine. He was a veteran of the NYPD with a solid reputation and a no-nonsense approach. Valentine had been the investigating officer in two of my other cases. He didn't play games, and he had no patience for prosecutors or defense attorneys who did.

He said in his voice mail that he was calling about Courtney because he had been assigned to investigate her death. That was a shocker, as he had already been tapped to take over the police work on the Dunning Kamera case after Detective Dutch Alreider screwed it up with his illegal search of Kamera's apartment.

It was highly unusual that Valentine would be permitted to investigate my wife's death, while at the same time posing as the point man for the police department on a murder case where I was counsel for the defendant. Didn't he realize that I could object and scream bloody murder about it being an investigatory conflict of interest, and demand that he be removed from one or even from both of the cases? I would wait to get back to him. I needed to think that one through.

When I arrived at the courthouse, I went down to the basement level and checked in with the jailer, telling him that I had an appointment to meet with Kamera. My client was already in a holding cell, but I would have to wait for a jail escort. Ten minutes later, a corrections officer showed up and walked me down the holding cell corridor, where I was treated to the usual torrent of obscene catcalls from other inmates, their voices echoing through the concrete tunnel and ricocheting off metal doors.

The jailer unlocked the holding cell and let me in, and then locked it after me. Kamera was waiting for me there, looking even paler than usual, dressed in his jail jumpsuit, sitting quietly with his hands folded, free and unmanacled, on top of a metal table. For reasons that seemed obvious, the legs of the table in the holding cell were secured to the cement floor with large machine bolts.

I greeted my client, but didn't shake his hand, and instead dropped my briefcase in the corner. By this time the full case file had grown considerably, filling up three brown ten-inch, expandable folders and a thick trial notebook that was taking shape. But I'd brought only one file that day, my working file.

Right out of the gate I told him I had some questions about the bloody handkerchief. I told him I would be filing a motion to suppress it from evidence because it had been obtained by the police illegally, and that I would announce my intention to the judge when we appeared before her shortly. Kamera grinned and nodded. He could see he was as good as acquitted.

I figured I might as well press the issue while he was in a good mood. "Mr. Kamera, there's one detail I need to know about." His grin faded a bit. "The blood on your handkerchief—where did it come from?"

Dunning Kamera looked away. "It was a few nights before the . . . incident. I met a young lady at a singles bar, and we got together. For a date. In the course of the evening, she had a nosebleed, and I naturally offered her my handkerchief."

The man looked positively satisfied with himself. "Obviously my date had the same blood type as Heather."

It struck me that this was the first time that Kamera mentioned Heather by name. So, in turn, I asked him for the name and address of the "date" he had supposedly been with.

Kamera twitched a little. I hadn't noticed before that he had a tic. He shot back, "Why is that important? I thought you were going to suppress the handkerchief from evidence?"

"I hope to get it suppressed," I replied. "But nothing is certain. Just to be safe, I'd like to interview the woman you met at the bar. The one with the nosebleed."

He let out a big sigh, but it came out in a series of panicked exhales. "Let's take things . . . one . . . step at a time."

I blew that off and told him he'd better produce the information about his bar date, and quick, if I was going to be able to effectively represent him, particularly if the judge didn't kick the bloody handkerchief out of evidence.

He didn't respond to that. At the same time he looked distracted, giving side-glances around the room, though what he kept looking for, I couldn't tell. The room was empty except for the two of us.

Second by second, things became very bizarre. Dunning Kamera twisted his head to the side and back again, back and forth, like it was being operated by mechanical control. Then he said something that made absolutely no sense. At least, not at the time.

"The life is in the blood. Or so they say." After he said that, he gurgled out something even more cryptic. "But that depends on why the blood is spilled. Right? And from what part of the body."

After that strange dictum, I wondered whether I had missed something in my defense strategy. Maybe my client needed a psychiatric evaluation. Perhaps I should consider a plea of not guilty by reason of mental defect or think about challenging his competency to stand trial.

But what happened next made me wonder about myself. And whether my coffee from the courthouse vending machine had been laced with LSD. Or if I really was mentally unhinged after all.

Because just then I was hit with that same odor. The foul stench of smoky incineration from the Manitou landfill. It filled my senses to the point of my nearly gagging.

I quickly surveyed the holding cell. No fire could be in the room, and of course there wasn't.

At that point, Kamera's hands were clasped together on the table so tightly that his knuckles were white, and his face was hard and troubled. Something was about to give way. I suppose I could have retreated at that point, but at the same time I couldn't turn away. I had to see this through. Find out what was behind the veil. A clammy dread crept up my spine as I recalled that long-ago phrase. It hadn't crossed my mind in more than twenty years.

So I steeled myself and proceeded to ask my client the question that I was pretty sure would light up the fireworks, whatever those might be. "Tell me, Dunning. Answer something for me, will you?"

His head twisted back toward me again, like an automaton's. "Yes?"

"Suppose you were to take Heather's dead body. And you also take a paintbrush. The thin kind, you know, like an artist might use to paint a picture on a canvas. Are you following me?"

No answer from my client. But his head was now slowly cranking backward with his eyes still glued on me.

I forged ahead, ignoring the fact that my skin was crawling. "And if you were to dip that paintbrush into Heather's blood . . . and you were to write a question on her body . . ."

Now Dunning Kamera's face was radically changing. From a pale sickly color to translucence, where I thought I could actually see the veins in his skull. I had to remind myself to keep breathing as my client continued to morph, with the flesh of his face becoming more and more transparent.

Some kind of nightmare was unfolding, but I had to see it through. I quickly spat out the rest of the question. "What would you write on her dead body?"

By then I wasn't simply smelling the putrid presence. I was beginning to see it. Visualizing a form that was arising from within my client. Something even more transparent than Kamera, but still visible, as if two images had been laid one on top of the other, slightly askew, the way you would see if you had double vision.

I watched as Kamera stumbled up to a standing position, knocking over the plastic chair in which he had been sitting. His head tilted back farther still, staring almost straight up. Something was pulling his strings. The creature that had emanated from his body was controlling him.

The head of the thing looked like some kind of animal. Hideous, resembling a huge, hairless jackal. With clear, vacant eyes; they were the eyes of the dead, and its mouth was yanked wide open with an interior of absolute blackness within.

Dumbfounded, I heard myself moan, "No, no, no."

Then it screamed.

The sound was a cacophony. Like cars dumped from a great height onto each other.

Then it spoke, and it was as if the sound of a car crash had been digitally remastered into a voice. In that voice the creature roared, "You're doomed."

Both Dunning Kamera and the creature that had enveloped him simultaneously grabbed ahold of the metal table and ripped it out of the floor, pulling the large machine bolts out of the concrete, and then lifted the table up high. As if the next move would be to bring it down onto my head and to bash my brains out.

I yelled out a plea. "God, please, no."

The voice of the creature was still reverberating in my ears. But Dunning and the horrid thing both seemed to be frozen momentarily in midpose, holding the table over my head.

I lunged toward the jail cell door and started banging on it, yelling at the top of my lungs for the guard. An eternity of seconds later, he ambled up to the door, unlocked it, and said with a weary tone, "What's the big emergency?"

Jerking around, I spotted Dunning Kamera. He

was seated at the table as if nothing had happened. Gone was the creature. The heavy metal table was back in its exact place. Kamera's hands were folded perfectly on the surface of the table.

The scene looked harmless. As if nothing extraordinary had occurred, and I had imagined all of it.

15

I was standing just outside the courtroom of Judge June Cavendish, leaning against the wall. The hearing was about to commence in five minutes. But I had to flush my brain first. Exorcise the grotesque images and plot out some kind of statement to the court. I already knew what I had to do next, once Dunning Kamera's case was called. I just didn't know how I was going to frame it. How to fit it into the straitjacket of the law. But who was I kidding? The law had neither procedure nor precedent for any of this.

Instinctively, I began cooking up a clever lie so I could confidently march in there and tell it to the court. Some crafty technical reason, totally unfounded, but plausible, giving legal support to what I was about to do. But the truth about Dunning Kamera was burning a hole in my insides, and for some reason, I found the idea of falsifying the facts strangely repugnant. This new me would, if pressed, have to tell it to the judge. The whole, honest-to-goodness truth.

Was this really me, thinking like this?

Then a voice.

"Don't think so hard, Trevor. You'll hurt yourself." It was the prosecutor, Betty Verring, short, middle-aged, with salt-and-pepper hair and small, intense eyes that were like those ultra-white, obnoxious headlights that some cars have. She was holding her own Kamera file under one arm. "Geez, Trevor, relax. It's only a status conference." Then she smiled.

But I couldn't smile back. I just nodded.

She came to a halt. A softer look broke over her face. "Hey, you all right?"

I nodded again. She gave a single shoulder shrug and trotted into the courtroom. After another half minute, I followed her.

Our case was the only one on the docket. Amazingly, the courtroom was empty except for the court reporter and the clerk, who were already in their places, and Betty, who was sitting at the plaintiff's table pulling a few papers out of her file. Best of all, no media.

I made my way to the defense table, dropped my fat briefcase to the ground, and slouched in the chair. This was not going to go well, I was sure of that.

Then Dunning Kamera shuffled in, his hands and feet manacled, with two jail guards, one on each side. One of the guards pointed to the chair next to me at the defense table. My client clumsily grabbed the back of the chair, pulled it out, and sat to my right. The word *eerie* seemed ridiculously inadequate to describe how it felt with him sitting next to me.

Judge June Cavendish, a judicial dictator with reading glasses set in place just above her hairline, breezed in, her black robe fluttering around her. The few of us in the courtroom rose to our feet. The judge dumped herself into the big black judicial chair, grabbed the file from the bench in front of her, and flipped it open. The clerk called the case, Betty announced her appearance for the state of New York, I did the same as counsel for the defense, and then we all sat down.

The judge started. "Okay. Status conference. Let's talk about defense motions first."

I stood up. "Your Honor, I would like to confer with the court." Then I added, "At sidebar."

The judge glanced around the room, obviously noting that there were no members of the public or the press. "Mr. Black, there's nobody here. The courtroom's empty. What's so mysterious that you need to approach the bench?"

"At sidebar," I reiterated. "Please, Your Honor."

"Fine." She waved both Betty and me up to the front. When we were standing at her judicial bench, I began with a voice dropped down to a hush. "Judge, I have to withdraw from this case."

114

"Why is that?"

I took a second. Then, "Your Honor, I am asking that you trust me on this."

Judge Cavendish crossed her arms in front of her and leaned over to me, bringing her face down real low. "Don't confuse me with one of your cocktail cronies. That would be a tragic mistake. Let's hear it again."

"Sorry, Your Honor." This time I polished it up a bit. "I am asking that I be permitted to withdraw as counsel on the grounds that my client and I have an irreconcilable conflict. It prevents me from being able to defend him zealously."

"What kind of conflict?"

I was trying to construct a lawyerly response in my head that might avoid putting an end to my legal career. The judge got tired of waiting, and after ten seconds she interrupted. "Let's get your client's take on this . . ."

"No," I blurted out. "Bad idea."

"Look, counsel. One way or another your client, Mr. Kamera, is probably going to have to be heard on your request. Either he consents and has some new lawyer waiting in the wings, in which case I'll probably let you withdraw, subject to any objections of the prosecution of course. Or else your client objects, in which case you'd better have a prizewinning reason that will convince me. Prizewinning, as in qualifying for the Pulitzer or the Medal of Honor. You get me?"

"My client . . . ," I began, wishing that I could just lay it all out—the whole insane thing—and be done with it.

But it didn't happen like that. Not quite that way.

"Your client . . . what?" Cavendish sputtered. "Finish the sentence."

"My client has . . ." But I couldn't finish the sentence. Betty Verring was watching the whole thing with astonishment. It struck me that I should have asked for an *in camera* conference with the judge in her chambers. Just her and me. It would have been a hard sell, but it would have been worth the try.

Instead, the prosecution would now be an eyewitness to my professional dissolution.

Judge Cavendish was moving from simmer to boil. "I am ordering you to spell this out for me, Mr. Black . . ."

"It's hard to explain," I mumbled.

She leaned back in her chair. "Are you mentally impaired in some way, counsel?"

"Of course not."

"Then what is it you're trying to say? Your client has . . . what?" she yelled.

The truth couldn't stay silent. I declared, "My client has a demon."

The judge winced a little as she considered what I had just said. Then a half smile when she replied, "Demon? Yeah, well, don't we all. What's his, a drug problem?"

116

"No."

"Then in what possible sense do you mean that your client has a demon?"

After taking a second, I replied. "I mean it literally, Your Honor. He is possessed by a demon."

Silence. I could hear the creaking of the leather on the gun belts of the guards as they shifted where they stood.

The judge must have been feeling beneficent that day, because she gave me a second chance. "I am giving you the opportunity, counsel, right now, to retract that statement. Or else to clarify it in some way that conforms to the twenty-first century, rather than the Middle Ages."

"I can't, Your Honor. I meant exactly what I said."

Cavendish eased back in her judicial chair and swiveled back and forth. Then she spoke. "It is always sad when this happens. Personal trauma. Or substance abuse. Whatever the reason, when a good lawyer—and you, Mr. Black, have a reputation as an accomplished defense attorney— when a lawyer unravels like this."

"You don't understand," I interjected.

"No, *you* don't understand," she blasted back. "I am removing you from this case. I am ordering the office of the public defender to take over representation of your client, Dunning Kamera, until such time as he is able to secure private counsel." She drummed her fingernails on the bench as she finished. "I also have no choice but to report your behavior to the ethics committee of the bar . . ."

"Join the club," I said.

"What did you say?" she blurted out.

For whatever reason, I stupidly repeated it.

· The judge gaveled me out of the courtroom. With gusto. In retrospect, I realized she could have ordered a bailiff to bundle me off to jail on contempt of court charges. But she didn't. Small blessings. I would be searching for those, from that point onward.

16

It wasn't surprising that the ethics committee of the New York Bar, after suspending me, gave me a chance to recover my law license, even after my slugging one client and calling another a demoniac in open court. The fact was, I had never suffered any discipline before and had an excellent professional reputation up to then. My partners weren't so easily mollified, though. Hal Tobit broke the news to me that I was out of the firm via a letter on my desk. "With sadness and regret," was how he wrote it.

It lit my fuse that I had to endure psychiatric "treatment" as a condition of applying for reinstatement of my license, but I was reluctantly willing to give it a shot. The morning that I was to report to the psychiatrist's office, I made myself a cup of coffee and quickly leafed through the newspaper. Something caught my eye as I flew through the arts and leisure section on the way to the sports.

It was a blurb about a jazz festival in Newark. Listed among the performers was the Jersey Dan Quartet. That would be New Jersey Dan Hoover, one of my blues band buddies from high school in Wisconsin. He was going by the shorter, simpler moniker of "Jersey Dan," having permanently relocated to the East Coast twenty years ago. His success didn't surprise me, as he was a phenomenal guitar talent, even when we were teenagers. Head and shoulders above the rest of us in The Assault.

All things being equal, I would have gone to the jazz fest just to see Dan in action. But then, I had my own miseries to attend to.

Two hours later I was sitting in the poorly decorated office of Dr. Roland Dumfrey, the appointed shrink, who busied himself with rocking back and forth in his chair during our first session. He spent the first hour on my background and personal history. It was during the second hour when things got interesting.

"Do you resent being here?"

"Of course."

"Because you feel you don't belong here?"

"Correct."

"Why is that?"

"I'm not psychotic."

"Who says you are?"

"You didn't have to. Neither did the ethics committee of the bar association. It's clearly implied in everything that has happened to me up to now."

"Implied?"

"If I am not delusional, or psychotic, then why was I ordered to submit myself to you?"

"You could have chosen your own mental health professional—"

"No, no," I replied. "I don't mean that. I mean that being ordered into mental health counseling presumes that I have a problem."

"Everyone has problems."

"Can everyone spot demons in the room?"

A small smile crept over the good doctor's mouth.

I continued. "Visualizing evil. beings from another dimension and talking to them, that presents only two alternatives. Number one, it is evidence of visual and auditory hallucinations. My drug screening in your file tells you that I don't take drugs. So then, you're thinking it must be a matter of psychosis or some schizoaffective disorder."

"Or?" he asked.

"Or, secondly, that I really did witness some kind of supernatural event."

I watched Dr. Dumfrey closely, but he did a good job of acting like he was made of plastic.

"And in that case," I went on, "well, the supernatural realm—that's not exactly in your wheelhouse. Am I correct?"

He moved a little in his swivel chair. "Let's talk about your wife." He glanced down at the file. "Courtney."

"Dead. Cocaine overdose. Broke my heart. I have some guilt and much regret about our relationship and the way it ended for her. I am still experiencing grief, but I am quite functional. Oh, and one more thing."

"What is that?"

"My wife and her tragic death have nothing to do with the incredulous things that I have witnessed."

"I have a suggestion," he said.

"Oh?"

"It's called risperidone. A newer-generation, generally effective medication . . ."

"I'm familiar. Good approach to treat psychosis. A few of my clients suffering from mental illness have experienced real improvement on those meds. But not a good prescription for me. At least for what ails me."

"And what is it, exactly, that ails you?"

I stood up to leave. "That's what I'm going to find out."

It was Wednesday, late afternoon, when I cut short the "therapy" session and trotted out of the medical building where Dr. Dumfrey had his office. I never returned. My exit from his treatment was AMA, as they say—against medical advice. After doing that, my chances of reviving my license to practice law were, to continue with the medical jargon, DOA, and I knew it.

My stomach was rumbling. I would grab a pastrami sandwich at the deli on that same block. Then I needed to pay a visit to somebody.

It's funny the things you forget in the middle of chaos. When Courtney died, and I picked up her personal belongings from the coroner's office, her iPhone was among them. In retrospect, I was a little surprised that Detective Valentine hadn't seized it, seeing as he was supposedly investigating Courtney's death. But I never thought to check her device until after that court hearing when Judge Cavendish yanked me off the Dunning Kamera case. When I got around to digging out her smartphone, I checked the incoming numbers for the day or two before her death.

One telephone number in particular leaped into sight like a scared rabbit. My world was getting exponentially stranger, with no ending point in sight. But if my suspicions about the cell number were correct, tragedy was about to be compounded. I would have to confront Elijah White.

17

Behind the pulpit in the Church of Christ the Holy King in Harlem, Rev. Jason Jambly stood dressed in a blue suit in front of a large lighted cross. Off to the side was a young man who had been playing licks on an electric guitar and who had some real talent. Another black teen was on the drums. Jambly was wrapping up with a song, his arms flung wide.

It was Wednesday night service, and I knew Elijah White would probably be there, so I had slipped into the back, behind the crowd of forty or so standing in the pews, swaying and head-bobbing and hand-raising. No one seemed to care that a stranger had joined them. An elderly lady with a hat who was in my row smiled and nodded in my direction when I stepped in.

I had to make sure that I could spot Elijah. Sure enough, he was in the front row.

Toward the end of the service, two folks stepped into the aisle and helped bring it to a close with some sanctified dancing. While people started to mingle, and before Rev. Jambly could descend on me as the newcomer in the crowd, I trotted down the side aisle and grabbed Elijah by the arm. "Got to talk. Outside. This is urgent."

He looked surprised. "Okay. Okay," he shouted

back. "Good to see you. Let's go out to the parking lot."

When we were alone, I stuck Courtney's iPhone up to Elijah's face and started to shout. "Your number is on Courtney's cell. You called her the day before she died. I want to know why. And it so happens that your call to Courtney was just a few hours before you called me and delivered your doomsday prophecy." Elijah started to respond, but I cut him off, still yelling. "I want to know if you supplied her with the coke. The stuff that killed her. Or whether you dealt the cocaine to that worthless scum Bradley Yelsin, who then gave it to Courtney."

Elijah started waving his hands in front of me. "Hold on."

"I won't hold on. I've got a dead wife. And some sick, really weird stuff has been happening to me. So you're going to give me some answers. Right now."

By then a couple of Elijah's fellow parishioners were in the parking lot, staring at us, sensing trouble. A big guy in the group started toward us. But Elijah told him it was okay, and not to interfere.

"Answers," I repeated.

"Okay," Elijah said. He plucked Courtney's iPhone out of my hand and looked at the number. "Yeah," he said. "That was the day. My last phone call to her. About group."

"What group?"

"Rehab group," he said. "I had been trying to get her into treatment. She called our drug rehab center a while ago but kept backing out. So I suggested maybe she just sit in on one of our addiction group meetings. Get a feel for it. Maybe change her mind."

It took a couple of seconds to process all of that. Then more anger bubbled up. "Why didn't you tell me any of this? Why'd you leave me in the dark?"

"We've got this confidentiality thing. Couldn't do it, man. Even with you. Really sorry about that."

Elijah's explanation was so obvious and so logical I wondered how I could have missed it. "So, you were trying to get her into rehab?"

"Of course, man. And I know you've been dealing with some major heartbreak since she died. That's why I didn't tell you before now. Even so, maybe I should have let you in on it after she was gone. That's my fault."

A weight had been lifted, even though I felt like an idiot and had to admit it. "No. It's my fault. I shouldn't have jumped to conclusions about you still dealing drugs. You're a good man, Elijah."

His face brightened. "Thanks. You know, I've known you awhile, Trevor, but never heard you say that before."

"You're going to be hearing a lot of things from me that you've never heard before."

He studied me close. Then he said, "Something's going on with you . . ."

"I've witnessed some wicked stuff. Not sure what it means."

"Wicked? Like what?"

"Some kind of . . . don't know exactly. Dark, evil force."

Now he was getting hyped. "You saw it? Actually *saw* it?"

"Not just that. I smelled it."

Elijah did a half twirl where he stood. "What? Oh, man, what are you saying?"

"I know it sounds nuts."

"No, that's not it. Not nuts at all. This is what I've tried to warn you about. The Spirit has been telling me this was coming. And here it is." He kept staring at me as if I had a Post-it note message stuck to my forehead and he was trying to read it. Finally he said, "You've had a Christ Jesus meeting."

"I'm not sure what I had."

"Don't deny it, man. You got to tell it proudly."

"All I know is that I was at rock bottom. I was desperate. Believe it or not, I remembered a few things you told me way back when. So I reached out, praying. Or up, actually. But then, not too long after that, bam, I find myself being dropped into something that's like a scene from *Beetlejuice*."

The look on Elijah's face told me he never saw the film. He skipped over my allusion and delivered a mini-sermon in a slow cadence. "What's of the flesh is flesh. And what's born of the Spirit is spirit. And I am of the belief that you, my man, have traveled through the spiritual birth canal. And as a result thereof, you are now seeing and smelling certain things—things of the unseen world, the world of the spirit—because you have been given something from on high. Never heard of anything just like this. Not exactly. You've been given a gift."

"It feels like a curse."

"Yeah, I got you. But the Lord don't make mistakes. You've been chosen. Given sanctuary. Of course, now you're a marked man. That means they're going to come after you. Only, you've this weapon. It's the sword of the Spirit. Don't forget."

It was dark, and the church was in a bad neighborhood, so I said a quick good-bye. Elijah made me promise that I would stay in contact with him. Then I jumped into my Aston Martin.

For all the good things about Elijah White, I didn't take him to be an expert on supernatural cosmology. For that, I was thinking about some-one else.

18

At home that evening, I scrolled through my contacts, hoping I'd kept the number for Dr. Harlow Tentsky, one of the curators at the Metropolitan Museum of Art. No luck, so I called the museum's main number and connected through the employee directory. I expected to get his voice mail, so it caught me off guard when Tentsky picked up the call.

"Dr. Tentsky, this is Trevor Black. We met at the gala last year, and there's a matter I'm hoping to discuss with you."

No response. Maybe I needed to grease the wheels a bit more.

"Our law firm, Tobit, Black, Dandridge & Swartz, was one of the major donors at the event, and I remember your presentation about occult mythology of the ancient Near East. You mentioned a few ghoulish relics you uncovered, and that detail stuck with me."

"Of course. Mr. Black. I remember now. You attended with Hal Tobit that night, if memory serves me."

Impressive. The man was sharp. "That's right." I decided not to mention that I was no longer with Hal. That information might not get me in the door.

"There was something you wished to discuss?"

128

"I'm looking for information on demonology. And it's rather time-sensitive, so I was hoping to meet soon."

He asked the obvious question. "Is this about one of your legal cases?"

"Partly, yes," I responded.

The fact was, even though I no longer represented Dunning Kamera, I still wanted answers about his dance with the devil.

"It's a bit late tonight, but I could spare a few minutes tomorrow morning, just after the museum opens, if that works for you. Gallery 403 would be apropos."

Promptly at 10:00, I strode through the Fifth Avenue entrance and navigated to Gallery 403, one of the exhibit rooms draped in dramatic mood lighting that illuminated the exhibits under glass but left shadows everywhere else. It appeared Tentsky was already waiting for me in the empty gallery when I arrived. He looked to be in his sixties, with long white hair pulled into a ponytail, and he was wearing a sport coat with jeans. I didn't recognize him at first, but then again, it had been a year since my single contact with him. He must have been expecting to go out on a hot date later that day, because he reeked of men's cologne. The cheap kind.

The curator with the ponytail smiled, introduced himself, and then directed me to a relic inside a glass case within arm's reach. "You are interested in demons?"

I nodded, thinking that should have been obvious from our phone call.

He motioned to the artifact in the case, an exotic piece of metalwork. It took me a few seconds to identify the three figures that were mounted on some kind of ceremonial ax head, which, according to the note on the glass case, was from the Bronze Age.

Tentsky explained. "On the right side of this piece is a boar, charging. On the left is a dragon advancing. Both of them are being defeated by the demon in the middle."

The winged demon had the body of a muscular man. But instead of hands and feet, it was armed with sharp talons. It had a set of small wings, and there were double bird heads sprouting from its neck.

He elaborated. "This is from around 2000 BC from the area of modern Uzbekistan. The common cultural consensus today, of course, is that demons are enemies. The Christian Bible rails against them. Movies like *The Exorcist* and countless other films and TV programs have reinforced that. Yet, in this beautifully preserved piece of metalwork, fashioned two thousand years before the birth of the Christian religion, we see something entirely different. The bird-demon as the hero. Protecting mankind. Isn't that fascinating?"

There are words in the English language that could describe the creature that I had seen rising out of Dunning Kamera. But *fascinating* isn't one of them. In any event, Tentsky was beginning to sound like a typical academic.

"I appreciate the insight, Doctor," I said, "but can we get practical for a moment?"

"How do you mean?"

"How can demons be recognized?"

Tentsky flashed his eyebrows. "That depends. They have taken on many manifestations over the ages. According to the anthropological data, that is."

"Like?"

"Sometimes animal forms, like this bird-demon in the glass case. Then there is the ghost-demon, the *udug*, which is a Sumerian word, later appearing in the Akkadian language as the *utukku*, part woman and part demon. Those date back seven thousand years. Every culture is different."

It was time to cut to the chase. "How can they be defeated?"

He laughed. I figured that by now he had pegged me for a nutcase. But his answer surprised me. "Defeated? According to established legend they can't be defeated. Not by mere mortals, which is the whole point. They have supernatural powers."

Things were getting interesting so I kept the ball rolling. "But, to my question again: Who, then, can defeat them?"

He spun around like he had just heard something; his eyes searched the room. Then he turned back. "Now what . . . ? Oh yes. Demons defeated? You mean that fairy tale."

"Which one?"

"Silly mythology."

"Humor me."

"There's an example, but it's not here. It's on display at the Chicago Art Institute."

"What is?"

"The artifact, or at least one of them. A small statue from around the eighth century. The Tang dynasty. Called a *lokapala* in the Sanskrit rendering. But other cultures mention him too. A nasty, recurring theme. A lie, really. The Guardian King." Then his face twisted up a bit, like he had just bitten his tongue. He added, "That there is somewhere a Guardian King, anointed to crush . . ." More facial contortions. "Crush the demons underfoot."

The professor suddenly looked ill. "Are you all right?" I asked.

But he wasn't. Because by then, the cologne was wearing off, and something else, a pungent odor, was detectable. It was the underlying stench of burning decay, and it was beginning to cut through the room. I whipped my head back to check the entrance to the gallery, looking for an escape route. Where were the crowds? The security guards?

I was prepared to sprint out of there. Until I looked back at Dr. Tentsky. And when I did, I saw something revolting.

He had been engulfed by a giant phantasm. I looked closer, trying to comprehend it. A creature so bizarre that it sent me reeling. I was staring into reptilian eyes that belonged to something with the head of a prehistoric monster with jagged fangs, a set of wings on its back, six-inch-long talons instead of fingers. It was a predator bird from hell.

And its voice was like the tectonic plates of an earthquake, groaning deep in the earth. "We are gods. Now you will die."

Then, in a blur of motion, it swiped its bird claw at me. There was an explosion of pain in my torso near my left ribs. I looked down. One of its razor talons had ripped into my body, and blood was spilling out through my shirt.

As I reeled, my legs buckling, the beast spoke again. "Dead already?"

I was still on my feet when it raised its claw again, getting ready to strike a deathblow. But the creature suddenly stopped and blinked its reptilian eyes. The slit irises of the beast were focused on the gallery entrance. I stumbled in that direction, where a man, a security guard, stood in the doorway, and his face was turned toward us like granite. The man looked miraculously calm while he held up his hand to the immense creature as if he were a traffic cop. I turned around clumsily to see if I was still being pursued.

But by then the creature was gone. Only the white-haired man with the ponytail remained in the room with me, and he was holding a knife in his hand—a knife with my blood on it.

There was a momentary thought. *Run.* But I took only two steps and then collapsed to my knees, clutching at the wound. I felt my attacker brush past me. Then a few seconds later—or a few minutes; I'm not sure which—someone knelt beside me as I lay on the floor. It wasn't my assailant, but a bald man with black horn-rimmed glasses who said in a pleading voice, "Help is on the way. Hold on."

I moaned, "Security guard," and tried to motion toward the doorway.

"Yes, yes," the bald man yelled. "The museum guard is on her way . . ."

"But that man, the guard . . . back there."

He shook his head. "No, not here yet. But don't worry, the security guard is on her way."

I was feeling woozy, but I managed to ask him a question. "Who are you?"

The man said clearly, "I'm Dr. Harlow Tentsky. A curator here."

My chest was on fire with searing pain, and I looked down and saw the blood continue to flow into the cloth that the curator was pressing into the wound. I mumbled some cryptic words. My utterance must have seemed unintelligible to this man, the real Dr. Tentsky. But in retrospect, my ramblings had summed my journey into a supernatural realm that I was not prepared for and that I sensed no power to overcome.

I later learned that I had been mumbling the same thing, over and over.

"Behind the veil, horror . . ."

19

During the two days that I spent in the hospital for my stab wound, I collected eighteen stitches and two visitors.

The first person to see me was Elijah White, who said that he had heard about the attack on the radio the day that it happened. I pulled up the news story on my iPhone and read the account.

Disbarred attorney Trevor Black, the former lawyer for accused murderer Dunning Kamera, was stabbed by a knife-wielding assailant in the Metropolitan Museum of Art today. His attacker was identified as Hanz Delpha, an unemployed anthropologist. Delpha, who previously worked at the museum, fled the scene and is still at large. Trevor Black is listed in stable condition.

Before Elijah left, he laid a Bible next to me on the bed and said that I needed to start reading it. "If you're going to war, Trevor, then you need a battle plan."

I picked it up and leafed through it. Elijah laughed.

"What's so funny?"

"Just that back when you represented me, a long time ago, getting me an early prison release, I offered you this same Bible. You wouldn't touch it. Like it was going to bite you. Like it was a snake. But now, Trevor, think about it. Now you're in the army of the Lord. And you're the one going after the snake." He laughed out loud at that.

As he wheeled around to leave, Elijah dropped another reminder. "Gotta remember: you're a new creature now, after your spiritual turnaround."

I shot back, "I'm not digging that word *creature,* you know."

Elijah laughed again, and as he waved good-bye, he pointed his index finger toward the Bible on my bed and said, "Don't forget, sword of the Spirit."

The other visitor was Dick Valentine, the NYPD detective with a widow's peak kind of receding hairline and the build of a retired linebacker. At the outset he explained that he had heard about the incident at the museum and wanted to check up on me. I pressed him on whether it was a professional visit or a personal one. He said it was both, and then pulled up a chair next to my hospital bed.

I poked back a little. "Let's see. First you are assigned to my Dunning Kamera case. Then you investigate my wife's death. And now this visit. I guess that makes you an official stalker."

"Maybe just curious."

"A perverse kind of curiosity."

Valentine smiled. "So let's get the official part over with. I know you already gave the patrol officer a report when you were admitted to the ER. I had only one question. Can you tell us anything else about the security guard you described, the one in the doorway of the gallery?"

"I already gave his description to the police."

"The museum says there is no such security guard."

"Right. I heard that. But I know I saw him."

"Your statement was pretty vague about how, or even why, Hanz Delpha knifed you."

"Purposely vague."

"Why is that?"

"Hey, I thought you only had one question."

"Yeah, but it has a lot of subparts to it. Why did you beat around the bush in describing the knifing?"

"Trial lawyers like me would call it plausible deniability."

Valentine pressed in. "I never pegged you for a guy who liked to blow smoke."

"Let's just say that I see things differently now. Anything beyond that, I'm going to have to enter the Forrest Gump plea."

Valentine looked lost, so I filled it in with my slow drawl à la Tom Hanks. " 'That's all I have tuh say about thay-ut.' "

He must have missed the humor, because with a deadpan expression he just rolled on. "So, that stuff about you seeing things differently now," Valentine said, repeating me. "You wanna talk about it?"

"I thought I just made my point with the clever Gump impersonation."

I could see the brawny detective was thinking hard about something. Eventually he said, "I heard some rumors about an incident that happened between you and Dunning Kamera in the holding cell. So I went down there and checked things out myself. The jailers showed me the room. Looked normal enough to me. Table in place. Two chairs, nothing weird. The guards told me that nothing happened."

I was still stuck on something the detective had just said. "Rumors?" I asked.

"Your little sidebar with Judge Cavendish," he said. "The court reporter took it all down. I read the transcript. That led me to conclude that something must have happened during that jail conference you had with your client right before the court appearance."

I waited.

Valentine continued. "I'm sort of old school, Trevor. Maybe it's the Catholic neighborhood I grew up in. Anyway, I'm open to some mysteries. The invisible kind, I mean."

"Really?"

Valentine rolled his eyes. "I said 'open.' Not gullible."

"Gotcha."

"I was thinking," he went on, "now that your license is suspended, and you can't practice law, maybe you ought to consider working as a private investigator."

"Private eye? So, what is that, like the sacred burial grounds for disbarred attorneys?"

"Not in your case."

"So, I'm different?"

Valentine bobbed his head back and forth, not quick to jump in, until he said, "I think so."

"I'd like to hear why."

Instead of answering that, he said, "Every once in a while the department gets a crime that is sort of, you know, special. You could help us out. On a confidential consulting basis. I could toss some work your way."

"Why would you do that?"

"I'm a nice guy." He stood up and looked like he was ready to leave. "You have any questions for me?"

"Actually I do," I replied. "About the Kamera

case. About what was written on Heather's body. I think it was some kind of question."

"You want to know about that?"

"I did, once upon a time. But I think I figured it out. Now I'm guessing the murderer wrote a two-word question: something like, 'Dead already?' Am I right?"

Valentine looked stunned. "I thought Betty Verring never gave you the rest of those photos."

"She didn't. I only had the ones without the writing, but there was enough for me to guess the assailant had written a question. Before I could pursue my discovery demand for the rest, I was off the case."

The detective had a crooked little smile on his face. "The writing on her body—we kept that part of the case close to the vest. Your version—close, but no cigar. The phrase was 'Already dead?' So, how'd you know about that question written on her body?"

I wasn't ready to describe what I had seen and heard in the art museum. "Let's just say a little birdie told me." After a moment's reflection, I modified that. "Actually, let's call it a really big, ugly birdie."

"That birdie of yours—anybody I know?"

"I hope not, for your sake."

Valentine nodded as if he understood, but his eyes told me he didn't. Before he walked out, I asked him again, "So, why do you think I'm different?"

This time Valentine gave me the straight answer. "About that holding cell that Kamera and you were in. It looked normal enough. Cleaned up. Unremarkable. Except for one thing: the holes in the floor. Where someone, or something, had pulled the big metal bolts clear out of the cement."

20

Two weeks after my discharge from the hospital, I was sitting in my condo, staring at the grainy remains of the espresso at the bottom of my cup and pondering my future. I decided to pursue Detective Valentine's suggestion about a new career, so I called him on his direct number. When he picked up, I didn't dive into the private investigator idea at first. Instead I asked him something even more personal. I wanted to know if he had ever found any evidence linking Bradley Yelsin to the cocaine that had taken Courtney's life.

But Valentine closed the door on that. "Sorry, nothing yet. We questioned him. He gave us permission to search his place, but it turned up zero. We're still looking."

I didn't want to let it go. "You sure? Bradley would have needed a Hazmat team to clean up all the drugs he kept at his place."

"For what it's worth, I was surprised too. But there is some good news about that guy."

I was in the mood to hear something positive.

Valentine said, "Yelsin was persuaded not to push for criminal battery charges against you. You know, for the punch in the nose you gave him."

"How did that happen?"

"I suggested to him that I could continue the investigation into his drug use. Or maybe not. His choice. And I strongly hinted at his making the right choice. As long as he was willing to forget about your knockout punch."

Another favor from Detective Valentine. "Thanks," I said. "And while I have you on the line, I'm interested in your idea. About being a private investigator."

"Okay. But if you don't mind, let's hold off on your getting licensed by the state of New York as a PI. That is probably not necessary for what we would have you doing."

"Which is what?"

"Using your talents, whatever they are, to help us."

I groaned. "You mean, like the psychics? The crackpots who live in basement apartments with too many cats and tell you where the bodies are buried?"

"Not exactly. You'd just screen some suspects for us. Bad people. And then tell us exactly how bad they are, and in what way."

"Oh. You mean, like a human Geiger counter?"

"There you go. I like that," he said.

I told him I was willing, but wondered if I could make a living doing that. And then there was also the public relations problem. "My being on the payroll, wouldn't that raise some eyebrows?"

"The NYPD accountants have a way of cutting checks to you without the public knowing we've hired a demon chaser."

"Is that what I am?"

"You tell me."

In truth, I couldn't. I had no idea what I was at that point.

Detective Valentine ended with a big flourish. "Oh. And some breaking news about Dunning Kamera. Just heard it on my private line. Not even on the police scanners yet."

"I'm all ears."

"Not sure if you knew, but yesterday in court, Kamera's new attorney was able to get him released on bail. Judge Cavendish had recused herself. Supposedly because of something that was said during your last repartee with her in court. Anyway, a new judge came on the case and reversed Cavendish's order and put Kamera back on the street."

"That's terrible news."

"I'm not done. An hour ago your former client, after getting released from jail, threw himself in front of the subway train at the South Ferry stop. Not exactly a clean way to go."

While I was weighing that news, Valentine

added, "I don't know what would have taken Kamera to that station. It wasn't even close to where he lived. The South Ferry stop is the end of the line. Literally."

The rest of my day, while tending to the necessities of my life, like checking on the balance of my retirement account and figuring out how I was going to make it financially, my mind kept drifting back to Dunning Kamera's death.

I had heard once about the suicide phenomenon that attracts people to the Golden Gate Bridge in San Francisco. How, according to some psychologists, the dreamers and drifters migrate to California thinking that they could discover the good life. When they didn't find it, and having come to the end of land and having run out of dreams, they would hike onto the bridge and jump off.

I had a different theory about Dunning Kamera. He may have traveled down to the South Ferry stop with the thought that once he was on the water, he would be safe. Then he realized that there was no escape. Because what he was trying to escape from seemed inescapable, because it had already inhabited him. And that's why he jumped.

The thoughts in my head were growing increasingly morbid.

Then, out of the blue, I received a text from Jersey Dan Hoover. Dan's message was about our Manitou teenage music crew that used to hang out together. A nice change.

> Hey Trevor. I've felt nostalgic lately, and finally looked up your contact info. How are ya? Been way too long. Am down at Muscle Shoals, AL right now. Doing a jazz/rock/blues festival. I connected with Bobby too. Just a quick text. He's some kind of environmental scientist now. What a gas! I'm still trying to link with Augie. Man, that guy's vanished. Do you know where he is? Are you still playing the blues harp? See ya. Dan

Dan. Bobby. Augie. For some reason I had also been thinking a lot about those guys recently.

But I had to laugh at Dan's text, because I never would have pegged him, with his skyrocketing music career, to have been such an impresario of high school memories. Go figure.

I should have realized it was more than coincidence that we both started thinking back to our old hometown.

Later that day I forced myself to finally go through Courtney's personal things. It was a task that I had deliberately put off, knowing that it would place me deeply inside the vacuum that had been left by her. Never mind that we had perfected the art of mutually assured destruction, with eventual infidelity by her and emotional abandonment by me way before that. None of that lessened the pain, just redirected it, like a nerve injury that sends the shock to the head rather than to the heart.

When I slowly entered her twenty-two-foot clothes closet, I could still detect the faint scent of her Clive Christian perfume. At first I toyed with selling all of her clothes on eBay, but decided instead to donate her fashion retinue to a worthy charity. So I started pawing my way through the racks of clothes and jotting it all down on a legal pad.

Every so often I would reach down or bend the wrong way, and there was that shooting pain again at the site of the wound in my chest.

More than once I would pull up my shirt and look at it again. As I studied the red, angry flesh and the sutured edges where I had been stabbed, there was the same thought. It had been plaguing me. The jagged cut on my torso was in the exact same location as the entry wound on Heather's body. The difference, of course, was that she had been killed first and then her heart had been cut out through that opening in her flesh. I, on the other hand, was still alive. But we were both slashed at the same spot.

All of that came from the objective side of my brain. But logic wasn't enough. Yes, there were some similarities between Heather's murder and my attack.

But it also meant something else. If Elijah White was right, it meant that I was now the target of demonic forces from the underworld. While I tried to hunt them, they would be hunting me.

So, that is where things stood. *Well then,* I thought, *if that's what life looks like, I might as well make a living at it.* I left a voice mail on Valentine's cell: "Let me know when we can start."

21

During the months that followed, Detective Dick Valentine was true to his word. He brought me into the precinct once or twice a week to eyeball a variety of suspects and arrestees who did the lineup routine: front view, turn to the right and turn to the left, while victims behind one-way glass tried to identify the perpetrator. There were holdup men, muggers, kidnappers, and wife beaters. I watched interrogations of gang members who had inflicted violence for no other reason than it was part of their initiation, as well as a stream of pickpockets, arsonists, serial rapists, and drug dealers (a lot of those).

But missing was the familiar stench reminiscent of the Manitou landfill fires—not a hint of it, despite the despicable things these suspects had done. I was beginning to wonder why I was being paid to traipse regularly into the cop shop at all, because I was adding nothing to the police effort.

At the same time I was being exposed to a flotilla of human depravity that topped anything I had ever experienced before, at least not since my short career as a public defender, my first sixteen months fresh out of law school before the firm snatched me up.

As a criminal defense lawyer I thought I had seen it all. But I hadn't. The only lowlifes I represented in private practice were the ones who could pay me my quarter-of-a-million-dollar initial retainer fee. That fact alone cordoned me off from a whole criminal underbelly of humanity.

During my stint as the NYPD's "special consultant," the title that was printed on my checks' memo line, there was one perp named Jimmy Delacroix. His specialty was residential burglaries, which he would execute through the use of a chimpanzee that he had trained to scamper up to windows and then find which ones were not securely locked.

Then there was Little Ted, a bearded dwarf with a photographic memory who stood in line at ATMs behind high rollers when they would dash out of their limos to get some cash; he memorized the passcodes as the victims typed them in, having a perfect line of sight for the keypad due to his short stature. Ted made his living selling the passcodes. Ted was hot for Little Betty, a nightclub entertainer who stood four feet tall in her high heels but who spurned his advances. When Betty disappeared, the police suspected foul play and fingered Ted, but their suspicions happily fizzled when Betty showed up very much alive after a trip to Vero Beach, Florida. You can't make this kind of stuff up.

At the same time, I felt like a freeloader in my work with Dick Valentine, given that I was feeding at the public trough while seemingly doing nothing productive for the privilege.

One day Dick Valentine and I walked out to our vehicles together at the end of his shift and I put the question to him. "Why are you keeping me on? I haven't given you once piece of information about these evildoers that you couldn't have figured out yourself."

Valentine was customarily a plain-talking man, but not then. He said, "It only takes one. That'll be worth it."

"One what?" I asked.

"That's what we're waiting for. For you to show us the one." Then he pointed an index finger up in the air.

While he stood next to his Ford Taurus, I kept up the conversation with another question. "As a cop, do you believe in demons? I mean, the real ones?"

While he fished his keys out of his pockets, he explained. "You remember Jeffrey Dahmer? Milwaukee serial killer?"

"Of course. The trial was covered on TV, gavel to gavel."

"He was into human desecration," Valentine continued, "body parts in the refrigerator. He emulsified the corpses in his own toxic vat. Cannibalism. I had a friend on the Milwaukee PD who sent me the police supplementals. One part of the report had portions of Dahmer's confession, the things that didn't get televised. Never made the papers. The way Dahmer explained it, there was this point in his life, before his rampage really started, when he knew he was at a crossroads. And he describes how he made this conscious choice to go to the dark side, and he says when he did, an irresistible evil force, a true demonic power, took over from that point on. After that, he said he felt helpless. This is not stuff I would ever say publicly, you understand. But there it is."

"Then you do believe?"

"I told you once that I was open to the super-natural because of the Catholic neighborhood I was raised in. Actually, that's only partly true. The other part is that I've done my own study. Dahmer wasn't alone. There are others."

"Like?"

"Henry Holmes, a doctor."

"Never heard of him."

"Most folks haven't," Valentine replied. "I read up on him. Holmes was around in the late 1800s in Chicago. The World's Fair was in his backyard at the time, and people started disappearing. He was a butcher. Huge numbers of victims. When he was caught and convicted, he confessed to having a devil inside of him. An actual devil. And I think he meant it. Not as a dodge, or an excuse, but as a fact."

Valentine climbed into his car as I stood there in the parking garage. I heard the echoes of squealing tires from cars below us taking the spiral turns, speeding home for dinner. I wondered whether or not in the end I would lead them to the "one" they were looking for. Apparently I needed patience. So I would wait, like Valentine said. As it turned out, I wouldn't have to wait long.

22

A week later—it was a Wednesday—Valentine and I were in the precinct station together. I had been asking him occasionally for updates on my assailant, Hanz Delpha. That particular day sticks in my mind for two reasons.

That was when he told me that they had finally tracked down Delpha at a cheap hotel on 47th Street. The guy had looped a rope over the top of the door to his rented room, closed it tight, looped the other end around his neck, and then must have kicked the chair out from under him. He had been dead for a while when they found him.

So, I thought to myself, *okay, two demoniacs, both came after me, and both killed themselves.* Of course, there were other similarities too. They both inflicted slashing wounds on the same part of their victims' anatomy. And they were both hung up on a similar phrase: One had used *Dead already?* and the other, *Already dead?*

I thanked Valentine for telling me about Delpha.

Valentine asked me to hang around late until he finished the interrogation of a drug entrepreneur by the name of Carlos Alvarez.

"We got him now, Black," Valentine said when he met me during a break in the interrogation. "This guy's the crown jewel. He's the main link between dealers and that cartel in Colombia. Shutting him down will choke some of that supply line at least. But the guy's cagey. Keeps saying the translator speaks the wrong dialect and he can't be sure of the questions. Yeah, sure."

The news about Alvarez was a huge relief. I had heard some of the gossip in the police stations about Alvarez. He was suspected of possibly being the person who carried out killings on his turf very recently—a string of grisly mutilations. Hearts being cut out.

"So what's Castor going to do now?" Sid Castor was an NYPD cop who'd been undercover with

Alvarez for two years. He probably deserved most of the credit for tagging him and bringing the cartel's operations to a halt.

"That guy has been in deep for a long time. But hopefully we've got plans for Castor." Valentine got up to head back into the debriefing room, and I told him that I was going to grab some coffee. I strolled into the lunchroom alone where the table was littered with sports sections from the newspaper. The coffeepot had a thin inch of stale coffee left in the bottom, so I poured it into a Styrofoam cup and smothered it with Sweet'N Low.

Most of the officers treated me pretty well. Only two of them gave me a hard time. Victor Chavez was one of them. He seemed like a decent guy, but a few years before that I had him on the stand during the defense of a client of mine who had been charged with armed robbery of a convenience store. During discovery I unearthed Chavez's daybook containing his handwritten notes and found that he had taken down a description of the robber from the store manager that differed radically from his description in the police report that he later typed up. The surveillance cameras in the shop were on the fritz during the robbery, so the ID of the bandit was a crucial issue. I made Chavez look silly on the stand, and my client was acquitted. Police officers have long memories, I guess.

The other one was Sid Castor himself. Every

time he saw me he tossed me a wisecrack. Castor was a swarthy-skinned guy of ambiguous ethnicity, but with a look that helped him gain access to the Alvarez drug cartel. He was handsome, with a swagger and an arrogant attitude.

That day, while I was in the lunchroom, Castor strolled in and spotted me. "Hey, Trevor, what's on the docket today? Palm reading?"

I smiled.

He kept it up. "Maybe with your Gypsy magic, you're after bigger stuff, like Wolfman or Dracula."

My smile was wearing out. Castor sauntered up closer to me, and pulled out a cigarette and lit it up.

I didn't miss that. I said, "I thought this was a no-smoking premises."

He tittered. Then he said, "Did you actually use the word *premises* just now? You lawyers are something else."

I nodded, still trying to be civil, but I was wondering where this was going.

Castor returned to the subject of smoking and said, "I do whatever I want. You know what I mean?"

I nodded again, but I really wasn't sure what he meant, only feeling the need to keep the dialogue going and see where it went.

"Okay," he said, "you're being a good sport. So, I've got this lead for you . . ." Then he started looking around the room. "I'm not sure I should tell you. At least not here. It's about your buddy Dick Valentine."

"What about him?"

"I said . . . not *here*. Let's walk."

He took me outside, to the alley behind the station, where there were a few parked cars, a dumpster, and a layer of oily filth on the pavement. Then he opened up. "Okay, how much do you know about Valentine anyway?"

I told him that I didn't know him personally. Only through his work on a few cases that we had in common, but that I trusted him.

"Well," he said. "Internal Affairs had some concern about him. You know, pushing his way into the investigation of your wife's death."

"Oh?"

"Yeah. You got to wonder what his interest was." Castor was rubbing his hands together, the cigarette hanging out of the corner of his mouth, and he took a step closer to me. "Ever wonder about that?"

"No. I've got better things to think about."

"Do you, now? Well, I'm just trying to give you some friendly advice."

"Like?"

"I'm not sure you belong here in the NYPD, swimming with the sharks. You could be somebody's dinner. Maybe it's time for you to head back to shore."

I shook my head. "I'm not ready to do that."

"Really?"

"Yeah."

Now Castor was about a foot away. He plucked the cigarette out of his mouth between two fingers, blew a thin stream of smoke in my direction, tapped the ash off the end, and then decided to drop it to the ground. He ducked his head and crushed the butt with his foot, taking a long time to study the dirty pavement of the alley as he did.

Then he looked up, and that is when I understood what this was all about.

Castor was changing. Into something else. And I felt my guts exhale, like a deflated tire, and I only had time for half of a thought.

Oh boy.

His eyes evaporated. Now they were just empty eye sockets. Black, ugly, gaping holes where his eyeballs had been. His lips were gray. His face, caulk white. He struck out at me with lightning speed, pinning me against the wall of the building and choking me with both hands while he spoke.

"Your wife, Courtney," he grunted as he squeezed tighter around my larynx, "her eyes had this scared look while she was dying. Wondering why you weren't there to save her. Think about that while you're taking your last breath."

I swung my fist in a blasting uppercut to his chin. It should have broken his jaw. But this

156

creature without eyes only twitched a little, like a dog with a tick. I slammed my fist into the monster's face again, and a trickle of thick black blood started oozing out of his nose. The thing that was strangling me twitched again, then squeezed harder and lifted me clear off my feet, holding me against the building while I dangled there.

The grip around my neck was too much. I tried to yank his wrists away from my throat, but I couldn't. I was getting woozy. Beginning to lose consciousness.

I tried to kick at him, sloppily kneeing him in the chest. Flailing. Nothing was stopping him. Somewhere in my head, I was saying, *The end.* Things went dark.

Then I felt my head hit the pavement of the alley. It jolted me back. Above me, I saw men fighting. Someone was growling like a mad dog. Ferocious.

Things came into focus, and I saw Dick Valentine and three uniformed cops wrestling with Castor and pinning him to the ground, snapping cuffs on his hands behind his back. More growling like the sounds of a mad dog. In the air there was the scent of the Manitou land-fill fires.

23

"Enough. I'm done." I spoke it with my mouth half-full, finishing a corned beef on rye at the sidewalk café deli. But I wasn't referring to the food.

Valentine was biting into an egg salad sandwich. I was thinking, kind of a strange lunch choice for a guy like him. I figured him for a carnivore. After swallowing, he said, "Just so you know, you were able to do what nobody else could have done."

"Being strangled by a zombie?"

"Bringing Castor to justice," Valentine said. "Nobody wanted to touch him. He was a hero with the guys in the force. But I had been tracking some recent bloodlust killings. Heart extractions without benefit of anesthetic. Interestingly, the newest batch of victims started showing up just after the suicide of Hanz Delpha."

What Valentine told me wasn't new. But it reinforced the question: what was the consistent link for all those similar mutilations, starting with poor Heather?

Valentine continued. "I matched those new cases to areas that were geographically close to where Castor had his undercover dealings with Alvarez. We had Alvarez under surveillance, so it couldn't have been him. But no one was watching Castor. It's always tough to suspect your own."

"But you did."

"Yeah, but it doesn't feel good."

I added things up. "Castor's mayhem against me—that was what gave you the probable cause you needed."

"Right. That, coupled with what he said to you about how your wife died. As if Castor had some special insight into the details of the death of your wife, even though, strangely, she died alone in her car and Castor wasn't anywhere near her location that day, which raises some very spooky questions, I guess. Anyway, we got a warrant to search his locker and his car. And his apartment. We found DNA evidence to link him to the mutilation killings." He wiped his mouth with a paper napkin. "So that's why I said that you did for us what we couldn't do."

It was good to hear that from Valentine. "I was glad to help," I said. "Maybe I was meant to be working with you for no other reason than that."

Valentine tossed his napkin onto his paper plate. "So . . . tell me again. About what Castor looked like. When he changed into that . . . that thing."

"Why? Are you trying to convince yourself it really happened?"

"Maybe."

"Honestly, I don't like talking about it."

"Fair enough."

I decided it was time to share my plans. "I've decided to hang it up. The 'consulting' business, I mean. I'm leaving the city."

"Where are you going?"

"I'm thinking North Carolina. Our firm had a client with a big place down there on the ocean, along the Outer Banks. Hatteras Island. He took me deep-sea fishing a few times. I think maybe I'll move down to that area."

"So, you're a fisherman?"

"When I was a young boy, my father would take me out on his little boat. River trout, and some lake fishing too, for bass, walleyes, muskies. But there's something about ocean fishing that appeals to me now."

"Hatteras, you said?"

"Actually, I'm looking for something on an island near there. A lot of sand and water, and sea grass and dunes. And quiet. Tourists come and go. But people leave you alone."

"Sounds remote."

"Exactly."

"Like a witness protection program?"

"Huh." I snickered. "I hadn't thought of it that way. Anyway, my wife's gone. My lawyering days are over. I finished the job for you. Time to move on."

"Too bad. You've done some good here in the city."

"Thanks for that. But I've also been stabbed in

the chest and nearly choked to death in an alley." I lifted up my swollen right hand. "And I think I may have broken a knuckle on that last one. Then there's the daily thing. What happens to me, for instance, when I'm walking almost anywhere in this city. Crowds passing by, shoulder to shoulder, on the sidewalk. Then suddenly I pick up the scent. I wonder where in the mob of humanity is the person with the demon. Who's going to butcher someone next. So I turn and look, trying to figure it out, knowing I can't ever find them all, or even most of them. It weighs on you."

Valentine had finished eating, and he was leaning back in the little chair at the sidewalk deli, studying me. As people streamed by, Valentine looked over at them, and then back at me. He just nodded, saying nothing.

I continued. "Dick, I think if I stay here and keep doing this, I'll lose my mind."

"Don't want that to happen. But I'm just thinking, maybe there's some reason you have this particular ability. Things have a reason. Higher purpose."

I'd never told him about my inner transformation. It wasn't just the dark, sinister things coming after me, but other things, good things too. I was on a path, though in terms of the immediate future, I had no idea where it was taking me. "Higher purpose?" I said. "I know that's true. I didn't used to believe that. But I do now." For a moment I had a sudden regret about leaving the city. Admitting defeat.

After a second or two, Detective Dick Valentine stood up and stretched out his husky hand to shake mine. "Good luck. Let me know where you settle."

24

The very next week, I cashed out my 401(k) and my mutual funds. Courtney's Benz had already been sold. Any hesitation about leaving Manhattan was quickly alleviated when the media got ahold of the Sid Castor arrest story. It didn't take long before my name was dragged into the press frenzy. Trevor Black, disbarred attorney, was dubbed the "demon-chasing defense attorney" who had been secretly employed by the NYPD.

I wanted out of town quick, but I figured it would take a while to sell the condo. Surprisingly, within four days of the listing my agent presented me with a married couple who were tired of renting. To top it off, they wanted to take the place furnished, so they paid extra for all of the designer furniture and artwork.

At the closing, I wished them well, and I truly meant it. The condo had been a place of extremes for Courtney and me, ranging from glowing newlywed love to cold indifference and militant confrontation. I hoped that home could become a consistently happy place for the two of them.

Patty, the wife, worked for a conglomerate that published several magazines, and her husband, Doug, was an account manager for a marketing outfit. They were friendly and asked me about my background. I told them I had left the practice of law.

Doug was talkative and prodded a little. "What now?"

"Oh," I said, "I guess I'm a traveler in search of a destination. But only figuratively. I don't want you good folks to think that I'm homeless and will be ringing you up from the lobby, asking if I can crash at your place for the night."

Patty gave out a hearty laugh. She had been eyeballing me closely, like she knew something about me but didn't want to say. She asked, "No professional plans?"

"Not really," I said. "Professional activities require a layer of professionalism—you know, the shiny coat of varnish. I'm afraid that's been stripped off of me. Like a worn desk at a flea market."

Now they both smiled. But I noticed my real estate broker wasn't amused. He had another closing right after mine. I rose and announced that we should let my agent get on his way, and shook both of their hands.

As we left the closing room, Patty said, "You've got an interesting way of expressing yourself. Ever think about doing some writing? I mean, other than legal briefs?"

In response, I shared a quick story about a court decision I had once read where the judge laid out his legal opinion in a lengthy rhyme, like a poem. "He was no Wordsworth," I said. "Most lawyers, and judges too, probably have an over-rated view of their own communication skills."

Ten days later I was riding over the series of bridges along the single highway that connects thin stretches of sandy turf and clusters of beach houses. The place where the Atlantic crashes into the shore on your left, and the marshy waters of the Pamlico Sound are on your right. At the Hatteras harbor I pulled my rig onto the car ferry that was bound for Ocracoke Island, North Carolina.

I had traded in my Aston Martin for some cash plus a Land Rover, and hitched it to a trailer full of possessions. I had honed things down. Travel light, I told myself. More books than I should have kept. Only one suit, the Armani. All the Tommy Bahama shirts, and lots of wrinkled shorts and faded blue jeans. And every ball cap I ever owned. Particularly the sweat-stained Mets cap.

I had bought, sight unseen, a cottage on the

island based on pictures that had been e-mailed to me. It was located off of a dirt lane down from a cemetery belonging to ancient mariner families. Over the ages the inscriptions on the tilted headstones had become illegible.

But my place had a clear view of the blue ocean just beyond the sea grass. I told myself that I had found contentment.

I paid an obscene amount of cash for an impressive fishing boat, and took the safety classes and learned how to handle it. After a couple of months, though, I realized that the price of this kind of self-imposed exile was loneliness. I made the effort to be sociable and met a friend down at Howard's Pub by the name of Roy Dance, and we would occasionally launch out to the Gulf Stream together where the fishing was legendary. I started hanging around every bar on the island, ignoring the internal gyroscope that had been guiding me since my spiritual awakening in my New York law office. In my new island life I was drinking too much bourbon, Fireball whiskey, and every rum drink ever made. Sadly, I was becoming a local barstool fixture. I knew down deep that there was a lot wrong with that picture, and that things had to change. When Elijah White gave me a call one day, out of the blue, asking me, "How are you traveling with Jesus?" it was like a punch in the spiritual solar plexus.

Eventually I did a few smart things. I decided to

get an actual job to keep me busy, so I left my seat at the barstool and started to wait tables at Howard's.

Then I started going to a little church called Port-of-Peace. The pastor, Banks Trumbly, was a part-timer who walked with a limp and had a day job on one of the commercial fishing boats.

For a while, even before visiting Port-of-Peace, I had been taking Elijah White's advice about reading the Bible. The book of Ecclesiastes struck a chord with me. A sort of low bass note. In one place it read, "Like fish caught in a treacherous net and birds trapped in a snare, so the sons of men are ensnared at an evil time when it suddenly falls on them." I thought about the evil times that were behind me, and my escape from New York City. Since coming to the island, I hadn't bumped into any of the dark forces. But then, it was just a matter of percentages, wasn't it? New York City has a population of well over eight million. The odds are much more likely that at any one time there might be a possessed soul or two in the mix. I didn't know the population of Ocracoke Island, but even at the height of the tourist season, it was minuscule.

From time to time I did wonder about future encounters. And about the other part in Ecclesiastes that makes an obvious point when it says a man "cannot dispute with him who is stronger than he is." Those supernatural ghouls were stronger, and I knew that. Yet I knew that God was stronger still. I was banking on that.

On the occupational side of things, I also gave some thought to what Patty had said to me at the real estate closing. One day I called her up. After asking how they were enjoying my former condo, I dove right into the reason for the call.

"Patty, remember when you talked about my doing some writing?"

"Sure."

"I'm thinking about it. Any advice?"

She told me that she knew someone, a friend of hers, who was looking for a reporter for a true-crime magazine, and would I be interested? She said it wouldn't get me rich, which was not my goal by then, so I said sure, I'd give it a try.

I had a six-week deadline. They needed fifteen hundred words. So I jumped onto the Internet to gobble up as much information as I could about writing like a journalist. The editor at *American Crime Digest* liked it and put me on as a regular contributor, specializing in reports about bizarre murder cases. A little later, a monthly legal magazine started shooting me some assignments to report on oddball lawsuits and out-of-the-ordinary courtroom stories. With my articles on all things weird, I was beginning to feel a little like the host of *Ripley's Believe It or Not!* But it paid the bills, and I found some pleasure in my modest career as a legal reporter.

I was starting to feel just about settled into my new island life when I got a text from Dan Hoover. I hadn't heard from him in over a year. He said that he had connected with Bobby Budleigh and learned that Bobby was heading back to Manitou, and maybe all of us could rendezvous there in a few weeks. Dan explained that he was cutting a record and then would be doing a one-night event in Chicago, which was only a few hours' drive from Manitou. Maybe, he said, we could all join up after that. He was still looking for Augie Bedders and wondered if I had any leads.

I told him no, regarding Augie's whereabouts, but absolutely, yes, I was hyped over the idea of our getting together. I asked him to keep me in the loop.

Suddenly, all of the old memories about our life as teens in Manitou came down on me like a rain shower. I didn't realize that the past had a long reach and was not over yet. Not by a long shot.

A week later, Dick Valentine called me. He said that the Sid Castor prosecution was finally resolved and he was free to talk to me about it. Castor's attorney had cut a deal with the DA for thirty years in prison in return for a guilty plea to one of the homicides and dismissal of the others. The forensic evidence was thin, and the circumstantial links were even thinner. Valentine said he was disappointed at first, because in his considered opinion he thought Castor deserved "a dirt nap." But then he added, "He ended up getting one anyway."

I asked what he meant and he explained that during his lockup, Sid Castor had been knifed to death by another prisoner who had used a homemade shiv. It happened shortly after Castor had started his prison sentence.

He asked me a little about how things were going, and I brought him up to speed. Then he told me something that I hadn't heard before. It was in response to my asking him if Castor had ever mentioned me during the case, before he was sentenced and shipped off to prison.

Valentine said, "Yeah, he did."

"What was that?" I asked.

"After the plea deal, Castor's lawyer let me talk to him. Castor said he was surprised that he hadn't finished you off when he was choking you in the alley. I told him no, that he didn't finish you. That you were just fine. Which was odd, because obviously Castor should have known that if he had killed you, he would have been charged with that too. Which he wasn't. Then Castor said something else to me."

I replied, "I'm waiting."

Valentine spoke slow at that point, like he knew it might be important. "Castor had this weird grin when he talked about you, Trevor. He said, and I quote—'I thought he was *dead already*.' Those were his exact words. Then he said, 'Be sure and tell Trevor Black what I just said,' and laughed."

I told Valentine that I was glad he told me. But inside I felt an electric shiver. When I left New York, I had assumed all of that was behind me, but it was only wishful thinking. I had been wrong about it, and not just about that. But also in failing to realize, until it was too late, how my hometown in Wisconsin, and the events of my life there, had everything to do with everything.

THE
DEVIL

25

After a few months with no further contact from Dick Valentine, I was hunched over my laptop at the desk in my bungalow on Ocracoke Island, working on a magazine piece. This one was on the plight of young runaways and their involvement in street crime. By then, Ocracoke Island was my home. But the memory of Heather, the young victim in New York who died at the hand of my client, still hovered over me as I worked on the assignment. I liked to think that other Heathers out there could still be rescued.

By eleven thirty that morning, having interviewed two authorities on juvenile delinquency by phone and finished a few pages, I decided to call it quits. I needed a break.

I phoned my friend Roy Dance and asked if he wanted to go fishing. His wife, Elaine, had respiratory problems and always needed to keep a tank of oxygen close to her, so Roy was careful to schedule his time out of the house. But he said his daughter happened to be visiting just then, and she could keep an eye on his wife, so he was free to hang out with me. Something stirred in me as I thought about the children Courtney and I never had the chance to raise, and I thought to myself, *What a blessing it is to have a daughter. I hope Roy feels that way too.*

When Roy arrived, we drove to my slip at the harbor and launched off the island on my fishing boat, heading for the Gulf Stream. I had struggled for a while to name the boat. I finally painted the single word *Unnamed* on the stern. People who read it remarked how I must have given up trying to decide on the right name. But that really wasn't it. It was the fact that certain mysterious things—some bad, some good—come to us without names attached.

Two hours later we were motoring into the deep waters looking for yellowfin tuna.

Roy had brought a cooler full of beer and a bottle of Scotch. I told him no thanks, that I was making an effort to dry out my brain and renew my soul, but maybe I'd help myself to a single beer once we had settled on a trolling spot. Roy said he wasn't up to fishing and offered to hang on to the wheel while I strapped myself into the fighting chair.

We baited my hook for tuna, but we didn't get any. Forty-five minutes later I hooked something better. It was a blue marlin that must have been three hundred pounds and that let us know he was there before I even felt him on my line, because we saw a big swirling dent in the water when he went after the bait.

Then the fight. He broke out of the water,

showed his white belly, and tossed his long saber of a bill, then dove down deep. *Oh no,* I thought, *he's going to go down and down forever, and I'm going to lose him.* "Roy!" I yelled. "Slow the boat down and come about. Stay close to the line." In the water, the marlin was stronger than me, and I knew it; if this monster fish had a mind to, he could have worn me out.

But for some reason, as I was trying to just hang on, the monster gave up and started surfacing. I fought him for a while. My arms were tired, but though I still had the strength to keep going, I didn't have to, because in less than an hour we had him up and into the boat.

We knew that we would throw him back. But first I gave Roy my iPhone to snap some pictures with me crouching next to the big fish.

There was plenty of blood flowing from his mouth, and it pooled on the deck and mixed with the seawater, forming a pink pond at my feet and soaking my deck shoes.

After the photos, we unhooked him and rolled him back into the dark blue of the Atlantic to see him streak off. I was still standing in the pool of seawater and blood when my iPhone rang. Roy handed me my cell. The area code was from New Jersey. Dan Hoover was calling.

I picked up with a hearty hello, because it was good to hear from him, and I was wondering about his plans to have all the band members of The

Assault assemble back in Manitou in a week or two for a reunion.

But Dan cut me off suddenly. His voice was troubled. "Hey. Listen. This is terrible, man. Rotten news. I feel like I got kicked in the stomach. You will too."

"What is it?"

"It's about Bobby."

"Bobby Budleigh? What about him?"

"Something terrible."

"Tell me."

"He's dead, man. He's gone."

A silent tornado. Mental debris and confusion. I had to take a few seconds to collect my head. "What happened? How . . . ?"

"I don't know the details," Dan admitted. "But it sounds bad. I tried to call his cell because I knew he should have arrived back in Manitou doing some kind of science thing for his consulting company. That's what his wife, Vicky, told me before, almost a month ago when I called his house in Colorado. But when I tried to call him yesterday, no answer. So I called Vicky again in Colorado. Vicky's sister picked up. I explained who I was. She told me that Bobby had been killed."

The boat was rocking slowly and the riggings were creaking as I stood there trying to process the shock and looking down at the deck where I was standing in the blood and the water from the big blue marlin.

I didn't say anything at first.

Dan broke the silence. "I'm trying to get more information."

"Where did he die?"

"In Manitou."

"You really don't know anything else?"

Dan said, "No, man. That's everything."

There was silence for a while.

Then Dan said, "Look, I know you're a lawyer . . ."

"Not anymore."

"Well, yeah. Okay. But weren't you some kind of private investigator for a while too?"

"Used to be. Left that. I write for legal magazines now." I was still numb.

"I know that you can get information. Right? You know how to do that."

"Yeah," I said. "I know how to do that."

More silence. Until I decided. "Okay, Dan. I'm going to get to the bottom of this. Find out what happened to Bobby. Then I'll let you know."

Dan thanked me. He said, "Maybe by then I'll hear back from Augie. I tracked down his aunt, who I knew because she used to work with my mom at the Red Owl in Manitou. I gave her the message to have him call me, wherever he is. When Augie connects, we'll have to tell him the news, in case he doesn't know."

I struggled to make conversation. I asked Dan how his tour was going.

"My Chicago thing is coming up. But right now . . . Man, I'm just so totally bummed about Bobby. Can't stop thinking about it."

I had another thought. About somebody else. "Does anybody know where Marilyn Parlow is these days? I lost track of her in college. I think she'd want to know about Bobby."

"Yeah, Marilyn. Haven't thought of her in ages. Don't have the faintest about her."

When we hung up, I asked Roy to start motoring us to shore. Meanwhile, I pulled up Detective Dick Valentine's number on my contact list and left a message on his voice mail telling him everything I knew about Bobby's death, which wasn't much. Maybe Dick could get the Manitou police department to tell him, as one cop shop to another, what had happened to my friend.

26

It was nine thirty in the morning the next day, and my usual routine would have had me slurping down coffee in my island cottage. But instead, I was just standing there, staring out beyond the tall sea grass on the little patch of sand that was my front yard and scanning the greenish-gray ocean all the way to the horizon. It was time to sit down at my laptop and get to work, but I couldn't. I felt cemented to the floor. The death of Bobby Budleigh was sinking in.

There was misery about it on multiple levels, even though I hadn't talked to Bobby in twenty years. I'd had the chance to connect with him, but I disregarded several notices over the years from the class reunion committee and had no contact with my high school friends until Dan Hoover started pursuing me.

So I stood there, holding my Mets cup in my hand, with the coffee growing cold. I heard my ringtone and had to hunt around the place, looking for my cell. When I found it, Dick Valentine's name was on the screen.

"Trevor, it's been a while."

"It has."

"Saw a crime magazine that had one of your articles in it."

"Did you buy a copy?"

"Naw. I deal with murder all day long. If I'm going to read, it's going to be something fun."

"I'm not fun?"

"You're an interesting guy. But fun? That's a stretch."

I laughed. It was good to talk to him. I asked him if he had a chance to check up on Bobby Budleigh's death. He said he did. "I've got some details for you."

"That was quick," I said.

"Like I said, you're always dragging interesting

stuff behind you." Then he added, "Like a beagle I used to own as a kid. Always coming into the house with some dead animal in his teeth. So yeah, you drag some interesting stuff to me. But definitely not fun. Not in this case."

I cleared my throat. "Tell me."

"Your friend Mr. Budleigh was the victim of some really foul play."

"How did he die?"

"Shot in the back of the head."

"Where was this?"

"Out in the sticks, at the municipal fringe of Manitou."

"Any suspects? Any motive for this?"

"Not so far. I spoke to the head honcho in the sheriff's department. They're working it."

"Anything else?"

"Yeah. There's more."

That didn't sound good. But then, how much worse could it be? Bobby had been murdered. "Okay," I said. "I want to hear."

"They found his body at the spot where they think he was killed. Sounds like they did the usual forensics."

"What did they find?"

"You don't need to be a pathologist to figure it out."

"Meaning?"

"This is going to sound familiar."

I waited.

Valentine said, "His heart had been sliced out. The incision was in the upper-left quadrant of his chest."

I let him finish.

"And . . . some writing on his body. They wouldn't tell me what. They don't want anything to leak out. They're still tracking suspects." When Dick was done with the facts, he added, "Really sorry."

"Thanks."

"You need anything else?"

"Not now," I said. "Maybe later."

"You got a plan in mind?"

I had made a promise to Dan Hoover. To find the truth about Bobby's death. But there was more to it than that. Dick Valentine hinted at it back in New York, maybe even inadvertently. The higher purpose for my special ability. I had often thought back on that. There are no accidents in God's plan.

"Yes. I've got a plan," I replied. "Tracking down a monster. The one that killed Bobby. That's what I'm going to do."

27

At the very end of the James Brown song "It's a Man's Man's Man's World," there's a line that goes like this: "He's lost in the wilderness; he's lost in bitterness." Bobby's murder was heavy on my mind.

The world is a broken place, and I felt as if I was being drawn into the deepest of the broken places.

It was a week after my talk with Dick Valentine. I had deplaned at the Milwaukee airport, and I pulled my roller bag behind me to the car rental desk. The only thing they had left was a little Fiat, which I took. As I squeezed in, I remembered the James Brown song. The lyrics captured something about the human condition. There was no template for what I was trying to do. No GPS for the dark territories where I was heading. I had only my sense of calling and the "sword of the Spirit" that Elijah White had talked about. It would be one step at a time. Faith walking.

Manitou was about two hours northwest. I hadn't been back to my hometown in more than two decades.

I drove into Manitou from the west end of town along the Little Bear River, where the weeping willows still hung along its banks. I noticed the quarry on the other side of the road, with a high tower that still had a big Christmas star at the top that had been lit up every December. It would stand out because there weren't any streetlights in that part of town. I wondered if the lighted Christmas star was still working.

I kept driving into town, past the row of industrial plants. But several looked closed now. Including the Opperdill Foundry, where my father had worked for almost thirty years, and where he took his last breath.

The road that approached the Opperdill Foundry was a long winding one, off the main road that led to the large industrial complex on the banks of the river. I slowed down and pulled into the opening of the driveway to the plant with half a mind to drive down and check it out. But there was a rusty chain across the drive blocking the entrance, and a red metal sign with a few bullet holes in it. The sign read *No Trespassing*. The cement drive had cracks, and there were weeds sprouting up in the broken spaces.

I pulled back into traffic and cruised toward downtown. Different shops. A few new strip malls, little ones. The row of little houses across from the lane of foundries had been replaced by a Starbucks, a 7-Eleven, and a big Walmart.

I did a tour of the residential area. Incredibly, the homes looked pretty much the same as I had remembered, including the house where I grew up. I thought about connecting with my mother by phone and asking her if she had ever returned to Manitou to see the house after she was remarried to Stanley, her current husband, who had made his money running a chain of carpet stores. Stanley and I never saw eye to eye, particularly after he made nasty remarks about my father. Stanley and my mother eventually moved to Boca, in Florida, years ago. After that, we rarely saw each other.

On my way to the hotel I rang her up on her home phone, but she didn't answer. I imagined that she must be over at the hospital where she helped as a volunteer, so I left a message. It was time to reach out. Try to patch things up.

The day was winding down, and I eventually made my way to the Holiday Inn Express on the other end of town, which was in the direction of the site where the police had found Bobby's body.

The desk manager looked like a semiretired fellow. He was friendly but moved slowly as I checked in. He was wearing an Atlanta Braves T-shirt and I remarked about that fact. The man said, "Don't care much for the Milwaukee Brewers. I moved to Milwaukee in the heyday of the Braves. Warren Spahn and that bunch. Eddie Mathews. Hank Aaron. Broke my heart when they moved to Atlanta. But I stuck with them anyway. Loyalty. That's what it's about."

"Yeah," I replied. "Loyalty's important."

It made me think of my dead friend. Loyal—that

was what Bobby Budleigh was. Among the other things that were good about him.

"Loyalty's rare," the desk clerk shot back. Then he passed me my room key and asked if I wanted a newspaper. I nodded and grabbed a copy of the *Manitou Times* off the stack on the front desk and tucked it under my arm.

My room was stuffy, and it was taking a while for the noisy air-conditioning unit to catch up, so I stripped down to my boxers, dropped into bed, and clicked through the TV channels. While I did, I mentally sorted out my questions about Bobby's murder. Why had he returned to Manitou? And what kind of motive could there possibly be for someone to do that to my friend? Or was it a random act of a psychotic killer? A copycat?

Dick Valentine was right. Of course the mutilation was familiar. But the other incidents like that were back in New York. Most recently at the hands of Sid Castor. Who was now dead. Before Castor it was Hanz Delpha trying to carve me up. But he committed suicide, and then Castor's reign of terror followed that. Before Delpha it was Dunning Kamera, my client. He took his life also. The whole thing was beginning to look like a wicked relay race.

Except for one big difference. The runners were homicidal, and they were dying. Several runners, but one baton. And yet somehow the baton was being passed from each bad actor only *after* he

185

was dead. A theory was forming, and it wasn't pretty.

I reached over to the nightstand next to me and snatched up the local newspaper. There it was, right on the front page: "Arrest in Murder of Former Local."

The article quoted the county sheriff, Butch Jardinsky, saying a suspect was now in custody for the killing of Bobby Budleigh, PhD, honor student and graduate of Manitou High School. The suspect in custody was somebody named Donny Ray Borzsted.

There was a feeling of relief, that maybe it was all over before I even got involved.

But I had the nagging feeling that it couldn't be that easy, that quick. The slim facts I already knew about Bobby's death told me something different. Maybe Donny Ray Borzsted was linked in some way to the murder, but a hideous force had to have been behind it, and had jammed the knife in and had plucked out Bobby's heart. The force that was carrying the baton.

I tossed the newspaper onto the floor and turned out the light. The only sound was the humming buzz coming out of the air-conditioning unit.

Then a random thought: Years ago I read a novel by Thomas Wolfe. He'd left behind an unfinished manuscript, and after he died, Wolfe's editor published an excerpt, calling it *You Can't Go Home Again*. Right then, in that hotel room in my hometown, I decided that the title was missing something. It struck me that even if you do go home, you don't expect the devil to be waiting for you when you get there.

28

The next day I discovered that the Manitou police station had not changed much. It was still a one-story redbrick building, except that they had built out the back end and expanded it.

After leaving my rented Fiat in the parking lot, I trotted into the lobby. I recognized the glass case with trophies from the police softball league and the historical display of law enforcement badges dating back seventy years. It was all still there. I remembered it from the day when a juvenile officer, a woman whose name I've since forgotten, towed me in as a sixteen-year-old for my high crimes and misdemeanors, and told me to sit tight in the lobby for a few minutes while she called my mother. I often wondered if it was a test. Seeing if I would bolt out of there if left to myself. If it was a test, then I passed, because there I sat, not moving, staring at the glass displays in the lobby. Those kinds of experiences get laser cut into your brain.

The desk sergeant yanked me back from yesteryear. "Sir? Can I help you?"

I collected my thoughts and gave her a professional card:

Trevor Black
Consultant to Law Enforcement Agencies

Underneath was my old home address in New York City. I'd had them printed up when I was working with Detective Dick Valentine, assuming that I would branch out to other police departments and make a living out of it, but that didn't happen.

I told her I needed to see Sheriff Jardinsky, and that I was a friend of Bobby Budleigh, the murder victim, and wanted to offer my help. She gave me the same unenthusiastic sideglance that I used to give to homeless guys milling in the borough courthouses who would ask me for hasty legal advice as I hustled to my court appearances.

The desk sergeant sighed and told me to sit tight. She called someone, presumably Jardinsky, speaking to him in a hushed tone. Two hours dragged by. Police lobbies are uninteresting places, even ones that hold personal memories. Finally she stood up and told me to follow her down the hall to Sheriff Jardinsky's office, where I met a barrel-chested guy in a brown-and-tan uniform who had a mustache and iron-gray hair cut into a flattop. He was waiting for me behind his cluttered desk.

He stood up slowly and we shook hands. He asked me, "Friend of the victim?"

"Yes."

"Then you'll be glad to know we've got the guy who did it."

"I read the headline. If that's true, then it's good news."

"It's true. You can believe it."

I noticed that he was fingering my business card in his hand while he spoke. I asked, "Any objections to letting me in on where your investigation is at?"

He tossed my card down onto the desk. "Where we're at is that we'll be filing a criminal complaint for murder in the criminal branch of the circuit court. That's where we're at."

"I just want to make sure you've got the right guy."

Sheriff Butch Jardinsky grew red-faced in a hurry. "And you think we don't?"

I ignored the mini-meltdown. "Who's your investigating officer?"

After eyeing me for a few seconds he answered, "Detective Linderman."

"Can I talk to him?"

"It's a 'her,' not a 'him,' and I'll pass that on to the detective. She can make the call whether to talk to you or not." Then, like a lawyer who suddenly realizes he needs to amend a too-hastily drafted document, he added, "Of course, after she consults with me first." He looked like he was still mulling the point, then asked, "You have any relevant evidence about the victim? This Mr. Budleigh?"

"Definitely," I replied, not particularly caring about legal evidence or anything else except getting to the bottom of Bobby's murder and talking to the investigating detective so she could help me get there.

The sheriff said he would tell Detective Linderman about me. I asked for my card back, and I penned my cell phone number on it and gave it back to him. I urged him to have the detective contact me.

As I left the police station I had my doubts about hearing from the detective. And if my efforts were to grind to a stop, it would be like a punch to the kidneys.

I drove away in search of a root beer stand I remembered from my youth. A little shack with clapboard siding that used to serve astounding root beer floats. But when I arrived at the street where I was sure it used to be, I found a little duplex instead.

Luckily, about two blocks away I spotted an ice cream stand called Otto's Creamery. There was a long line, but I was willing to wait it out. I planned to drown the disappointment over my stalled investigation with a chocolate malt.

The shake was great, worth the wait. But even a

great shake tasted a little sour with my inner turmoil over Bobby. While I was sitting in my rental, slurping up the last bit of melted ice cream from the bottom of my paper cup, my cell rang. It read *Restricted*. Detective Linderman was on the line.

"I understand you stopped by the station, and you were a friend of Bobby Budleigh."

"Yes. We were close friends back in high school."

"And you're doing an investigation for who, exactly?"

"Myself. In honor of a really good guy."

"Sounds noble."

"I wouldn't go that far. But I am on a mission. Compelled, you might say."

"Where are you now?"

"Ice cream stand. Not far from the station."

"I know it. I could do with an ice cream cone. Be there in five or ten."

She arrived in seven, driving an unmarked black Dodge with no whitewall tires and a prominent antenna. Then Detective Ashley Linderman stepped out and swept the aviator sunglasses off her face. Before I could wave, she spotted me and stepped over to my car. I wondered if I had been that obvious, as the place was crawling with customers and the picnic tables were crammed too. How had she picked me out?

She was in good shape, thin, about my height,

and wore a dark suit coat and pants, and a white blouse. She had a pretty face and wore her hair pulled back in a sloppy ponytail wrapped with a red elastic band. By the time she was at my window, I noticed she had a long, thin scar on her left cheek.

She smiled and reached out to shake hands through the open window. "Trevor Black?"

"Yes. Thanks for meeting, Detective."

"My colleagues call me Ashley."

"If you're calling me a colleague, I'm honored. Seeing as we're meeting for the first time."

"Well, your card calls you a consultant to law enforcement, doesn't it?"

"Right."

"I take people at their word. Unless I find out differently. And if I find out they've lied, I put them in jail." Her smile broadened.

I suggested that we find a table to sit down at and talk, even though they all looked occupied.

She had a better idea. "Follow me." She strolled over to the side door of the ice cream shack and pulled it open. "Hey, Otto," she yelled. I heard a loud man's voice call out her name from inside. He stayed hidden from view as they bantered for a few seconds. She pulled out a couple of one-dollar bills and passed them over to a man's hand that reached out through the open door. "The usual," she added. Then she waved for me to follow her. There was a single picnic table behind the ice cream shack, and it was empty. We both sat down.

I said, "Restaurants in New York have special booths they keep open for celebrities. So this is yours?"

"I wouldn't know much about New York. I don't get out of Manitou very much. I've only been to New York City twice, both times for law enforcement conferences. Believe me, we didn't eat in any celebrity booths."

I decided to ask, "How'd you recognize me?"

"There's this great invention called the World Wide Web."

"You worked fast."

"Full disclosure: My second conference in New York was a few years ago. I picked up the paper at my hotel, checked the local news, and there was this article about a demon-chasing ex–criminal defense lawyer. So when Butch, my boss, told me that you had stopped by and wanted to talk, I already had the scoop on you. Then I did a little more Internet snooping today."

"Considering what you found there, I'm surprised you agreed to meet."

"Train wrecks. Car crashes. Embarrassing celebrity bloopers. It's hard to look away from real messes." She smiled wide enough to flash a dimple on the other, unmarred cheek.

Otto, a short, balding guy, came out and handed Ashley Linderman her ice cream cone, a strawberry and vanilla swirl, along with her change in coins, then nodded to me before disappearing back into the shack.

Without embarrassment, she tore into the ice cream, demolishing it from the top down to the edge of the cake cone and getting some ice cream on her nose in the process. She demurely swept it away and went back to finishing it off. She paused to ask about my defense practice in New York, so I gave her a breezy overview but avoided anything about my infamous Dunning Kamera case. While she was crunching down on the cake cone with her mouth full, she asked me an almost-indecipherable question and, after swallowing, repeated it. "Did you really punch that stock-broker in the face, the one who was your client?"

"Former client. And yes, I did."

"I suppose you feel vindicated."

"What, by having my license to practice law taken away?"

"No. Because the guy's just been indicted for selling dope to the rich and famous."

"Really? Bradley Yelsin?"

"I thought you would have known. Just happened. I picked that up in my online search. They mentioned you in the article—said that you had decked him because he sold drugs to your wife, and that, well, you know, she·died from an overdose."

My reaction must have given me away. Ashley

bit the corner of her lip. "Sorry. Didn't mean to dig up bad memories."

"I've been avoiding the news from New York. But I'm glad they nailed him."

She wiped her mouth with a napkin and asked, "So, you actually chase demons?"

"I used to."

She raised an eyebrow way up. "Really?"

"Really."

She laughed and shook her head. "Not anymore?"

"I've retired."

She got serious. "Why are you in Manitou, exactly?"

"I want to make sure whoever killed my friend gets caught."

"Well," she said, "I don't know anything about demons, or that sort of thing. Not my bag. But as far as the Bobby Budleigh murder, what happened to him, I suppose an ex–defense lawyer hotshot who thinks he can track demons is not a bad way to go."

That sounded vaguely like a compliment, and I was searching for some kind of reply, but before it came out, her police radio started squawking. Ashley plucked it out of her jacket, listened, and then replied, saying she'd check it out.

She studied me for a few seconds, like she was sifting me through a sieve. "Want to tag along on an investigation? Just received a call."

"Absolutely."

"I suppose I could call you a background source to the Bobby Budleigh murder. Have you ride in the backseat of my unmarked, behind the screen."

"That sounds like a plan."

She kept eyeing me. Then she shook her head and said, "No. You're a consultant. Come on. Ride in the front."

We walked together over to her black Dodge.

I asked a simple question. "What's this about?"

"They found a body. A dead male."

"Where?"

Ashley Linderman had no idea, she couldn't have, about the impact her next words would have on me. "Over at the town incinerator. You know, at the Manitou landfill."

29

The windows in Ashley Linderman's unmarked squad were down as we entered the Manitou sanitation landfill. There was a stench in the air of dead things, mingled with smoke. Ashley drove her black Dodge over the gravel road that cut between a high plateau of dirt on the right, and on the left the three-story-high incinerator, an ugly concrete structure with a smokestack in the back.

"That smell," she said, "is because today is dead animal day. Roadkill, dead dogs and cats, skunks, woodchucks, and whatever else the cat dragged in. Plus, bigger animals like deer and horses and cows. They are all burned the same day each week. They used to be tossed into the incinerator. But then the thing malfunctioned. An environmental group got involved. They targeted this operation and, before that, a factory down along the river. There's been a legal dispute for years about levels of pollution in the air from the incinerator, so it's been shut down. Protesters flocked here, the whole nine yards. Now it's back to the old-school type of burning. All kinds of dead animals dumped into a ground pit and set on fire. The incinerator has been cleared to start up again, though, I guess."

Just beyond the plateau there was a thick vortex of smoke winding its way up into the sky. The irony was hard to miss. "So, open-field burning of animal carcasses, that's supposed to be more eco-friendly?" I said sarcastically.

Ashley shook her head. "I think it's Manitou's way of sticking it to the protesters. But don't quote me on that."

She took a turn off the road and headed down a drive that led toward the front of the incinerator. Two county sheriff's squads were already there, with their lights flashing, parked in front of the mammoth entrance to the cement incineration tower. I also noticed an EMT vehicle and a red fire truck parked off to the side.

"Gang's all here," Ashley said, and she slammed the Dodge into park. "Wait by the car while I check in." Ashley stepped over to the two uniformed deputies and spoke to them.

My eyes wandered, and I noticed to my right there was a white sign with the hours of the landfill and incinerator operation printed on it in black letters, but a line had been carefully painted through the hours for the incinerator. Some protester had scrawled a message in red on the sign, and an effort had been made to paint over it with a thin coat of white paint, but the message was still legible underneath: *The devil doesn't recycle. He burns instead.*

I was distracted by a black fly that was buzzing around me. I swatted at it. Then swatted at another. And another. In a matter of minutes they were coming in squadrons. The air was filled with fat, buzzing flies.

Before I could duck back into the car, Ashley turned around and waved for me to join her. As I left the swarm of flies behind me and hustled to catch up to her, the two deputies led the way.

I followed Ashley into the cavernous interior of the building, which was roomy enough for garbage trucks to roll in and then dump their loads into a concrete pit. High above the pit was a three-pronged industrial claw hanging from a hydraulic arm that would have been used to grab the garbage, then swing it over to the spot where it would be dumped into the furnace. I could see a glass enclosure up above the pit, probably a control booth for the whole operation.

But over to the right, I spotted the reason we were there: Three firefighters in their helmets and bulky jackets were huddled together. They were talking to an EMT. Even from my position across the room I could see why they were grim-faced. Lying at their feet was a form. It looked as if it had been human once, and it was curled up, as black as coal. Next to it was a rubber body bag, zipped open, ready for loading.

Ashley told the deputies to hang back, and she summoned me to follow her with a flip of her index finger. As she approached the firefighters and the EMT, she said, "I'll take it from here, guys. I'll meet you outside when I'm done."

After they left, Ashley bent down to study the blackened, incinerated form on the cement floor that no longer bore any recognizable features.

As she studied it with forensic detachment, I looked on with horror. I could faintly hear the charred corpse hissing internally from the smoldering heat.

Ashley looked up at me. "Who would kill themselves this way?"

After examining the remains of this poor soul, who had been reduced to black cinder, she stood up. A forensics officer shuffled in with his camera, and Ashley directed the angles that he was to capture, then led me toward the open garage door, talking as we walked.

"The landfill engineer was outside at the time," she explained, "and he caught a glimpse of the deceased entering the building. Apparently the guy used to work here," she said. "Must have known how to get in, and how to kickstart the incinerator, which he did from the glass control booth. Once the furnace was fully fired up, he climbed over to the chute . . ." Ashley turned to point out the top of the metal chute, where garbage would be dumped into the furnace. "Looks like he slid down the chute right into the belly of the fire. The engineer had run into the building just in time to see the guy take the plunge. He ran up and shut off the furnace, then called the fire department and the EMT."

Instead of leading me out of the building, she took a right turn. "The dead man has a deep gash running in a linear fashion up his right forearm. Even in his charred state, that part is visible. A bloody knife was found up at the control booth. There's a blood trail leading up there. The trail started here." She stopped about fifty feet down the corridor, at a spot with police tape marking the cement floor, where it looked like something had been written on the floor in blood. There was a single word scrawled there: *Judas*. The victim apparently cut himself, and then wrote this one-word message on the floor in his own blood before igniting the furnace and jumping in.

Ashley started toward the open garage door, and by the time we got there, one of the deputies approached us holding a fat wallet in his hand. "Detective, this is from the car that's parked around back. A 1997 Chevy Blazer. Presumably the deceased's. We're checking the registration now. The wallet's packed with hundred-dollar bills."

While Ashley was checking the contents of the wallet, I looked around the incinerator. Somehow my former hometown had morphed into something horrible. A place belonging to the lower circles of hell.

But then the circles began to descend even lower. Ashley plucked the driver's license out of the wallet, held it up to my face, and asked if I knew this person. At first I couldn't answer. I had to blink several times and look closer and closer at the picture ID on the driver's license until I was finally willing to accept the reality of it. I was staring at the name and face of my high school friend and former band member Augie Bedders.

30

My head was reeling. I tried to give Detective Ashley a short course on my friendship with Augie, including how Dan Hoover had tried to look Augie up but couldn't find him. Augie had been more or less off the grid.

When we were seated next to each other in the black Dodge, Ashley asked, "What do you think the word *Judas* meant to Augie Bedders?"

"I couldn't tell you."

She had a second question. When she asked it, the smiles were gone and the dimples weren't showing. It was the tough girl instead. "Augie and Bobby Budleigh were friends of each other and also friends of yours. Now they're both dead. And here you are."

I waited for the shoe to drop.

She asked, "How are you involved in these deaths?"

Even after being kidney punched by the sight of Augie's incinerated body, and hit with the reality that people I knew and cared about were dying around me—despite that—I didn't miss her point. The triangulation of Bobby-Augie-me. Then, right in the middle of their two deaths, I sail into Manitou with uncanny timing.

"Here's how I'm involved," I replied. "Two of

my friends are gone. I've been kicked in the stomach. And now I get the feeling that you're trying to implicate me in this."

"Have you told me everything you know?" she asked.

"Everything you need to know."

That didn't sit well. She shot back, "We'll be returning sometime to your evasive answer. But meanwhile, I don't want to hear any crap about demons from you. Just the facts."

"I'll give you the facts," I replied. "But the rest of it is up to you."

"The rest of what?"

"The rest of the story, which you're probably not going to like. That the real message behind the death of these two men could have a post-mark from hell."

Another of my responses that Ashley didn't like. She pulled into the ice cream stand where my car was parked and slammed her car to a stop. By that time it was early evening, though customers were still lined up at the window. "Don't leave town without telling me first," she ordered.

I nodded and climbed out, but needing to stay on the case, I took a shot. "Am I still a consultant? I'd like to see some of your investigative leads. I could help. With Bobby's death and maybe even Augie's too."

"Good day, Mr. Black," she replied, and drove off.

· · ·

On the way back to my hotel, I sized up the unpretentious female detective with the pretty yet subtly scarred face, wondering why she had just turned on me.

I had nothing to hide, and yet, things being as they were in my life, concepts like evidence, logic, and objective thinking didn't always prevail. Things unseen can trump the visible.

As I parked my rental and crossed the hotel parking lot toward the lobby, dark clouds were building, and off in the distance there was a quick flash of brilliant light in the sky, but no rumble. The storm must have been a ways off at that point. I trudged into my hotel room, dumped my suitcase, and dropped into bed. I toyed with ordering a delivery pizza, but I had no appetite for food, so I mindlessly clicked through the TV menu of programs.

I landed on a reality show about survivalists in Alaska. A bearded loner named Big Jim Torley was trying to figure out a way to keep the brown bears and the wolves away from his food stash of elk meat, which he had hanging in several bags from a tree.

Feeling fatigued and emotionally gutted, I clicked off the TV and the light next to my bed. But in the darkness my mind kept whirling. About my mission in Manitou. And how the events in that town were making no sense. At least Big Jim Torley knew who his Alaskan predators were. I didn't. Not precisely.

And then there was the image that I couldn't shake. Augie's charred corpse, curled up in the fetal position, like the dead of Pompeii who had been buried under the volcanic ash of Mount Vesuvius.

The air-conditioning unit on the wall was buzzing loudly. I fiddled with the control knob but couldn't fix it. I lay in bed listening to the rush of air blowing out of the air conditioner and the intermittent sound of vibrating metal. After flip-flopping in bed, I fluffed the semi-starched pillows under my head and then shuffled them like a deck of cards, looking for the right combination.

Eventually my body relaxed and my eyes closed. A few minutes passed. But then a flash of light. The curtains in my room faced the parking lot and were parted a few inches, letting in the flashes of lightning in the distance. I was too tired to get out of bed and close the curtains the rest of the way. I would be asleep soon anyway.

Then thunder the next time with another flash of lightning. Followed by darkness and quiet. Then another flash. Between the curtains, I saw a jagged trace of white electricity wriggle across the sky and then disappear. I turned over to face the door to my room before shutting my eyes again. Another streak of lightning crackled across the sky.

Instinctively I half opened my eyes. But when I did, something was illuminated near the door of my room. A half second later the room was in blackness again. It looked like a shape by the closet area. I listened for a noise. An intruder? But I heard nothing. I lay there waiting.

Then a big flash of lightning with a bang. That was when I saw it. An outline, like a man in the shadows. But not a man, because in his head there were eyes like two burning lasers, and where the mouth should have been, a red glowing orifice in the shape of a smile. I bolted upright in bed and yelled for the creature to show himself.

Then I clicked on the nightstand light. But there was no one in my room. No evidence of him by the door, nor by the closet, nor anywhere else. Nothing, except for the smoldering odor of the fires of the Manitou landfill.

31

I lay in bed with my eyes open until the lightning stopped and I could no longer hear the distant pounding of thunder in the sky. When exhaustion took over, I dropped into sleep. But I never turned off the light.

The next morning, I dangled my feet over the edge of the bed until I had enough energy to fire up the cheap one-cup coffeemaker. When my

Styrofoam cup was filled, I sat down at the round mini-table and slurped down my coffee. When I was younger, I used to take it straight black, but over the past few years, I'd started taking my coffee with creamer and sugar substitute. Life had enough bitterness. I didn't need it in my coffee.

I had some reading to do. Ever since Elijah had given me his Bible, I had kept it with me. From New York to Ocracoke Island. And then to Manitou. I would dig into it whenever I could. Flipping through it in the hotel room, I considered the one-word message left on the incinerator floor—*Judas*—that had been written in the blood of the man who dumped himself into a furnace. After checking out the Gospel accounts about Judas, I saw a sobering explanation for it.

Bobby's death was obscenely cruel and unfair. But the double tragedy was the thought plaguing me at the time—that Augie may have killed himself so shortly after Bobby's murder because he felt responsible in some way.

I regretted that I hadn't kept in contact with both of them over the years. Yet I also knew that those thoughts were a dangerous quicksand. Years go by, and people change. Things go inexorably bad, and before you know it a friend does something desperate and incomprehensible.

I could beat myself up, but ultimately I wasn't in control. Even in all the mud and mire through which we plow, there is a benevolent heavenly

Father holding us up with an invisible hand, guiding our ends from our beginnings and nudging us toward the light rather than the darkness. Giving us a thousand chances to make a thousand good choices if we will only take them. And yet, despite that, people make terrible choices all the time. I've made my fair share.

The day I arrived in Manitou was the day that Bobby Budleigh was being buried in Denver. He left his wife, Vicky, and a ten-year-old son. I chose not to fly out to Colorado for the funeral, deciding to hunt down his killer instead. Perhaps that was yet another regret. But if it was, I had to shuck it off, sweep it away like a wasp. Because if you leave it clinging to you, it will sting you and keep on stinging you. Besides, I think Bobby would have wanted me to get to the truth, whatever it was.

I telephoned Detective Ashley Linderman, got her voice mail, and left a message. It wasn't a long one, but enough to let her know that, as a result of my Bible reading, I might have had a kind of "revelation" about Augie and his death and the message on the incinerator floor, and we needed to talk as soon as possible. There was a chance that my use of the word *revelation* might put her off, but it was too late to worry about that. Besides, it was time for Ashley Linderman to know what I believed.

I hung around the hotel room for an hour, but

no call back from Detective Linderman. I knew that Dan Hoover might still be down in Chicago. It was about a three-hour drive from Manitou, depending on traffic. Maybe four. I toyed with the idea of driving down to see Dan if I didn't hear back from Ashley soon. But I would have to break the news to Dan about Augie first.

32

It was late afternoon, and I was driving south on I-94 toward Chicago when I remembered her warning me about not leaving town without telling her.

So I left another message on her voice mail.

"Hi, Trevor Black here again. I'm trying to be cooperative. Thought you would like to know that I'm on my way down to Chicago to catch up with a friend of mine. But I haven't checked out of my hotel room yet, because I plan on returning to Manitou tomorrow and staying for a while. If you have some problem with my plans, you need to call me soon, because in about an hour or two I will be crossing into Illinois." After a slight pause I added, "I would like to stay in contact. Can you call me?"

But she never did. Not that day.

I had connected with Dan Hoover via text messages and told him I'd stop by the club where he was playing, which was on Hubbard, not too far from the Chicago River. I had missed seeing him perform with his group back when I was in New York. Of course, back then I was drowning in my own sea of troubles. But now it was time to catch his music, and I was looking forward to it. He texted me back, saying he would be playing two sets in the second slot, from 9:30 p.m. to 1 a.m., and that I should make sure to catch his second set at eleven thirty.

I tried to call Dan personally and tell him about Augie, but when I received his voice mail I was forced to leave a message. "Dan, sorry to add more bad news to our reunion, but it's about Augie. I found out as soon as I arrived in Manitou. We'll talk. Bad stuff happening. I'll see you tonight."

In Chicago I checked into my hotel room at the Courtyard on Hubbard across the street from the club. By the time I dropped my bags off, took a quick shower, changed my clothes, and made it to the big yellow awning that read *Live Jazz,* it was almost time for Dan's set to begin. Dan told me to introduce myself when I arrived, which I did, and as he had promised, a little place had been reserved for me near the front, squeezed in among the other tables.

After ordering some bar food, against my better judgment I put in for a glass of Dark 'N Stormy, a concoction of dark rum and ginger beer. For the last several months I had been drying myself out and feeling good about it, but somehow I figured it wouldn't hurt now to fudge a little. The drink came before my food, and I downed it straight-away, so on an empty stomach and coupled with my physical exhaustion, it did a number on me quickly.

To the left of the stage was a neon lighted sign that proclaimed *Wall of Fame* over a scad of framed pictures of music celebrities who have played the club. As I studied the photos, I wondered if Dan was in one of them by now, and if not yet, then soon. And yet I also thought about the lives of others that I knew and how things had changed radically in the last few decades. And how, given enough time with the passage of the years, the flesh sags, marriages can fail or go cold, businesses can go bust, health fails, and then the end comes. I must have been in the clutches of the Dark 'N Stormy view of life.

Yet, on the surface at least, the facts were hard to ignore. My wife had died of a drug overdose. I had been disbarred from the practice of law. Around the same time, I experienced a series of confrontations with spirit beings from hell. Bobby had been murdered, and Augie had killed himself. Which had left Dan Hoover, with his busy, successful music career and a demeanor that seemed content with life.

About fifteen minutes before Dan was to start

playing, my food arrived, but it wasn't what I had ordered. Instead of the simple burger that I had asked for, she brought out short ribs and mashed potatoes, my personal favorite. The server then said it was compliments of the band. A nice touch on Dan's part. I wondered how he had convinced the kitchen to stay open for a full meal so late. I was suddenly ravenous and I devoured everything.

I was on the last bite when the Jersey Dan Quartet took the stage. I had seen a few recent pictures of Dan, but up close he looked different. His hair, receding, was cut short. He had kept himself slim, and he had a close-cropped beard. In jeans and a sport coat, he looked like he could have been a college prof or a computer consultant, except for the haggard face.

Dan was always a virtuoso, but that night he impressed me all over again. His guitar work reminded me a little of Eric Clapton—infinitely effortless and smooth yet always on the verge of shimmying to the edge. He finished his last set with his rendition of the Dave Brubeck Quartet's "Take Five," but instead of the keyboard or the sax leading the way, Dan recreated the song on his Fender guitar. It was masterful.

After Dan ended the set and the applause and the crowds slowly cleared away, it was just Dan and me at a table in the middle of the empty room, with two cups of coffee. The staff was cleaning up but told us there was no rush.

Before I could give him fist bumps for his superb musicianship, Dan immediately asked about Augie, and I told him most of what I knew, although I spared him the gory details about what was left of Augie as he lay on the floor of the incinerator building. Unfortunately I had to explain how he did it.

Dan was shell-shocked. Finally he said, "Nobody does something like that, man. Not that way."

He looked pensive when I told him how Augie left the *Judas* message in his own blood. And how I had speculated about the possible parallels between Judas and Augie, Bible-wise, and how, no matter which way you looked at it, that one-word message looked like a confession.

"Confession of what?"

"Here's the other bad news. Don't ask me specifics, but the *Judas* thing and the timing makes me think that Augie may have been connected in some way to Bobby's murder."

A change of expression flashed across Dan's face. Cynical anger. After a somber minute of silence, Dan asked, "What are the cops doing about all of this?"

"They have a suspect in custody. I don't know if he's actually the guy who did it, or if he is, whether he's the only guy involved. At first, the detective was bringing me into the guts of the investigation, but now I've been shut out. No matter. I'm going to find out what really happened." I took a sip of my coffee. "Did you learn anything when you tried to locate Augie a while ago?"

"I was on tour, so I asked my agent if he could help. He knew this guy who's a skip tracer and got him to do a favor for us. The skip tracer said that the local court records showed a divorce filed against him by his wife, Susan . . . You remember, Susan Cambridge from high school?"

Yes, of course I remembered.

Dan continued. "But he said the divorce was dismissed, so I guess they got back together. The only other thing he could find out was the fact that, in the last year or so, Augie had been running a local head shop in Manitou. You know how, back in high school, Augie was always hooked up. Always knew where to get the stuff. I'm surprised he stayed clean during football season. Or maybe he didn't." Then Dan exhaled and added, "This is really heavy."

I nodded.

"Speaking of drugs," Dan said, "you look clean and sober."

"After high school, drugs weren't my particular poison," I replied. "I struggled with other things."

"Well," Dan said, "it was my poison all right. Definitely." He clasped his hands on the tabletop and looked directly at me. "Still is my poison. I'm working on that. One of the reasons me and Nancy—my ex—we didn't make it. That, and also my being on the road all the time. By the way, I heard about your wife. Really sorry about that."

I said, "You're like the town crier, with all the local news. How do you know all of this?"

Dan said, "I keep up with our high school class on social media."

I told him that in my criminal defense practice the only time I used Facebook was to size up prosecution witnesses and prospective jurors in my cases, so I could pick them apart.

Dan smiled. "You lawyers are so nasty."

"Was," I replied. "I'm not lawyering anymore, remember? Anyway, the path I am on now, even with the disturbing things I have been dealing with—even with all that, I've got some peace."

The instant the words came out of my mouth I knew they were true. And I knew that even in the middle of the dark and stormy parts of life, some good things had happened to me along the way.

Dan stared at me. It was late, almost three in the morning, and he started to yawn, but even as he did, he kept looking straight at me. "You've changed, I think."

"Oh?"

"Yeah. I think so."

"How?"

"You were the restless one. Always trying to figure things out. And don't let this go to your big fat head, but maybe you were the smart one too."

"Naw, that was Bobby. Straight As in class. Mr. PhD in environmental science."

Dan said, "I don't mean it that way. I mean, like you were always trying to figure out the big stuff. Trevor Black, mystery chaser. Mister 'searching for the meaning of life.' Now I'm looking at you. Listening. You look like you've gotten some answers."

"It's not about being smart."

"Then what's it about?" Dan asked.

"Seeing things the way they really are. The things that I used to ridicule, I now buy into. There are spiritual forces—and some are very dangerous—but God's at work too. So you have to choose sides. Neutrality isn't an option. Not really."

Dan leaned back with a half smile. "Well, I've learned surprising stuff. Never thought I'd have to go through rehab. And maybe I'll be going there again. My promoters and my agent, they keep threatening to pull the plug on me unless I go back into treatment. So I'm enjoying the music. Obviously. Sometimes, though, I feel a little like I'm going in circles. Drifting."

I didn't respond, just listened.

"You, on the other hand . . . You look like a man on a mission."

"You want it straight?" I asked.

"Why not."

"I'm on a mission from God."

Dan's face lit up, and he chuckled. "You mean like Belushi and Aykroyd?"

"Too late for movie trivia," I said. "And no, not really like that."

The club manager poked his head into the room and said he was ready to lock the doors. So we closed down the conversation.

"My gear is already packed up," Dan said, rising slowly to his feet. "So I'll say adios right here." He gave me a fist bump and then looked like he remembered something. "Oh, I almost forgot to tell you about Susan, Augie's wife. More bad stuff. Where's my head? You hear about her?"

"No."

Dan winced. "Killed in a car accident. I guess it was a few years ago. Ran through the stop sign on the Manitou bypass—you know that tricky hill that intersects Highway A? Hit broadside by a truck. I heard they put up a stoplight there after that."

Before I could ask how Dan knew about that, he answered like a mind reader. "Facebook."

As he walked away Dan shouted back to me, perhaps to end on an upbeat note. "Brush up on your blues harp again, and one of these days you and I could jam together."

33

The next day—or later that same day, depending how you look at it—on the drive back to Wisconsin, Detective Ashley Linderman was on my mind. She still hadn't called me back.

But I knew at least one reason why she might be avoiding me. Ashley could have been grappling with Augie's possible criminal involvement in Bobby's death and how it would destroy their case against Donny Ray Borzsted, the defendant they had indicted. That was reason enough.

As I drove north on I-94 toward the Wisconsin border, I hooked up my earbuds with my cell and made a series of calls until I tracked down the defense lawyer for Donny Ray Borzsted. Donny Ray had been found indigent and had been given a public defender, a lawyer by the name of Howard Taggley. At a tollway oasis, I pulled out my iPad and checked him out on the Web. He was a career public defender, never rising above the level of assistant deputy PD.

I called Taggley and explained to him my background as a former criminal defense lawyer, my personal connection to Bobby Budleigh, and my desire to get to the truth. After that, I cut to the chase, even though I knew the legal pitfalls: "I was wondering if you would permit me to interview your client, under conditions of strict confidentiality, of course."

"Only way to enforce confidentiality," he replied, "is to make you a part of our defense team for Mr. Borzsted."

"I can't do that. I've got to remain impartial."

After a few seconds, Taggley lowered his voice and slowed down to a sly cadence, like he was telling a dirty joke. "Now, you're the lawyer who got disbarred. Right? And you got disbarred in New York City, as I understand it, for telling a judge that your client had a demon inside of him. I think I've got that straight, right?"

Somehow all that had sounded better when it had come out of Ashley Linderman's mouth rather than Taggley's. I replied only, "Bad news travels fast."

"I had heard you were in town nosing around. I'm not surprised you called."

"Oh?"

Then the public defender held out a ray of hope. "Okay, listen, I'm supposed to meet with Borzsted shortly. In jail. I'll bring this up with him. I'll get back to you."

After we ended the call, I thought it over. If I were in Taggley's position, and I had any kind of reasonable defense at all in the case, I would never let me interview this client. Not in a million years. There was no legal privilege that would protect my conversation with him; the prosecution could subpoena me and force me to spit out everything Borzsted had said in our meeting. I figured, when all was said and done, my request would hit a dead end.

But three hours later, Taggley called me back. "We may have a deal."

"What kind of a deal?"

"You sign a confidentiality agreement, pledging not to voluntarily divulge your conversation with my client to anyone—not the prosecution, or Detective Linderman or any law enforcement person, or the press, or anyone else in the universe—and you agree to defend vigorously against any attempt by the prosecution to force you to share your conversation with Borzsted."

"And if I get subpoenaed, and we file a motion to quash the subpoena, and the court disagrees and orders me to testify? Then what?"

"Then you're off the hook."

"So, that's it?" I said.

"With just one more caveat."

"What's that?"

"I sit in on the interview. And you can expect me to instruct my witness not to share certain information as we go along."

I was dumbstruck at the door that had just opened. "You've got a deal. So, when?"

"I'll get back to you promptly."

"One other thing," I said, deciding to push for more. "How about sharing the discovery you've obtained so far?"

"Rather than that, how about I give you the criminal indictment. It's public now."

I thanked him for the courtesy.

After pulling into the hotel in Manitou and stepping back into my room, I thought about dinner. A steak and seafood place down the road looked like an option. But a telephone call interrupted my dinner plans.

It was Howard Taggley. He was shifting things into fourth gear. "We can see you in an hour."

"Where? The county jail?"

"That's it. You know where it is, I suppose; you used to live here."

"I remember. The annex next to the courthouse." Then I asked him, "What about the confidentiality agreement?"

"I'll have it typed up and ready for you to sign."

34

Howard Taggley was in the lobby, waiting for me outside the check-in window. He was wearing a wrinkled suit coat and a loud tie that had been loosened at the neck. He looked to be in his fifties. After popping open his briefcase, he yanked out a two-page document that was stapled in the corner.

He handed it to me. "Here's the agreement. Look it over. Then sign. No changes. No cross-outs. I had a tough time convincing my client to go along with this." Then he reached into his briefcase and also pulled out my copy of the criminal indictment. "Remember: my client was reluctant to cooperate with you."

I waved the papers in the air. "If your client is innocent, he has nothing to lose by this and everything to gain."

Taggley was skeptical. "Mr. Black, with all due respect, I know you had a reputation in New York for pulling rabbits out of hats for your clients, but do you really expect me to buy that? What you just said?"

I smiled and looked over the agreement, and as I did I was thinking to myself how I had always played my cards close to the vest as a defense attorney. Don't take excessive chances. Control everything. So, either Taggley was being monumentally sloppy in letting me interview his client, or else he thought he had something to gain. Something valuable.

The terms of the agreement were exactly as Taggley had represented, so I signed it, and so did he. Then he stuffed it into his briefcase, told me he had e-mailed a copy to me already, and announced us to the jail clerk who was behind the glass window. We both dropped our driver's licenses into the aluminum slide tray so the clerk could verify our IDs. Taggley also tossed in his professional Wisconsin State Bar card, his evidence of being a licensed attorney. I noticed that fact and remembered that I no longer had one. As memories of my life in New York flashed past me, for an instant there was that momentary pang of regret about my past. But I shook it off. Things were different now. And so was I.

While we waited for the clerk to check us in, and as we rode the clunking jail elevator to the basement level, I quickly scanned the indictment.

Bobby's body had been found at the border where Manitou met the countryside about a quarter of a mile from Country Club Road, off a farmers' service road, and a few feet from the banks of Pebble Creek. The charging document said he was shot in the head by a pistol, but it omitted mentioning the caliber of the weapon that had been used.

A witness who was driving down Country Club Road shortly after sunset, around the time Bobby's death had occurred, had noticed two men, a tall one and a short one, walking down the service road in the direction where Bobby's body was later found. The short one was in front. Bobby was five feet nine inches, and the witness identified him later from a photo. The witness said the taller one, well over six feet tall, with long hair, was walking right behind him. Borzsted was six-one—not exactly "well over" six feet. The headlights illuminated the men, and Bobby turned around, but the indictment failed to say anything about the tall man turning around. The witness identified Donny Ray Borzsted as the taller man from a photographic array supplied by the police.

The indictment also indicated that the boot-prints found in the mud matched a pair of boots that Borzsted owned. When he was arrested, his apartment was searched, and the police found a handgun in a dresser drawer—make and caliber also unspecified.

But the criminal charging document failed to mention what Dick Valentine had privately told me: about a message, written in Bobby's blood, having been left on his body. Nor did it say that Bobby's heart had been extracted. I was sure that Detective Valentine, who had spoken with the county sheriff's department, had his information correct. Not surprisingly, the prosecutor had chosen *not* to feed that information to the grand jury. He was obviously saving that for later, for the trial. Nothing unusual about that.

When we exited the elevator, we walked down to the jail conference room reserved for attorneys. Donny Ray was already waiting for us, sitting at the table with a deputy on either side. The deputies stepped out, and Howard Taggley sat at the head of the table and introduced me.

Donny Ray was a big fellow with long greasy hair that fell down to his shoulders, and he had tattoos of fierce mythical creatures running up and down both arms and around his neck. He didn't get up to greet me. Didn't shake my hand. But stared me down as he fingered his lit cigarette, from which he took long drags with exquisite delight.

Donny Ray said, "My attorney here okayed with the jailers that I can smoke. And that's sweet, you know, 'cuz they don't usually let us smoke. Least not in this room."

I explained that I had some questions. But before I could continue, Howard Taggley interrupted.

"Now, Mr. Black, first off I've got some questions for you."

"That wasn't part of the deal," I said.

"I know you thought this was your show, but it's not. It's mine. I call the shots."

Donny Ray started to giggle.

I asked, "What kind of questions?"

"How long have you known Detective Ashley Linderman?"

Donny Ray giggled louder.

I said, "Only since I arrived here in Manitou. Never knew who she was before that."

"Really?" Then Taggley said it again, louder. "Really?"

"You sound surprised," I replied. By the tone of Taggley's voice, it was as if I didn't know who Madonna was, or Angelina Jolie.

"Everybody here in Manitou knows who Ashley Linderman is. I thought you were from here originally."

"I was."

"The Red Owl robbery? That ring a bell?"

"Not at all. Must have been after I left."

"Sheriff Daniel Linderman? It was in all the papers."

"Like I said, I may have left for the East Coast by then."

"Never mind," he said. "Are you working with Detective Ashley Linderman on this case?"

"Not really."

"What does that mean?"

"I was shown the corpse of a deceased person at the Manitou incinerator who may or may not have anything to do with this case."

"Anything else?"

"Detective Linderman and I had ice cream together."

Donny Ray jumped in. "Aw . . . lovebirds." And he giggled some more.

I'd had enough. "Where are you going with this?"

"I've got the same question for you," Taggley said.

"I'm not an agent of the sheriff's department, and I'm not formally working with them to prosecute your client, if that's what you're after."

"Good to know. Did they tell you anything else about the murder?"

"No. Nothing."

Taggley hadn't bothered to ask me about

hearsay information from a secondary source, so I didn't feel compelled to tell him what Dick Valentine had told me.

That was all Taggley wanted from me, which, in the end, was pretty paltry. So I started in on Donny Ray.

"Were you at the scene of the crime, and if not, where were you and who were you with?"

"I wasn't there. Okay? Got that? I was with my brother Karlin. Drinking. At my place. Watching the ball game."

"Which one?"

"Brewers and Cardinals."

"Who won?"

"Geez, I don't know. We both finished off a pint of brandy apiece, and a case of beer too, partying pretty good, so I dunno . . ."

"You don't know who won?"

"I just told you that. Don't you got ears? You know, I don't have to tell you nothing."

"Yes, you do. I've got a piece of paper from your lawyer with his signature on it that says you do."

"How about I give you a brain concussion right now?" Donny Ray put a fist in front of my face. His lawyer calmed him down.

I ignored the tough-guy routine. "What time did the game start?"

"I can't remember."

"Where were they playing?"

"Not in Milwaukee."

"Okay, so in St. Louis, right?"

"Duhhhh," Donny Ray said, laughing and sneering.

"Which means central time."

Donny Ray cocked his head to the side. "Maybe eight or something, at night. Like I said, Karlin and I were drinking hard and blasted out of our gourds."

If he was telling the truth, that would have been when Bobby, on the other side of town, miles away, had just been killed. "Okay. Anyone else see you in your apartment that night?"

"Nope."

"Do you know of any other evidence that would prove your innocence, other than your alibi? That at the time of the murder of Bobby Budleigh, you and Karlin were in your apartment drinking and watching the Brewers game?"

Taggley shouted, "Don't answer that." Then he turned to me. "I'm not having my client give you my whole theory of defense. You think I'm crazy? What kind of lawyer do you take me for?"

I was tempted to answer Taggley's question candidly, but I refrained.

When we were done, and Howard Taggley and I were back in the basement lobby of the jail, I had a question for him. "Is Karlin Borzsted, Donny Ray's brother, around?"

"Sure. He lives here in Manitou."

"An upright citizen?"

Howard Taggley laughed. "Just got out of prison, like his brother. You figure it out."

"What else can you tell me about Karlin?"

"He's bigger than Donny Ray."

"Anything else?"

"Yeah, he's meaner."

35

By the time I arrived back at my hotel I knew that the surf 'n' turf restaurant had stopped serving. That left only the late-night pizza delivery guy. Fifty-five minutes later he arrived at my room with a medium-size thin-crust margherita pizza that was no longer hot and had left a grease spot on the inside of the soggy pizza box. But I was famished. Lukewarm pizza is still tasty if you're hungry enough.

I silenced my phone and fell asleep quickly, this time with the lights turned off but with the air-conditioning unit still buzzing.

The next morning I slept late and awoke to a message on my cell. It was the one I had been waiting for. The one I had been hoping for.

Detective Ashley Linderman said she wanted to talk and would swing by at 11:30 a.m. sharp. So I was there by the sliding-glass doors at the front of the hotel, waiting at exactly 11:30, holding the

Styrofoam cup of coffee that I had grabbed from the complimentary breakfast bar just off the lobby. I knew Detective Ashley Linderman would be all business and that lunch wasn't going to happen.

Ashley swung her unmarked patrol car beneath the hotel carport, and as I approached her window, she told me to hop into the front, so I figured it was good news that I wasn't relegated to the backseat behind the metal mesh; at least I wasn't going to be arrested. But she had something else in mind. I was about to be treated like an insect hitting one of those electric zapper boxes that you hang outside in the summer, and you forget are hanging there until you hear the zap as the bugs get the shock treatment.

"Tell me," she said as she swooped her black Dodge into traffic, "how was your little chat with Donny Ray Borzsted?"

ZAP.

I played it cool. "I wish I could tell you. But I signed a piece of paper that says I can't voluntarily disclose that to you. Not without an order from the court, and not until after I put up a fight in court first. Any disclosure has to be, you know, involuntary."

"Then I could make it involuntary," she said. "I could Taser you until you talk." I studied her when she said that. She never broke a smile.

ZAP.

"Let's get real," I shot back. "You're going

to have to honor my agreement with Howard Taggley or else file a motion with the judge. Those are your two options."

"I've got a third option."

"Oh?"

"I could start pressuring you, squeezing you like a pimple till you spill everything."

"Thanks for the word picture," I said. For an attractive female detective, Ashley was still rough around the edges.

After a while I noticed that she had taken a route that was heading west, toward the bypass that eventually led out to Country Club Road.

I tried to bridge the silence. "Sorry I can't tell you much."

No response.

My mind was clicking. I needed Detective Ashley in my mission to find out about Bobby's murderer. And I needed Howard Taggley. And Taggley's seedy client too. Somehow I had to find a way to straddle all of that.

"You know," I led off, "my criminal defense practice was in New York."

She glanced in my direction.

"So, I was wondering," I said, "whether here in Wisconsin, you've got a notice of alibi law. Requiring defense counsel to give notice to the prosecution, a certain amount of time before trial, that the defendant is going to claim that he was not at the scene of the crime when it happened, but was somewhere else. Just a hypothetical question."

She looked at me again.

"Just wondering," I added.

"Yes. We've got a statute like that." She kept throwing me side-glances as she continued. "If the defendant claims he was somewhere else."

"Another question," I said. "Just curious. I was also wondering what you might know about Donny Ray's family."

"Mom's out of state. Dad's in some kind of long-term assisted living facility. Donny also has a brother."

I smiled and nodded. "I bet he's an interesting fellow."

"His name is Karlin. Just got out of prison."

"You don't say." Then I asked, "You watch much baseball?"

"Some. But my job keeps me pretty busy."

"I bet a lot of people around here watch the Brewers games. You know, with family members and all. A brother watching with a brother. National pastime."

As she listened to me, there was movement at the corners of her lips. Not exactly a smile, but close.

"Now, from hereafter," I said, "if you want to know anything about my contact with Taggley or his client Donny Ray Borzsted, I'm going to have to enter the Forrest Gump plea."

I planned on having to give an explanation. But Ashley got there first. "You mean, 'That's all I have tuh say about thayut'?" she said in an impressive Tom Hanks impersonation, and I chuckled. A detective with a sense of humor.

After a while we reached the intersection of the Highway A bypass and Country Club Road, and we stopped at the light.

I decided to resurrect something about my late friend from high school. "Augie Bedders, the deceased man at the incinerator—I learned that his wife, Susan, was killed at this intersection," I reported. "That's why the stoplight is here now."

"Donny Ray told you that?"

"No. Somebody else."

She drove straight ahead on Country Club Road for a mile or two and then pulled over to the side of the road where there was a cattle grate in the ground at the opening to a farmers' service road. I knew why we had stopped.

I looked over to the hill a half mile away and recognized the spot in the trees where so many years ago Bobby and Marilyn and I had our picnic, overlooking Pebble Creek. I knew the stream was nearby because I could hear it trickling and flowing somewhere, accompanied by the sour odor of decay in the warm summer air from the muddy swamp of the wetlands.

"This is where it happened, isn't it?" I asked.

Ashley nodded. Then she reached under her seat, produced an envelope, and pulled out a photograph and handed it to me. "Sorry I have to show this to you," she said. "But this envelope is about you."

It contained a police forensics photo of Bobby Budleigh as he lay dead along the banks of the creek. He was on his back and he was bare-chested. An open gash, ragged and red, was evident on the left side of his chest, where the heart must have been extracted. Underneath the open wound, there was a message scribbled in blood on his body. And when I read it, the breath was sucked from my lungs.

Wrong side, Trevor.

ZAP.

36

Ashley wasn't talking as she drove me to my hotel. Neither was I.

After seeing the photo of Bobby's lifeless body and visiting the area where he had been slain, death seemed to be everywhere. I found myself repeating in my head something that I had read in the Psalms. "I shall walk before the Lord in the land of the living." For me, it was a prayer, steeling me against the message written on Bobby's corpse. It was clear that the someone, or something, that had murdered Bobby also knew I would be coming to Manitou.

When Ashley Linderman pulled up to the hotel, and before I could climb out of the front seat, she asked me a question. The same question she had put to me back on Country Club Road. "You're telling me you don't know why your name was written on Bobby Budleigh's body? And that message—the business about 'wrong side'—you don't know what that means?"

I gave the same answer. "Like I said, maybe Augie did it, maybe he didn't, but I'm not going to give you some wild guess about why it was written on his body or what it means. All I know is that back in New York, I defended a guy who wrote a question on his victim, but it was different from the message here." I took a second, then added, "But I have this inescapable feeling that there are forces at work that link all these killings together. Location of the mutilations on the body. Lack of motive. And most important, the sequential timing."

"What does that tell you?" she asked.

"It's the dreaded *D* word, Ashley. I'm thinking demons. You asked, so I answered. God and the devil. The battle between heaven and hell. Ever since Jesus gave me a U-turn, I can't see these types of cases any other way."

Ashley's jaw tightened, but she remained silent.

I had my own questions for the detective. "Okay.

Now it's my turn. Can you tell me about the Red Owl robbery and Sheriff Daniel Linderman? Was he your father?"

She raised an eyebrow and tapped her fingers on the steering wheel. I hadn't noticed before that her nails were painted. Red, but not flashy red. Soft red. Like the color of a rose.

She said simply, "I don't know you well enough yet."

But as I cranked open the passenger door and began to climb out she added, "Maybe later, sometime."

"One more question," I said, still half in the car. "I'm convinced about God being who he is and about the devil being who he is. So, just wondering, off the record, where do you stand on that?"

"Same answer. Some other time."

As I entered the lobby, I nodded to the desk clerk, trudged into my room, and after throwing some water on my face, I dumped into bed. I could have ordered another pizza to be delivered, lukewarm and greasy, but I wasn't in the mood for food.

So I caught another reality TV episode of Big Jim Torley, the Alaskan mountain man. This time he was concerned about a pack of gray Yukon wolves that were prowling around his cabin. Big Jim said that wolves were a "top predator . . . top of the food chain," and that even though the experts discounted any real risk to humans by healthy wolves, Big Jim wasn't buying it.

Looking straight at the camera, he said in his big, barrel-chested, basso profundo voice, "Them nature 'experts' don't know what they're talking about. I heard about a boy at Icy Bay getting attacked by a wolf. For no reason. No provocation. Then there was this guy on a bicycle riding down the Alcan Highway. A big gray comes out of nowhere charging at him, snapping and snarling. So the man on the bike blasts the big gray in the face with some bear repellent. Thinks, *Okay, that's that.* But it wasn't. A couple of seconds later, the Yukon wolf comes back and jumps up on the back of the bike and starts biting at him like the thing was possessed."

On the TV screen there were images of Alaska late in the day, with shadows growing and the sunlight getting low and dusky, but of course the sun was not going to fully set, and Big Jim had his favorite wolf-hunting rifle, the AR-15, tucked across his arm as he paced around the outside of his cabin, surrounded by thick forest. He was looking for wolf tracks on ground that had been covered with a light dusting of snow. Then he stopped and said out loud so that the camera could catch it, "I hate them wolves when they come in packs, 'cuz they are especially bold and take no prisoners. And I hate 'em specially in the daylight when there's woods around, like out yonder . . . ," and he pointed to the tree line about fifty feet from his cabin. "'Cuz they're mixed colors, gray and white, and they blend in when there's snow on the ground and when the trees and underbrush is all gray-like. So, if they're standin' still in the woods in the daytime, you can't hardly see 'em."

Then he stops and looks at the camera and grins so you can see his yellowed teeth. "Prefer 'em at night . . . 'cuz with a flashlight mounted on your gun barrel, you can shine 'em, and you know where they are 'cuz you can see them devil eyes glowing in the dark."

After Big Jim's program was over, I did more channel flipping and then the late news. Meanwhile I took two bites from a breakfast bar that I had picked up at a quicky-stop store as Ashley was driving me home. That was all I could stomach. The forensic photo of Bobby's corpse had broken my heart and killed my appetite.

Around midnight I clicked off the television and then the light next to my bed. I had set my alarm for a decent rising time the next morning because I knew what my next move would be. I needed to track down Donny Ray Borzsted's brother, Karlin, the guy who held the key to Donny Ray's alibi. I wanted to get resolution, yes or no: Did Donny Ray have anything to do with Bobby's murder, including any connection with Augie Bedders, who, tragically, may have played some part?

Sleep came slow. After tossing and turning I could finally feel myself start to sink into the bed. Muscles relaxed. I had managed to shut off the thinking machine in my skull, almost. In the dark of the room, darker than I had remembered the night before for some reason, I heard only my own labored breathing and the crinkle of the starched pillows under my head as I shifted position.

A sensation began to materialize. But I tried to ignore it. From the part of the thinking machine that had still not been shut down entirely, I ordered myself to stop thinking, and to ignore it and go to sleep, which of course then guaranteed that I could not. Especially after the next thing that happened in that room.

When I actually felt something hovering over me.

Then I heard my name spoken, but not by a human voice. More like someone saying *Trevor Black* while coughing up a blood clot.

Then hands around my neck squeezing down to the larynx and two red eyes glowing in the dark and coming down close to my face. I screamed and bashed out with both fists, sending round-house punches that connected with something solid and in a humanoid form, banging my knuckles. I tried to scramble out of bed but was caught in the sheets and tumbled to the ground, face-first.

While I was on the floor I heard the voice again,

and it was chuckling and making a gurgling, guttural noise.

I tried to scramble to my feet, but I was picked up and then tossed back down to the floor like a wet bath towel. Then a crushing force on my chest. There was a foot pressing on me, and I couldn't breathe.

A simple thought. *This is it.*

Then a flash from behind me in the room like a comet hitting the atmosphere. A blinding light that lit up the room. Whatever was crushing the life out of me was gone, along with the blood-clot voice and the glowing eyes.

When I looked up, there, above my head, was a little round laser light in the ceiling that belonged to the fire alarm.

After flicking the lights on, I found nothing but a nightstand tipped over—possibly, I wondered, the surface that I had hit with my fist?

I sat down on the couch, heart pumping wildly. A logical assessment of the situation seemed impossible, reduced merely to *What was that?* A nightmare? I wanted to believe it, but I knew it wasn't true. I looked up again at the alarm in the ceiling. Maybe it had been a dream, and I had been stumbling around in a state of half sleep.

But as I stared at the ceiling alarm I realized that there was no red light. The light in the smoke alarm was actually green.

It was time to switch gears. To size up my

predator. My enemy with the glowing red eyes. True enough: he would be easier to spot in the dark, at night. Big Jim Torley was right. So I kept the lights off and sat in the dark on the little couch, looking for his reappearance. And strained to keep my eyes open until daybreak.

37

After a few hours of sleep, I was on the move, on the way to the new Manitou courthouse. I drove through the old downtown section along the Little Bear River and past the old historic courthouse that had long ago been converted into the Manitou Museum.

After parking and trotting inside the Manitou Justice Center, I struck up a conversation with the harried-looking assistant clerk of courts.

My request was simple. "Good morning. I'd like to see *State v. Borzsted*, 015 CR 239, the criminal file in the Donny Ray Borzsted case."

In a weary voice she asked, "Are you a reporter?"

"No."

"What's your interest in this?"

I had already checked out the state law on open records and court files, so I was prepared for that. "I used to be a New York criminal defense lawyer. But I'm not here as a lawyer. I'm here as an investigator."

"This isn't New York."

Of course it wasn't, but I knew my rights. "No," I said. "But under Wisconsin law I have a right to check out a pending criminal file."

"Investigator for who, exactly?"

"The man who was murdered. The victim. Bobby Budleigh."

"Well, the DA who prosecutes this case is the one who represents the victim—"

"Not exactly," I cut in. "Actually, prosecutors represent the state." I was tired, low on sleep, and wanted to ring the bell on this useless bout. "Ma'am, I was a high school friend of the victim. Very close. Please let me take a peek at the court file. I'll only be a few minutes."

She shrugged, then waved me around the counter and into the file room and pointed to the computer screen where the files were digitally indexed. She would be no help and I was on my own, but it didn't take me long to locate the court file. Donny Ray's attorney had already filed a notice of alibi indicating his client was not at the scene of the crime when it occurred, and that his brother Karlin was his witness to that fact. Karlin's address was listed in the court filing as 607 Central Avenue, Apartment C. That was all I needed.

I motored over to Central Avenue, remembering how I used to bike around that area when I was a kid. The block was filled with old two-story houses that had been subdivided into apartments. At number 607, a house sided with asphalt roofing tiles, there was a front apartment with a porch entrance and a big black letter A on the mailbox.

When I made my way around back where apartment B was located, I found an outside set of stairs running along the side of the house up to a second-story door. I trotted up to the next level, to apartment C, and saw no doorbell, so I banged loudly on the door. No answer. So I kept banging. Still no answer. I returned to ground level and around to apartment A and rang the doorbell. An elderly woman answered the door but opened it only a crack.

"Good day. I am looking for Karlin Borzsted. He lives up in apartment C, right?"

"You the law?"

"No."

"Process server?"

"I'm not that either. Just want to talk to him. Do you rent here too?"

"I'm the rental manager. But I don't think Karlin's here."

"Where would he be?"

She shrugged. "I don't know his business."

"You know anywhere he might possibly be? Places he frequents?"

"Frequents?"

"Places he likes to visit."

She thought a moment. "Casey's Pool and Tap."

I knew generally where it was. When I was a teenager in Manitou I would lounge around the pool hall with my delinquent friends during my troubled-youth stage, watching tough guys and pool sharks playing for fifty-dollar bets. There was a bar with stools, which was out of bounds for minors. But as long as my teenage gang and I hung in the area with the pool tables and stayed away from the bar, we were left alone.

I couldn't believe the place was still standing. There was a Harley cycle parked out front, along with a pickup truck and a damaged compact.

I strolled into the place and was hit with a hazy smog zone of cigarette smoke. The decor was strictly old-school: lighted beer signs, mounted fish on the walls, and a girlie calendar next to the dartboard. The female bartender was in a black T-shirt that read, *I'm Katie and You're Not*. She was a bleached blonde who probably lifted weights and looked like she could take care of herself. Katie the bartender eyed me as I made for the pool table area.

Two guys were playing at one of the tables. The test now was to figure out if either of them was Karlin. But neither looked big enough or mean enough to qualify.

Then the men's bathroom door banged open. A man around six foot four stomped out, bald-headed with a full beard, a sleeveless denim jacket, and bulging biceps. I had just located Karlin Borzsted.

"You punks not done yet?" he shouted to the two men still playing.

There was some nervous laughter from them and a retort that I couldn't hear.

I started toward Karlin, and his head snapped around to eye me. When I was a few feet away, looking right at him, he said, "What you starin' at?"

"Karlin Borzsted?" I asked.

The two guys with pool cues straightened up and stopped playing.

He took a step toward me. "Who wants to know?"

"Somebody who may be able to help your brother."

"You don't say."

"Can we talk?"

"Isn't that what we're doing? Or are you stupid or something?" Now all the men were laughing. "Or maybe," he said, "you want to talk to these." With that, he held out his two fists. The knuckles were adorned with homemade tattoos—the kind of amateur ink artistry that gets inscribed in prison. Four letters on each fist:

FROM HELL

I tried to keep my cool. "I'd rather talk privately. Just you and me."

Someone in the group gave out a phony I'm-so-scared kind of moan. "Whooo . . ."

Karlin and I stepped aside. I started first. "I'm

trying to find out who killed Bobby Budleigh. If not your brother, then I want to know who."

Karlin growled. "It wasn't Donny. Conversation over."

The big guy was missing my point. "Bobby Budleigh was my friend," I shot back.

"I couldn't care less," he said, and started walking away.

"My name is Trevor Black. I'm in town to get to the bottom of this."

Karlin whipped around and started striding back to me. "You're the one who's been driving around with the little tramp whore Ashley Linderman?"

Something clicked all of a sudden, like a switch, surprising even me. Maybe it was a venting of my frustration and anger. Something that had been buried, that now was exploding to the surface. Or maybe it was something about Ashley.

But whatever it was, it caused me to grab a pool cue from the table next to me, ram it across Karlin's throat, and push him backward on the pool table, pressing it against his larynx. I shouted, "She's a decent woman, but maybe you don't know what that is. My friend was murdered, and I don't know what the matter is with you people, because I'm trying to help—"

I never finished my sentence because Karlin knocked me back into the air like a freight train hitting a shopping cart. And I was the shopping cart. I landed on my back on the floor, with the breath knocked out of me, gasping for air.

He snatched me off the ground, stood me up, and hauled back to throw a punch in my direction, but I managed to feint to the left and then duck to the right, so when his fist came flying it missed my face but clipped my left ear, which exploded with pain like it had been smashed with a mallet. I stumbled backward, with my hand landing on a tall wooden stool. As Karlin came charging at me, I instantly thought about using the stool, but then there was this voice in my head whizzing out of the wreckage of my legal training, and it was telling me, *Smack him in the head with that stool, and you could go to prison.*

Instead, I swung the stool with both hands right into his chest like I was hitting a line drive. He bounced backward against the pool table, leaning against it and grabbing his ribs as he moaned.

I thought I had tamed this brute, so I was feeling confident. "Look," I said, still struggling to regain my breath, "let's cut this—"

But I never saw his fist. What I did see was the explosion of light like a star nebula as his knuckles hit me just above my right eye. Then the whirligig sensation of being dragged like a manikin and tossed onto the pool table. My eyesight was clearing just in time to see him pulling back his fist to play smash-a-pumpkin with my face. But that is when I heard big Katie the bartender scream for him to stop. And he did. Even in my decimated state, I wondered why. Then I saw the double-barreled shotgun in Katie's hands.

Right before I blacked out.

38

The next day I was lying on a hospital bed, eyes closed, when I heard her voice. I must have been dozing, but Detective Ashley Linderman woke me up with something that sounded like a question. I opened my eyes.

She asked again, "So, you really don't want to press charges?"

I was looking up at the attractive face of the female detective as she stood at my bedside. I didn't answer at first. She just shook her head and gave half a laugh as she watched me struggle to sit up.

"Why am I still here?" I asked. "I'm not hurt that bad." As I shifted, I felt the deep ache in my upper back and shoulder, and then the ugly spinning sensation inside my skull.

"Concussion. Loss of consciousness for a while. A bad contusion over your eye. Dislocated shoulder, which they snapped back into place. Other than that, you're tip-top." Then she asked me again, "No charges, really? After what Karlin did to you?"

"The truth is, I feel kind of sorry."

She squinted. "For what?"

"For what I did to poor Karlin."

Ashley practically busted a gut laughing. Then she said, "Seriously, he could be facing an aggravated battery charge, and that's just the beginning. We could have piled it on him."

"I knew the risk."

"What were you thinking? He could have killed you."

"He's the alibi for his brother."

"And?"

"If his alibi sticks, then someone else must have killed Bobby."

She looked at me awhile, then said, "So, you're on the case?"

"I never left. You're the one who left me in the dust."

She shook her head. "Not me."

I couldn't figure her out. I shot back, "You cut me off. Didn't answer my calls."

"I had to settle some things."

"Like what?"

"I'll tell you later."

"Well," I said, "I've got things to do. I wonder when I can get out of here."

"Later today. The doctors just want to make sure you're not going goofy in the head."

"Too late for that."

Ashley flashed a smile, then looked like she

was about to leave. But instead she turned back toward my bed, and her eyes widened and lit up. "The bartender said Karlin made some remark. About me. And that you defended my honor."

"Do I get a medal for that?"

"No. Just dinner. If you're up to it."

"That's even better."

"Tonight," she said brightly. "An Italian place here in town."

Things were looking up.

Then Ashley said something else. "Over dinner, I'll catch you up on some new developments."

"Can you give me a hint?"

"It's about that charred corpse we found at the Manitou incinerator."

I wasn't in the mood for a tease. Especially about the burned remains of Augie Bedders. "This is my friend we're talking about. Can you give me something more?" .

"Well, that's just the thing," she said. "About the body, I mean. You see, it wasn't Augie Bedders."

39

When I checked out of the hospital that afternoon, the discharge nurse gave me a printed sheet about how to handle myself post-concussion. She asked me if I had someone picking me up, and I just nodded and smiled and stuffed the hospital discharge papers in my pocket and called a cab to take me back to the Holiday Inn. On the way, I kept thinking about Ashley Linderman's last comment.

I had just put on a change of clothes when Ashley rang me up and said she'd drop by in ten minutes to pick me up for dinner. As usual, she was on time, and I climbed into the passenger seat of her unmarked, acting like I wasn't hurting all over.

"Thanks for driving," I said as we wheeled away.

"How's your head?"

"I'll live."

"And the rest of you?"

"Sore." Then I added, "Hey, do you always drive this unmarked, or do you have a personal vehicle?"

"The department lets me use it off duty. For personal things."

"Is that what this is tonight? Personal?"

"Nice move, Mr. Black."

"I thought so," I responded. "Sorry I didn't bring flowers."

"That's okay," she said coyly. "I fully intend to stick you with the bill for dinner. I'm old-fashioned that way."

She told me we were going to an Italian eatery called Carmello's, in the center of the old downtown section of Manitou. When she pulled into the parking lot I remembered the place. When I was a kid my parents took me to dinner there a few times. It used to be called Emile's and was considered moderately fancy. I recalled that it had a kind of European café look inside. Never set foot inside again after my dad died. When I was in high school, it changed hands and was turned into Carmello's. As we walked in the front door, it all came back to me. Maybe some new paint and woodwork, but the same faux Tuscan decor. Some things do stay the same after all.

They showed us to an empty booth, and we ordered an antipasto salad big enough to split and a bigger pizza. I am usually particular about my pizza, at least when I have a choice and I'm not holed up late at night in a hotel. I've always believed that Little Italy in New York is tops, with Chicago second. I learned long ago it's not the cheese that makes the difference; it's the sauce. After that, maybe the crust, but definitely the sauce.

We made small talk about my hospital stay and her schedule at the police department. The food came out quick, and Ashley dove in. I like a woman with a good appetite. For a skinny thing she really packed it away. The pizza was probably the third best one I had ever had. Maybe even the second. Of course it also could have been the company I was with.

She ordered a bottle of wine. I had a glass. She

had a lot more. At one point I noticed her hand shaking a bit, even before the wine.

There were a thousand questions I had about the Bobby Budleigh murder case, but at that moment I wasn't in a hurry to get into any of it. Instead, I asked her how long she had been a detective and whether she had found it hard breaking into such a male-dominated field, especially in Manitou.

"Yes, it was hard," she said. "But I guess it was in my DNA."

"Your dad?"

"Right. He was my hero. And he died that way too: as a hero."

Just then I felt my cell vibrating in my pocket. I didn't want to be rude and answer it. But I had a feeling it might be important. "Excuse me," I said. "I have to run to the boys' room for a sec."

I started toward the men's room. But I stopped. No, I was not going to bluff it with Ashley. I was going to be honest with her. No pretense. No shady stuff. That was the old Trevor Black. Things were different now. I was different.

Instead, I turned and headed back to our booth. I don't think Ashley had noticed that I turned around, because she had a pill bottle in her hand, and she shook out a little pill, then popped it in her mouth and washed it down with a gulp from her water glass. Then she looked up when I was almost at the booth, and our eyes locked, and when that happened, she quickly stashed the pill bottle in her purse.

After dumping myself back into the booth across from her, I looked into her face, that slim, perfectly beautiful face that seemed way too pretty to belong to a police detective. A face that was marred only minimally, almost imperceptibly, by a single intriguing mark.

I glanced at my cell, then said, "Truthfully, I really didn't need to run to the men's room. I got a call from a friend of mine back in New York. Dick Valentine. He's with the NYPD. I didn't want to take the call in front of you. Didn't think that would look cool. The fact is, I care about what you think about me."

She looked at me closely and took a sip from her water glass. "Honesty?" she said. "That's a refreshing change for an ex–criminal defense attorney. All right, let me reciprocate. Valentine is probably calling you because I called him. I wanted to get his take on your 'consulting' work for the police force. He said some good things about you. Then I pushed him about the weird stuff that you investigated. He hedged."

"Do you blame him?"

"Not really. But I pushed harder anyway. He opened up a little. From what he says, in New York you were dealing with some real-life Halloween horror stories."

"Well put."

"I told you that I had to settle some things before we could work any closer together. I needed to check you out. So, Detective Valentine was the last item on my checklist."

Things were looking up, way up. I asked, hopefully, "And?"

"Just don't embarrass me, that's all."

"No guarantees."

"Then at least don't get me fired."

"I can roll with that."

She relaxed in the booth and said, "Your turn now. Tell me what else is on your mind. Besides confessing to me, like a bad boy, that you lied about having to go potty."

I took a second. Then I laid it out for her. "Okay, one question. That thin scar on your face—was that from something that happened in the line of duty? Police-force related?"

Her back stiffened. Her tone changed. "Gee, Trevor, you really know how to treat a lady."

"Sorry. I didn't know how to ease into it. You see, if I were totally open about what I think about you—about the way you look and how you think about it—well, it would spoil the beginning of a wonderful friendship. Not to mention a great partnership."

Ashley pushed herself back from the table like she was about to hike out of there. Then she erupted. "You're arrogant and insulting, do you know that? And by the way, what gives you the idea that you know anything about me? You know absolutely nothing about who I am or what I'm thinking."

"I suppose you're right," I added quickly. "About everything you just said. The thing is, if I told you how beautiful you were, and how that infinitesimally thin white line on your face doesn't change anything about you, then you'd think I was a creepy stalker. But I'm boxed, don't you see? Because I also figure that this might be the only chance I have to actually find out things about you, which is what people do when they care about the other person. Which includes that little scar, and wanting to know whether some very bad person, somebody out of a creep show, might have given it to you while you were being a police hero, sort of like your dad. Because you strike me as that kind of person." I paused. "But then, what do I know?"

There was a tense, confused look on her face. Seconds went by. She turned to the side in the direction of the window that looked out to the street, to where it was getting dusky and a streetlight had just lit up. When she started talking, she kept looking in that direction. As if she wanted to be outside at that moment, far away from me, yet at the same time also be inside, talking.

After a long moment of silence, she said, "It happened while I was on the force."

I was about to tell her that it didn't matter. That she didn't have to tell me.

But before I got the words out, she told me anyway. "There was a serial rapist on the loose," she explained. "I volunteered to pose as his next target. Acting like I was inebriated, coming out of some bars. Looking vulnerable. Meanwhile, we had some fellow officers staked out around me. Ready to follow me. I was wired at the time, and we had a code word I was to say when I wanted the guys to close in and grab him."

"Did you ever give the code?"

"I couldn't. Never had the chance. I thought I could handle him. I was cocky and sure of myself, and I wanted to collar that vile pig myself, but he hit me from behind. It was a rookie mistake. The next thing I knew I was in the back of his van, tape over my mouth and hog-tied. He had found the police audio wire on me. Gerard Voxly, that was the guy's name—he knew right then that I was a police plant, and he went berserk. He cut my face with a razor just for fun. But that was just the beginning."

"I'm so sorry."

"Eventually the guys from the force tracked us down. They saved my life for sure. There is no doubt in my mind about that."

"So, all that ugly stuff. How did you handle it?"

"I think you mean to say, am I 'coping' with it in a healthy way? Which is what my doctor would say. Not a shrink, mind you, but my GP. A friend of mine. She asks me that."

"On the other hand, there's nothing wrong with getting help from a psychiatrist when you need it."

"Which is why I go to one of those too."

I didn't respond, but then I didn't need to.

"And yes," she added, "I know that you saw me take my meds here in the restaurant," she said. "So . . . oh, wow, Trevor. Nice. You have all the good stuff on me now."

"It's not like that at all," I assured her. "I don't work for the defense. I simply agreed not to disclose my conversation with Donny Ray Borzsted, that's all. This conversation between us is off limits. This is personal. You said it yourself. Just so you know, I would face a contempt of court order and some jail time rather than divulge to anyone what you're sharing with me tonight."

She looked skeptical.

So I added, "Hey, I've faced a lot worse than a scolding from a judge. After all, I jousted with Karlin Borzsted, right? I was the guy riding the white horse, defending your name."

She was fighting back a smile.

"You got to admit: chivalry's not quite dead. True?"

On the other side of the table, a grin at my banter. "Okay. Yes. You were the real deal." She nodded at something to herself, something private. Then she said, "It's called GAD."

"What is?"

"My diagnosis. As in, ye GAD, I've got generalized anxiety disorder. G-A-D."

"You've got guts," I said, "talking about this."

She straightened up again where she sat. "Well, that's all we are going to discuss on that subject. Change of topics. So, what is it exactly that you need to know about the Bobby Budleigh murder?"

I was ready for that. "I assume from your comment at the hospital that it was the dental records that did it. Proving that the corpse didn't belong to Augie?"

"Correct, along with blood type of the message on the floor. I should know by tomorrow who the dead man really was."

"About the state's case. The indictment said there were bootprints in the mud where you found Bobby's body, linking Donny Ray to the scene."

"Clear imprints from size 12 Sierra Trading Post hiking boots. We found a pair in Donny Ray's apartment."

"Any traces of mud on those boots, even microscopic?"

"No. Clean as a whistle. Practically brand-new."

"Tire prints at the scene?"

"Yes, but not matching the defendant's car. Next, I suppose you'll ask about the gun used to shoot Bobby in the head, so I'll tell you about that too. We found a .38 in Donny Ray's apartment. But ballistics tells us that the bullet that struck Bobby was from a nine-millimeter."

"What about the eyewitness?"

"A female driving alone at least forty miles an hour past a car that she couldn't describe and that was parked along Pebble Creek. She saw two men, a shorter one—presumably Bobby Budleigh—with a taller one, which she later photo ID'd at the police station as Donny Ray."

"Did your eyewitness have any prior knowledge about Donny Ray before the photo ID?"

Ashley brightened. "Smart thinking. Here is how it came down. A couple of months before, she had seen a picture of Donny Ray in the newspaper. It was an article about a couple of Manitou residents who had all been given early parole, causing a community ruckus. The photo may have stuck. Anyway, it could have tainted her identification. And without going into the weeds too much, there were problems with the way the ID at the police station went down."

Then she added, "Of course possession of a weapon is a violation of Donny Ray's parole. Which is why we are extending his rest stop in the county jail until his parole violation hearing. But all in all, I think the case for murder against him is very thin."

She changed gears. "Now I need your help

locating your high school buddy Augie Bedders."

I shot back, "But if the corpse wasn't Augie, then the writing on the floor at the incinerator, which I took to be a confession, wasn't written by Augie either. So he's in the clear."

Ashley cocked an eyebrow and said, "It's complicated. If forensics tells me tomorrow what I expect to hear about that dead man at the land-fill incinerator, then we need to find Augie Bedders, and in a hurry."

40

While we waited for the server to come back with my credit card, Ashley said that was all she could tell me about Augie for the time being. But then she added, "We need to find out more about Bobby Budleigh."

I thought she meant more information from his wife back in Colorado, or from his son, or about his environmental work at his Colorado foundation. But no.

"I mean," she explained, "about Bobby's connection to Manitou. You were friends in high school. Like you, he left to pursue his professional life. Then he comes back, after all that time, and then we have a homicide. Our reports indicate that his return had something to do with his environmental interests. So where's the motive? Just some random psycho killing? Or was it something else?"

I had already begun sketching out in my mind an explanation, one that Ashley wasn't going to like. "What do you think?" I asked.

"The mutilation of his body, the heart extraction, is exactly like several homicides in New York. Ones you know more about than I do."

"Dick Valentine?"

"Sure, he told me all about it."

"So . . ."

"We've got a copycat murderer." After saying that, she stared into my face like she was a mind reader and she was trying to hack into my cerebral cortex. "And your take?"

"Depends," I said, "on how you define *copycat,* I guess."

"Lawyers."

I could tell Ashley didn't appreciate my playing close to the vest. I assured her that if I knew anything concrete about the identity of the perpetrator, I would tell her immediately.

While she drove me back to my hotel, she said, "I bet you already have a theory about Bobby Budleigh's death. Something weird. Otherworldly. But you're being cagey and don't want to tell me about it. Trevor, the fact is, you're still chasing demons. Or at least you think you are."

The car pulled up to the entrance. We looked at each other. I took on a mock-solemn expression and said, "Well, if I'm chasing demons, then that makes you my perfect partner."

"And why is that?"

"What better partner than an angel disguised as a cop?"

Ashley rolled her eyes and gave a loud groan. "Did you steal that from some old black-and-white Bogart movie?"

"Naw. He was way too smooth to say anything like that."

I suddenly had this crazy idea to kiss her good night in the circle drive before I climbed out. But I'm glad I didn't, as it wasn't a real date. Though it wasn't strictly business either.

I would have to sort all that out later. Along with something else.

Her suggestion about Bobby had sparked a thought. His parents had moved out of Manitou years before, so they couldn't fill in any gaps about Bobby. But there might be one person in particular who had a connection to Bobby and to his family back in the old Manitou days. And he might still be in the area.

After I climbed out of Ashley's unmarked, I stuck my head back in the window and said two things.

"I really liked our time together tonight."

She replied only, "I'm glad."

Then the second thing. "Also, I'm pursuing a lead tomorrow. In case you were thinking about our teaming up together again."

"Actually, I wasn't. This isn't my only case. I'm also working some others. I'll be in touch."

"Sure."

As I unlocked my room door I knew that Ashley's parting words had been a blow-off.

I threw some water on my face and looked at myself in the bathroom mirror. My ear was red and swollen from Karlin Borzsted having clipped me there with his fist. It didn't look human. It looked like it belonged under glass in a butcher shop. And I was wearing a goose egg over my eye. No wonder Ashley gave me a rain check.

I dropped into bed feeling sore all over, gave a last look at the green laser light in the ceiling fire alarm, and wondered whether I would get a visit from *them* again.

That was when I told myself it was time for me to hammer a stubborn fact into my stubborn brain: that, just as surely as if I had been a train set upon iron rails, something much bigger than even my friendship with Bobby had set me on this journey. If God was in this mission, and he most certainly had to be, then he was in that room with me too.

I pulled out my cell phone and noticed that I had inadvertently turned the volume off. There was a message. I hit the voice mail icon. When I was halfway through it, I began to laugh. Not because it was funny—except in a divine-appointment kind of way.

"Trevor, Elijah White here, brother. Was praying about you today and had a thought. A God-planted seed, I do believe. Whatever you're up to now, God wants you to know the peace that belongs to Jesus followers like you. Even if you're a warrior who's banging on the gates of hell. Check out the Gospel of John. Chapter 16."

Then I heard Elijah break into a hearty laugh. "Overcome," he said. "Oh yeah, that's what you're going to read there, brother Trevor, in John 16. Overcome. Bless you, my man."

I pulled out Elijah's Bible and turned to the sixteenth chapter of the Gospel of John, where Jesus was telling his disciples about peace, even though it was right before the hammer was about to fall: his arrest, torture, and death were soon to follow. He said the world was full of tribulation, but they should cheer up because "I have overcome the world." A paradox on the surface considering that, despite his innocence, Jesus was marching into a bloody execution. Unless, of course, by "overcoming the world" he meant something different. Something other than just escaping the pain of tribulation. Something miraculous.

I closed the Bible, flooded with a sense of safety. And even more, with a joyful realization that I was actually being watched. Protected. Guided.

It was late, but I decided to call Elijah back anyway and got his voice mail. My message to my friend was emotional.

"This is Trevor calling. Listen, Elijah, you just delivered a message to me straight from the throne room. Faster than overnight delivery. Better than a winning lottery ticket. You have no idea . . ." But I started to choke up a little and had to take a second. Then I ended with, "Thank you, Elijah. Things have been a little rough at my end. You just made my day."

I clicked off the light on the nightstand and fell into slumber land.

The next morning, after a decent sleep, I drove across town, past buildings I hadn't seen for decades, like the county fairgrounds where my family and I would go every summer when I was a young boy—the place with the amphitheater and the animal barns and the big corrugated-metal exhibit building.

When I arrived at the Covenant Retirement Village, I found a discreet parking spot for my Fiat behind the nursing home, hidden behind some small trees and bushes. It looked to be an overflow parking area. I hustled into the front lobby of the single-story tan brick building.

I told the receptionist who I was and who I was looking for, and that I wanted to talk to him about Bobby Budleigh. She made a call and sat there on the phone for a full minute until someone answered. After giving my message to the person on the other end, she listened, then hung up and told me, "I'll take you to the music room. He's on his way."

She led me into a room with plenty of windows and sunshine, a piano at one end, and two music stands, three rows of folding chairs, and a sofa in the corner.

My escort disappeared, so I strolled around, looking at the wall decorations: paintings of musical instruments and a still life of flowers arranged in a bowl. I wondered if I was wasting my time coming there. I wondered, after all the years that had passed since the one and only time I had ever met this man, whether he would even remember me.

After maybe ten minutes I heard the slow, methodical clumping of a walker coming down the hall. I turned around.

Rev. John Cannon, former pastor of Good Shepherd Lutheran Church of Manitou, had come to a halt in the wide opening to the room and was gripping his walker with both hands. Even though it was summer, he was wearing a button-down cardigan sweater, and he was huffing and puffing. When he caught his breath he said, "Legs are the first thing to go. Can you help me over to the sofa there?"

After the old man was settled on the couch, I pulled up a wooden chair and started in, explaining who I was and about my high school friendship with Bobby. I reminded him of my one visit with him as a teenager when Bobby had led me into his pastor's study. Cannon stared at me, appearing unable to conjure up the connection. I finally told him that I had come back to Manitou to help find Bobby Budleigh's killer.

Time and gravity had laid deep, soft creases into Rev. Cannon's face, but I could still recognize him. Our meeting in the pastor's study must have made more of an impression on me than I had realized.

Cannon moved his mouth around, a little like a cow chewing its cud. After a moment he asked, "Don't you trust the police?"

"I'm actually working with them, in a way."

"Terrible thing," he said. "I read about it. Broke my heart. Bobby was a fine young man. Went into a scientific field of some sort . . ."

"Environmental studies."

"I thought they caught the man who did it."

"They have someone in custody. But I just want to make sure. So do the police."

"What can I do for you?"

"Anything you can remember about Bobby or his family that might indicate a reason why someone would want to take his life? Or take it so brutally?"

He thought on that for a while. "I'm sorry, but I have no idea. Other than the usual."

"What would that be?"

The Reverend looked at me hard, like he might

be trying to remember something. "Did you say you went to Good Shepherd?"

"No. Just came to your church that one time to meet with you. It was Bobby's idea."

He nodded. But then something distracted him. He zeroed in on my swollen ear and the bump on my forehead. "Looks like you were in a car crash."

"No. I just crashed into someone bigger than me."

Cannon seemed to be searching for the trail that he had wandered off, then found it. "What you were saying before . . ."

"I was asking about what you just said. About the 'usual' reason for someone getting murdered."

"Yes. Well, I was with a missionary organization before I was ordained. Before the synod. Working in South America. Along the Amazon in Brazil. Mostly among the indigenous tribes. While I was there, I encountered the powers of darkness. Demonic evil."

"I recall Bobby mentioning that to me way back when."

"We did exorcisms in the jungle. God worked miracles. So many people were set free."

"Did you ever talk to Bobby directly about that? The exorcisms?"

He gave a half chuckle. "Not that I can recall. I wouldn't have. My background caused quite enough of a stir among the congregation. As you can imagine. Gossip spreads fast."

Then out of the blue, he mentioned something else. "Missionaries have to study the language. Culture. The pagan lifestyle of the tribes. A common bond of communication and trust must be created before you can go deeper. Into the real spiritual issues, that is. When I came to Manitou to pastor the church, I did that. Went to the county museum here in town. Studied up on the area."

"The museum in the building that used to be the old courthouse?"

"Yes, that's it. Do you know where the word *manitou* comes from?"

"They must have taught us something about it here in the schools, but I can't remember."

He said, "It comes from Indian tribes. Algonquian mostly, I think."

"What does it mean?"

"Supernatural spirit."

Images flashed in my head. The photographs of Heather's mutilated body, and Bobby's too. Maybe Cannon's experience with jungle demonism as a missionary could give me a lead.

I asked, "Your time in South America—did you ever encounter a situation where the hearts were cut out of victims?"

He thought on it and said, "Not personally. But we heard of that sort of thing. There's plenty of that in pagan cultures. Even in tribes today."

Then Cannon threw something else at me unexpectedly. "I had my own idea about those kinds of horrible practices."

"I'd like to hear it."

"This is not inspired. Just the gospel according to John Cannon. But I think that kind of practice—the removal of the heart—is the private joke of the devil. His demonstration of power. Over the world. And over flesh. And a repudiation of God. He mocks anything that is good and pure. Does it, I think, with a cynical grin. He has an appetite for devouring things. And people."

I wasn't following, so I asked him to explain.

Cannon said, "In the Gospels. The Roman soldier thrust a spear into the chest of Jesus. To make sure he was dead. And blood and water poured out, from a heart that had burst. You know, I believe Jesus died from a broken heart. Rent apart, having taken on himself all that evil, that blight of sin of the human race."

"But those pagan practices we were talking about . . ."

"The heart," he said, raising his voice. "It's about mutilating the heart, don't you see? Mocking the Savior."

Again, the images. Heather, Dunning Kamera's victim, and Bobby too. And even the knife attack against me in the art museum in New York, a thrust that came into the same part of my body.

Only the extraordinary appearance of some museum guard, or whoever he was, stopped me from being a homicide victim myself. I was lucky to be alive. Several times over.

There was a sinking feeling in my gut. My bravado about solving Bobby's case and coming to Manitou in search of the killer. Was I a fool on a fool's errand, thinking I could handle this?

I found myself suddenly longing to get back home. Longing for the peace that I felt in my cabin on the edge of the Atlantic. Especially on those days when the ocean was calm and grayish blue, and it would be so still that the expanse of water would bleed into the horizon. The peaceful-looking place where the sky meets the sea.

Cannon disrupted all of that. "Do you have any other questions?"

I told him yes, I did. "What side of Jesus' chest was punctured by the spear?"

Just then the sound of a bell rang through the building. Rev. Cannon's eyes brightened. "Have to go. That's the lunch bell. It's meat loaf day today. It's not half-bad either." Then he looked back at me. "Oh, your question?"

I repeated it, and Cannon took only a second or two before answering. "The Gospel accounts actually don't answer that question. Tradition says the entry was on his right side, opposite the side where his heart was. But as I said, just a matter of traditional church thinking. I seem to recall it was bolstered by other medical facts, though I can't remember them right now."

I stood up and said, "About what you said, Rev. Cannon. About the word *manitou* meaning 'supernatural spirit.' You didn't say whether that meant a good spirit or an evil one."

I was now aware that an aide from the retirement home had swept into the room. She offered to help Rev. Cannon to the cafeteria. He struggled to get to his feet, and when he did, he planted them under the walker and prepared to walk.

Once he had mounted the walker he returned to my question. *"Manitou,"* he said. "Now, about that word. For me, there's only one Spirit that's truly good. But many that are bad. Now, what those Indian tribes meant by it, I'm not sure."

I thanked him and turned to leave. But there was something else that was bugging me, and I needed to get Rev. Cannon's take on it while I had him. So I decided to walk alongside him while he made his slow shuffle toward the cafeteria.

"Rev. Cannon, just one last question. Treat it like a game. Trivial Pursuit perhaps."

His eyes lit up.

By then I had been thinking back to that very similar message that had been delivered by three violent and possessed souls, all of them in New York: Dunning Kamera, Hanz Delpha, and Sid Castor.

So I started out, "If I were to use the phrase

'dead already'—or something similar, like, for instance, 'already dead'—would that mean anything to you?"

The old pastor scrunched up his face, then turned to me with a bright expression. "Got it. Yes. Dead already. Jesus was on the cross, and the Roman soldiers were about to break his legs to hasten his demise, but then they noticed, according to the Gospels, that he was dead already. As a result they didn't bother, and thus they fulfilled the prophecy that no bones of the Messiah would be broken."

I stopped, grappling with that last bit from Rev. Cannon as he kept moving toward the cafeteria. Cannon twisted half around in my direction with a great effort and said, "Good game. I like that. Any more questions like that one?"

I told him no, but thanked him for his time.

Then it was Cannon's turn. He suddenly shouted back to me, saying, "I remember you. You were the smart aleck."

I stopped in my tracks.

He added, "You and Bobby were together that day in my study at the church. And you were the smart-aleck one."

I smiled. "Yes, sir, I was. You've got a better memory than you think."

"I always was fond of Bobby," he said. "That boy had a bright future. And he always kept his eyes on the prize."

"He was the real deal, even when the girls were practically throwing themselves at him."

Rev. Cannon nodded and gazed down the hall the way we'd come. "I seem to recall that pretty blonde, Marilyn, kept batting her eyelashes at him. But he never gave her the time of day."

I did a bit of a double take. "You knew Marilyn Parlow?"

"You were friends? Marilyn's parents were longtime members at Good Shepherd, and she was sweet on Bobby. Since elementary school. Poor girl. Went through two or three marriages. Always looking for love, I think. Not finding it. Not the real kind. Right up to the day she passed."

A deadweight dropped in my stomach, and my face must have gone pale because the reverend responded with concern. "I'm sorry. You hadn't heard that news? Marilyn died a few years back. Cervical cancer, I was told."

He stepped closer and patted me on the arm. "It is sad when you start losing friends and peers. Believe me—" he extended his other hand, taking in the sterile hallways and shuffling retirees around us—"I know what it is to see people pass beyond the veil. We still grieve, but with hope, if our trust is in the Lord." He gave my arm one final squeeze, then turned and continued toward the cafeteria. "Trust him, son. All other ground is sinking sand."

As I exited the building and started toward my

Fiat rental car, I realized that Rev. Cannon never got around to explaining something. How the brutal murder of innocent people in Manitou, or anywhere else, could ever be considered "usual." But my mind was already on fire with everything else Cannon had just told me.

On the drive back to the Holiday Inn, my cell rang. It was Dan Hoover, and he said that he was in Seattle, had a day off before his jazz tour started up again, and wanted to know how things were coming in my investigation.

I pulled over and shut off the engine, then took a breath and told him first about Augie. That I'd thought he was dead, possible suicide. Then it turned out the corpse wasn't his after all.

Dan made me repeat it again. When I did, I said, "I know this whole thing is confusing. And bizarre. And doesn't make much sense—"

"I don't get it. What's going on in Manitou, anyway?"

"Something evil." I left it at that for the time being. But I had more news to share. "Remember Marilyn?"

"Wow, yeah. Blast from the past. Hot on you, right? Or was it Bobby?"

"Complicated," I replied. "Anyway, I found out she died too. Cancer."

"Geez. Sad, man." Then, "Well, what about the guy who did that to Bobby, anyway? Are you making headway?"

I told him that the guy who the police had in custody probably didn't do it.

Dan was thunderstruck. "Wow. Man. Where does that leave us? Got me looking over my shoulder."

In spite of myself, I found myself repeating my pledge again. "I'm not leaving till this is done."

Dan said, "Man, Bobby's gone. Susan, Augie's wife, she's gone. Any idea, then, where Augie is? I'm worried he might be in trouble too."

"The detective I am working with thinks the same. We need to get to him before something bad happens."

I ended the call by reassuring Dan that I would not give up on nailing Bobby's killer and also locating Augie.

When I got back to the hotel, I figured I'd head over to the Ranch Roundup Steak House for dinner, but first I pulled my Bible off the nightstand and turned to Ecclesiastes. I had been going back to this book of the Bible lately, and I flipped to a passage that had been lingering in my thoughts for a few days now: that God has placed eternity into the human heart. The echoes of the supernatural that we sense. But like everything else, enemy forces have twisted that yearning and turned it into something ugly. And dangerous. The question was how to navigate that.

But as I pondered and prayed, my belly was rumbling. I decided to navigate my way to the steak joint that was walking distance from the hotel. The great questions of life would still be there when I returned.

41

While I ate my T-bone dinner at the Ranch Roundup, I leafed through the local news in the *Manitou Times* that I had picked up in the metal newspaper box outside the restaurant. Two things caught my eye; they seemed only tangentially related. One was a full-page advertisement for the Opperdill Real Estate Development Company. It was the land business of Jeffery Opperdill, who I recalled was the son of Hoskins Opperdill, the man who owned the foundry where my father was killed in his industrial accident. The ad sported a big, full-color picture of Jeffery Opperdill. He looked fit, was smiling broadly, and seemed to be about my age, with blond hair and mustache. A little too blond. Probably a dye job.

The other news that I spotted in between bites of steak was farther back in the paper near the sports section: a notice of an upcoming Manitou City Council meeting about the future of the abandoned Opperdill Foundry located along the Little Bear River. Those two bits of information didn't seem connected at the time, except for the fact that the Opperdill family name was involved in both.

When I finished dinner, I put in a call to Dick Valentine back in New York. I presumed his years in homicide would have likely put him into contact with a variety of doctors and medical professionals. He didn't pick up, so I left a message on his voice mail.

"Trevor Black here, friend. Would love to catch up with you sometime. So, here's the reason for my call. I am still working the case involving the murder of my high school friend here in Wisconsin. I've got an unusual request. Remember the Bible story about the crucifixion? The Roman soldier jams a spear into the side of Jesus and blood and water pours out. I need a medical opinion. Why the separation of blood and water? How would the puncture wound have produced that kind of result? There's lots of information on the Internet, but I'm not sure what's valid. Would actually like a professional opinion that I could trust. Do you know any people in medical forensics who might be able to give me some answers? Not sure how or why it seems important to me, but there it is. Anyway, let me know. And I'd also like to know if you're staying safe and still catching bad guys. You've got my number."

As I started to amble back to the Holiday Inn,

which was about half a mile away along the bypass, I wondered why I hadn't driven instead. There was no sidewalk, so I walked just off the edge of the shoulder of the highway to make sure I didn't become a squashed bug on someone's front windshield. I fished out my cell and put in a call to Ashley as I walked. Again, no answer. I was starting to feel like people were avoiding me. The prompt beeped, and I left a message telling her that I would like to reconnect about the Bobby Budleigh case and had been wondering how she was doing on her other cases. Not that she could discuss those with me, of course, but I was just thinking about her. And that I really enjoyed our dinner together. I ended by asking her to call me.

When I reached the grounds of the hotel, I headed for the keyed-access entrance at the rear of the building rather than walking all the way around to the front lobby. I saw a few cars parked in that part of the lot, but I was alone, and the only sound that I heard at first was the echo of my own footsteps. Then, when I was about twenty feet from the rear door, my cell rang. I looked down at the little luminous screen—a restricted number. *Could be Dick Valentine calling back,* I thought. As I brought my cell up to my ear, I was about to tap the Accept button.

Then the sensation. The scent of smoky incineration and putrid rot.

And the feeling of a presence behind me. And

then two hands coming around my neck in a choke hold from a guy who was bigger than me and stronger. So much bigger and stronger that I was lifted up off the ground at least six inches as I clawed at the hands to release me. The hands were squeezing the breath from my throat. I couldn't speak. I was shaken like a wet dishrag until I thought my brains would be scrambled in my skull.

Next came a voice. But it was more of a cacophony, like a piano hitting the pavement after falling three stories.

Yet the words were clear. "If you stay, Trevor, I'll make you my slave."

Then my short flight through the air.

I was tossed forward to the asphalt, and as I fell, my arms were out, and they kept my face and nose from being busted when I hit. I gasped for breath, flipped myself over, and tried to find my attacker. He was gone.

My cell was on the ground, and I heard someone on the other end, but by the time I picked it up, the incoming call had ended.

I stumbled to my feet, a little unsteady, wondering if my shoulder had been dislocated again when I fell. I rotated it slowly around, but no, it just felt like a sprain. Bruised forearms, but that was it. I heard myself explode with a burst of profanity. An unpleasant reminder that the old me wasn't quite gone. I was tired of being ambushed. Punched and kicked. Handled like a side of beef in a meat locker.

A beam of light from the headlights of a car came swooping into the parking lot and approached. I saw Ashley Linderman's unmarked car pulling up to me.

Ashley jumped out with her hand under her suit coat and on her sidearm, then approached me cautiously as she tossed a look in all directions. "Are you all right? You look a little shook up."

"I think so. What are you doing here?"

"I was cruising, and I called your cell. Then I heard a sound. Like you were choking."

"Yeah, that was me choking all right. I must have clicked on your call when I was being manhandled."

"By who?"

"He came from behind. I couldn't see him."

"Any idea who it was?"

"No. But he said something. He said that if I hung around here, he'd make me his slave."

"Sounds medieval," she said.

"You have no idea."

Ashley's expression changed. A gentle look. I felt something wet dripping down my upper lip, and as I did, Ashley reached in her pocket and pulled out a handkerchief. She dabbed it to my lip, and I saw bright-red blood. I must have banged my nose when I hit the ground. I noticed Ashley's hand trembling as she held the handkerchief, but I knew it wasn't fear. Probably her ongoing struggle with GAD. *Must be hard,* I thought, *considering the job brings her into contact with a parade of dangerously bad actors.*

"Keep the handkerchief," she said. "You know, Trevor, maybe you'd be safer finding somewhere else to crash tonight."

"Funny. I had been thinking the same thing."

"Don't get any ideas, okay? But I've got a spare bedroom in my apartment. Maybe you'd be better off there. At least for tonight."

Everything in my physical and psychological being was telling me to run with this. No need to catalog all the reasons. "You know, Ashley, I'm glad you're here. I was hoping we could see each other again."

"You mean so I could rescue you from another beat-down?" We both laughed.

"No," I said, "because I wanted to see you."

"Okay, okay. We can talk it over at my place over a glass of wine."

She turned toward her car. But I didn't move. "You coming? Or not?"

"Not," I said.

She threw me a look. One part hurt, perhaps. And maybe two parts confusion.

I tried to clear it up. "You know, when I was a trial lawyer, I learned something about putting in a case. When things are going your way, don't overreach. Don't take a lily and then try to gild it with gold plating. The lily is perfect just as it is."

She went snake-eyed. "You must be talking Portuguese, because I don't speak the language. What are you saying?"

"Let me translate. We've got a chance to start off on the right foot, and I don't want to spoil it by making wrong choices. You deserve better. Your reputation. Who you are. And how I am now, compared to who I used to be." Then I asked, "But can I see you tomorrow?"

She snorted out a laugh. "Trevor, you're an interesting case. Such a major mess of a man. Maybe a good mess. But still a mess. Okay, let's team up tomorrow. But I'll call you. Don't call me."

42

Ashley didn't call me, but she did text. I saw it when I woke the next morning after getting a relatively good sleep—meaning no nightmare visitors entering my room to attack me in the dead of night.

Her text had two parts. The first part raised some serious questions in my mind. **Come right down to the sheriff's office this morning. Sheriff Jardinsky needs to talk with you.**

Then the next part: **And after that, come over to the Sunrise Cafe and meet me for breakfast. It's my day off.**

• • •

The sheriff was waiting for me in his office when I arrived. No handshake, but a quick hello and then asking me to take a seat as he strolled over to the door and closed it before sitting down behind his desk. He opened up the button on one of the two chest pockets of his tan sheriff's uniform and plucked out a stubby little yellow pencil. It looked like he had cut it in half so it could fit into his shirt pocket. There was a pad of paper on the desk in front of him, and he laid the pencil on the pad. Then he started to talk.

He asked me if I was part of the defense team for Donny Ray Borzsted, and I quickly and accurately denied it.

"But you met with Donny Ray in jail?" he asked.

"Certainly," I said, "as an independent investigator."

"There is no such thing. You're either with the defense or with the prosecution."

I didn't want to argue the finer points of the law with him, but in fact there is a third alternative, one that values truth over victory in court. I told him I fit nicely into that third option.

"Okay, then are you working as an assistant to Detective Ashley Linderman?"

"Not really."

"But you've been spending time with her."

"True. Because I want to find the killer of my friend."

"We already have the man who killed your friend. You spoke to him in jail, remember?"

"You've got the wrong man."

"Our DA doesn't think so."

Given my prior life as a criminal defense attorney, I had heard that kind of retort before. I told him, "I will be glad to instruct your district attorney on the fact that the eyewitness who supposedly saw Donny Ray by Pebble Creek that night with Bobby, when she's cross-examined, will fold up like a bad poker hand. And the forensic evidence that you possess does nothing to connect Donny Ray to the scene of the crime."

Jardinsky stroked his hand over his graying flattop, then reached for his pencil, picked it up, but laid it back down. Then he leaned back in his chair. "I trust our DA. He's a good prosecutor."

"I'm sure he is. But occasionally a good prosecutor is stuck with a really bad case. Like this one."

"All right. Here's the situation," the sheriff said, suddenly scooting forward with his forearms on top of the desk. "Number one, you are not to leave this jurisdiction for the time being. You are officially a person of interest in the murder of Bobby Budleigh."

I recognized the lingo. Keeping my discomfort hidden, I quickly asked why.

"Because we know that you were here, at least very shortly after Mr. Budleigh's death. Who knows, maybe you were even in Manitou when it happened."

"I can prove I wasn't."

The sheriff rolled on. "Well, also you knew him—the victim. And your first name was written on his body. And also you're out doing your own shadow investigation, and that bothers me. And then there's the fact that a man who drove a car registered to Augie Bedders, and who had Bedders's wallet and ID in the car, ended up being incinerated at the Manitou landfill, and you were a friend of Augie Bedders, which puts you only one degree of separation from the victim in the incinerator. Plus there's the fact that frankly, Mr. Black, you have a very strange background in New York. And I find you to be a very strange man."

I saw no basis for the sheriff's holding me in Manitou, but no matter, I wasn't going anywhere for the time being. I changed gears. "I'm guessing that you have located Augie Bedders by now?"

Jardinsky didn't bite on that.

I said, "You've given me the order about staying in Manitou, but was there something else?"

"Yes, there is. You are to keep your distance from Detective Ashley Linderman's official investigation."

I speculated that Sheriff Jardinsky's last directive was the real reason he had brought me in. But as I walked out of his office, I concluded there was a bright side. Nothing I had said had caused him to pick up his little yellow pencil to jot any notes down.

With the help of my GPS, I found the Sunrise Café. It was a green one-story restaurant with a rising sun painted over the front door and was attached to a greenhouse operation. Most important, it was twenty miles out of town on Highway 18, nestled between farmers' fields and down the road from an agricultural co-op, which placed it just outside of the county jurisdiction and therefore outside the official reach of Sheriff Jardinsky. Ashley was in a booth next to the window with a view of the highway, and she had already ordered coffee for both of us. When the server swooped over to us, we said that we were fine with coffee for the time being.

As I recounted my conversation with the sheriff, Ashley didn't look surprised. Then I pieced it all together: Ashley must have known all along that it was coming, hence her "day off" and her choice of a restaurant in the next county.

I said, "A day off? You really mean that you were suspended, don't you?"

She nodded. "Good deduction on your part. Only one day. Without pay."

"Because of me?"

"No," she said. "Because of me. I knew the risks of working so closely with you. I knew Butch would look for any reason to come down on me. That's life."

"So, why meet with me now?"

"Butch said no 'official' relationship with you."

I explained how Butch Jardinsky had told me the same thing.

"Seeing as I am suspended today," she said, "that would make this an unofficial meeting, wouldn't it?"

I couldn't argue with that, and didn't want to anyway. It was good to see her. She asked me for more details about my attack in the parking lot the night before, and I went over it again. But this time I felt the urge, at some point in the rendezvous, to share something else about the incident.

But that would have to wait. I knew, in light of Jardinsky's edict, it might be my last official sit-down with Ashley, and I needed as much information as she felt comfortable sharing.

I asked her about the identity of the corpse at the incinerator, and what she knew about Augie Bedders's whereabouts, and why the dead man at the landfill had Augie's car and driver's license.

She explained that the dead man was determined from dental records to be Wendell Quarlet, aged thirty-two, with a drug conviction on his record. He had worked with Augie at a local Manitou shop called Exotica.

"Was the shop a front for drugs?"

"Probably," she said.

"What about Augie?" I asked.

I wondered if my old friend had wandered back into drugs after the car-crash death of his high school sweetheart and wife, Susan. From what Ashley explained to me, the timing sounded like it. She told me that Augie had two drug-related misdemeanors on his record, had no visible means of employment for long periods. Then, surprisingly, he started running Exotica a few months prior to Bobby's murder. But after Bobby's death, Augie disappeared and had become persona absentia.

There was something I had to ask. "Do you think the same person who killed Bobby was also after Augie? That something happened to him too?"

"That was my first thought," she said. "It seemed that Augie could have been in danger, considering that the corpse belonged to Wendell Quarlet and that they had worked together at Exotica. Especially because Wendell had Augie's car and his wallet and driver's license and a wad of money that could have been stolen from the Exotica shop."

"But why Wendell's suicide?"

"I wondered," she said, "whether it was guilt over the theft and a possible killing of Augie, and maybe even the murder of Bobby Budleigh too. His *Judas* message left in his own blood at the incinerator might support that, the same conjecture we had when we thought the body was

Bedders. And yet, why in the world would he have picked that way to go, jumping into an incinerator? It's crazy."

I shared one theory. "Maybe he was on a drug trip."

She nodded. But there was a look in her eye that told me she still had things she had not shared with me. Not yet.

So I asked, "What do you know about Augie?"

"He's not dead. He's very much alive."

"Where is he?"

"He's returned to Manitou. He's running the Exotica shop again." Then Ashley shoved her coffee cup aside and asked, "Now, about that guy who assaulted you last night, I get the feeling there is more from you too."

It was time for me to get real with Ashley. "There is something I need to tell you."

"I'd love to hear it. Was your attacker Karlin Borzsted? Or even Augie Bedders?"

She had no idea where I was about to go with this. "No, couldn't have been. Let me explain. When we first met, you said that you didn't want me to talk to you about certain things. About my special ability—the supernatural one, for detecting demons."

She sighed. "Fine. Hit me with your best shot."

"I can smell them, the demons. And I mean that literally." I paused. Her eyes widened like she was in the path of an oncoming car. I continued. "Don't ask me how or why. But I can."

Ashley took her time responding. "Okay, I guess I asked for that. Look, I live fully in this world, not the next. I put my trust into what I can see, touch, hear—"

"And smell?" I added.

She smirked. "I should know better than to banter with an ex–trial lawyer. But you get my point."

"Of course. The physical world. Sticking to the strictly empirical. Suspicious about the spiritual. I get you. I was there once too."

I could tell Ashley wasn't satisfied with that. She said, "I'm going to ignore your don't-ask-me-why part. So, I'm going to ask you the 'why' part: Why you? And why . . . whatever that ability is . . . Why that?"

"On the first question, I don't know. On the second, I have this idea: I know there's a God in heaven, and he has given me this ability for a reason, even though it feels like more of a burden than a gift. But there it is. My attacker last night was one of them. A demon walking around inside someone it has occupied."

If faces were billboards, hers would have read, *Dubious*. She asked, "Uh, okay, so how did you get out of that attack?"

"That's what's strange. In every other situation I've been rescued through a variety of . . . let's call them interventions. But this time, no. I'm just not sure how I escaped."

Ashley couldn't resist and shot back with a smirk, "Were you maybe wearing garlic around your neck?"

I flashed a smile. But I thought to myself that there was no way for her to understand the real-life terror of those beings from the other side. So I unfortunately started letting the words come out of my mouth. "It's hard to describe to anyone unless they have experienced real horror." Then, just as quickly, I reversed myself as I looked into her slender, perfectly proportioned face, but the face that also bore that thin white scar across her cheek, inflicted by a real-life monster of a different kind.

I quickly added, "But then, you're different. You're a surviving member of that club. You could even be president of it."

Her face softened. "Thanks," she said in a voice that was matter-of-fact and quiet.

But I knew what I had to do next, so I told her. "I think you should know that I'm going to stop by the Exotica shop and see my old friend Augie Bedders."

"And just so you know, I didn't just hear that." Ashley waved to the staff so she could pay for our two coffees and added, "I'll find a way to be in touch with you."

I volleyed back, "And just so you know, I will

be looking forward to that very much. Hopefully very soon too. And I hope it's not just about this case."

She gave me this look just then that was more than a smile, a look that I would want to remember for a long time.

43

Exotica was on the back side of a row of stores in the old section of downtown Manitou. It faced the Little Bear River but was several blocks away from the part of town where the riverfront had been renovated with artsy sculptures, and buildings had been refurbished into nice condos. In the Exotica neighborhood, by contrast, peeling paint and drab little stores were the standard, and the area included a pawnshop, a bail bondsman's office, and a few vacant shops with For Rent signs in the windows.

When I strolled into Exotica, I found it to be a combination retro head shop out of the Haight-Ashbury '60s mixed with the musty ambience of an antique store. I was greeted with beads hanging everywhere, racks of tie-dyed shirts, a poster of Jimi Hendrix on the wall, and, naturally, the powerful scent of burning incense. There were boxes of old vinyl records for sale, a scattering of very dated furniture, and imported objects displayed everywhere with little price tags hanging on them by strings. The collection of carved and sculpted objects—mostly dragons, wizards, and a variety of mythic creatures— looked like they might have been imported from Africa, India, or the Middle East.

I spotted a cluttered counter with a cash register but no one manning it. Then I heard some movement from the back room and rang the little copper bell on the counter.

A bearded man stepped through the doorway in the wall. He was my age. Taller than me, with long, thinning hair in need of combing. A pale face that was gaunt, bearing the ravages, no doubt, of personal loss, addiction, and jail time. He was wearing an untucked construction-grade shirt with a circular logo on the pocket and ripped jeans.

We looked at each other. I gave him a moment to put it all together as I stood there at the counter.

Then I said, "Augie Bedders. Good grief. It has been a long time. Too long. How are you, friend? I've missed you. Been thinking about you."

A weary smile spread over his face. "Oh, man, Trevor. Geez. Been so long . . ."

He reached over the counter awkwardly and took my right hand into his two hands and squeezed hard. "Wow, yeah, missing you too."

"Is this a good time?" I asked. "I can come back if not."

"No, this is perfect. Really. So, Trevor Black, here you are. In the flesh."

I nodded.

"No, really," he said again, "in the flesh and blood. Back here in Manitou. What's going on, man?"

"Well, I'd love to talk to you . . ."

"Sure, fine. Right. No customers, as you can see." Then he laughed hard, and I recognized that laugh. "So, shoot."

"Well, first, I'm sure you know about Bobby."

"Oh, man, so mind-blowing. Gone, man. Totally gone. What can you say? He was one of us, you know?"

"I know. We were the band."

He lit up. "The Soul Assault. Those were the days."

I hadn't heard the name of our band out loud in so long. It sounded like someone else's life. Distant. Foreign.

Augie asked, "So you're here in our fair city about that? About Bobby?"

"I am. Trying to figure things out. Why he was killed."

Augie was nodding athletically.

I continued. "And something else. Maybe unrelated, I just don't know. Are you okay talking about this?"

"Sure, yeah. Go for it."

"I'm referring to Wendell Quarlet. The guy who worked here with you. At Exotica."

"Oh, that was really disturbing. Right. Worked here. Then took my stuff. A bunch of money from the register. My wallet. My car. Goes totally nuts and drives to that place . . ."

"The city incinerator. At the landfill."

"Right," Augie shot back. His eyes were wide, his mouth drawn back, tight. "Drove there and then lit himself on fire. Insane."

"What was going on with that guy? Do you know?"

Augie leaned forward like he was going to say something, but stopped and looked around. Side to side. As if he wanted to make sure we were alone. But of course we were. Then he motioned for me to follow him through the doorway behind the counter and into the back room.

He pulled a string from a hanging bulb and the room lit up. There were boxes stacked in the corner, a rack with a few hangers full of clothes that looked like they were from a Goodwill store, and on the other side of the room there was a dusty desk.

Augie pointed to a bulletin board that hung over the desk. It was stuffed with papers and news clippings that were pinned to the corkboard. He wagged a finger for me to come closer and read them, so I did.

There was a news article about an Ohio mother who had decapitated her infant and claimed it was because of demons. And a piece about a demonic man in Gambia in West Africa who underwent an exorcism. Another one about a fire set by a man in Oklahoma, also because of demons, and a similar one about an arsonist who set fire to his cabin in Maine under the direction of supernatural forces. There were others. But buried in the middle was a newspaper article from a New York City paper with the headline, "Disbarred Attorney Is Demon Hunter for NYPD."

Augie smiled again. "You made the papers, bro."

I shrugged, then asked, "What is all this?"

"I told you," Augie said, "Wendell was bat crazy. You know, he used to work at the incinerator. That's how he got in. Anyway," Augie said, pointing to the newspaper clippings, "like I said, he was into this stuff. Very scary. For me especially, working with him."

Then he added, "And scary for you, too, Trevor."

"Why me?"

Then he pointed to the article about me on the bulletin board. "Because it was put up, right here on the board, like I said. The stuff about you and all that junk about demons. I told you, this is very scary. Look what happened to Bobby. And Wendell. I've got the shivers just talking about it."

Augie rubbed his hand over one of his arms, as

if he had been locked up in a walk-in deep freezer. "Listen, man," he said. "I could be next."

He pointed toward the shop area, and we both walked out together. I caught a closer look at the logo on his shirt: *Opperdill Real Estate Development Co.*

"So," I asked, "you own this place?"

"Not really. Just work here."

"Oh?" Then I pointed to the logo on his shirt. "You work with Opperdill, the real estate mogul?"

Augie scrunched up his lips. "Sort of. Kind of set me up. He, like, owns half of the city." Then he laughed again and quickly said, "The Opperdill Foundry. That's where your dad died, right?"

I nodded. Yet thought that the site of my father's death was a strange thing for Augie to remember. On the other hand, it was clear that over the years Augie Bedders's life had been fractured. Perhaps things for him were being viewed through shattered glass.

"Also, Augie, I am so sorry about your losing Susan the way that you did. And sorry about how long it has taken me to acknowledge your loss, or even to look you up."

"Everything's changed to the bad since then. Everything's, like, in darkness around here. You know?"

My reply was simple. "Then it's time to turn on the light."

44

While I was standing with Augie, my cell rang. I was going to let it go to voice mail, but just then a young customer and his girlfriend sauntered into Exotica and started looking around. I decided to leave Augie to his business. "I'll take this call," I told Augie, "and be back with you later. Great to see you."

I stepped outside. The man on the other end of the call was Dr. Kirby Twilliger, a pathologist in New York City. He had testified in a few homicide cases handled by Detective Dick Valentine and was calling me as a favor to Dick about my medical question.

Twilliger said he was not a religious person and didn't know much about what the Bible said about the crucifixion of Jesus. I told him that was fine and just wanted to get his medical opinion.

He started out, "In terms of the separation of blood and water through a chest wound, if that's what you want to know?"

"That, and also your opinion about which side of the body it would be easier to pierce with a sharp object like a spear or a knife in order to produce that effect."

"The right side, I would think," he said. "Opposite the side where the heart is located. A thrusting incision into the right upper quadrant chest area can produce a blood flow much easier than the left, where the heart is located, because the distended thin-walled right atrium or the ventricle could much more easily be ruptured by a sharp piercing object than the left side, which is thick-walled."

"Okay. Got it. Maybe the Roman executioners had learned that by experience," I speculated out loud. "And maybe that was SOP for them when it was time to make sure the crucified person was dead."

"Well, I hope I've been helpful."

I cut in. "Before you go, about the separation of blood and water . . ."

"Oh. Well, when they used the term *water,* they probably meant serous pleural and pericardial fluids. We call those effusions. A spear into the right side would drain the pleural effusions from the lungs first, with the blood flowing after, from the heart and then out through the wound."

I had one last question. "And the reason for blood to have flowed out of the wound?"

"Maybe there was a cardiac rupture of the heart. Torture and crucifixion would be traumatic to the extreme. I suppose that could have triggered something like an acute transmural myocardial infarction."

I thanked Dr. Twilliger for his time and clicked off. It seemed clear, at least circumstantially, that

Jesus was probably impaled with a spear after his death on his *right* side. On the other hand, Bobby had his heart removed from the *left* side, through a wound directly under the heart. And the same was true of Heather, the victim of Dunning Kamera. And also the victims of NYPD under-cover officer gone haywire, Sid Castor. And the same was true about the location of that wound I had incurred in the New York museum when Hanz Delpha attacked me.

Based on that, the attacks didn't look like a bizarre copycat of the spearing of Christ on the cross. Still, the mutilations had popped up around me in New York and then landed in my hometown of Manitou, involving my high school friend, and it made for a deeply disturbing pattern. They seemed to be following me. But then I knew Elijah had been right about that back in New York—that I would be a target. Well, I may have been a defense attorney in my former life, but now God had me playing offense instead, going after destroyers. I liked the feeling.

At the same time, the words of Rev. Cannon were echoing in my head. What he had said about certain rituals, where the heart is cut from the victim, and how he thought that those mutilations were the devil's private joke. An obscene mocking of the crucifixion of Christ and of the piercing wound to his body.

I was back in my car, and I caught sight of my

hair in the rearview mirror, untrimmed and curling over my collar. I remembered an old-school barbershop on the opposite side of the downtown area, complete with a striped barber's pole outside. I would get my hair cut there. But not just because I needed to clean up my act. There was another reason.

I parked on the street and walked up the concrete steps that were cracked and tilted. The three barbers wore the old-fashioned uniform—slick green tops, like pharmacists' smocks. They were all white-haired, and the customers were lined up in aluminum-armed chairs reading *Field & Stream* or true crime magazines. I wondered if any of them carried my articles. After almost an hour, I had my turn.

And then the real reason for my being there. During my criminal defense practice I had learned that there were certain kinds of places where you could get the real scoop on the locals. Places that gushed with a font of information. Old school– type barbershops were one such place.

After shooting the breeze with my barber about sports and television programs and some politics, I came out with the opening volley. It had been triggered by my meeting with Augie. And the logo on his shirt. And his interesting and somewhat obscure relationship with Jeffery Opperdill.

"So," I asked, "I'm a visitor, and I noticed this

Jeffery Opperdill seems to be a big real estate guy."

"Yup."

"Daddy owned the foundry down at the river?"

"Yup. Hoskins, the father, he was a good man."

"Son took it over?"

One of the other barbers guffawed loudly. My barber said, "Took it over? I guess you could call it that."

"Not good?" I remarked.

"The kid ran the foundry into the ground. Layoffs. Lawsuits. EPA came in and poked their nose around. Some talk about income tax problems. But somehow young Jeffery, he comes out of it, all of it, smelling like a rose and richer than ever."

"Jeffery sounds like an interesting man."

One of the other barbers laughed.

My barber said, more or less directed to his hair-cuttery partners, "Remember the funeral of old Hoskins Opperdill?" At that point all three of them were laughing loudly.

I didn't want to miss the inside joke. "Okay, this you have to share with me."

My barber obliged. "When Hoskins was alive he used to fill his pockets with big rolls of hundred-dollar bills. Whenever he came on a person who was down on his luck, he'd yank a bunch of hundreds out and give them to the person. No questions asked. He was like that."

Suddenly I was back at my dad's funeral. At the grave side. Hoskins Opperdill sticking a wad of hundred-dollar bills in my hand to help my family. I nodded to the barber.

"So," he continued, "then Old Man Hoskins dies, and in his will, supposedly, he says that he wants to be buried like he lived—with big rolls of money in his pockets."

"Pretty much in character," I replied.

"But there was something else," my barber said. I waited. One of his colleagues started to chuckle again. My guy continued. "Old Hoskins also said in his will that an armed guard had to be placed at his grave for a full six months after his burial."

I waited for the punch line, apparently missing the elephant that had just entered the room. I twisted my head to look at my barber, to see if he was going to finish the story.

He must have seen that I wasn't getting it, so he connected the dots. "Old Man Hoskins knew his son, knew what kind of man he was, and knew that his kid, Jeffery, would dig up the old man's grave to get the money that was buried in his pockets."

The barber went back to cutting my hair, and I meditated on that for a while.

Nice fellow, that Jeffery Opperdill.

45

I assumed I'd have to do a bit of sleuthing to locate Jeffery Opperdill, but surprisingly, when I flipped through the phone book in my hotel room I found him. He had a house on Country Club Road. Funny how many things connected to my life had happened right out there, near the edge of town.

My interest in Jeffery Opperdill had been piqued by the comments of the trio at the barbershop and also by the fact that Augie had some vague business association with him. Which seemed odd. But more important, Opperdill sounded like a guy with the knack of escaping from one gallows after another, just to end up not only surviving, but flourishing to the point of becoming a local legend. Where did that kind of magic come from?

When the GPS announced I had arrived at Opperdill's address, his house was invisible from the road. There was a big wrought-iron gate across the driveway with stone pillars on each side and an intercom. I pressed the button. After a woman with a Hispanic accent answered, I told her my name, and that I was a private investigator dealing with the Bobby Budleigh murder and needed to talk to Mr. Opperdill. I expected a roadblock. Imagine my surprise when the gates opened.

At the end of the long driveway, at least an eighth of a mile, there was a circle approach in front. His house was huge and white, and boasted a Southern mansion look to it, with four towering pillars, a big veranda wrapping around the first floor, and a second-story porch too. The house-keeper greeted me at the door and led me to a massive library paneled in mahogany. If Opperdill's goal was to impress visitors, he'd succeeded.

I was offered a drink but declined. Ten or fifteen minutes later, Jeffery Opperdill strode in with bleached-blond hair and matching mustache, but looking taller than I expected, and he was wearing a short-sleeved golf shirt that flaunted his powerful build. Looked like gym sculpting, though, not the kind of muscle that comes from hard labor. I noticed his expensive slip-on foot-wear. *Didn't they outlaw real alligator shoes?*

After going through the drill about my status as a private investigator, my personal connection with Bobby, and my interest in his murder, he asked how he could help me.

"I'm not sure," I said. "I just know that you are a very prominent member of the community. And was hoping you could give me some information."

Opperdill let out a belly laugh. And he kept on laughing for a few seconds. "Prominent? Is that how you'd describe me?"

I didn't get the joke.

He explained. "I am a controversial fellow in this city. I rub people the wrong way. But I get things done. 'Prominent'? That's what some of the businessmen in the Rotary Club are. That's not me. Better that you call me successful."

Trying to be amiable, I apologized for the mischaracterization. Then I asked how he got to know my high school friend Augie Bedders.

He sat and thought on it for a while, then brightened with a smile and shook his head. "Augie. Yeah. He worked doing odd jobs in my real estate development company for a while. I told him he needed to go to rehab and shake off the drugs before he got arrested. He didn't listen to me and ended up in jail. When he got out I leased him that little shop downtown, the Exotica. You ever go in that place? Weird. But Augie likes it. Squeezes out a living, who knows how. He's a nice guy, though. The kind that just needs a break or two. My dad, Hoskins Opperdill, used to help people out. Took me a while to realize that there was something nice in doing that. So I try to carry on that tradition myself."

"What do you know about the death of Bobby Budleigh?"

"Honestly, nothing. Except for one thing. Mr. Budleigh happened to show up along Pebble Creek one day. The reason I know that is because he was doing something close to the property line of some of my real estate acreage, not far from here. You may have passed it on the way. It's an area I want to develop commercially. Henry, my expediter at the time, spotted him and approached him. Just to make sure he wasn't trespassing."

"What did Bobby tell him?"

"That he was a nature lover. Grew up here as a boy. Was back in the area studying the land or something. I'm really not sure what else. He could have been counting salamanders for all I know."

"Did you tell the police what you just told me?"

"Sure did. In fact, when I found out what happened, I called the sheriff myself and told him about it, and that I thought he ought to know. In case it helped him catch the killer."

Jeffery shot up from his chair just then and bellowed, "I think I'll grab a bourbon. Care to join me?" I declined. He fixed his drink, asking me if I had anything else, and I said no. Then he escorted me to the front door, with the ice cubes tinkling in the glass as he walked.

"Thank you for your time, Mr. Opperdill. I'm just trying to be thorough—contact everyone who might have information about Bobby."

"As I said, always happy to help the community. Take care, Mr. Black." With that, the door shut.

As I drove back to the hotel, the sun was setting and I was ruminating on the empty feeling you get when you have just hit a dead end. Opperdill only corroborated what Ashley had already told me. That Bobby was doing some kind of environ-mental study, and that was why he was back in Manitou.

When I was in my room, I pondered my next step. Dinner, most likely, as night was falling. Then my cell rang, but from a number I didn't recognize. I picked up, and it was Ashley.

I was feeling down, so it was good to hear her voice. I started on an upbeat note. "You couldn't have called at a better time. I know we're not supposed to consort together, not officially, but how about some unofficial dinner plans?"

But she cut me off. "Where are you?"

"At the hotel."

"Get out of there."

"Why?"

"Butch is coming after you. Just heard it."

"Who?"

"Sheriff Butch Jardinsky."

"What for?"

"Did you pay a visit to Jeffery Opperdill?"

"I just left his house."

"Apparently Opperdill was on the horn seconds after you left, calling Butch."

"I didn't know that conversation was illegal in this city."

"It sounds like Opperdill is accusing you of harassing him."

I was about to make another jaded remark until the lightbulb went on. Sure, conversations were protected by the First Amendment. But from what Jeffery Opperdill told me, he had a paper-thin slice of information about Bobby showing up along Pebble Creek before his murder, which was enough to make him a potential prosecution witness. Which meant that if Opperdill postured my visit as an attempt to pressure him, I could be looking at a charge of interfering with a witness in a criminal case. A felony. Sheriff Butch Jardinsky had a hook to hang me on after all.

I saw the light. "Okay, I get it. Though I don't know why Sheriff Jardinsky is so hot on this."

"Jeffery Opperdill helped get Butch elected. He was a major contributor to his campaign. You've got to check out of that hotel right now. He'll have deputies in marked cruisers coming after you."

"I'm out of here in five minutes. How do we stay in contact?"

"You can call me back on this number."

"I didn't recognize it."

"This is my special cell. For super-secret conversations."

I couldn't resist. "Does that mean I'm super-special?"

"Knock it off, Trevor. Get moving."

She was right. But more than that, she was a friend. "You're risking a lot by telling me this. You'd better watch your step."

"Too late," Ashley said, and I gave a tight-lipped smile.

I tossed my belongings and my shaving kit in my overnight bag, snatched my laptop, and trotted down to the front desk and checked out. The desk guy was still wearing his Braves cap. I wished him well for the rest of the baseball season, then fast-walked to my rental.

I pulled out of the parking lot and headed away. In my rearview mirror I noticed a brown sheriff's deputy cruiser slowly pulling up to the lobby.

46

The task was to find a place to crash for the night. But a new hotel didn't seem like a good idea, as the deputies could put out a quick APB to every hotel in the area. I entertained the idea of simply giving myself up. What's the worst that could happen?

But the consequences were obvious. The sheriff could lock me up for a while and keep me from ever getting to the bottom of Bobby's death, while their flimsy case proceeded against a conveniently undesirable defendant who was almost certainly innocent.

I did a quick mental checklist. Bobby was my friend. God had given me a strange gift to sift out the demons among us. Because Bobby's death had the same hallmarks as the demonic killings in New York, I was in the position to put this all together, to track down the hellish source and achieve some justice for my murdered friend. Ipso facto, I must be in Manitou because I was on a mission from God.

Given that, and considering the ethical balance that had been taking place in my mind ever since my great awakening, I landed on the side of non-violent civil disobedience, at least until I came up with some answers. Then Butch Jardinsky could do whatever he wanted with me. I even entertained the thought that I could finish my magazine article in jail at that point. Joining the ranks of some notables who had penned powerful stuff behind bars. Saint Paul, the apostle. John Bunyan. Dietrich Bonhoeffer. Martin Luther King Jr.

But, no, I didn't belong in their ranks. Besides, I knew too much about jail. Not something to take lightly, especially considering that I was innocent of whatever Jeffery Opperdill had fabricated for the sheriff about our conversation. I needed a bed for the night. I knew I could always leave the jurisdiction of Manitou. The problem would be getting back in again.

Then I remembered something. The back side of the parking area behind the Covenant Retirement Village, where Rev. Cannon lived. A parking spot hidden from view.

I took a turn into an industrial area, heading for the opposite side of town, where the nursing home was located.

As I rolled down the unlighted boulevard that cut through the industrial park, I glanced in my rearview mirror. I saw some headlights about a half mile behind me, coming through the intersection that was illuminated by the overhead streetlight. It was the brown squad car of the sheriff's deputy, and he was coming up on me fast. At that point he hadn't engaged his flashing blue lights yet.

I needed to think fast. Was I committing a crime? Eluding an officer? One of my first criminal defense cases was exactly that, a guy chased by an officer over a curvy road where the officer took too long to turn on his lights. The jury acquitted my client, whereupon I advised my appreciative client to quickly plead guilty to the simple speeding ticket and be glad about it.

The boulevard took a long curve to the left, and I floored my little Fiat. But it would be another couple of miles through the industrial area before I would reach the bypass that would take me to the retirement village. By then, out there in the open, the squad car would have its lights on and would be catching up to me and pulling me over.

Funny the things that you remember in a pinch. This was the same part of the city where late at night I would recklessly race my '68 Ford Fairlane down that wide-open boulevard when I was in high school. And I remembered something else. There was a shortcut to the bypass.

It was an alley that cut in from the left, and it ran through an area full of warehouses on each side and ended up at a stop sign, right at the bypass.

The alley appeared on my left, and I slowed down slightly, then turned my headlights off and skidded into a turn with my tires squealing as I entered the alley. I gunned my little Fiat straight down the narrow asphalt lane. There were a few yellow overhead lights among the warehouses, not enough to light the alley, but at least enough to give me a shadowy sense of whether I was staying on the asphalt.

I throttled up the Fiat. To fifty miles an hour. Fifty-five. Sixty. Sixty-five. The outlines of buildings were whizzing by. *I hope the alley is clear ahead.*

I looked in my rearview mirror. There was nothing behind me. Where was the squad? Maybe he had passed the alley that I was on.

I looked ahead.

But now, only seconds to react.

Oh no . . .

In the shadows, an empty trailer with its ramp down in my direction appeared in the middle of the alley. Just feet away. No time to avoid it.

I jammed the accelerator down. My Fiat reached the ramp at aircraft takeoff speed and launched up the ramp and into the air over the trailer. I was airborne. Midair, the Fiat started to tilt backward. Impact upside down would crush me. I begged God for survival.

But instead of flipping backward, the Fiat righted itself and then came down on all four tires with a bone-crushing crash. The Fiat skipped a few times like a stone on a lake. It was still running, but something was grinding under the hood. Was it the transmission?

I hobbled to the end of the alley, then took the service road to the bypass and drove in the slow lane with my flashers on until I saw the turn-in to the nursing home. There were only a handful of cars in the front lot of the Covenant Retirement Village. I limped my Fiat to the back, behind the trees, parked it, and shut the engine off. I decided to spend the night there, and would have to figure things out in the morning.

After my stunt driving, sleep was the last thing on my mind. So I booted up my laptop.

Then, with my face bathed in the electronic glow of my laptop screen, a memory came to mind.

Maybe the Fiat crash had jarred something loose in my head. Or maybe it was my race around that familiar industrial boulevard. Or simply being back in Manitou.

Whatever the cause, at that moment it was right there in front of me, as if all those years had evaporated. And I was a teenager again, standing there in Mason Krim's house. Looking at a painting on the wall. A picture of a dead Jesus who had just been taken off the cross.

Thinking back to that painting, this one thing I was sure about: the wound depicted in the painting was on the left side of Jesus' chest, just at the heart. The same place where the horribles had mutilated all their victims.

And opposite the side where, according to Christian tradition, the spear had entered Jesus' chest, as confirmed by Dr. Twilliger.

So why did the painting in Mason Krim's house have it the other way around? And why did he have a painting like that hanging in his house in the first place? He didn't seem like the church-going type.

Luckily I found a WiFi signal on my laptop, and I discovered the retirement village wasn't particular about Internet security—no password required. I did an online search for paintings of Jesus, amazed at the massive number of depictions through the ages. I had to narrow my search. So I typed in a new keyword phrase: *Dead Christ wound wrong side.*

That was when I found it, the famous painting. And Krim had a reproduction of it hanging in his house.

I kept reading. The painting was by artist Édouard Manet back in the 1800s. It caused a scandal when it was publicly unveiled. First, because Manet attributed the inspiration for the painting to the Gospel of John, chapter 20, verse 12, which proved to be the wrong verse. In fact, that is the verse in John's Gospel that says that Mary Magdalene ran to the tomb of Jesus but merely found it empty.

But the second artistic mistake was even more fatal. Manet had depicted the wound from the soldier's stabbing on the left side of Jesus' chest, right by the heart. Critics derided Manet. The grotesque, ultra-realistic portrayal of the pale corpse of Christ, with its attribution to a Gospel verse that mentions only an empty tomb, and the placement of the wound on the wrong side of his chest could easily create the impression, right or wrong, that the artist may have had a hidden intent, a message mocking the death of Christ.

I clicked off my laptop and moved the handle in the Fiat to lower the seat as far as it would go. Maybe I could get a few hours of sleep before daybreak. I knew what had to be done the next morning. There was one more aspect of my mysterious former neighbor Mason Krim that still had to be unraveled.

47

When daylight forced my eyes open, I called in the incident to the car rental office at the Milwaukee airport, followed quickly by a call to my insurance agent.

Last was the call to a towing service. When I

had tried to start the Fiat, I was greeted with a gritty, grinding noise and a pool of oil on the cement. Not that I needed to drive anywhere soon. I had business to take care of at the Covenant Retirement Village first.

In the lobby I asked to see Rev. John Cannon. No, I told the desk person, he wasn't expecting me, but I said it was urgent.

A half hour later, Cannon and I were in the cafeteria together. I told Rev. Cannon that, yes, I would be more than happy to get him that extra serving of fruit that he wanted and another cup of coffee from the cafeteria breakfast bar. As I wandered over to fetch it for him, I wondered how exactly I was going to launch into my conversation. But with a wrecked rental car, sheriff's deputies after me, and too many unanswered questions about my friend's death, I decided to dive in feet first.

So many years ago, my strange neighbor Mason Krim had mentioned something to me, and as I spoke with Rev. Cannon it weighed heavy on my mind. Something about Lutherans. So I asked him, "Did you make any enemies back when you were pastor of your church?"

"As I told you last time . . . whenever that was . . . some of the members of Good Shepherd and the higher-ups in the synod, they were nervous when I preached about Satan and about demonic activity. And when, from time to time, I would share stories of my experiences with the powers of darkness on the mission field."

"Sure," I shot back. "But I'm actually talking about more personal kinds of enemies. People who didn't care for Lutherans like you for some reason."

He took a long time to think while he scraped the last bit of fruit out of the plastic cup with the spoon. Finally he shook his head.

I dug deeper. "Does the name Mason Krim mean anything to you?"

He put his spoon down. There was a look of recognition on his face. "How do you know that name?"

"He was a neighbor of mine."

"I haven't thought about Mason for a very long time."

"How did you know him, Rev. Cannon?"

"He and his wife, and daughter too, were members of my church."

I had to take a moment to absorb that. "Tell me more."

"How important is this?" he asked. "I'm hesitant to talk about internal church business. Or about former members . . ."

"It may be very important to my investigation."

Cannon took a moment. "Well, Mason's wife died, and then his daughter, and of course he took it very hard, understandably. And became bitter. Angry. Probably at God, I suppose. But certainly aimed it at me. That can happen following a loss. Grief is such a heavy weight to bear. Then after that, he left the church."

"His wife and daughter died, how?"

"His wife from cancer, as I recall. Then his daughter from kidney problems. As I understand it, the transplants failed."

I was trying to wrap this all together. It had to mean something. I decided to come clean about things.

"Rev. Cannon, I believe that Bobby Budleigh was a target of demonic activity. He was mutilated in the same way as others back in New York City, where I used to live." Then for the clincher. "The point is, I have this peculiar ability. And I am trying to use it in order to track down Bobby's killer."

"Peculiar? Exactly how peculiar?"

I explained in detail. After that, Cannon's face told me that my use of the word *peculiar* may have been an understatement.

"This ability of yours. I'm not sure I understand. When did it start?"

"When my life back in New York City was collapsing. My marriage. My law practice. Everything. I had this moment when I prayed, sitting there in my office. Pleading with God."

"Tell me about that. About your pleading."

"I had this client, Elijah White. His life had been turned around in a dramatic way, and he told me once how it had happened. So that day, at my desk, I remembered it and it made sense. Or at least enough sense to give it a try. So I prayed."

"Prayed about what?"

"About Jesus. And his death on the cross. As a pardon for every rotten thing I had ever done, and even for all the rotten things I had forgotten about. I sealed the deal. And somewhere in my mind I knew that I was entering into a completely different kind of transaction. An encounter. But not like any other. Sacred. The feeling that, at the other end of this, was the Creator of the universe, and that from then on things would never be the same."

"And they weren't?"

"Things changed. Including discovering my peculiar ability. To the point where I could sense when a particularly bad person had been taken over. Inhabited demonically. And then actually see them. The demons would become visible to me."

Cannon leaned back, his eyes transfixed inside the soft folds of flesh. "Become visible," he said, repeating me.

I nodded.

Cannon shrugged. "The Bible speaks of a variety of gifts that the Lord bestows when a man 'seals the deal' in his heart about Jesus the Savior, as you put it. Discernment is one of them. Discerning the spirits. But in all my days, I have never heard it manifested like this. I'm not sure what to say."

I knew it was a big deal when a preacher found himself at a loss for words.

He added, "Except to say this. You, sir, are walking on the edge. You must walk it straight."

"How do you mean?"

"God's Word is the road map. But the walking is left up to you. You are not alone. God does not fail. He empowers you. Christ in you, the everlasting hope. But the way is narrow. Sometimes daunting. A thin line, like a razor's edge."

Razor's edge. The phrase rang in my head and held no comfort. "These enemies that I encounter, they're incredibly powerful."

"Yes," Cannon agreed. "Part of the trio of forces you must deal with."

"Oh?"

"Yes. One force is the world. Created in perfection. But now corrupted."

I had experienced enough of the world to understand that one.

"Second," Cannon went on, "is the flesh. The physical organism created to operate magnificently in a perfect world. But no more, because your physical being, your reasoning, and your senses are critically flawed—all of ours, from the very beginning. Since the fall of man."

"And the third?"

"His name is Beelzebub."

For some reason that hit me funny, and I laughed at the arcane name. It sounded like something I had read in college. A deadly boring class on sixteenth-century literature.

Cannon wasn't perturbed by my reaction. He asked me, "Do you know what that name—that particular name of the devil—what it means?"

I shook my head.

"Lord of flies," he replied.

I suddenly remembered the filth and the stench and the death that was in the Manitou landfill, and the flies too. No more laughing.

Cannon added, "We are no match for him."

More bad news. But then, that was no surprise. "What hope is there, then?"

Cannon dipped his head. "There is a parable about an empty house. Jesus told the story. By 'house' he meant the body of a man. The house was swept temporarily clean by the best of human efforts. But because it was empty, unoccupied, it could still be overcome by demonic forces that are wandering in dry, barren places invisible to the eye, and seeking someone to inhabit."

I asked him again, "Where's the hope? My enemy can crush me at any moment. Or worse, take me over."

"Not anymore," he said. "Only empty, unoccupied houses are at risk. But you, on the other hand, are occupied by Christ. By God's grace, and your faith. You see, it is not what comes against you that matters. It is who occupies you that counts. Christ, the guardian of your soul."

That triggered a memory. New York. The Metropolitan Museum of Art. My bizarre chat with Hanz Delpha as he paraded himself as the curator, just before he morphed into one of the horribles and attacked me.

"The Guardian King," I said, repeating the phrase that had given Delpha convulsions when he struggled to speak it. "The Guardian King who crushes demons underfoot."

"Interesting," Cannon said. "I like that." He leaned forward and once more patted me on the arm. "Take heart. He commands powerful angels, messengers of light to guard you. Tell me about the demons you've seen."

I shuddered and told him about each hideous appearance.

"How perfect," he said in a hushed voice, "how accurate are those portraits of the demonic."

I missed his point.

He explained. "That demonic wild beast, like a hyena that breaks in from the dry, empty wilderness as a murderous scavenger. Next, the violent bird god, figurehead from a doctrine of demons, worshipped ignorantly in ages past. And last, the demon you encountered in the alley in New York, the one without eyes. Demons are blind to the truth."

At that point he raised a wrinkled hand and

pointed his finger at me. "But beware the demon who brings to you the lie that is beguiling. The most dangerous demon of all."

Then, changing directions quickly, Cannon asked how I had avoided destruction during those encounters. I told him how, during the jail conference with Dunning Kamera, one minute he had morphed into an angel of death and the next, after I cried out to heaven in a panic, he was transformed into my client again. And then there was the mysterious guard in the museum in New York who appeared from nowhere. And again, in my hotel in Manitou, a flash of light that drove a shadowy creature from my room.

"Well," he said, "that's what I mean. Rescue can be visibly spectacular or appear to be very normal. Powerful angelic protectors. In either case, it is heaven-sent."

Then he added a warning. "As you walk your razor's edge, there are two extremes. And you must avoid them both. One, wishful thinking. Wishing away all the dark realities of the supernatural war that you are in. On the other side, the equally dangerous obsession with the darkness, allowing the thought of it to dominate your life."

"My enemy is formidable. You said it yourself. The battle is enormous."

"Perhaps," he said. "But not that different, in a sense, from the daily skirmishes with the flesh and the world. The lies we tell and we brush off as trifles. The greedy, unethical deal. The prideful conceit. Manipulating others for gain. The cruel word spoken in anger. You don't realize the great gift you have been given."

"And what is that?"

"To visualize the true ugliness of the other side. To see evil and sin at its core, as repulsive as it must be to God. And then to be thankful that you have the power not to be its slave."

Before I left, Cannon thanked me for coming and talking to him. Then he added something else. Our talks had given him, he explained to me, "a chance to feel useful again."

I was glad for the old minister. But the conversation simply reinforced that there was a savage force out there with immense, almost unmatched power. And that one of them, without a soul and without mercy, had written my name in blood on my high school friend's corpse.

48

My dilemma was how to get around. I called Ashley's super-secret cell and she picked up. I explained about my damaged Fiat. She sounded nonplussed and said simply, "Jim has a second car that he doesn't need."

"Who is Jim?"

"My brother."

"You never told me you had a brother."

"You never asked."

She told me that when her brother, Jim, had left for military duty in Iraq, he had a classic car, but after he had returned he decided to buy a new car, though he still didn't want to part with his 1975 Ford Fairlane, which was an official antique. I guffawed, and Ashley asked why.

"I drove a Ford Fairlane, a '68, back when I was a wild child here in Manitou." Then I added, "You sure he trusts me with it?"

"I'll vouch for you."

Two hours later Jim came cruising into the parking lot in his Fairlane. He was much bigger than Ashley, broad-shouldered, but his face resembled hers a bit.

"Mr. Black?" Jim extended a hand, and I shook it. "Ashley's told me all about you."

"Probably a terrible shame she had to go that far." We both had a laugh over that.

As he drove me to the hardware store where he was an assistant manager and where his new car was parked, we chatted briefly before he cut to the chase. "Mr. Black, Ashley told me some of what you believe about God, the devil, heaven and hell, and all that."

"Yes, all of that. And more. Jesus came to put a stake through the heart of the devil. And death. And the grave. And sin. But he had to suffer torture and execution on a cross in order to do it.

The sacrificial lamb. But also a lion, who's going to put an end to the evil empire."

He broke into a grin. "I gotta say, I'm in tune with all that. I'm fighting the good fight, same as you." But then he added, "My sister, though? Not so much." As we pulled into a parking spot, he shut off the engine and turned to face me. "I can tell my sister has a lot of respect for you. Maybe even more than just respect. Not many men she'd go to bat for. And that pulls a lot of weight with me. But I'm still her big brother, so I have to tell you, she's had too much heartbreak already."

I inhaled a long, slow breath, picturing the brokenhearted people in my wake: Marilyn, Courtney. Women I thought I'd loved. Maybe I did love them in some way, but not the right way. "I've had some heartbreak myself. I'm not interested in causing any more—especially to your sister."

Jim nodded sharply and extended his hand. Nuff said.

"Can't believe you'd entrust a beauty like this to a stranger," I said, patting the dashboard.

"You're no stranger," he answered with a big grin. "You're a brother soldier, fighting against the dark side and standing for the light."

Before setting out in the Fairlane, I put a call in to the Opperdill Real Estate Development Company. A secretary answered. I asked for "Henry, the expediter." That was the name mentioned by Opperdill during our chat in his mini-mansion.

She paused. "I don't know who you mean."

"Sure you do," I said confidently, and repeated it. "You know, the expediter . . . Oh, wait," I added. "Henry doesn't work there anymore."

"I am afraid not," she said. "Henry Franklin's been gone for a while."

Armed with Henry's last name, I drove the Fairlane over to the Manitou courthouse again. This time to the real estate office, where I did a title check and located a piece of property out in the country that was listed to him. A plot in a trailer park.

In search of Henry Franklin, I drove along Route 59 until it intersected Shore Road. The surrounding area was remote, with open farmland. There was a storage facility on the other side of Route 59 across from the entrance to Shore Road. It had a few rows of big metal pods and some yellow safety lights and what looked like a surveillance camera on top of a metal pole.

Taking a turn down Shore Road, I found that it ultimately transitioned into a dirt driveway, marked with a rusting sign that read, *Water's Edge Trailer Park.*

But the "park" was now history. Instead, I found several cement pads with weeds growing around them and electric plugin posts for trailers, most of them bent or with wires hanging out of them.

There was a black, three-legged barbecue tipped on its side, a few broken toys, and a trash can. The trees and bushes had overgrown the area from both sides, and there was a tangle of spindly willow branches hanging down like bony fingers and growing into each other from opposite sides, creating a tunnel effect. The place was scoring high on the creep factor.

At the very end of this tunnel of unchecked growth there was a pickup truck. But it was parked in front of something that was oddly out of sync with the trashy ambience of the place: a gleaming forty-five-foot Zephyr RV with an artisan paint job. It must have cost Franklin, or someone, a bundle.

As I approached, I heard the rushing water of Little Bear River in the distance. I also noticed, not far from Franklin's luxury RV, a fire pit that was rimmed with large rocks, and around it a scattering of empty bottles and globs of melted wax. Something that had once been alive had been recently burned there, a fact that I found to be both disgusting and intriguing. I would ask Franklin about that if I had the chance, but not at first.

I knocked on the door of his RV, and Henry Franklin opened the door a few inches and asked who I was and what I wanted. He was an unshaven man in a T-shirt, somewhere in his fifties or sixties, but hard to tell because his face had a weatherworn look to it.

"I'm a private investigator looking into the Bobby Budleigh murder, and I heard that you saw Bobby shortly before the murder."

He eyed me carefully, then asked, "You from the defense lawyers?"

I put on my best placid, reassuring face. "I'm neither with the defense nor with the prosecution. I'm just after the truth, which is the least I could do for my old school pal Bobby. Is there anything you can tell me about your conversa-tion with him?"

He said, simply, "I don't know where you got your information."

"Didn't you talk to Bobby Budleigh, the murder victim?"

"Yeah."

"Shortly before the murder?"

He snorted. "Course not."

"Then when?"

"A bunch of months before I read about it, you know, about how they found his body by the creek."

"Pebble Creek?"

"Yeah."

"Is that where you met him, several months before?"

"Listen, mister, I don't know what you're after."

"But it was in that area, right? Near the boundary line of the land owned by Opperdill Real Estate Development Company?"

He nodded, then began to close the door slightly. But then something must have snapped in his head, and he suddenly swung open the door and stepped halfway out. "Are you from Opperdill?"

I assured him that I wasn't there on behalf of his former employer. Then I told him that what I really wanted to know was why Bobby was out there in the first place.

Franklin stared me down. Finally he gave me one word. "Environmental." There it was again, the same thing I had heard before.

"Bobby said that to you?"

"Yup."

"Anything else?"

"Can't remember." Then he added, "I got to go . . . ," and started to close the door again.

I shouted through the two-inch opening, "You know this makes you a witness in the murder case."

"So what?"

"It means the defense is going to dig up any dirt they can against you. It's called impeachment. And they'll make it very public. Are you ready for that?"

"So?" Franklin said, and then twisted his head slightly to one side like he had a kink in his neck. "I got nothing to hide."

I glanced over at the fire pit.

"Really?" I said.

Franklin reversed directions and was coming

out the door again. He was squinting and rotating his head some more. I am guessing that he hadn't taken me for someone who knew a few things about criminal law. He shouted, "Get off my property."

I motioned back to the fire pit and the charred remains in the middle of it. "By the way, is that the carcass of a dog that was burned in that pit?"

"What's it to you?"

"Just curious." Then I added, "Your dog?"

I could see the wheels turning. He had to give me some kind of dodge, anything, or else he'd have to face the animal warden. "Sick dog. Old. Put him out of his misery."

I nodded. "Just seems odd, that's all."

Henry Franklin went even more slit-eyed. "Why's that?"

I finished. "You know, because of those long knives sticking out of that dog's side. Three of them. And with ornate handles too."

Franklin barked back. "Like I said, sick dog. Don't have money for vet bills."

I couldn't resist one last question. "How did you come by this fancy RV?"

His jugular was pumping when he yelled, "Get outta here!"

As I drove away, I noticed in my rearview mirror that Franklin was bending over the dead dog in the fire pit, yanking the knives out of the carcass.

When I drove to the end of Shore Road and turned onto Route 59, I noticed once again the yellow security lights of the storage facility across the road. And I made a point again of checking out the security camera on top of the pole.

But I was still thinking about Franklin's place back there. An occult-looking fire pit complete with melted candles and a sacrificed dog. Henry Franklin's outpost was oppressive. Like visiting an ancient place made famous for violence or defilement. Not knowing the particulars, I was somehow certain that evil resided there.

49

I texted a message to Ashley's super-private cell number. I apologized for bugging her on "official" business contrary to Sheriff Butch Jardinsky's directive, but I needed to know what Henry Franklin told the police about Bobby Budleigh's explanation for tromping around the Pebble Creek area in Manitou.

A few minutes later I received the reply. Yes, Mr. Black, you should apologize. But okay, just this once: the supplemental statement from Franklin to our department quoted Bobby Budleigh as telling him that he was there on environmental business. So, you're welcome.

That matched what both Jeffery Opperdill and

Henry Franklin had told me. And it moved me not an inch further in solving Bobby's murder.

I was coming up with zero. I tried another angle.

Okay, just one more. In return, I will take you out to another fine dining experience. Money is no object (not literally). Storage facility at the intersection of Route 59 & Shore Road. Surveillance camera pointing toward the entrance to Shore Road. Let's check license plates of the cars going in/out of Shore Road. Begin a day or two before Wendell Quarlet's death & end a few days after that. FYI—Shore Road only leads to one house, the RV home of Henry Franklin in a weird (spooky) setup in a former trailer park. I have a feeling about this.

A feeling? You have to be kidding. Getting a warrant for the surveillance footage of a private company? Based on what?

Franklin was the only witness having contact with Bobby Budleigh during his prior visit to Manitou a few months before his death. When

Bobby returned the second time, just recently, he was murdered. Let's identify who has been visiting Henry Franklin. Find out the company he keeps.

It took thirty seconds for Ashley to respond this time.

Seriously?

How could I reply to that?

Forty-five minutes later Ashley texted me back, saying she would look into it, but I shouldn't count on anything because it was a real stretch, and if she lost her job because of me, she would come looking for me, and when she did, she would come "locked and loaded . . ."

It was impossible to tell whether she was joking.

I checked into the YMCA in Manitou, an old six-story building that had tiny rooms for rent with one communal bathroom per floor. I was hoping that the deputies, if they were still looking for me, would pass over that kind of place. They'd assume it would be below the dignity of a former high-priced lawyer from New York City to stay at the Y. Once upon a time, they'd have been right.

In my little room I spent that evening reviewing my situation.

Bobby's death was not just another homicide. I,

of all people, knew better. The circumstantial facts about his murder and mutilation were part of a blood trail. And it traced all the way back to New York City and to the nasty men there who had been occupied by fallen creatures. But there was still more, and the dark specter that had appeared in my hotel room proved it. They were tracking me. Exactly as Elijah had said.

I had Elijah's Bible in hand, which by then was my Bible, actually, so I buckled down to study. I counted about a hundred New Testament mentions of demonic activity. Jesus exorcised demons at will, and they knew him by name, and they knew the names of some of his followers too. Sometimes they came in legions. Sometimes alone. Nonphysical beings, wandering in a state of invisible, forsaken desolation, seeking humans to inhabit. Why was that? I wasn't sure. Maybe for relief, or to enlarge their power. But I had met them myself. I knew their hideous power.

I also knew that the modern scientific approach rejected all of that and resorted to psychology or sociology to explain it. Demon activity passed off as mental illness or social dysfunction, or even drug addiction. I didn't have the expertise to parse that all out. Except to conclude that the science could not explain it. Behind the physical, empirical world was an unseen spiritual one. I was certain of that, not only from what I had seen and heard and now knew to be true from the surety of my own journey, but also from what was written there, in black-and-white, in the New Testament accounts from the testimony of multiple eye-witnesses.

The question was next steps. My ten-by-ten room in the YMCA was feeling too cramped, so I took the fire exit stairs down to the first-floor lobby to get some air. Two of the local residents of the Y were playing a lively game of foosball at a game table. I picked up a copy of the local newspaper from the stack on the lobby desk and walked outside as I leafed through the first few pages.

On page two, I ran into the story about the murder charges against Donny Ray Borzsted. A preliminary hearing was scheduled in his case for the next day, with Judge Martha Prescott presiding. The timing of my reading the article couldn't be an accident.

My next move was painfully obvious. Preliminary hearings are usually open to the public. As an ex–criminal defense attorney, I needed to be there. I couldn't rely on the details in newspaper reports or on secondhand information from Ashley, even if she was free to share it with me. I needed to hear the testimony myself and then sort it out. Decide, once and for all, if someone other than Borzsted was Bobby's killer as I suspected.

Which raised the issue of Sheriff Butch

Jardinsky's order for my apprehension. The courtroom would be packed for the prelim. Could I slip through the police security check at the front door unnoticed and then seat myself inconspicuously in the crowded courtroom?

The more I thought on it, the nuttier it sounded. The easy thing would be to stay away from a courthouse full of police and prosecution lawyers. That way I could remain free, presumably to get to the truth. But how was I going to do that if I avoided getting a front-row view of the prosecution's evidence involving Bobby's death?

One alternative was good, but risky. The other was safe, but ineffectual.

As I looked at the cars passing in the night along Grant Avenue, the newspaper clutched in my hand, I needed a tiebreaker.

Minutes went by. More car lights cruising past. The slow, lazy sound of bugs in the night gathering at the portico light where I was standing. Then things cleared in my head.

In Chicago I told Dan Hoover that I was on a mission from God, and if that was true, and if I had to be in that courtroom the next day, then okay, done. Decision made. It was time to put faith into action.

50

When I arrived at the Manitou courthouse the next day, there was good news. The city police were doing the security checks at the front entrance. I knew that Sheriff Jardinsky had sent the request for my apprehension to those officers, too, not just to his county sheriff's deputies. But even so, different law enforcement agencies had different priorities. Possibly less vigilance at the court-house entrance. Maybe I could slip through.

I stood in the X-ray machine line. I was carrying no coins. Nothing to cause a delay. The only thing to toss into the bowl on the conveyor belt would be car keys. I waited. A police officer beckoned me through the doorframe of the body scanner. I passed through without a hitch. The officer took a long look at me.

Then he waved me through.

I headed for the second floor, breathing easier. A crowd was squeezing in, and I joined them, deliberately picking an empty spot toward the back. It was in the middle of a bench already jammed with court watchers, and I had to step over legs and shoes to get there.

Howard Taggley, the public defender, was already seated at the counsel's table on the left. Donny Ray was sitting next to him in an ill-fitting suit that the defense must have provided for him. At the prosecution table was Steve Sandusky, the deputy DA. I had checked out Sandusky's credentials online before going to sleep at the YMCA the night before. He was a veteran prosecutor who obviously knew his craft.

At this stage, the burden of proof is never high for the prosecution. At the preliminary hearing Sandusky only needed to show that a homicide had probably occurred and that Donny Ray was probably the one who had committed it, and once that low threshold was crossed, then, next stop, pretrial motions and the inevitable march toward a jury trial.

And if the case against Donny Ray didn't get booted and he was bound over for trial, the sheriff's department would have no motivation to search for another killer. The case against Donny Ray would drag on. Delays. More motions. I knew the drill. Meanwhile the trail to Bobby's murderer would grow cold. And for Butch Jardinsky, what little tolerance he had left for my independent investigation would come to a screeching halt. Bobby deserved better. The truth, not a show trial.

The white-haired judge for the preliminary, Martha Prescott, appeared at the bench and announced the case in her soft voice.

Sandusky began his case predictably, putting on the senior investigating deputy who was first on the scene along with his partner. He described the initial call from some nature lovers who had been looking for wildflowers and berries and found a dead body instead.

The deputies arrived and then slogged through the marshy land along Pebble Creek until they found Bobby, naked from the waist up, on the bank of that tiny tributary of the Little Bear River. Next, the description of the corpse. The gunshot wound to the head. The gaping slash across the left side of his chest, below the heart.

Then testimony from the pathologist who did the autopsy. Determining it to be a death by the hand of another. A graphic explanation of the entrance wound in the back of the head, execution style. Description of the post-death torso wound through which the heart of the victim had been removed. No evidence of a struggle on Bobby's corpse: his fingernails showed no signs of having scraped at the flesh of the assailant—thus, no DNA—and no other bruises or abrasions indicating a fight with his aggressor.

On the surface, the courtroom rhetoric should have plucked a chord familiar to my trial lawyer's ear. But this time when they talked about "the victim," they were referring to my high school friend. As the testimony droned on mechanically, I would rather have been somewhere else.

The second-to-last witness was Colin Jennings, the investigating detective who searched the home of Donny Ray and found a handgun on the premises. He was a decisive, articulate, reliable witness. Detective Jennings ended by describing the size 12 Sierra Trading Post hiking boots that he found in Donny Ray's closet. Taggley calmly rose to his feet and said he would stipulate that the prints in the mud found at the crime scene were from a size 12 Sierra Trading Post boot.

Then Taggley went to town cross-examining Jennings. Several bullets fired at the prosecution's case. Each time, Taggley hit the target.

Did those boots bear any trace whatsoever of mud, soil sample, or vegetation of the types that exist in the Pebble Creek area?

No.

Is it a fact that the bullet that killed Bobby Budleigh came from a nine-millimeter handgun?

Yes.

Did you ever find such a weapon in Donny Ray's apartment?

No.

Was the handgun in Donny Ray's apartment a different weapon, namely a thirty-eight caliber?

Yes.

Boom.

The final witness for the prosecution was Ada Johnson, the middle-aged woman who had driven by Pebble Creek when the sun was going down on the night of the murder. In her testimony she said that in the dusky last light of day she glanced to the right and noticed a tall man with long hair walking next to a shorter man, and they both were stepping through the high grass of the open field that ran adjacent to the creek. The short man, Bobby, turned around and looked at her car, and she recognized his face from a later viewing of his photograph in the sheriff's department.

Sandusky asked her, "And the other man, the taller one you saw that night, is he in the courtroom today?"

She nodded and responded, "Yes, sir."

"Can you point him out?"

Ada pointed to Donny Ray and described the clothes he was now wearing in court. Judge Prescott announced that the defendant had been identified.

Taggley launched into his cross.

"Mrs. Johnson, how fast were you driving that night on that section of the road when you saw the two men?"

"Forty, maybe slightly faster."

"It was getting dark?"

"Sun just beginning to set. I'd call it dusk."

"You were able to identify Bobby Budleigh because he turned around and you could see his face?"

"That's right."

"That taller man next to him, though, he never turned around, right?"

A pause as Ada looked over at the prosecutor. At the bench, Judge Prescott leaned toward her.

"Mrs. Johnson, don't look to the deputy district attorney for the answer. Either you know the answer or you don't. Do you understand the question?"

"I do, Your Honor."

"What is your answer?" the judge asked.

Another pause. "I'm sorry, I don't recall. Don't remember if he turned around."

Taggley jumped on that. "Would you agree that while you identified the defendant in this courtroom just now, you actually have an uncertain memory regarding whether you saw his face that night or not?"

"I'm mixed up."

"Then how," Taggley asked, "did you know to point to Mr. Borzsted just now?"

"From the photographs at the sheriff's office."

"You mean the visit to the sheriff's office when they showed you several photographs of several different men?"

"Yes, that's it."

"But is it true that you saw Donny Ray's picture in the local newspaper a few months before? In an article about some prison inmates from Manitou who had recently been paroled?"

She bobbed her head a bit. "I think so."

"And that fixed Donny Ray's face in your mind?"

"Uh, well, no, I can't say that's what happened."

"Then let's go to your meeting in the sheriff's office. That is when you pointed to one photograph of one man and you said that he was the taller man with long hair who you had seen that night out by the country club and by Pebble Creek, right?"

"Right."

"But then the deputies asked you if you were sure, and you said, 'No, I am not sure.' "

"I guess that's what happened."

"Then you pointed to another photograph of a different man, and you said, 'That's him,' right?"

"Yes."

"And when asked if you were certain, you said once again, 'No, I'm not.' "

She tilted her head. "Something like that, yes."

"Then," Taggley said, going in for the kill, "finally, you pointed to a third photo of a third man—this time it was the photo of the defendant, Donny Ray Borzsted—and you said that he was the taller man with long hair that you saw that night?"

She nodded. "That's exactly right."

"But that time, after saying that, the deputy who was talking to you, he never asked you if you were certain about that particular photo, unlike the other photos, right?"

Ada squirmed a bit in the witness chair. "I'm not sure . . . Maybe that's true."

"The truth is, Mrs. Johnson, you really aren't sure whether the defendant seated here is the man that you saw on that early evening at sunset in dusky light conditions, while you were driving by the scene going forty miles per hour, right?"

The witness looked to the judge.

Judge Prescott said, "The truth, Mrs. Johnson, as you can best recall it, and if you cannot answer, simply say so."

Several seconds ticked by in silence. Finally Ada Johnson said, "I just can't be sure what I remember about that taller man. But I feel pretty sure that the defendant right there is the man I saw that night. He's the right height, I guess. And hair too."

Taggley quit while he was ahead. On redirect Sandusky labored to rehabilitate his witness, with moderate success.

The state rested. Then the defense rested, with Taggley having called no witnesses of his own. Smart move.

Judge Prescott was pondering something up there on the bench, her hands folded and her gaze seeming to travel beyond the courtroom. Then she asked the prosecutor a question. "Mr. Sandusky, help me out here. What exactly is the prosecution's theory of this case?"

Nothing compelled the prosecutor to explain it at that early stage of the case. But I was betting that the prosecution would make the effort anyway. I was right. They needed to show the judge they were the side wearing the white hat. Nothing to hide.

Sandusky rose to his feet, smiling confidently. "That there is probable cause to believe that the defendant is the man who committed this crime. Though he has filed a notice of alibi, he has offered no alibi evidence yet that he was somewhere else at the time of the crime. There's the fact that he has been identified by Mrs. Johnson. He owns boots of the type that left boot marks at the crime scene. He is a gun owner, and a bullet from a handgun was found in the back of the victim's head."

"But what's your theory," the judge snapped, "on why Dr. Bobby Budleigh was tramping around that part of Pebble Creek that early evening?"

"He is an environmental expert. And a former resident of Manitou."

"So?"

"Well, our information is that a few months before, he had told a witness by the name of Henry Franklin that he was walking around in that area because of an 'environmental' reason."

"Namely, what?"

"We aren't certain, Your Honor. But just yesterday Mrs. Budleigh, the victim's wife, came across an e-mail on her late husband's computer and informed us of its existence."

"And?"

"The e-mail was to his partner in his environmental consulting business explaining that he was going back to Manitou a second time and indicating why."

Silence. Sandusky looked down at his file, apparently reviewing the e-mail. I was about to hear, at last, the best evidence of why Bobby had returned to Manitou.

"Unfortunately," Sandusky continued, "the e-mail was a little vague."

"Give it a try, Mr. Sandusky," the judge said. "And the defense needn't worry, Mr. Taggley," the judge went on. "This information is outside the record at this preliminary, so it will play no part in my decision. Now, Mr. Sandusky, proceed."

"The e-mail simply said, 'I will be out of town for a week. Heading back to my hometown of Manitou, Wisconsin. Primarily business, but also very personal.'"

"That's it?" the judge asked.

Sandusky said that was it.

"I know you aren't required," the judge went on, "to prove motive for the crime. But regardless, any theory of motive, Mr. Sandusky?"

The deputy district attorney shook his head. "Not at this time, Your Honor."

The judge was poker-faced when she noted, "No matter. As we all know, motive is not essential. Moreover, at this stage of the case, it doesn't take much to satisfy the low burden of proof. Just probability. Nothing more. Thank you for elaborating, Mr. Sandusky."

The prosecution and defense summed up. Nothing new. I was getting the uneasy feeling that the prosecution's case against Donny Ray's case may have crossed over the necessary threshold, though just barely. If that was true, my ability to keep digging would be stymied.

Judge Prescott adjourned the hearing for ten minutes and whisked off the bench and through the door to her chambers, leaving the gathered crowd to wait in awkward murmurs.

Judge Prescott returned to the bench, tidying up her court file in front of her, framing it with her two hands like a picture, first top and bottom, then side to side. She looked out at the courtroom. "Anything else before I make my ruling?"

Both counsel agreed there was nothing more to add. The judge began to summarize the evidence dispassionately. I listened for some clue where she was heading. Some glimmer. A turn of a phrase. But the judge was giving me nothing.

Until she announced her ruling. "The state's case, at this preliminary stage," she said, "is riddled with problems. The failure to show, within the range of reasonable probabilities, any concrete link between the defendant's gun, or the defendant's boots, or even the defendant's presence, and the crime itself or the crime scene." She stopped talking. I stopped breathing.

Then she finished. "Those missing links are

not just material. They are fatal. Accordingly," Judge Prescott announced, "I am dismissing the criminal complaint against the defendant, Donny Ray Borzsted. But I am dismissing it *without* prejudice. The state can refile a criminal complaint if additional evidence is presented."

Donny Ray was looking up at the ceiling with a big grin on his face. But the thrill of victory wouldn't last long.

Sandusky was on his feet. He announced that the probation department had issued a hold against Donny Ray for possession of a firearm, a violation of the terms of his probation. Sandusky turned to look Donny Ray in the eye. "We ask that the defendant be held in jail until that probation revocation hearing. I'm confident that Mr. Borzsted will be found in violation and shipped back to prison where he belongs."

Judge Prescott didn't give it a second thought. "Motion to detain defendant in custody in the county jail pending the probation hearing is granted." Then she gaveled the hearing to a close. Everyone rose.

The crowded courtroom began to disperse as onlookers moved toward the aisles to leave. My row was packed in tight, and I had to wait for the others to file out. That is when I noticed a deputy with a sidearm standing in the aisle. He pointed his finger in my direction. "You need to come with me, Mr. Black," he said as the court watchers quickly shuffled out of my row, some of them glancing back at me with suspicion. The jig was up.

Up at the front, Taggley was on his feet. And so was Donny Ray, who I noticed had been unshackled during the hearing. A young deputy approached him and reached out with the cuffs as Donny Ray held his wrists out.

But in that next fraction of a second, things went berserk.

Donny Ray lunged for the deputy's handgun, and an instant later he had it in his hand, and the deputy was struggling with him while the service revolver was pointed into the air. Shrieks and screams from the people in the courtroom. Taggley tripped over his chair at counsel's table in a frantic attempt to get away from the fracas.

The deputy by me had unholstered his service handgun and was blowing through the crowd, running to the front, his weapon dropped to his side as he reached for the stunner on his belt with his other hand and yelled for everyone to get down.

A moment later he was on top of Donny Ray and zapping him in the neck with his stun gun. Donny Ray dropped like a sack of potatoes.

More uniformed officers poured into the courtroom. Onlookers were ordered to stay in the courtroom as the shackled and dazed Donny Ray Borzsted was dragged out.

For an hour, deputies filed through the court-room taking down names and addresses from each of us, together with the accounts of what we had just witnessed.

As the room was beginning to thin out, the deputy who had disabled Donny Ray approached me.

"Great work, Deputy," I said. "You deserve a commendation. At a minimum." Then, resigned to the inevitable, I told him that I was ready to go with him.

He looked around the room. "We still have to finish our reports here. Tell you what, you can take off. I'm sure we can find you." Then he said with a smirk, "If not, Detective Ashley Linderman will obviously know where you are."

I wondered at the locker-room banter that had to be going on in the sheriff's department about the two of us.

Driving back to the YMCA, it struck me that I was no longer on the run. I could find a nicer place to stay for the night. After giving it some thought, though, I decided against it. There was something about the dormitory aura of my tiny room at the Y and the stark realism of the place, even the common bathroom at the end of the hall that we all used. It seemed strangely right for another night. A kind of monastery atmosphere.

Which would make me the monk tasked with hunting down a ruthless demon. But I was convinced that Donny Ray, nasty as he and his brother Karlin were, was not one of them.

51

The next morning, I walked until I found a donut and coffee place called The Java Shop a few blocks from the YMCA, then hunkered down to a cinnamon twist and a double espresso, joining the host of patrons in their twenties and thirties who had their laptops open.

Mine was open to the Manitou High School class reunion Facebook page. I was on an uncharted fishing expedition, trying to find out why Bobby had been a target. Looking for anything.

I scanned backward through the postings, looking for a unifying thread regarding Bobby Budleigh. There were multiple messages grieving over Bobby's murder. And epithets against the vile person responsible for it, whoever it was.

One post in particular clicked the light on for me. It was from Jerry Cunningham, who I didn't know, but who ended up marrying Kelly Pillter, a classmate of mine. Jerry described himself as a biologist with an interest in ecology. He wrote that he happened to have read a research paper that Bobby wrote on the subject of wetlands, a personal interest of Jerry's, so he contacted Bobby, praised his work, and said that the Pebble Creek area of Manitou, Bobby's old stomping ground, would be a prime area for further research on the value of wetlands to the local environment.

Jerry concluded by writing, "Please forgive me, all, if somehow Bobby's decision to take me up on my idea to investigate the Pebble Creek marsh area ended up leading to his death."

A long trail of postings resulted from that, assuring Jerry that he shouldn't feel guilty.

Jerry filled in some of the blanks in Bobby's e-mail that his wife had discovered, the one mentioned in Judge Prescott's courtroom. "Primarily business, but very personal." There it was. He had returned to Manitou, and to his roots, to do some seemingly innocuous research on the wetlands along Pebble Creek. But it didn't explain exactly why Bobby had made a follow-up trip to the area—one that ended with a bullet in his head.

I glanced over the high school class Facebook page once again, just to make sure I had caught everything. In the process, my mind wandered through high school memories and eventually landed on Marilyn Parlow.

I sat there at the high-top table with my empty espresso cup and the screen of my laptop staring at me.

Marilyn's death was sinking in. And I thought about my much younger longings for Marilyn, our ill-conceived tryst that night in my college dorm room, and the termination of the life that would have been the one valuable thing, the only good thing, that could have resulted from any of it.

Reaching for my cell, I texted Ashley, At The Java Shop for another 30 min. or so. Let's talk? Just personal, not business.

I ordered a second espresso and read one of the newspapers that had already been rifled through, but the front page was still intact, containing an above-the-fold account of the court hearing from the day before, and, of course, Donny Ray's attempt to escape.

I slowly leafed through the rest, then laid the paper down and stepped over to the counter to pick up my espresso, which was now ready. A familiar female voice at the *Order Here* station next to me at the counter was putting in for a vanilla latte.

I turned to Ashley. "Latte?" I said. "That's a bit lacy and fluffy for a tough detective, isn't it?"

She replied, "They know me here. They spike it with a triple shot of espresso."

"Too strong for me," I said with a smirk.

"Don't patronize me, Trevor." She looked around. "Where are you sitting?"

I pointed to the high-top table.

The two of us sat down. Then she asked, "What's so personal?"

I took a moment. "You were once very up-front with me about your GAD diagnosis. That took courage. Thinking back, I never told you anything personal about me."

She said, "Every day's a new day."

"Right. So here I am. And you too. Thanks for coming."

Then I launched into my past, laying it all on the table. My whirlwind marriage to Courtney and our inability to have children; how we'd grown distant and cold. I got emotional when I told her about Courtney's tragic death, my subsequent bottoming-out, and all the regrets I'd discovered about that relationship in the time since I'd started following Jesus—wishing I'd been a better husband, a better person. I even dug further into the past, including my backstory with Marilyn. How Marilyn had become pregnant after our one-night stand back in college, had an abortion with my passive support, and I'd never heard from her again. Then how I'd just learned of Marilyn's death, yet another person in my life gone forever.

Ashley asked a lot of questions. First about Courtney—how long we were married. Whether I still thought about her. Of course I did, and I still struggled with regret. And also about Marilyn, our short-lived relationship and some strangely detailed questions about the pregnancy and the dates when it all had happened.

"Regrets," Ashley said. "Those will kill you."

"Right."

"And your feelings about Marilyn now?"

"Truly sorry she's gone, obviously. But not because I ever thought we could get together again. Or should. Or wanted to, because I didn't."

"That's important to hear." She said that with a serious tone, with a kind of finality to it.

I wanted to explore that. "So, that's important to you?"

"Yes, it is."

"Can you expand on that?"

She laughed loudly. "Sorry, but for some reason that sounds like a direct-examination question from a trial lawyer."

I laughed too. "Right. Okay. Look, anything you have to say about me is high priority because I think very highly of you. In fact, I have been thinking about you a lot."

"Then we have something in common," she said. "You know, Trevor, you blow into town out of nowhere, suck me into this bizarre case . . ."

"Me? That's not how I remember it. Butch Jardinsky told me on day one that you were the detective assigned to the case."

"Not true," she shot back. "That didn't happen until after he talked to you for the first time. Then he took Detective Colin Jennings off the case and put me in charge of the investigation."

"Why?"

"It seemed weird at first until I figured out the reason. Colin's a veteran detective. Sharp and aggressive and was doing a really intensive investigation into Bobby Budleigh's death. He was pushing it hard. Leaving no stone unturned in the short time that he was in charge. Then you come to Manitou and meet with Butch, and then suddenly Colin's out and I'm in. That's how it happened."

"So, again, what's behind that?"

"This case was already sensational by Manitou standards, and I think Butch saw it escalating when a former New York City criminal defense attorney showed up and started asking questions."

"But why you?"

Ashley's animation was building. "Because I'm a woman. Butch thought I would follow orders like a good little girl and wouldn't stick my nose in where it didn't belong, which, for some reason, was the end result that Butch was after. On the other hand, Butch feared that Colin would push the investigation hard. Because Colin's a man. Of course."

"Obviously Butch had you pegged wrong."

"Tell me about it." She was staring down at her latte, which she had cupped between her hands. Then she said, "But now Butch knows I won't rest until I hit pay dirt in solving Bobby Budleigh's murder. And as a result, he's pushing back."

"Meaning?"

"Butch is threatening to suspend me from the force. He found out about my GAD diagnosis somehow, my taking medication, the whole shootin' match. None of which I ever told anyone in the department. He's saying I'm unfit for service. Plus, he thinks I compromised this investigation by working too closely with you."

"That's obscene. A rotten way to treat a hero like you. I'm sorry. I feel responsible."

"No, Trevor. It's not about you. It's all about Butch." Then she reached out and squeezed my hand. "I don't know what any of this means about us. Except you're probably the most unique guy I've ever met. My brother, who only met you once, is now totally hyped about how I need to get to know you better." She tilted her head to the side slightly. "Honestly, I think it's about the God thing, the Jesus business that the two of you seem to have in common."

Then there was a sly grin on her face. "Just reassure me. You aren't into snake handling, or trances, or levitating, or anything like that, are you?"

"Well, I've got this friend, Elijah White, who has dreams about me, and he says they are messages from God. Does that count?"

"Not even close. Too tame." Then Ashley became intense. "Hey. What was the reason you were checking out the Facebook page of your high school class?"

I explained it all. "I think I found out why Bobby may have come back to Manitou. Simply to check out the wetlands along Pebble Creek for a research subject he specializes in."

"How does that give us anything on his murder?"

"It doesn't." Then I thought about something else. "I keep mulling over the pieces in this case, trying to make them fit. That area along Pebble Creek abuts a real estate development area owned by Jeffery Opperdill. One of Opperdill's men, Henry Franklin, ran into Bobby and asked what he was doing."

She asked, "Was Bobby's research a threat to Opperdill?"

"Not that I know of. The point is that Franklin reported to Opperdill that Bobby was in the area."

"But we already knew that," she said. "Opperdill informed Butch Jardinsky about it after the murder became public."

I agreed. "Opperdill told me that too." Then I added, "Maybe Bobby posed some kind of threat to Opperdill that we've missed. I was getting a haircut downtown and I heard the local scuttlebutt that the Environmental Protection Agency was investigating Opperdill."

Ashley lit up. "I have a contact in the regional office for the EPA, a sort of middle-level staffer. There was an EPA case involving illegal dumping in our area. I ended up becoming the Manitou law enforcement liaison with the EPA."

"So," I said, wanting to make things very clear,

"are we moving into the business side of things now, official law enforcement matters? Despite Sheriff Butch's warnings?"

"Absolutely."

"Terrific. I'd like to hear what your contact has to say about Opperdill. Oh, and one other thing. Have you come up with anything on the license plates of the cars going in and out of Henry Franklin's trailer park?"

"I had the subpoena served for the surveillance camera footage of that storage facility. We should hear anytime. Possibly as early as today."

"Good."

Ashley was eyeing me. "What else is on your mind?"

"I get the feeling that Bobby walked into a trap."

"Spell that out," she said.

"Are you sure? It's the kind of story that once upon a time you said you didn't want to hear."

I looked at Ashley, and she was staring into my eyes, maybe trying to decide if I was actually serious about what I was about to tell her.

I made it plain. "What I'm learning is that demons leave a trail, like slugs leave slime. Except in blood. There is a demonic trail from New York to Manitou. And I'm following it," I told her. "I'm not stopping until I expose the dark, twisted center of this. Anyway," I continued, figuring I'd better ease up, "thanks for risking so much. For putting your job on the line for me."

She cocked her head and grinned. "Yeah, well, it's not all about you, you know." She reached over the table and patted my hand. But just as quick, Ashley dropped the smile. "I don't know about this supernatural obsession of yours. Just be careful." Then, like an afterthought, "Oh, and about the old girlfriend, Marilyn, and the ill-fated pregnancy . . ." She took a second or two, then added, "I've got a hunch."

52

When I was back in my borrowed Ford Fairlane, I had a brainstorm. I put in a call to defense attorney Howard Taggley, knowing at that point he was probably locked in an inescapable conflict of interest, forced to withdraw from representing Donny Ray because he was now an eyewitness to his own client's criminal chaos in Judge Prescott's courtroom. As a result, he might play it cagey with me. But there was also Judge Prescott's comment at the end of the hearing. I could use that.

The public defender took my call, and I asked whether he had gained any information in his defense of Donny Ray about the identity of the real killer. But I cushioned it with a qualification. "Of course, if it is privileged by the attorney-client relationship, I know you won't be able to share it."

"Privileged?" Taggley said, repeating me. "No, it's not privileged. My client authorized me to release it to the other side, to the deputy district attorney. So we waived any privilege."

"When was that?"

"Just before the preliminary hearing. I was betting that they knew the case against Donny Ray was flimsy, so I sweetened the deal by handing over some exculpatory information about other possible killers. But when I told it to Prosecutor Sandusky, he said it was not compelling enough to drop the charges against Donny Ray. Hence the preliminary hearing that ensued. And the victory in Donny Ray's favor."

"And his Wild West fight in the courtroom."

Taggley started to pull the drawbridge up. "I can't comment on that. I now find myself a potential witness for the prosecution in the next round of charges against Donny Ray regarding his conduct in Judge Prescott's courtroom. That places me in an uncomfortable position, as you can imagine."

No more hedging. I asked him, "What did you tell the deputy DA about Bobby Budleigh's real killer?"

There was a half minute of silence, at least. Then Taggley finally said, "Why would I share that with you, Mr. Black? You're an outsider to this proceeding. You don't have legal standing."

"What I have," I shot back, "is moral conviction. My high school friend was shot in the head and then dissected in a swamp. You and I know that Donny Ray didn't do it. Which means the person responsible is still out there. You know my history, and you may not believe it, but there are forces at work here much meaner and much scarier than the Borzsted brothers. I am telling you right now, I'm not just some man with a personal vendetta; God himself has sent me on a mission to stop the fiend who did it."

More silence. Then I added, "And by the way, we both know that at the end of the hearing Judge Prescott dismissed the homicide case against Donny Ray *without prejudice*. The charges could be resurrected against your former client at any time. How would Donny Ray feel about you standing in the way of my campaign to exonerate him?"

That did it. The drawbridge came down again. Taggley began talking. "I told Sandusky exactly what Donny Ray had confided to me. Just rumors. Something he heard while he was in jail awaiting the preliminary hearing. Gossip among some of the other inmates."

"Gossip, like what?"

"About some small group in Manitou called the Club."

"What about it?"

"It wasn't clear. But it wasn't good. They were powerful."

"Powerful how? Rich people? Political insiders in town?"

"Not like that, exactly. Sounded like something else."

"Like . . ."

Taggley hedged. "I'm not going to speculate."

"So about this 'club'—what was the point?"

"They were involved in your friend's death."

"What are the details?"

"Can't give you any because I don't have any," Taggley said. "Except for the leader of the Club."

"What about him?"

"I don't know his identity. Only that Donny Ray heard the other inmates talking about him. People call him the Chief. That's all I know."

"Nothing else?"

"Nothing."

I pressed. "Are you sure?"

"Well," Taggley finally said, "I guess there's one other thing."

"Which is?"

"The people in the Club, those who know him, are careful of him. The Chief, I mean."

"Careful of him, in what way?"

"Careful in the way that people act when they are very, very afraid of a person."

53

Because my arrest was no longer imminent, I checked into the hotel that was in downtown Manitou, in the heart of the Three Points area, named, we were told back in school, for the three Indian trails there. My last talk with Rev. Cannon had jarred my memory, and I'd finally placed it. As schoolkids we learned that the tribes would convene there, in that meeting place, where they would then summon up spirits.

The hotel was an odd refurb of a turn-of-the-century commercial tower with lots of strange twists and turns, but my room had a big, comfortable king bed, and a desk with a view of the street below and of the hotel entrance, so I was satisfied. I needed a vantage point to spot people looking for me. And not just Sheriff Butch Jardinsky's men either.

I checked in early. Once I had washed up, stripped down to my gym shorts, and plunked down at the desk, I noticed that I had a missed call from Harlem on my cell.

I returned the call from Elijah White. It was good to hear his voice.

"I know you're busy, brother Trevor."

"Not too busy for you. How's life?"

"I am still working at the drug center. And

heading up the jail ministry at church. Oh, and I got a new lady in my life."

"Congratulations."

"Church secretary. Very pretty and very gracious. We're thinking, we're definitely thinking . . ."

"Yeah, sounds like you're thinking about it."

"I believe she's the one. God's gift, for sure." Then Elijah changed his tone and dropped his voice low, as he would often do when he was about to impart something about me. "I had this dream, Trevor. It was another one about you. I need to ask you a question."

"Shoot."

"Is your daddy dead or alive?"

A strange question. "He died when I was a boy. Why?"

"Just wondering. I think he was in my dream. And so were you."

"How did you know it was my father?"

"I don't know."

"Describe him to me."

"Handsome man, balding, white hair on the sides, no glasses, broad face, stocky build, like you. Oh, and a scar across his upper lip."

It sounded like a good likeness of my father. "What happened in the dream?"

"He was reaching out to you. With his hand. Smiling."

"What was I doing?"

"You were just standing there with a look on

your face—not reaching out, though, but looking like a man who had to decide something deadly serious. Like a matter of life and death."

"I'm not sure what to make of it. Maybe it's positive. My memories of my father are good ones."

Elijah took his time before he added, "All I know is when I woke up from the dream I was drenched. In a cold sweat. With all due respect to soul brother James Brown, of course."

I laughed out loud at that.

"Well," he said. "For what it's worth, I didn't have a very good feeling about it. Take that any way you will."

There was a call-waiting blip on my cell, so I said my good-byes to Elijah and took it.

It was Ashley Linderman. "We have the surveillance footage from the security camera across the road from Henry Franklin's place. It's been posted online to a restricted law enforcement cloud site, so other detectives around the country can view it and can weigh in with additional data about the vehicles or the drivers."

That's where she stopped.

"Let me guess," I said. "You can't bring me into the loop."

"Right. At least it can't come from me. You're persona non grata. And who knows what my future looks like. But I did happen to reach out with a voice mail to this detective I know in New

York, who handled a related homicide case. He has the passcode now to get into the site. You may know him."

Nice end run, Ashley. "You're brilliant."

"Say hello to Dick Valentine for me."

"Have you seen the footage?"

"I have. Valentine can give you access to view it. Then just look at it, that's all. You'll see for yourself."

Dick Valentine gave me the passcode immediately. "I'm not under any dumb directives that stop me from talking to you," he said, then added, "Unlike another law enforcement agency in Wisconsin, which shall remain nameless."

"I wish you could have been helping out more during this investigation."

"Naw," he shot back, "as far as the Bobby Budleigh homicide goes, you're better off going with your instincts. Or whatever you call that sixth sense of yours."

"Stay in touch, Dick. And I hope I can return the favor someday."

"You already have," he said. "My wife's got me going back to church regularly. When Momma's happy, everybody's happy. I think you had something to do with it."

I grinned, picturing Dick Valentine trying to sing hymns. "That *is* good news. But I hope it's not just about placating the missus."

"Don't worry, preacher. I'm the proverbial

iceberg. Plenty under the surface." Then he made a hard left turn in the subject matter. "You know, in recent months, no more of those murders with hearts being ripped out. At least not here. They stopped when you left New York."

"Like it's all following me," I suggested.

Dick didn't reply.

I wanted to get real with him. "I'm prepared to do whatever it takes. And with God's help, to stop it. It's vile. It has to end."

"Don't do anything reckless."

"Too late."

It was good to have my friend on the line. I trusted him. So I let him inside. "This thing, this evil force, is coming after me. I can feel it, and it's getting closer. Things have turned. Wondering if I'm the hunter or the prey."

"Any idea who's behind it?"

"Not yet. But it's as if this thing has an obsession with me. Which means I have to get there first. Reach into the darkness. Trusting God to turn on the light so I can stop the monster. Kill it. Ram a stake through it."

"So, enlighten me. Who's the obsessed one?" Dick sounded stone-cold serious.

He ended the call by saying that he was about to send me a text message listing the vehicle registrations on the cars heading into Henry Franklin's trailer park.

I booted up my laptop, accessed the site on the

cloud, and entered the passcode. A minute later the screen went black, then lit up with a banner that said, "Manitou Sheriff's Department, Manitou, Wisconsin—Secure Site—Security Surveillance Camera Footage from Able Storage Facility, Highway 59," followed by the date, which was the day before Wendell Quarlet set himself on fire at the incinerator.

I touched the arrow icon on the screen, ready to find out who had been partying with Henry Franklin at his weird fire pit.

The opening shot on the surveillance video showed the intersection of Highway 59 and Shore Road. After several minutes, a car passed down Highway 59, and a few minutes later, in the opposite direction, another.

Then nothing. I waited, staring at an empty intersection in rural Wisconsin. Then something important happened.

First, a Mercedes-Benz slowed down and pulled onto Shore Road. The footage stopped, showing the rear of the Benz. On the screen, in the upper corner, was the banner "Forensic Enlargement." Ashley had arranged to have the state forensic guys do an enhancement of the license plate. I jotted down the license number.

Ten minutes later another vehicle pulled up and slowly turned onto Shore Road.

I said out loud, "You're kidding, is that a Bentley?" Once again the footage stopped with the same banner in the upper corner of the screen. I wrote down that license plate too. But there was something interesting about the Bentley. It had tinted windows, so dark that I wondered if they were legal.

Then the footage sped up, with the digital time indicator showing that two hours and ten minutes later, the Benz and the Bentley both left Franklin's trailer park.

I heard my cell ding. I checked the text message. It was from Dick Valentine. No personal tidings. Just the facts. The listing of the two cars and their registered owners: Mercedes-Benz—Wisconsin registration: Jeffery Opperdill. Bentley (Flying Spur)—Wisconsin registration: Wendell Quarlet.

My mind raced. I stared at the information about the second vehicle and wondered how Wendell Quarlet, an employee at the Exotica shop with Augie, could afford a Bentley. Also inexplicable was the fact that the following day, Wendell would steal Augie's Chevy Blazer and drive it to the incinerator where he would kill himself.

It was intriguing. And screwy.

I stood up and stretched, walked to the window to get a perfect view of the sidewalk outside the hotel lobby and the street. Nothing going on there. I strode around the room, trying to figure out the Henry Franklin–Jeffery Opperdill–Wendell Quarlet connection.

Then a knock on the door. I looked through the

tiny, circular view window in my door, but saw no face outside. I waited.

I grabbed my room key, not a plastic card but an actual key, one of those long, metal, old-fashioned skeleton key–looking things with a plastic tag attached with my room number on it. I slid the safety chain off the door and opened it, stepping out into the empty hall. Halfway down the corridor, the elevator doors were closing. I sprinted in that direction, trying to catch a glimpse of the occupants. But I was too late. The doors had closed and the elevator was already heading down. I watched until I saw on the screen above the elevator doors that the car had made it all the way to the lobby, where it had stopped.

As I stepped back, I felt someone standing behind me. But there was another sense too, and it told me instantly that I was in for trouble. There was that noxious, smoky scent of burning death. Out of my peripheral vision I caught the sight of a hulking figure behind me.

Before I could respond there was a deep, guttural voice, powerful enough to resonate in my chest.

"You were warned."

A large hand tightened around my neck, choking me from behind and hoisting me off the ground, while the other reached past me for the closed elevator doors and began to pry them open single-handedly.

Still locked in a choke hold and held six inches off the ground, my room key in my hand, I was swung off to the side as if I were a kid's stuffed animal. My assailant's right foot was lodged into the space that he had created between the elevator doors with his hand. The doors were banged open wider, and even wider, with his foot and his hand. Wide enough so that—*Oh no,* I screamed silently in my head, *he is going to toss me . . .*

And he did. Throwing me through the opening. My key dropped from my hand as I fell into the darkness of the elevator shaft. My hands grappled wildly until they landed on the vertical elevator cables, and I clutched the cables for dear life, dangling there, several stories up. But my hands were beginning to slip on the cables. Inch by inch, I was sliding down.

Where was the elevator door to my floor? I looked up. I was hanging below it now, too far to reach. The doors were banging open, then closed, and then open again, against my room key, which was lodged in the floor track of the doors.

"Oh, God, help me!" I yelled, and it echoed through the shaft. I tried to pull myself up, but my hands were sweaty, and the cables were greased. It was only a matter of seconds before I would slip off the cables entirely and then begin tumbling through the air and down to my death.

I wish I could describe my cool, calm demeanor, my heroism in the face of destruction. But I'd be lying. I was in an imminent-death panic.

Then a metallic groaning sound. The shaft shuddered as the cables moved, now bringing the elevator from the lobby, rising upward, and me with it. My hands were still slipping, but I hung on as tight as I could, being lifted upward until the elevator doors of my floor, banging open, were within reach. My rescue, engineered by the upward dynamic of a power accomplishing what I could not.

With my left hand I reached out to the space between the banging elevator doors and laid hold of the threshold, then released my slippery grip on the cables with my right. I swung against the wall of the shaft, hanging on with both hands, and pulled myself upward until I could see the color of the carpet in the hallway and feel the blast of hotel air against my face.

Squeezing myself frantically into the space between the doors, first on my belly, then on my knees, I finally stumbled to my feet, safely in the hallway. At the end of the corridor, an elderly man was standing at the door of his room, transfixed at the sight of someone climbing out of the elevator shaft.

Less than ten minutes later I was standing at the lobby desk, still in my gym shorts, with my overnight bag and laptop, checking out.

The clerk tried to be cordial. "How was your stay?"

"Exciting."

The cordial expression disappeared. "Do you have your room key, sir? They are antiques, the old-fashioned kind."

"Which I'm really glad about." I beamed.

"Do you have it with you?"

I told him, with regrets, that my big metal key was jammed in the floor track for the elevator door and that they'd have to call their maintenance crew.

"Was there a problem with your key, sir?" he asked as I turned to stride out of the lobby.

I yelled back, "No. It was a lifesaver."

54

The call to my cell caught me just as I was climbing into the Ford Fairlane.

"Trevor Black?"

"Yes."

"Detective Colin Jennings here. I need you to come down to the sheriff's department."

I quickly deduced that he had been placed back in charge of the investigation into Bobby's death, and that Ashley was out. Before getting to his office, I stopped at a gas station to change into some pants and a shirt.

At the sheriff's office I was seated, without explanation, in front of a one-way pane of glass that looked into an interrogation room with a table and a few chairs.

Then, through the glass, I saw Henry Franklin being escorted into the room and seated by Detective Colin Jennings, who sat next to him and began to ask questions. He spent the first ten or fifteen minutes diving into Franklin's business relationship with Opperdill and his working for Opperdill as an independent contractor and foreman on various real estate ventures.

Then things got really interesting.

"Tell me, Mr. Franklin, about a group called 'the Club' that you are involved in."

Franklin started out cagey, using a dodge that was the equivalent of "it depends on what the definition of *is* is." But after some persistent drilling, Jennings got him to admit that there really was such a group. "We have drinks around the fire pit. At my trailer park. That kind of thing."

Franklin hemmed and hawed at first about Opperdill. Jennings pushed, reminding him that failure to cooperate would go very badly for him. So, was Opperdill part of the Club, or wasn't he?

Finally Franklin fessed up that Jeffery Opperdill was in the group.

"And you told Jeffery Opperdill about your encounter with Bobby Budleigh?"

Franklin's eyes darted, but he couldn't see any

trap in the truth. "Yes, I informed Mr. Opperdill. Bobby Budleigh said he was checking into environmental things."

The detective looked away casually. "Was Jeffery Opperdill concerned about the EPA?"

"I couldn't tell you what was in Mr. Opperdill's mind," Franklin retorted.

Jennings tried it another way. "Okay, so did Opperdill look happy, sad, or mad about Bobby Budleigh's research in Manitou?"

"He didn't look bothered. Just real interested. Asked me a bunch of questions about the guy. You know, about whether he was that Manitou kid from years before who had grown up here. Whether he was 'that Bobby Budleigh.' That's the way Opperdill put it."

Jennings switched gears again. "Who is the person in the Club known as the Chief?"

Franklin balked. Jennings pushed harder and then suggested a name. "Was Wendell Quarlet the Chief? The leader of this club?"

Franklin scoffed at that. "You kidding? That punk? Don't mean any disrespect, of course, his being deceased. But, hey, he couldn't be the Chief."

Jennings followed up. "Then who?"

Franklin pulled the plug. "Okay. I've done all the talking I'm going to do till I call my lawyer."

Jennings smiled, read him his Miranda rights, and said he was free to call his lawyer. But he added that Franklin was no longer free to leave the office and that he was now in custody for possible complicity in the death of Bobby Budleigh.

Even through the one-way glass, I could tell that the color drained from Franklin's face like he had just seen a ghost.

Then Jennings asked him again if he was willing to share the identity of the Chief. I knew, and I'm sure Jennings also knew, that whatever Henry Franklin answered at that point couldn't be used against him in court under Miranda. But it didn't matter.

Franklin shook his head furiously. "Nope," he said. "Not telling you anything about this Chief stuff. No way."

Henry Franklin apparently was more frightened of the Chief than being charged with murder. More than seeing a ghost.

55

After the interrogation, Detective Jennings swooped back into the debriefing room where I was sitting and wanted to know my reaction to Henry Franklin's comments. I told him that there was little new in what Franklin had said, except for his comment about Wendell Quarlet. "Wendell was a pawn," I explained.

"Go on," Jennings said.

"Based on Franklin's comments. You heard it too. Of course I saw the newspaper clippings that were kept in a back room at Exotica. So I know something about his interests."

"Us too," Jennings added. "We checked out his workplace after his death. I saw the newspaper collage on the wall. Not cute. Augie Bedders made a point of showing it to us and telling us how and when Wendell put it there. Your thoughts on this Club that Franklin and Opperdill were part of?"

"No Boy Scout jamboree. They were majoring in the occult."

"Based on?"

"My trip to their meeting place. Franklin's haunted Halloween trailer park. A fire pit full of melted candle wax, a nasty animal sacrifice, and some very un-nice people who gather there. And yes, I have seen the surveillance video, complete with license plates. And no, Detective Ashley Linderman did not supply it to me. I've got other contacts."

"Any other thoughts?" Jennings asked.

"Something very otherworldly is going down. Call it what you want, but I call it demonic activity. The kind of thing that detectives like you joke about when guys like me aren't in the room."

"Not true," Jennings barked back with a crooked smile. "We joke about it even when

382

guys like you *are* in the room." Then he added, "Me, personally? I have this thing that I quote."

"Which is?"

" 'There are more things in heaven and earth, Horatio, than are dreamt of in your philosophy.' "

I was impressed. A sheriff's detective who quoted *Hamlet*?

We parted ways, with no orders given about my not leaving town. As I climbed into the Fairlane, I was thinking about new lodgings. There was a motel in the city that I hadn't tried yet. One where I could get to my room by a stairwell. No elevators for a while, thank you very much. I took a shortcut through a residential area that was thick with trees. I was beginning to recognize some of the houses, and they looked as if they had been frozen in time. I was suddenly struck with the fact that I was only two blocks from my boyhood home. I had driven past it only once since coming to Manitou, and then I had just breezed by quickly.

I knew I would regret it if I didn't swing by 207 Wilson Street this one last time.

The two-story tan brick house where I grew up hadn't changed much. The trim was now white rather than gray, and the landscaping was tidy, with some bushes that I didn't remember. I cruised past it, then headed down the block toward the intersection with West Avenue.

But there was another house on that block, and

I slowed to see it. A big red mansion built in a Spanish motif. The former home of Mason Krim. My last memory was the overgrowth from the trees and bushes and the unmowed lawn. But now it looked different. Flowers had been planted everywhere in bright colored pots, the lawn was cut like a golf course, and there were two children's bicycles in the driveway. Life had been breathed into the place, it seemed. That was a good thing. A restoration.

The house also prompted a thought. There were only two cemeteries in Manitou. A big Catholic one on the western edge of town. Mason Krim had attended Rev. Cannon's Lutheran church at one time but left on bad terms. He didn't strike me as the kind to convert to Catholicism or to insist in his will to be buried there. That left Pioneer's Rest, the community cemetery on the north end of Manitou.

When I arrived at Pioneer's Rest, it was almost closing time, so I quickly told the elderly caretaker in the little stone entrance building that I needed to see the grave of a neighbor of mine for just a minute. He slowly booted up a map of the grave plots on the screen of his computer, then asked for a name. I told him I was there to see the last resting place of Mason Krim. Then I added, "It may be a double plot. His wife died a number of years before Mr. Krim did."

The caretaker took his eyes off the screen and

looked at me. "Mrs. Krim, his wife, was buried outside of Manitou. I've been here for more than forty years, so I remember some burials more than others. Mr. Krim wanted her buried here, but her final wishes were to be buried somewhere else, according to the estate attorney. She and her daughter were finally buried together in Omaha, where she was born. A Lutheran cemetery, I think."

"In any event, I'm just here to see Mason Krim's grave."

"Yes," the caretaker said somberly. "I remember that one too." Then he pulled out a printed map of the grave plots and circled one at the far end of the cemetery, almost to the fence line that separated it from a neighboring subdivision.

I drove along the curves and well-tended paths studded with trees and lined with gravestones and markers until I came to the place. Map in hand, I trotted up to the spot. There were no other grave markers close by. Mason Krim's grave was marked with a tall, white marble obelisk, and at the top was a chiseled arm with a hand projecting upward from it, fingers out stretched as if trying desperately to grasp something.

I came closer and read the name of the departed and date of death, just to make sure. Yes, it was his.

Then I read the inscription on the face of the obelisk. A weird poem that seemed vaguely familiar.

To all who hunger for secrets to keep,
and yearn for a realm of shadows deep,
and scoff at the wound of a fallen king,
but bow to a prince, his power to bring.

Then I scanned down to read the source of the poem, which had been etched in the stone just below the last line. When I did, I experienced one of those almost-out-of-body sensations, where the clocks seem to stop. And the noises of the world grow strangely quiet.

The marble obelisk attributed the poem to a book. The title of the book was *Piercing the Supernatural Veil*.

I read the poem again. The "fallen king"— Christ, the crucified. And his chest wound, as depicted in the Édouard Manet painting in Krim's house, a wound on the wrong side, which had caused a scandal in the 1800s when the painting was first shown publicly. There was the scoffing part.

The painting had the same kind of chest wound, and in the same location, as had been inflicted on Heather, the street waif in New York City, butchered by the possessed Dunning Kamera. The same with the victims of demon-occupied Sid Castor, not to mention my own wound inflicted in the New York museum by Hanz Delpha, the former academic who had been inhabited by that creature of darkness, and lastly Bobby

Budleigh's chest laceration too. All of them on the left side of the chest.

It was easy to figure out who the hellish prince was, who would bring power to the scoffers.

Rev. Cannon's words were ringing in my head. A series of mutilation killings in New York, and now one in my hometown. It had all the earmarks of a perverse Satanic joke, perpetrated through a demonic lieutenant who had inhabited humans, one after another, to execute the plan. And I was in the center of it.

There was a noise at the entrance gate. The caretaker was calling out to me that it was closing time and that the cemetery was about to be locked. I waved back to let him know I was going.

But just then I was hit with a physical sensation, a shiver shooting over my body the instant that I fully considered the hideous power that I was challenging. I questioned, at that moment, whether I was up to the task.

56

After reserving my motel room, a sense of gloom fell over me. Too many hours thinking about ghouls that possess and then ravage human flesh, and how to track them and what to do if I found them, and meanwhile, through it all, how to survive.

I wanted to connect with the one person in Manitou I could trust, who also happened to be the one person I couldn't get off my mind. So I called Ashley again. When she answered, she sounded unenthusiastic and distant.

I asked her if I could buy her an ice cream sundae with chocolate sauce and a cherry on top, said I knew this great ice cream parlor where we had first met, and did she want to meet me there? She agreed in a monotone and ended by saying she'd be there in ten minutes, then added, "And this isn't a date. So I'm not showering or putting on makeup. And I'm not putting on some cute outfit. Right now I'm wearing an old sagging pair of sweatpants and a tank top. I'm not changing and really don't care. Just so you know."

All of that was fine with me and I said so. Darkness was falling as I drove straight to Otto's Creamery, and the little ice cream stand had already turned on their crazy Christmas lights that outlined the frame of the hut. A few minutes after I arrived, Ashley was at the passenger-side door of my car knocking and looking perturbed, perhaps because I had left the car door locked, a habit I had acquired after a number of encounters with those who wished me ill. I unlocked the door, and she jumped into the passenger seat. She was holding a piece of notepaper.

I started off on a high note, trying not to stare at her baggy sweatpants and struck by the fact that she always looked good no matter what she was wearing. "It's really good to see you. I've been thinking about you."

Ashley didn't respond to that. Skipping over the pleasantries, she jumped right into reading from her notes. "I spoke to my contact at the EPA. There was an investigation. At least an initial one. Had nothing to do with Pebble Creek or wetlands, though. The concern was that Jeffery Opperdill might have allowed toxins to be released directly into the Little Bear River after he took over the foundry when his father died. Opperdill did a lot of dodging and weaving. Also, he had a powerful front man who was messing with the EPA on his behalf."

"A lawyer?"

"No, although he had plenty of those. Somebody else. Someone who had power of attorney to appear for him on the investigation, but not as an attorney. My contact told me the EPA was frustrated at every turn. The next thing they knew, the lead investigator drowned in a boating accident on Lake Michigan. Then, files, including digital ones, went missing. They couldn't even resurrect information from the backup data on the hard drives of their computers. She said she had never seen anything like it. Practically 'black magic.' Her words, not mine. In the end, Jeffery Opperdill quietly shut down the foundry, and the whole investigation fizzled out."

"So, who was this powerful agent for Jeffery Opperdill?"

"We don't know. That's part of the missing data."

I took a hard look at Ashley. She looked like she was in the grip of something. The hand that was holding the note was shaking. Her face was drawn.

Treading out on thin ice, I asked, "Tell me what's going on with you."

She refused, calling it irrelevant, so I pushed a little more. Telling her that, to the contrary, I considered everything about her to be relevant. Then she unloaded. "How about this. How about, ye GAD, I'm having a bad day. Remember? I opened up to you, unfortunately, about my diagnosis. Now the whole department knows. Butch knows."

"You don't think I said anything . . ."

"No, I'm not saying that. I am just saying that I am having a lousy day. It happens. So, I take my medication. I struggle through."

"I wish I knew what you were going through . . ."

"Do you really want to know?"

"Of course I do."

"It's like swimming in a pool that you think is safe, and the next thing you know there are ropes all around and you get all tangled up in them and you can't breathe and there's the feeling of drowning."

"That's what it feels like?"

"No. Not all the time. That is just one of the wonderful sensations. There are plenty more."

What happened next I never would have wished even on the nastiest legal opponent I have ever encountered in court, let alone see it happen to Ashley.

A brown unmarked sheriff's vehicle glided into the parking lot at Otto's Creamery and pulled up next to us. Sheriff Butch Jardinsky climbed out slowly. He had something in his hand and strolled over to Ashley's window. Today he was in full dress uniform: white starched shirt with epaulets, tie, and gold star on his chest.

Butch handed the papers to Ashley. "You have been served. Notice of suspension from the sheriff's department. The date and time of the hearing before the disciplinary committee is right there in the paperwork." Then he ducked his head down to address me. "And you, Mr. Black. You have twenty-four hours to clear out of Manitou. Or I will sit down with the district attorney to figure out the charges we'll be bringing against you." Then he turned back to Ashley. "As soon as possible I need your service weapon and your badge. Please turn them in immediately."

When Jardinsky had driven off, Ashley looked up at the sky and exclaimed in a burst of raging sarcasm, "This is so excellent. What a wonderful day."

I was ready to jump in and try to fix it. I was ready to launch my plan to hire the best law enforcement attorney for her I could find and to fight the phony disciplinary charges.

But before I could, Ashley turned to me with a kind of resolve I had not seen in her eyes before. "Hear me very carefully, Trevor. I am going home to my apartment. I am turning off my cell phones. Both of them. I will not be answering them. I simply want to be left alone. Please don't bother trying to find out where I live. Do not attempt to contact me."

She jumped out of her brother's car, which I had been driving, slammed the door, and headed over to her vehicle, her baggy sweatpants fluttering around her skinny legs.

In the old days, at a minimum I would have arrogantly confronted the sheriff for his ignorance and his malice. Verbally reducing him to an oil stain on the cement. But no more. My job at that point of my life was to lay all the muck and mire of things, the mess of life, before an inscrutable God. I was on a mission to do the right thing, not the natural thing. But that course of action was always the hardest thing, and I knew it.

Then my cell rang.

Augie Bedders was going ballistic on the phone. "Trevor, help. Please, you gotta help me!"

57

"Augie, calm down. Where are you?"

"I can't say much over the phone. You never know who's listening in. I'm in trouble, though, man. Please, you gotta meet me. Down by the river behind Exotica—you know, the shop I work at?"

"I'll be there in ten minutes. Hang tight."

When I arrived, Augie was there, waiting for me. But this time he was cleaned up. His shoulder-length hair was combed and washed, and he was wearing a starched dress shirt and a new pair of jeans. He looked good, and I told him that.

"Getting ready for a special thing, sort of a date . . ." He sounded calmer than he had been on the phone. Must have had a chance to think through whatever had spooked him.

"That's good to hear, Augie. I figured that after what happened to Susan, you know, that you might eventually find somebody else and settle down."

"Yeah, Susan," he said in a quiet voice. "Right." And then he just looked at me funny.

But I was suddenly distracted by the distinct odor of smoldering, decaying death drifting in from somewhere. I looked around frantically, expecting to see one of the horribles looming ever nearer.

Augie must have seen the disgust on my face.

"Yeah, stinks, eh? They finally got the Manitou incinerator working again. The bad news is we're downwind, and that smell floats all the way down the river."

I exhaled my relief. No supernatural assassins, just the honest scent of physical death and flames. "So, you sounded upset on the phone."

"I am upset. Because of what happened to me. I was freaking out."

"Just tell me."

"I was up on the roof today, of this building. We have a leak up there, and I was checking it out. Then, the next thing I know, suddenly this big dude is behind me on the roof. At least the size of me. Maybe bigger. And he grabs me from behind and jerks me over to the edge of the building and holds me out, dangling there, off the edge of the building, like he's going to drop me. And I'm not a small guy, mind you."

"Did you see his face?"

"No, I couldn't. He got me from behind. And as he's holding me off the edge of the roof like I was nothing, he says that if I don't do what he tells me to, he's going to throw me down to the sidewalk and crack my head like an egg."

"What did he want you to do?"

"To give you a message."

"Me? What message?"

"If you are not out of Manitou immediately, then someone you care for is going to die."

"Did he say who?"

"No. But he said these exact words. He said, 'She's going to pay for his sins.' That's exactly what he said."

"Anything else?"

"Yeah. He said that he would enjoy doing it." Then Augie added, "Do you know what any of this means?"

"I think so. Listen, I need you to get in touch with Detective Jennings."

"Yeah, absolutely," Augie said. "I need protection."

I gave Augie Detective Jennings's card and told him to call him right away. I didn't know what shift Jennings was working, but I said that he was a good man and would be very interested in what Augie had to say.

Before I left Augie, I decided to ask him something. He had been in and out of jail and rehab too. Maybe he had heard something. So I took a chance.

"Have you even heard of some secret group here in the area called the Club?"

Augie's eyes widened. "It was like some weird ghost story or something, so I thought it was just bull. But then I heard it was real. With somebody powerful who's in charge. Could make things happen. Like magic. Except worse."

"Was that person called the Chief?"

Augie eyed me. "How do you know about that?"

"Never mind. If you have any idea how I can find out who that person is, would you let me know?"

Augie promised he would. I told him to be safe and to leave a message for Detective Jennings immediately.

I could tell that I had Augie thinking. He said one last thing. "I might know a guy who could tell you about this Chief person. If he is willing to talk with you, what should I do?"

"Call me. Night or day. The sooner the better."

On the way to my motel I called Jennings. There was no one else in the sheriff's department that I could trust at that point. I left a detailed message on his voice mail that I thought Ashley's life had been threatened and that it was because of me. I also described Augie Bedders's conversation with me, emphasizing that he should expect a call from Augie any minute.

Then I left the same voice mail message for Ashley, but in big capital letters saying loudly that she needed to connect with me right away because she was in extreme danger, that someone wanted to kill her, and I would leave my cell on all night long. But, of course, true to her word, both of her cell phones went right to voice mail. That was all I could do. I had no idea where she lived. I felt quicksand under my feet.

At the motel, I went up the stairwell and right into my room, but I knew I couldn't sleep. I paced, watched a little TV, and paced some more. Finally I sat down in the fake-leather chair and pulled out Elijah's Bible. Eventually I must have fallen asleep in the chair, because the next thing I remember my cell was ringing at 3:04 a.m. It was Augie.

I tried to clear the fog in my head. "Talk to me, Augie."

"I've got the guy. The guy who knows about the Chief."

"Have him call me."

"No. He doesn't want that. Wants to meet you in person and tell you what he knows. Wants to meet right now. But somewhere safe. Where there is no chance of police surveillance or being bugged or whatever."

"Do you have any idea where I can meet him?"

"Yeah. I know exactly the place. He wants me there too because he trusts me. You remember the old Opperdill Foundry?"

"Really? That place? It's three in the morning."

Augie was sure about it. "I used to be a building caretaker. I'd patrol the grounds and the building after Opperdill closed it. I've still got a key."

It was agreed. We would meet in thirty minutes at the side door of the foundry next to the old guard shack.

I had already decided, whoever this Chief was, that any promise of his that Ashley would be spared if I would just leave town stunk like the

Manitou landfill. I had to get to him before he could get to Ashley. I had failed to protect other people in my life. But not this time.

I made one final, frantic attempt to reach Ashley on her cell, describing where I was going, and who I was planning on meeting, and warning her about threats against her. Again, it went right to voice mail.

58

My car lights hit the long drive leading down to the Opperdill Foundry. But the rusty gate with the No Trespassing sign had already been swung open, so I headed straight down to the foundry complex, my high beams lighting the prickly weeds two feet high, which had the look of thorn bushes sprouting up from the cracks in the pavement. I could hear them scraping the underside of the Fairlane as I passed over them.

So many years had passed since my last memory of the place as a boy, when my father had taken me to work one day for some reason I couldn't recall. He and I had checked in at the guardhouse, and then he escorted me to his area in the factory, a place of overwhelming size. It was a big, industrial cavern full of oily machinery, cranes overhead, and infernal noise. Most of all, I remember my father's hand on my shoulder as we walked. Good memories. But also mixed with pain, even after all those years, over his death at the foundry.

When I climbed out of the Fairlane on the way to my meeting with Augie's informant, I walked past that same guardhouse. But now it was unlighted, and even in the darkness I could tell that the windows were filthy with neglect. I noticed that the side door of the foundry was half-open, and there was light coming from the inside.

I understood, vaguely, the danger of this rendezvous. Augie knew the person I was to meet, but I didn't. I also wondered if Augie knew enough about our contact, and whether he might be a threat to Augie and me.

As a precaution, I did some reconnaissance. I walked past the half-open door, and made my way through the tall weeds and around the side of the building until I reached the back. The moon was full, and I could see the glimmer of it off the surface of the Little Bear River that ran just behind the foundry.

A vehicle was parked at the back end of the foundry. But it was not the 1997 Chevy Blazer that I had expected, the one that had been registered to Augie and that Wendell Quarlet had driven to the incinerator the day he killed himself. It wasn't that one at all.

The vehicle parked behind the foundry was the Bentley Flying Spur. The same one caught on the surveillance footage heading into Henry Franklin's trailer park. The one with the dark tinted windows. Listing price about two hundred thousand dollars.

There are those moments when logic flees and the flesh rushes into survival mode. That was one of those moments, and it was telling me not to enter that foundry.

But something else was at play. I had come all this way, to this time and this place, for a reason. And I couldn't shake the feeling that this encounter in the abandoned foundry had been fixed in heaven before the galaxies had ever been formed. I faced a doorway to some answers, convinced that God would be my strength, though at the same time I was also convinced that God wanted my fist to do the knocking.

I strode back to the doorway where the dim light was emanating. There, I uttered a prayer and walked inside.

The interior was bathed in a ghostly illumination from overhead safety lights that Augie must have turned on. I looked around the place. A dusty odor of oil and grime greeted my senses. On the ground level were rows of disabled machines that had been cannibalized, probably for the value of their parts. Overhead, massive cranes hung lifeless from beams. I wondered, for just an instant, which one of them had crushed my father on the day of his death. But I had to get that out of my head. I needed to stick to the mission. I had no idea what I was going to do, facing off against powers so far beyond me. But I had the sense that this was going to be the final reckoning.

Fear. It was suddenly palpable. I was ashamed to admit it. It was hovering over me. All around me. Threatening to paralyze me. This was the testing place, I found myself thinking. I wouldn't have figured it to happen like this, in the foundry where my father had died. But then again, the place wasn't important. What was important was how I would choose. Either faith or fear.

I walked through the cavernous space, listening for Augie, but heard nothing. So I called out, and my voice echoed in the shadows. I yelled again.

Then a voice. I looked up to locate the source of the voice and saw Augie standing high above on a catwalk that stretched across the fourth story of the foundry. Behind him was a wall of grimy windows where the hazy outline of the moon could still be seen.

"Come up here," Augie shouted.

"Why don't you come down?" I countered.

"Someone else is calling the shots. I'm just the messenger."

I looked around for a stairway and found a metal ladder that led straight up to the next level, so I climbed up until I reached a catwalk.

"Two more levels," Augie shouted. "Sorry about the climb."

I went up another fixed ladder taking me to another catwalk, and finally a steel stairway that took me all the way up to the dizzying height where Augie was waiting for me. When I reached it, Augie was standing fifty feet away, next to a huge iron girder that was at least four feet wide. He was still dressed in his jeans and dress shirt.

"Where's our guy?" I asked.

I stood still and waited.

"He's near," Augie said.

I looked at the foundry floor below, then down the length of the cavernous plant. Looking for someone who might be standing in the shadows but finding nobody visible. "How near, exactly?"

"Very close," Augie said in a husky whisper.

59

Augie started giggling.

My momentary thought, just then, was that this whole thing was Augie's sick sense of humor again. Toying with me. And it would have been better that way, had it only been a waste of my time and a twisted joke from a broken man. But it wasn't.

More giggles from Augie. The same as when we were in Mason Krim's house as teenagers after Krim's death, and Augie had grabbed the telephone from my hand while I was listening to someone on the other end, some unknown caller whose timing had spooked us out of our skins.

But standing there on the catwalk in the foundry, Augie's grin faded fast and he straightened up. "Just to set things straight," he said. "About Susan. My wife. The love of my life."

"What?" I asked. The dialogue seemed incomprehensible.

"Susan and I had a fight that night," Augie said. "The reason was because she had chased you-know-who clear across the country, even though she knew he was married. I guess she always had a thing for him."

"Help me understand—"

But Augie was unstoppable. "So I confronted her about it," he said. "We were both hitting the Jack Daniel's and smoking weed. We fought. She ran out and got in the car and I heard the tires squealing. Then later I get a show-up by the state patrol. Telling me about her car accident. Killed. But not just her. Something in me died too."

The conversation had turned strange. Was this Augie talking? He sounded different.

Augie kept going. "So when you told me earlier today that you thought maybe I would find someone else after Susan died, well, no. That was never in the cards. Ever."

"I'm sorry," I shot back. "I didn't mean anything by that. Look, I just want to interview your person about the Chief and be done with it."

"Oh yes, you're going to be done with it, leader of the band. Big man on the high school campus."

I shook my head. "No, not 'big man.' I was mostly a jerk back then, I think."

"Too late," he said. "Except for you to learn a few things. For one, that Susan died because of Bobby Budleigh."

By then it was making sense, painfully. I pleaded with him. "Augie, you can't blame Bobby for that. He would never have cheated on his wife, or on you. And he wouldn't have encouraged Susan to chase after him."

"Of course not," Augie roared. "Not Bobby. The little church boy. The virgin chick magnet. The perfect man. Blessed in the sight of the God who gave him everything he ever wanted."

I had to settle some things quickly. "Augie. The Bentley that is parked outside. Who owns it?"

"Who do you think?" Augie screamed, his face flushed. "Not Wendell, that little worm. It was a simple car registration forgery. You think I would ever drive that piece-of-junk Chevy Blazer? A man in my position? Or ever allow Wendell to drive my Bentley? Him? The gutless traitor . . ."

"Don't you mean Wendell Quarlet, the Judas?"

It was clear to me by then what the message in blood had meant. The one that had been scrawled on the floor of the incinerator.

"And just like Judas getting the order," Augie shouted, "Wendell got the order. But this time, no hanging from a tree like Judas. That'd be too good for Wendell. He knew the rules. Once you're in, you're in for good. Wendell got the indwelling, then suddenly he wants out. And was going to talk. So the Club convened, and the order was delivered: go, thou worm, and sacrifice yourself on the burning pyre." Augie roared with laughter. "Just for good measure, he was ordered to leave his own epitaph on the floor. In his own blood. When one of the visitors gets inside you, you obey. Wendell had to obey. Right down to the leap into the fire."

"Was it Jeffery Opperdill? He gave the order? Or Henry Franklin?"

Augie shook his head violently. "No, no, no. What's wrong with you? Henry Franklin was just a foot soldier for me. I took real good care of him for that too. Set him up well. And Opperdill? He works for me too. Don't you see?"

The three members of the Club, I thought. Then I said it. "The fire pit at Franklin's trailer park. The three knives. The sacrifice."

"Good for you, Trevor. Now you're getting it. A dog killed. Meaning, Wendell is a dead dog. A burning fire pit, and next thing you know, there's Wendell diving into the fire. Kinda melodramatic, but effective. It helps keep the foot soldiers in line."

"But Opperdill. And Bobby . . ."

"Come on, Trevor. Sharpen up. I'm the one with

the power from the visitor, not Opperdill. I waited a long time. Years. But finally I get the indwelling, and just in time to take care of Bobby. Opperdill? He's just my money guy. I solved his EPA problem and made it all go away. As a member of the Club, he had to pay up. And he did. He knew my wrath against Bobby. And what I wanted to do. So he gave me the scoop about Bobby coming back into town, and where I could find him. And you know what? When I pulled the trigger and then cut into Bobby that night, it was like I was just a butcher in a butcher shop. Nothing more. No guilt. No remorse. Just . . . nothing. Look me in my face, Trevor. See me now. I'm the judge. I'm the executioner."

"You . . . ," I stammered. "You're the Chief. Oh, God, have mercy."

"Are you kidding me?" Augie roared. "Would a merciful God have allowed Bobby to get wasted by me? It was so easy to take him down, Trevor, really, just a breeze the way he trusted me to join him along the creek."

I was horrified. The thought of my own complicity so many years before. "It must have started that night," I said. "At Mason Krim's place. That stupid séance game I was playing, with Krim's book. And then the phone rang, and I heard that voice on the other end. And then you grabbed the phone from me and listened. But you never told me—"

"Of course I didn't!" he bellowed. "You think I'd tell you? The secrets of real power, when it opened up to me? To me? Imagine my surprise. Why would I share it with you? I was always the second-stringer in your book. In everybody's book. But you're right about one thing. It did start with you. You're the guilty one. Responsible for all the bad that happened from that night at Mason Krim's house. So, deal with it. Feel really bad about it."

Then Augie started to rotate his shoulders around, like he had been forced into a shirt that didn't fit. "You wanted to know what's behind all this. Well, you're going to meet him. Right now. And, wonder of wonders, won't you be surprised."

A stench filled the foundry. Decay and death, and burning flesh. I watched as Augie began to change. His face lost its features. It was becoming a mound of rotting skin, like a corpse long buried, now exhumed from the grave.

The face continued to change and take shape. And it began to take on human features. A resemblance. *No, no,* I thought. *It can't be. Not him.* It was becoming a likeness. And I knew that face. The bald head, the handsome features, the grayish-white sideburns and the scar across his upper lip.

I bent forward, staring. Shocked and unable to speak. As my father stood in front of me. And he spoke. In a voice that was the very voice of my father.

"Trevor. I have missed you, Son."

I wanted to speak to him, but no words came out.

"I've traveled such a great distance to be here."

I spoke the word. "Heaven?"

He winced. As if I were a boy again and I had just uttered a filthy word. "No, Son. There is no heaven. No hell. Nothing but endless possibilities. Where you can become anything. A god, if you wish. Would you like to become a god?" Then he held his hand out toward me. "Take my hand, Son. I will show you such wonderful things."

A thought flashed with the speed of light. Elijah's dream. Suddenly, as if on a mountaintop, I could see the stark choice I had. I could practically hear the wind whistling past me and visualize the outstretched earth below. Leaving only me, and the God in whom I had entrusted everything, and the will, just then, to say the truth out loud.

I looked at the figure of my father and I shouted, "The greatest trick of all. Whoever you are, whatever your demon name, with your magic act, masquerading as my father . . . You're a lie. You come from the father of lies. But I'm occupied already. Occupied by Christ. You don't have any power here. Take your lie back to hell."

The likeness of my father vanished. It was only Augie standing in front of me. For a moment he struggled to smile, but then his face quickly transformed into a mask of grotesque anguish, and he screamed, swinging his arms. "No power here?" he raged. As he did, the massive cranes hanging from the ceiling of the foundry began to swing wildly back and forth, giving a metallic groan as if they were about to break free and fall to the floor.

The catwalk started to sway. I held tight to the railing and stood my ground.

Augie pulled a handgun from his pocket and pointed it at me. The nine-millimeter Beretta that he had used on Bobby. There was a voice that came out of Augie, but it was not Augie's—it wasn't anything from earth—and it screamed, "We gave you warnings. You didn't listen. Now I'm in charge. It's a bullet to your head. Then I rip your heart out. Just like the others. A perfect finish. A work of art. To mock your Christ. To hail the great prince of the air. And there is nothing you can do to stop it."

Then the creature inside Augie spoke in a low, hollow voice. "But something first. First, we take your soul."

I cried out, "Too late. Christ owns it. Not going to happen."

But as I said that, I realized something was all wrong. Even in the midst of the freak show in front of me, the flaw was obvious. Before I could think, it flew out of my mouth. "You need a gun to kill me? Really? What about all your power? Your magic tricks?"

The thing inside Augie shook his head back and forth, while the long hair cascaded around his face. His voice was suddenly whiny and simpering. "Rules . . . I didn't make them. Don't blame us. Restrictions. We hate them. With a hatred hotter than fire. Blame your God. For all of that. The limits on our reach. A temporary setback. But our prince is going to fix things, good and final."

I knew it was not Augie speaking. But an unholy other, a creature that left the dry wasteland of wandering and found victims to inhabit, one after another. Mason Krim. Then those in New York. Then back in Manitou with Augie. All the time killing and mutilating. More and more victims, both the dead and the possessed.

"Augie," I shouted. "I know you are in there. Tortured. Controlled by the evil inside."

The demon roared back, baring its teeth and shaking the gun at me.

But then, instantly, the face was no longer in a rage. It was Augie, struggling against an unspeakable horror within. "I want this to end," he murmured in a voice that was tearing at me because it was the one I recognized from years ago.

"It can end," I cried. "Reach out to Christ. The One greater than the demon inside . . ."

But the expression changed again. The face exploded with hellish anger, eyes bugging out as

Augie was overcome. The nine-millimeter Beretta, with a full clip, was pointed at my chest. "You're the one who is going to end."

From somewhere there was a cry. "Drop the gun!"

The voice came from the floor, far below. Down among the disabled machines. Then in the dim yellow light I saw her. Ashley, in her baggy sweat-pants and wearing her police-issue Kevlar vest, holding her clip-loaded semiautomatic between her two outstretched hands in perfect firing position.

But Augie, the possessed, didn't wait. He whirled half around and aimed at Ashley. She shouted once more for him to drop it. Instead, he fired, and a bullet rang off a piece of machinery with a spark inches from Ashley. When it did, Ashley let loose with a round that struck Augie in the upper-left quadrant of his chest, and he crumpled to the ground.

I could see that he was bleeding out badly. She may have struck his heart, and I rushed over to him, took the gun from his hand, and bent over him as I heard Ashley down below calling for an EMT and for backup.

I thrust my hand over his chest where the bullet had pierced him and pressed as hard as I could, trying to slow the bleeding, but it was a horrific flood tide of red, and I couldn't plug the dike.

Augie looked at me, the pallor of his face

quickly fading into a grayish white. Then he asked a question, and it burned into my soul. "Bobby? He's okay?"

I answered, "I believe with all my heart that he is."

Augie mumbled something that I couldn't understand. But, bending over him, I told him to hold on. And then I told him everything that was important: about who had rescued me, and about sin, and about redemption, and finding peace, and where to find it, and about Jesus on the cross, and how even while suffering himself Jesus had granted forgiveness to the dying criminal hanging next to him, and how Augie needed to open his heart and receive from God the only redemption that matters, and that it wasn't too late. His eyes were glassing over and I didn't know how much he could hear, but I kept talking. Until finally the pupils in his eyes were fixed and dilated and his body was absolutely still.

Only then did I stop talking and begin to weep.

60

I stayed in Manitou after the incident at the foundry until the shooting investigation was complete. I needed to be there for Ashley, and not just as a witness to the events.

As we met again for ice cream one evening four

days after the incident at the foundry, she said, "I'm sorry I had to shoot. And I'm sorry it was your friend who died."

I told her that she did what she had to do, and she was brave in doing it. And I owed her my life.

But I did ask her whether she saw anything unusual happening up on that catwalk that night. She told me she entered that area of the foundry just as Augie was screaming about something and pointing a gun at me. I decided not to share with her the supernatural cacophony that had preceded her arrival. Best to save it for another time.

During those days, just waiting around in my old hometown, I realized that I had to break the bad news to Dan Hoover. I called him and had to tell him about Bobby's killer. About Augie. I kept it to the bare facts. They were brutal and disturbing enough. Dan was deeply shaken, I could tell.

So, when Dan called me a week later, after I had returned to the island, I was surprised to hear from him so soon. I was even more surprised at his invitation.

"My band and I are going to be playing down in Norfolk, Virginia, next month. That's close to you, isn't it?"

"Only a few hours away," I said. "I can take the ferry to Hatteras and then drive up to hear you. Just tell me when and where."

"That's not exactly what I'm thinking."

"What are you saying?"

"How long would it take to brush up on your blues harp?"

"How long would it take," I shot back, "for you to restore your reputation after I destroy it in Norfolk?"

He roared. "Come on, Trevor. Let's do this thing. For old times' sake." Then he paused and added, "You know, and for our fallen comrades too."

Dan got me with that one. I reluctantly agreed. My magazine article was done; I had time to kill and the blues harp to relearn all over again. I told him that I'd do it. Dan said he'd pick a music set in the key of B, so I would need my E harmonica.

As I hustled to brush up musical skills that were all but gone for good, Ashley and I exchanged a few e-mails. Sheriff Butch Jardinsky had been suspended pending an investigation into his conduct, and Detective Colin Jennings had been named the interim sheriff. When I asked Ashley why she wasn't appointed instead of Jennings, she said, "Hey, I just received my second medal for heroism. I'm on easy street. Who would want all the paperwork and administrative headaches, and then have to run for sheriff every couple of years?"

I couldn't argue with that. One day, out of the blue, instead of an e-mail, Ashley's name lit up on my iPhone. I picked up, eager to hear her voice.

"To what do I owe this call?"

"Two things, Mr. Black."

"I can't wait."

"I told you I had a hunch about your high school sweetheart," Ashley said brightly. "A hunch, along with some good detective work."

I struggled to place the reference.

"You told me about Marilyn Parlow, and I checked up on the details."

I stopped breathing. What was she getting at?

Ashley paused a moment, then dropped a bombshell. "No abortion," she reported matter-of-factly, telling me that, instead, there had been a live birth. "Your baby daughter was adopted as an infant into a good family."

I couldn't respond. Not at first. The world was spinning.

"Are you still there?" she asked.

I stammered, "This is . . . Oh my heavens, this is fantastic. Unbelievable."

Then the rest. "When she turned eighteen," Ashley explained, "she went out on her own. Sort of disappeared for a while. Oh, and your daughter's name—I almost forgot. It's Heather."

Just then a crashing reversal of fortunes. The world, and everything in it, suddenly turned to night. An overwhelming sense of foreboding. "Ashley," I shouted, "I have a terrible feeling about this."

"Hey, Trevor, I bring you great news, and you're going all upset and funky on me?"

"You don't understand. She was named Heather, you say. But there was this case I was involved with in New York. A nineteen-year-old named Heather. Street kid. Hooked on drugs. Doing prostitution. A horrible death."

"Whoa, whoa," she shot back. "Put on the brakes."

"How? First you tell me that I have a daughter. The best news I have had for such a long time. The next minute I'm wondering whether she's a murder victim."

"Trevor, slow down. First of all, your daughter is in her twenties, not nineteen. Second, I'm here to tell you that she is alive and well. She's currently living in Florida."

"You're sure?"

"Sure, I'm sure."

I walked away from the edge of disaster. The sky shone blue again.

Ashley continued. "At this point I just need to know one thing from you."

"The answer is yes. Yes. If she's willing to see me, yes, please tell her I want to meet her."

"A mind reader too," Ashley laughed. "A man of many talents."

"Speaking of my many talents . . ." When I told her about the Norfolk gig with Dan Hoover, she went ballistic, laughing and asking me for all the details.

"I'll be in touch, Trevor."

But before we hung up, I asked, "So, Ashley, tell me, what about us?"

Silence. So long, I wondered whether the connection had been severed. But eventually she responded. "No matter how this turns out, Trevor, just remember: we will always have Manitou. Not Paris, I know, but there you have it."

I laughed at her retooling of the line from *Casablanca*. But after I hung up, I stopped laughing. Didn't Bogart end up splitting with Ingrid Bergman in the end?

The jazz and blues concert in Norfolk was in a small warehouse on Tazewell Street that had been converted into a restaurant and music hall called Live Stream Café. I was glad to sit out the first two sets. When Dan beckoned me up to the stage for the last one, I picked my way through the sea of tables in the dimly lit restaurant, with my key-of-E blues harp clutched in my sweaty fist.

The place was sold out, and there were even standees lined up against the wall by the entrance.

We did a variation on several Paul Butterfield Blues Band classics. I had been cramming eight hours a day for the two weeks leading up to the gig, trying to pick it up again, and Dan had e-mailed me a music file with his renditions from one of his albums so I could practice. Still, as we played, I felt like a kite flyer matched up with jet pilots. Dan and his guys were generous and ended up following me rather than vice versa just to make things easy. We ended the official set with our version of Butterfield's "One More Heartache," and Dan and I shared the vocals. Dan's guitar riff was musical brilliance.

But then, as an encore, Dan gave in to a number I had discovered and that we had practiced earlier that day. An African piece of gospel jazz called "Satan Fall Down," by blind musician Lasana Kanneh and his group IJenNeh.

Our rendition was pretty loose, more like a jam session, but the crowd loved it. The song has a killer beat, sort of Nigerian-blues-reggae fusion. Best of all is the simplicity of lyrics addressed to the devil himself—"Jesus done beat you two thousand years ago."

When we got to that part, because the house lights had started to come up, I could see the lineup of standees at the other end of the room by the entrance. And that was when I recognized Ashley standing there, grinning and clapping wildly. I think she couldn't help but laugh and applaud at the song that told about beating the devil and about who it was who had beaten him.

The ovation at the end was for New Jersey Dan Hoover and his group. I was just along for the ride, and it was a rush for me simply to be there.

Then I noticed that Ashley had begun to point. She was pointing next to her. To a young blonde woman in jeans and a leather jacket. The face, now visible in the glare of the overhead house lights, was a face I had seen before. So much like her mother. So very much.

I stumbled through the crowd and past a few well-wishers until I found myself standing inches away from her. Miraculous. Heather had been delivered. One of life's most important messages, lost in the mail, now recovered and standing in front of me.

I told myself to hold it together, for whatever reason, but it didn't work because my eyes blurred over and I could feel my chin starting to wobble. I strained to read her. Heather had a strange kind of calm. Keeping her distance. No tears. No hugs. Just an awkward moment as she studied me.

Then Heather said, "I understand that you're my dad. I guess you have been looking for me?"

All I could say—all that could be said—was simple. "Yes, I have. In one way or another, for most of my life."

Neither of us spoke for several seconds. Ashley broke the ice. "Okay. It's clear I am going to have to be the ringleader for this circus. Let's grab a table. Or do you two want some time alone?"

Both of us said no, that the three of us would be just fine together. Hopefully there would be plenty of time for Heather and me to get to know each other after that. We grabbed an open table in the noisy music hall.

How do you cover the distance of lives that have

been lived apart, an entire lifetime? We couldn't. Not in one night. I did most of the talking, along with Ashley. Heather did most of the listening. At the end of the night, Heather reached out her hand and shook mine. I had hoped for a catharsis, but none came. But my daughter had come. That was the important thing.

EPILOGUE

Through all the murders and mutilations, I had thought I was pursuing a monster. It turned out that I had been chasing my friend. He wasn't the enemy. Not really. He was just taken hostage by the enemy.

That weighs heavy on my mind as I sit in my Land Rover. The North Carolina ferry is sliding through the water toward the harbor of Ocracoke Island, which is now in sight.

Other things try to crowd their way into my mind, too, like the big man who was hovering at the window of my car, earlier on this ferry ride. One of the horribles.

Now a ferry master in the tan uniform is waving us forward. I take my car out of park, keeping my foot down on the brake, and when the cars ahead of me start moving, I creep forward and eventually over the metal drawbridge on the ferry until my tires hit solid ground.

There is only one road that leads to the one tiny hamlet of a town on my island, and I am traveling on it, following behind a line of cars. But something stirs in me, and instead of heading directly home, I stop my car at the marina. The sea is calling.

I have much to ponder as I prepare to embark.

There is still an ocean of distance between my daughter and me. But I pray for the lost years between us to somehow be restored.

That is on my mind as I motor toward the Gulf Stream. The engines throb heavy in my ears, and the wind is laced with salt spray. The good news is that Ashley and Heather have announced a joint visit to my little island hideaway. The plans are already under way. I am hopeful.

But then there are the consequences of life in a fallen world and the loss of people I have cared for, some of them brutally lost; the ache is still there, as if at a fracture line. So the world toils on. The flesh fails. And demons rage, but only for a while. Until the Guardian King finally crushes them underfoot.

Until then I will be buoyed, like a sail that is billowing full, captured by a good wind and plowing forward under a power that is not my own. Despite the treacherous waters all around, there is still joy. A paradox.

A catamaran cruises past me, tilting, its double hull cutting the water and its sail filled with a good wind. It is full of islanders, and they all wave. The man at the helm points to the newly painted name on the stern of my boat. He seems to be enjoying a good laugh at the new name that I have given my fishing vessel. He points to himself, creating his own interpretation, perhaps. But the name on my vessel carries a truth beyond the visible world.

I'M OCCUPIED

At the wheel, I daydream about hooking a yellowfin tuna today and about the vastness of the great blue rolling Atlantic. Even with the uncertainty of where things will go from here, I find myself hopeful and at peace.

Then my cell phone rings. I never considered I would have reception way out here. It's Dick Valentine on the line, asking me a question, although it begins with a statement. "Trevor, I'm investigating this crime, another grim one. The kind that troubles the soul. The kind that cuts a wake. I thought you might be interested. Are you?"

I listen as my friend gives me just the headlines, but enough to remind me that the destroyer is still out there and that I will have to make a decision soon. I steel myself as I look out to the horizon where the sea meets the sky. No sense in calculating the risks. After all, no matter how many forces the enemy brings, what really matters is who occupies me.

I respond to the NYPD detective.

"Tell me more."

DISCUSSION QUESTIONS

1. The novel is divided into three sections: "The World," "The Flesh," and "The Devil." Identify where these three elements appear in Ephesians 2:2-3. Now read the following Scripture passages about supernatural activity in our world: Hebrews 1:14; 1 Timothy 4:1-3; Luke 11:24-26; Ephesians 6:12. What does the Bible say about supernatural forces like angels and demons?

2. By the time Trevor meets Mason Krim, the man has dabbled with demons for a while. He tells Trevor, "You have to be the one in control. You. Not them." Considering what we know about Krim, what is foolish about this statement? Is there any wisdom to it?

3. Think of some of the choices Trevor makes throughout his life. Which ones are the right choices? Which ones are wrong? How do you see God's hand guiding him, even before he puts his faith in God?

4. What drives Trevor during his childhood and adolescence? What motivates him as an adult? When is human ambition a positive

thing? How does it become negative? Is it ever a sin to be ambitious?

5. How would you describe Trevor's romantic relationships with women? How do they change throughout the story?

6. When Trevor is at the end of his rope, he realizes, "I had just been at a crossroads. Taken one route, and not another. And there was something numinous yet real going on." If you are a follower of Jesus, think of the time you put your life in Christ's hands. How was it similar to Trevor's experience? How was it different?

7. When Trevor's defenses break down and he admits his need of Christ, how does his life change? What changes take a while to come into play?

8. Trevor calls his new ability to perceive demonic forces both a curse and a gift. Have you identified any spiritual gifts that God has given you? How can those responsibilities be a burden? In what way are they a blessing?

9. Trevor feels compelled to return to Manitou, not just because of his friend's death but because he knows God has given him this

task. Have you ever faced something—large or small—that felt like a "mission from God"? How did you respond?

10. Ashley Linderman faces generalized anxiety disorder after her violent attack. How does she handle this setback? Is there a role for prescribed medication for such issues, or perhaps counseling? Why or why not?

11. What kind of father do you expect Trevor will be? What kind of relationship will he have with his child? What challenges will he meet?

12. James 2:19 says, "You believe that God is one. You do well; the demons also believe, and shudder." What does this verse say about God's sovereignty? How should a Christian's belief in God differ from a demon's?

ACKNOWLEDGMENTS

In this novel I tried to paint a unique fictional picture of spiritual warfare. Given that, Tyndale House Publishers impressed me not only by the way it boldly embraced the vision behind this story but also how its staff actively encouraged and nurtured it. Karen Watson and Jan Stob deserve great thanks for the insights they brought to the project and their enthusiasm for the book. While my Tyndale editor, Caleb Sjogren, did a great job catching the usual technical "oops" that occur in every novel, he did more than that; he inserted himself into the world I was trying to create, as well as its message, and creatively urged it forward. Cheryl Kerwin and Maggie Rowe, marketing and publicity stars at Tyndale, were a delight to work with.

Many thanks to blind Liberian musician Lasana Kanneh and his group, IJenNeh (http://ijenneh .wordpress.com), for permission to use a few lyrics from their African gospel jazz piece, "Satan Fall Down." Lasana's own journey is a remarkable story in itself. I'm honored to have connected with him. I am grateful also to my agents, AGI Vigliano Literary, for their excellent representation.

Writers don't work in a vacuum. My fiction

work is blessed and inspired by the spectacular support of my family. My daughter, Sarah Parshall Perry, an accomplished writer in her own right, helped me with a key segment of this story. My son, Joseph, often assumed responsibilities so I could be cut free to keep fingers to the keyboard. My wife, Janet, has been the inspiration behind all my novels. But this one, with its portrayal of spiritual conflict, is a journey that has special meaning for both of us. Her life and her broadcast ministry have reminded me how the gospel of truth is more relevant now than ever before, and although the dominion of darkness is very real, its days are numbered because the Alpha and the Omega—the "Guardian King"—is real too, and he is victorious.

ABOUT THE AUTHOR

Craig Parshall is a fiction writer who has authored or coauthored eleven suspense novels. He has appeared on the *New York Times* Best Sellers List, and his novels have appeared regularly on the CBA bestseller list. *The Occupied* is his twelfth work of suspense fiction. He has also coauthored several nonfiction books and is a regular current events columnist for *Israel My Glory* magazine. Craig is a cum laude graduate of Carroll College (English/Philosophy/Religion) and Marquette University Law School, where he received his JD.

Craig is also a commentator on issues involving culture, faith, freedom, law, media, and technology, and he frequently debates the most controversial and engaging issues of the day with atheist groups and separation-of-church-and-state leaders. He addresses Christian worldview subjects and speaks nationally on topics as far-ranging as Washington policy and politics, Internet freedom, and artistic issues in films, which he debates with movie directors in Hollywood.

Craig Parshall currently serves as special counsel to the American Center for Law and Justice (ACLJ) and provides Washington-related consulting as the principal of Parshall Policy. He was the founding director of the John Milton Project for Free Speech, a pioneering venture on matters of religious expression on the Internet, which he launched in his previous capacity as senior vice president and general counsel for National Religious Broadcasters (NRB), where he was also the executive editor of its publications, later serving as senior adviser for law and policy. Craig has testified frequently before committees of the US Senate and the House of Representatives on constitutional and First Amendment issues, as well as before the Federal Communications Commission (FCC) on broadcasting freedoms and the future of media in America. As a veteran civil liberties trial and appellate attorney, Craig has represented clients in civil liberty and church-state cases before the US Supreme Court, the majority of the US Courts of Appeal across the United States, and numerous federal trial courts and state supreme courts.

Craig's appearances on legal and constitutional issues on mainstream media include FOX News, CBS television and CBS radio, CNN, NBC's *Today* show, *Inside Edition*, PBS, NPR, and Court TV among others. His cases have been featured in major newspapers and magazines, including the *New York Times*, the *National Law Journal*, the *Chicago Tribune*, the *LA Times*, the *Boston Herald*, the *Boston Globe*, the *Milwaukee Journal Sentinel*, the *Atlanta Journal-Constitution*, the

Charlotte Observer, the *Des Moines Register*, *Newsweek*, and *U.S. News & World Report*.

Craig is married to Janet Parshall, a nationally syndicated radio talk-show host who is heard over the Moody Radio network.

On Facebook: Craig Parshall Author
On Twitter: @Craig Parshall
On LinkedIn: Craig Parshall—
    Principal at Parshall Policy

Center Point Large Print
600 Brooks Road / PO Box 1
Thorndike, ME 04986-0001 USA

(207) 568-3717

US & Canada:
1 800 929-9108
www.centerpointlargeprint.com